Wrongful Deaths

Drake Cody Suspense-Thrillers, Volume 3

Tom Combs

Published by Evoke Publishing, 2018.

D1502778

WRONGFUL DEATHS

First edition. July 4, 2018.

ISBN: 978-0990336068

Written by Tom Combs.

As with book one, NERVE DAMAGE, and book two, HARD TO BREATH, I dedicate this book to the special people committed to helping others when needed most. Thank you!

Chapter 1

Memorial Hospital, ER

Fear radiated from the boy like heat from glowing coals.

"It's getting worse." The teenager leaned forward on the edge of the Emergency Room bed. "This morning I told my friend. He said I needed to shut up. When I told him it was real, he got mad." His words came halting and soft. He had dark hair, long eyelashes and looked younger than the sixteen years noted on the chart. "Tonight I told my parents." He kept his eyes down as he twisted the distinctive ring he wore. "They brought me here."

The ER chart resting on Dr. Drake Cody's lap identified the reason for the ER visit as "parents concerned about drug use." The boy's name was Bryce.

"What did you tell them?" Drake asked. The teenager's anguish assured the answer would not be good.

He shook his head, and continued to twist his ring.

"It's okay, Bryce," Drake said. "You can tell me. I want to help."

The boy swallowed, pursed his lips, then spoke so softly Drake had to strain to hear.

"My room is downstairs, so at first I tried to believe it was noises from the air ducts. At school I pretended it was just other kids' voices." He looked up. "It's not." His lip trembled. "I don't know what's happening."

The air left the room. The noise of the ER outside the door disappeared.

"The voices are real, and they won't stop." His voice cracked. "My parents think I'm taking drugs. I thought about trying some to see if it would stop what was happening." He looked at Drake with eyes that were pools of desperation and pain. "Can you please make them stop?"

Drake's stomach dropped. Dread gripped his heart.

He wished the boy had been taking drugs. He wished there was an explanation other than what he sensed with grim certainty. He'd look under every stone, but he knew he wouldn't find anything to alter what the voices meant. This young man was descending into the nightmare of mental illness. This evening, at this very moment, the grip of schizophrenia was tightening around him.

1

Why this boy? Why anyone?

The boy's realization that what he'd been experiencing was horribly, terrifyingly wrong would disappear. This polite young man—this innocent victim—was losing his ability to distinguish delusion from reality. Nothing would ever be the same for him or for those who loved him.

"I know something bad is happening—" The boy stopped and cocked his head as if listening. He bent forward and gripped his hands over his ears. "No!"

Drake sat next to Bryce, putting an arm around him. The boy's shoulders quaked as tears dotted the faded blue of his jeans.

Drake's insides fell away.

***

Drake exited the minor trauma room, brushing plaster dust off his scrubs. He'd just applied a splint to a child's broken wrist. Overhead pages, chattering printers, beeping phones, and the voices of patients, families, and caregivers hummed. The smell of disinfectant and the stink of an earlier GI bleed hung in the air. Memorial Hospital ER, the biggest and busiest in the Twin Cities, was packed.

"Dr. Cody." The mental health worker who'd been making calls and helping the parents of the disturbed boy held a clipboard. "Adolescent Psyche at Abbott hospital could have a bed for Bryce as soon as an hour or two, but if not, they'll have one for sure in the morning."

"Good work. Fingers crossed," Drake said. There were never enough inpatient beds to take care of mental health patients—especially adolescents. Waits of more than twenty-four hours were common. "Can you let him and his parents know?"

"I will," she said. "Can you sign the transfer?" She held out the clipboard.

He felt the hollowness of having so little to offer the boy and his family. Bryce was the same age as Drake's brother had been when he died. The boy triggered some of the same feelings—that Drake hadn't done enough.

He had multiple other sick and hurting patients, a stream of incoming ambulances, and a packed waiting room. The best he could do for Bryce was to transfer him to the care of psychiatric specialists.

"Dr. Cody?" the mental health worker remained holding the clipboard and pen outstretched.

"Sorry." He signed. "Thanks so much for your help."

"Sure thing. If—"

An electronic alarm shrilled overhead, causing the worker to flinch and Drake to scramble toward the radio room.

The signal meant an ambulance with a critically ill patient was hurtling with lights and siren toward the ER. The paramedics needed a doctor immediately.

Someone in the worst kind of trouble was racing Drake's way.

Chapter 2

Drake slapped the switch, silencing the overhead alarm with one hand as he pressed the transmit key of the radio with the other. "Dr. Cody here."

"Ambulance 724. Three minutes out with a twenties-year-old black female, narcotic overdose, status post Narcan." Drake knew this paramedic. The veteran's voice sounded tight. "She was down, looked dead, zero respirations. She snapped to after the Narcan and is now out of control." Drake heard shrieking in the background. "She's got a little belly bump—could be early pregnancy. She's too wild to assess, but I think something bad besides the OD is going on. She needs the Crash Room. ETA two minutes."

"10-4." Drake pivoted toward the Crash Room.

The station secretary stood across the corridor with headset on and hand poised over her console.

"Please call a Med Team Stat to Crash Room three," Drake said.

The secretary's hospital-wide page sounded overhead as Drake entered the Crash Room. His mind flashed through the likeliest of the life-threatening conditions that might be headed his way. He reflexively linked each possibility to the critical interventions that might be needed.

Nurses, EMTs, and the rest of the resuscitation team scrambled into the room and made ready. The Life Clock above bay three had been triggered, and large red numerals flashed the seconds and minutes since the radio call. For patients needing the Crash Room, every second mattered.

Drake moved to the head of the bed and flicked on the high-intensity lights, illuminating the white linens, monitors, and wall-mounted array of glistening chrome instruments. The team looked his way. He spoke as he ripped open packaging and pulled on a sterile gown and gloves.

"Ambulance 724 is a minute out with a twenties-year-old, female overdose patient found near-dead. She's awake and screaming after Narcan. Unknown history. The medics think she could be pregnant and something bad beyond the OD is happening." Drake scanned the area making sure the airway equipment and other instruments he might need were at hand.

"Let's roll the ultrasound over here in case I need to check for pregnancy. If she's pregnant, let's remember that good care of the mother is always what's best for the ba—"

The doors exploded open as 724 rammed the gurney into the Crash Room. A wiry, young female paramedic pushed from the rear while her large male partner entered backpedaling while bent over the cart. His mass blocked the patient from view. As they reached the bedside, Drake saw beyond the big man.

My God!

An ultrasound exam to check for pregnancy would not be needed.

The blood-covered legs, buttocks, and abdomen of a tiny male infant protruded from the woman's birth canal. The protruding parts and a short section of umbilical cord were supported in one of the paramedic's gloved hands. The yet-to-be-born, clearly premature infant's head, shoulders, upper chest, and arms were still within the mother's body.

Rivulets of sweat ran down the medic's face. He held one hand cupped beneath the tiny infant and the other gloved, bloody hand alongside the infant and pressed against the birth canal.

"Her water burst and he popped out to here a minute ago but he's hung up. He's moving his feet some, and his color looks okay as long as my finger keeps the cord from being squished. It's all I can do."

The female paramedic nodded toward the mother. "She quieted in the last minute, vitals okay but not great. She might need more Narcan soon, but we figured as long as she's breathing we'd hold off."

"Good call," Drake said. Right now the mother's drugged state was in everyone's best interest. He turned to one of the nurses. "Please give neonatal intensive care a heads-up."

The patient moaned but didn't move or open her eyes. The sickly, grayish cast to her dark skin showed her to be on the edge of shock. Her gaunt body and small belly did not suggest good health or a normal pregnancy. For an instant Drake imagined the life this addicted woman must have. His gut went hollow.

Nurses called out the blood pressure and respirations. The mother's pulse showed on the monitor.

Drake checked the airway, then listened to the patient's lungs as the team supplied oxygen, checked the IVs, and drew blood.

"Full labs including type and cross for two units," Drake said. "Give a liter of fluids wide open."

Patients who OD on narcotics die because they quit breathing. This patient's airway was clear, her breathing currently adequate, and her blood pressure okay. She was not dying this instant.

He turned to the tiny infant struggling to be born.

This baby weighed no more than four pounds. One of the doll-sized feet claimed his gaze as he grasped the umbilical cord and counted the heart rate he felt pulsing there. A rate of sixty. Desperately low...

A heart rate this slow promised imminent death or disaster.

Drake's throat clenched and his mind raced to thoughts of his brother Kevin and the childbirth-related cerebral palsy that had made his every movement a challenge. That or worse could be happening to the infant right now.

Was the baby's distress due to the mother's overdose, the pinched umbilical cord, or one of dozens other possibilities?

In the immediacy of the Crash Room, there was no time to "prove" exactly what was happening. Tests were a luxury that the ticking of the Life Clock and the baby's pulse made impossible. The imperative was to do what needed to be done despite the unknowns. Inaction assured tragedy.

He needed to do the right thing and do it now.

"I need to get in there." Drake wedged shoulder-to-shoulder with the medic. The smell of sweat mingled with the raw odors of blood and birth tissue.

The medic shifted. Drake advanced his gloved finger along the baby's trunk and into the jammed birth canal. The infant's arms were trapped in a hands-above-head position. The width of the infant's shoulders, arms, and head had him lodged like a cork in a bottle. There was no chance he could pass.

"Pulse is fifty, Dr. Cody," the nurse said.

"He's not moving anymore, Doc," the paramedic said, his voice strained. "His color's bad."

No time. *Don't let this baby die!*

Drake forced his index finger further into the birth canal along the infant's chest. He felt the tiny collarbone that supported the nearer shoulder like a strut. He knew what he needed to do but had never done it before. A small thing compared to much of what his job demanded, but inside he recoiled. He grit his teeth as he drove the tip of his finger against the infant's bone, forcing it to flex like a green twig. He pushed harder, then harder still.

Crack!

The snapping of the collarbone sounded impossibly loud. Members of the resuscitation team groaned. The baby's body shifted slightly. Drake extended his finger further, finding the infant's chin and the tiny opening of the mouth.

"I need to take him now," Drake said as he pressed forward. The medic slid back, completing the hand-off as Drake slipped his free hand under and around the little one's protruding body.

Using his fingertip as a hook in the baby's mouth, Drake moved the babe's chin down, flexing the neck. He rotated the infant's trunk and pulled. Nothing! Lodged tight.

Drake ratcheted up his strength and pulled, primarily using his grasp of the trunk and body so as to avoid dislocating the baby's jaw. The ends of the broken collarbone telescoped over one another, allowing the shoulder to collapse inward. Drake continually increased the power with which he pulled, knowing that the babe would die if he could not be freed.

Drake braced his legs, and his arms were cables pulling so strongly that he feared he would tear the little person apart. *Lord, no. Please!*

The doll-sized body shifted a fraction, then broke free, sluicing out in a rush of blood and fluids.

Drake held the limp, dusky babe in one hand, supporting the head and neck with his fingers. A nurse held oxygen tubing near his mouth. *Breathe, little guy!*

Drake suctioned the babe's mouth and airway clear. He laid the tiny infant on the warm blanket, gently shook, and then briskly rubbed the tiny feet as the medic kept the oxygen tubing near the face. *Breathe, baby, breathe!*

No response. No time.

Drake bent and put his mouth over the mouth and nose of the infant and delivered a measured breath to the delicate premature lungs—the tiny chest expanded.

The baby remained limp. Nothing. Dead weight in his hand. *No!*

He delivered another rescue breath.

Lifeless, nothing—wait! Did he feel a stirring? Had there been movement?

As Drake prepared for a third breath, the little chest expanded and then a shrill, jittery cry sounded. A surge like an electric current passed through Drake. The birdlike chest continued to pump and the infant's limbs moved.

"Hell, yeah." The paramedic whose work had kept the little one alive squeezed Drake's shoulder. Team members cheered or gasped.

"How's the mom?" Drake asked as he put his stethoscope on the little one, the bell covering the entire chest.

"Her breathing is adequate. Pressure 90," said one of the nurses.

"Have we heard from the neonatal intensive care unit?" Drake said. "We've got a little friend for them."

At that moment, two nurses with miniature stethoscopes around their necks wheeled a warmer through the Crash Room doors.

"Great timing," Drake said. The nearer nurse came to his side. Drake put the babe and blanket into her hands. "Watch the cord—I'll cut it in a minute."

He glanced at the mother as he picked up a clamp and scalpel.

"We don't know much," Drake said to the NICU nurses. "A narcotic-overdosed mother. Premature babe with a feet-first presentation, prolapsed cord, heart rate to fifties. Had to break his collarbone. We have no other history."

Drake cut and clamped the cord, leaving adequate length for IV lines as the nurses expertly tended to the little one in the warmer.

"As you know, he'll need respiratory support and maybe a tube," Drake said. This new one's battles were just beginning.

"The neonatologist is waiting in the unit," the nearer nurse said. "We'll race him straight up there."

They remained bent over the infant as they rolled out.

Handing a neonate to a NICU nurse was like handing him to a high priest, except the nurses were more committed. The hard-luck little man was in good hands.

The numerals of the Life Clock continued to flash. No time for high-fives.

He turned to the mother.

Blood spilled from the edge of the bed to the floor.

Chapter 3

Memorial Hospital, administrative office wing

Jim Torrins, MD, stood before the CEO's office door. The oversized gold-plated placard reading *Stuart Kline, CEO* hung at eye level. Apparently, Kline was concerned people would forget he was CEO in the six feet since passing the six-inch-high *Stuart Kline, CEO* sign perched on the counter in front of his secretary's desk. Jim knew that behind the door there was another title reminder sitting on Kline's oak desk.

Kline was an accountant who'd somehow jumped from a position in the University's Patent and Royalties office to CEO of Memorial Hospital. In the months since, Jim had not seen anything to suggest the new CEO had leadership ability or dedication to healthcare. More perplexing still, Kline had survived involvement in a failed scheme to pirate the breakthrough drug of Dr. Drake Cody and his two emergency physician partners. The man should have been fired and criminally prosecuted.

Kline had called Jim ten minutes earlier and commanded that he to report to his office "on the double." Jim waited ten minutes before making the short trip from his office to Kline's.

He knocked once and opened the door without waiting.

Kline glanced up from the spreadsheet on his desk and frowned.

The fiftyish, fit-appearing CEO reminded Jim of a department store manikin—his face unnaturally tan, his eyes too close together, and definitely a poser in his expensive, meant-to-impress wardrobe.

"What took you so long?" Kline asked, his gaze returning to the spreadsheet.

As a physician and president of Medical Affairs, it was Jim Torrins' responsibility to oversee the Memorial Hospital's medical staff and patient care activities. Bad outcomes, angry patients, and all real or perceived issues involving the medical staff were his to address. His position also made him the conduit between the CEO and the medical caregivers.

After only months on the job, Kline had Memorial Hospital's nurses and doctors near revolt.

"What's today's problem?" Jim asked. With Kline there was always a problem.

"Incompetence is the problem." Kline pointed at Jim. "The doctors and nurses of Memorial Hospital are the problem. They're inept."

Each encounter with the CEO challenged the civility and calm Jim prided himself on. He took a deep breath and kept his voice as soft as possible.

"That's nonsense."

"Nonsense? Millions of dollars in malpractice related claims is not nonsense!"

"There have been some unfortunate—"

"Unfortunate?" Kline's eyes bulged. "It's a full-blown crisis! We still have one death and four lesser claims pending, and who knows what those will cost? Clete Venjer's personal injury firm could set up an office in the hospital lobby. Your doctors and nurses are so bad our malpractice insurer is threatening to drop us."

Jim flushed hot. Kline pushed his buttons like no one else.

"Our doctors and nurses are excellent," Jim said. "Saying otherwise is irresponsible. There has been a rash of tragedies. Patients died. The doctors and nurses involved—"

"Are incompetent." Kline's volume climbed. "Millions in settlements and claims worth of incompetent, *Doctor* Torrins. That doesn't happen with quality physicians and nurses."

Jim took another deep breath.

"You're wrong," he said. "None of the three deaths could have been foreseen. Freakish equipment failures contributed in two of the cases. I know the doctors and nurses involved. They're skilled and caring. Even in hindsight, it's difficult to see how anything could have been done. The deaths are mysterious and tragic, but they are not malpractice."

"You're making excuses," Kline said. "If nobody did anything wrong, the patients would be fine and there wouldn't be any lawsuits."

The deaths and bad outcomes were heartbreaking, but to suggest that malpractice must have been the cause was ridiculous. Kline was one of those who believed if sick or injured patients die or don't recover fully, it had to be someone's fault. People are supposed to live forever.

"A patient dying does not mean malpractice occurred," Jim said. "Bad things happen to sick and injured people. Because someone files a suit doesn't mean anyone did anything wrong." Jim looked Kline in the eye. "We've had a number of bad outcomes and some freakish, tragic deaths. The best physicians in the world could not have predicted any of them, but they happened. It's devastating for the patients and their families and causes sleepless nights for the doctors and nurses involved."

"It's more than that—the hospital settled or lost in court and paid big money," Kline said.

"Malpractice attorneys found 'medical experts,'" Jim did the air quote gesture, "who testified for money that there was negligence. The truth is there was not. The insurer recommended settling several cases to avoid the possibility of them losing big money." Jim paused. "The courts are not a reasonable place to decide malpractice. The guilty sometimes go free, while the innocent face personal ruin and astronomical money judgments. The Memorial Hospital deaths were not the result of malpractice. It's been unlucky and heartbreaking."

"Unlucky?" The CEO blinked rapidly. "Millions in losses, the hospital in danger of going under, and my chief medical guy says we're *unlucky*? Are you joking?"

"Patients dying is no joke." Jim took a deep breath. *How is this guy CEO?* "I need to correct something else you have wrong."

"What's that?" Kline said.

"I am not 'your' chief medical guy. I'm Dr. Jim Torrins, president of Medical Affairs for Memorial Hospital. I'm head of the medical staff and I serve at the discretion of the hospital board. I'm committed to the well-being of our patients, doctors, and nurses. I'm not 'your' anything."

Kline's face reddened.

"Excuse me if I don't kiss your ring, *doctor*," Kline said. "You think you're so superior. You can't understand how a lowly, non-doctor like me was hired to run this hospital. The reason is, I get it—you doctor and nurse types don't. Running a hospital isn't about your high and mighty notions—it's about giving the customer what they want. It's about dollars and cents and making a profit."

"Medical care is not McDonald's," Jim said. "Patients aren't simply 'customers.' Medical caregivers are not assembly-line workers. It's work that demands brains and heart. It's a special responsibility."

"Whatever. They get paid to do a job."

"A unique job. And it's about more than money for them. They care, and it's a big part of who they are."

"Spare me the 'what we do is so special' crap you doctors and nurses hide behind." Kline shook his head. "Get over yourselves. It's just like any other business—it's about customer satisfaction, marketing, and the bottom line."

"You're wrong."

"Believe what you want, but I've talked to the hospital board about the malpractice mess," Kline said. "As of today, you are in charge of the Memorial Hospital Malpractice Investigatory Committee. You have one month to get to the bottom of the incompetence problem and correct it."

Jim froze as the political animal's strategy became clear.

If Jim and the committee succeeded—and Lord knows how that would be decided—CEO Stuart Kline would look good. If they 'failed,' Jim would take the fall. Either way, Kline would survive.

Jim's deeper concern was that Kline was right in one respect. Patients were getting hurt and dying mysteriously at Memorial Hospital—more than at any time in his decades-long career. It didn't appear to be malpractice, but he had no idea as to why.

"By the way, Torrins," Kline said, "if you fail, you won't be 'my' medical guy. You won't be Memorial Hospital's medical guy. You won't be anybody's anything. You'll be unemployed."

Chapter 4

"What's her blood pressure now?" Drake asked. The baby was en route to the NICU. The mother looked bad.

"80 over 60. Pulse is 125."

Overdosed on narcotics, a brutal premature delivery, and bleeding heavily—how had she gotten to this point?

Maybe she hadn't recognized she was in labor and took the narcotics because of the pain? Maybe she was too high to recognize when labor had begun? Or, more likely, her hunger for the drugs overrode all reason. That's what opioid addiction did.

He continued his head-to-toes examination. Other than drug-addicted, chronically ill-appearing, and having just delivered a premature baby, they knew nothing about her. Medically, there could be damn near anything going on.

"Did you talk with anyone at the scene?" Drake asked the paramedics as he continued his exam.

"She was alone," the fit-looking paramedic said as her partner loaded their gear onto the gurney. "We've pulled ODs out of that house before. Whoever called didn't stick around. She was as close to dead as you can get. Less than two minutes after Narcan, she was wild and screaming—but we see that fairly often when we reverse them."

Narcotics killed primarily by shutting down a person's drive to breathe. Narcan was the miraculous anti-opioid that in high-enough doses reversed the narcotic effects immediately. In addition to saving lives, it often triggered marked withdrawal symptoms in regular narcotic users. Each opioid drug's effects lasted for varying lengths of time. No one knew what she'd taken, so there was no way to know if and when more Narcan might be needed.

"The first liter of fluid is in," the nurse said. Drake scanned the patient and monitors. The respirations had slowed—her drive to breathe was fading.

"She's going down," Drake said. Whatever she had on board was outlasting the initial Narcan. "Secure her wrists in soft restraints then give 0.4 milligrams of Narcan. We'll go with low doses and try to keep her breathing without having her freak."

He checked her vaginal bleeding. The blood pooled on the bed and the placenta still had not passed. He checked her mouth, then examined the lower lid of her eye. The tissues were almost white rather than the beefy red of health.

"Have we got blood yet? Hang another liter of saline and transfuse two units of blood as soon as we can get it."

The Life Clock continued to tick.

"Please page the OB/GYN doc on call," Drake said.

"Already done," said the nurse. "I talked to her while you were busy with the baby. She's on the way from labor and delivery. It's Dr. Stone."

Great nurses and responsive doctors—reasons why he loved working at Memorial Hospital. The state Medical Board's punitive action and his probationary license status passed through his mind like a dark shadow.

The patient's breathing rate had improved after the low-dose Narcan. Her eyes remained closed and she was not fighting. The zone between not breathing and agitation was best for her and them.

"Where's that blood? She's going to need it. If there's a holdup, get me two units of O negative." Universal donor blood was not ideal, but this patient would die without adequate red blood cells.

"That's a bad idea."

The heads of the resuscitation team swung as one to the entryway of the Crash Room from where the shocking words had come.

Drake looked up at the source—Clara Zeitman, the hollow-cheeked, sharp-featured chief of laboratory services. The thirty-something lab and information technology supervisor wore a white lab coat and stood at the foot of the bed as if she were in charge.

As the team's eyes speared her, the woman's expression and posture changed.

"I'm Dr. Zeitman, head of laboratory services. What I meant to say is, we're having a hard time matching her blood. If you can hold off for a few minutes, it may be wise. She may react to the O negative."

Drake knew a little bit about "doctor" Clara Zeitman. She oversaw the hospital's computer network and also headed laboratory services. She had a PhD in laboratory science but was not a MD. Drake generally didn't care about titles, but in patient care settings, Zeitman's use of the title could be confusing—and dangerous. She had no direct patient care authority, and "doctor" could be misunderstood by others.

"How soon for the blood?" Drake asked.

"Perhaps it's available now. I can check."

Drake looked at the monitors. Pulse and blood pressure were not good but holding.

"Do that," Drake said. "You've got two minutes. If there's going to be any further delay, bring the O negative."

"I will," she said as she exited.

Claire Zeitman had delivered useful information, but in an inappropriate way—issues to be addressed later. Drake's partner Rizz had been on a hospital committee with her and had said she was brilliant but a control freak with a gold medal in "weirdness." At the moment, the only thing that mattered to Drake was getting his patient stabilized, and Zeitman looked to be trying to help.

He picked up the clamp attached to the umbilical cord and exerted gentle traction with one hand while supporting the uterus with the other. A wave of blood gushed out as the afterbirth passed out of the birth canal.

He examined the placenta. If the entire placenta did not pass, the retained tissue could trigger runaway bleeding. The placenta looked complete.

He rechecked the mother's bleeding. With the placenta out, it had already slowed.

Might things be starting to go right for his patient?

Chapter 5

Uptown Minneapolis

"What you looking at?" Quentin glared at the gawking white guy in the car alongside him at the stoplight.

The staring punk looked away.

The light changed, and Q turned onto Lake Street. This evening there'd be lines at the nightclub entrances and people holding drinks crossing mid-block under the streetlamps.

Young white people loved the Uptown area. He smiled. They were his fastest-growing market, but just one of many—his business had exploded.

The Uptown Minneapolis area was high rent compared to the north side, but it fit well with his new operations. He'd leased a fine house with an option to buy, bought a new ride, and his piles of cash continued to grow.

He'd made big changes in his life.

One thing hadn't changed—despite getting rid of his dreadlocks, losing the street talk, covering his tattoos, and generally going Better Business Bureau, wherever he went he still drew the looks. Most Minnesotans were like the white dude at the stoplight. They viewed his blackness with suspicion and fear.

Even growing up in suburban Minnetonka, he'd felt the stares. Lots of Minnesota people bragged about their state being one of the most liberal in the country. They voted liberal, but Q had lived the reality of being black in their state. The smug folks in the suburbs were just fine with black people—they just didn't know or interact with any. Outside of the Minneapolis and St. Paul inner cities, the metropolitan and outstate regions were as white as the ass-freezing winters.

Q had seen the newspaper and TV reports of statistics that proved to anyone the bias of the state's police and courts. He knew his conviction and time behind bars in Stillwater wouldn't have happened if he were white.

He had to be ready for a shakedown or worse at any time. Hell, black men got shot in this town.

When it got down to it, Minnesota wasn't much different than anywhere else.

And why do hard time for selling drugs? It was a victimless crime—not really a crime at all.

He sold a product to people who'd made a choice about what they wanted to put in their bodies. It was their right as citizens of what was supposedly a free country.

He had skills, ambitions and supplied a product—his business based on supply and demand—like any other.

He was one of the most successful young businessmen in the state yet he had to keep his success in the shadows. Getting crazy rich while being his own man made it more than worth it.

Screw the law, the hypocrites, and any who would oppose him. He wouldn't let anyone or anything stop him.

***

Drake looked up as the OB/GYN, Dr. Julie Stone, rushed into the Crash Room in scrubs with her operating mask hanging loose from her neck and surgical booties still over her shoes. Even in a crisis she triggered a double-take.

He'd thought of her a number of times in the weeks since they'd collaborated in saving the anchorwoman. Each memory of her had brought a smile—and a twinge of guilt. Rizz would laugh at Drake's altar-boy conscience. He wished Julie was not so likable.

"The message said a delivery." Her brow knitted as she surveyed the open surgical trays and blood-soaked linens strewn about the Crash Room bay. It furrowed further as she neared the ashen, gaunt, and motionless patient. The placenta was in a stainless basin on a surgical stand. "Looks like I'm late."

"Paramedics got a call for an overdose and found our patient near-dead," Drake said. "They gave her Narcan and she snapped to and started screaming. As they neared the hospital, the baby presented legs-first but he was hung up. Delivery was complicated. He was premature, for sure less than four pounds, and in trouble with a heart rate to the 50s—not a cheery greeting to the world. We got him delivered and he's up in the NICU now."

Dr. Stone moved to the still sedated patient. She raised the sheet and viewed the bleeding.

"She's getting fluids and Pitocin now, with blood on the way," Drake said.

"Good." Dr. Stone placed her hand on the patient's abdomen. "The bleeding's brisk but not too bad right now. We need to get that uterus contracted." She looked toward the patient's head. "Has she said anything?"

"No. We know nothing about her—not even a name."

"It sounds like she's intensive-care sick and her main problems aren't obstetrical—"

The Crash Room door swung open. Clara Zeitman entered, carrying two units of blood. The nurses grabbed them and initiated the check-offs and transfusion process.

"I agree," Drake continued with Dr. Stone. "She needs the ICU. I've talked with the intensivist, Dr. Vijay Gupta. He'll oversee the overdose treatment and all the other critical care issues. I was hoping you'd take care of her obstetric issues."

"For sure," Dr. Stone said, sounding relieved. "OB doctors hate the ICU, and overdoses are definitely not my thing."

"Understood," Drake said. "Can you take a look at the placenta? It looks intact to me, but it's not my thing." He smiled.

"We always check to see if there's a big tissue loss, but it's inexact," she said. "It's rare they get sent to the lab, but even then, pathology has a hard time telling if they're complete." She slipped on gloves as she bent over the basin. She turned the tissue over. "It looks good to me."

The nurses had the blood transfusions running in. Drake did a recheck of the patient's vital signs, bleeding, and appearance.

"We'll transfer her to the unit soon," Drake said. "Her bleeding is better, and as each minute passes, the overdose should become less of a threat. Dr. Gupta will see her up there."

"I'm confident the medication and uterine massage will get the bleeding stopped," Dr. Stone said. "I'll write some orders, then go up to the unit with her." She shook her head. "A mother with a near-fatal narcotic overdose, precipitous labor with bleeding, and the complicated delivery of a drugged, high-risk preemie—the stork ran into some rough weather on this one." Sadness claimed her striking features.

Clara Zeitman stepped forward. "I can take the placenta to pathology," she said.

"Pathology exam seems reasonable in this case," Dr. Stone said.

Clara stepped forward, stripped patient labels from the chart, then picked up the basin, her movements practiced and sure. There was definitely something strange and socially awkward about her, but she exuded competence.

Drake could handle odd people if they helped his patients.

Chapter 6

Clara had seen how they'd looked at her in the Crash Room. It didn't matter how smart or good at her job she was, the nurses and doctors would never give her the respect she deserved.

She wasn't one of the chosen.

She used her key card to open the door to her office while she balanced the placenta-bearing container in her off hand. She glanced at the placard next to her office door:

Clara Zeitman

PhD, Clinical Laboratory Science, MS Health Informatics

Chief – Laboratory Services

Chief – Health Information Management

Despite her impressive credentials, she didn't have "MD" after her name, so she'd always be a second-class citizen in the medical world. *Screw them.*

Inside her office, she worked at the counter, her movements quick and sure. One aspect of the placenta was maroon and beefy, while the other side was a mass of vessels covered by a grayish membrane. The tissue smelled like rusted iron.

When she'd finished her deft manipulation, she put the approximately one-pound mass into the plastic container, then cleaned the counter. No mistakes. She smiled. She'd told Dan she knew more than almost all the doctors on staff. It was true.

Dan Ogren—they said he'd been a brute and a killer. He'd been a man. A man who had loved her—the only one. When he died, a part of her had been torn away—a part that would never return. And there was no doubt who was responsible for her loss.

Dan's ER arrest for domestic abuse had triggered the cascade of events that had ended with her watching him die in the ICU, his handsome face and flawless body ravaged by a bullet he did not deserve.

Drake Cody had made that happen. Being in the Crash Room with him it had taken all her restraint to hide her white-hot hatred of him.

She removed her gloves, took the patient's lab paperwork from her pocket, and stripped off a label. She double-checked that the "Jane Doe" information and order request were accurate. *The precision of a surgeon.* She exited her office, backtracked down the hall, then entered the pathology specimen-receiving area. A technologist looked up, then got to her feet quickly.

"Yes, Dr. Zeitman. What can I do for you?"

"This is directly from the ER." Clara held out the container and the lab slip. "Make sure it gets straight to pathology intake. No mistakes. Understood?"

"Of course, Dr. Zeitman." The technologist took the specimen and slip.

Clara didn't try to be warm or friendly to those under her. Lab technologists tended to be perfectionists by nature. Clara found maintaining distance and a cold judgmental posture worked best. It came naturally to her.

After reentering her office, she took her seat in front of the keyboard and dual-screen display on her desk. From here she could monitor virtually all hospital activities at a glance—even viewing content others thought was password protected. She'd overseen the installation of the system as well as the introduction and conversion to electronic medical records. Her position as chief of health information management and her prodigious skills had earned her autonomy. Even the giant software vendors and support staff did not question the system alterations she suggested. After sixteen years at Memorial Hospital, she was the computer network's undisputed master.

Clara pulled up the overdosed mother's lab results on the screen. The drug screen lit up positives for illicit drugs. The drug-addicted woman's infant would likely die or end up forever damaged. The mother's selfishness was the cause.

Did the label "mother" really apply? Did giving birth earn her that title? No way. Just as when Clara's mother, Dr. Frieda Zeitman, had interrupted her clinical schedule to give birth, it was a biologic event that signaled nothing.

As she evaluated the laboratory results, Clara recognized that her flash-quick Crash Room plan had been more inspired than she could have hoped. Dan would have been proud. He'd trusted her medical knowledge enough to put it to bold use before he'd been killed.

Her memories of Dan helped her overcome the slights constantly directed her way. She was so much more than her parents, those in the hospital, and particularly the medical school admissions committees years ago had judged her to be.

She no longer let the judgment of others tear her down. Dan's limitless love, trust, and admiration had validated her as nothing before ever had. Their relationship had been secret but incredible. What he'd done to her physically was... Her body flushed warm and her breath quickened.

He'd proved to her that all the others were wrong. He was the only person who'd ever loved her.

Rejection and lack of recognition had always been her burden. After the medical school refusals, she'd buried herself in work. She'd seen herself as an unattractive, fat woman who wasn't "good enough" but was tolerated because she did brilliant and unending work. Insecurity had driven her.

Dan had opened her eyes. What he'd made her feel had flooded her senses to where she'd overcome her self-consciousness about her dumpy body. She'd been a woman desired. He'd marveled at her mind and believed in her. But Dan had been killed.

As the memories surged, she felt that she might cry, that she should cry. It didn't happen—ever.

Dan was dead, but he had not left her.

She had special plans for herself. But Dan wouldn't be with her, and that was a crime.

He hadn't pulled the trigger, but she knew who was responsible.

Drake Cody would pay—forever.

Chapter 7

Children's Hospital outpatient clinic

Doctors, counselors, psychologists, social workers, and others had been a big part of Rachelle's life as a troubled orphan ward of the state.

This warm, colorful clinic and the people who staffed it were very different from the worn, glum welfare and charity institutions where she'd received "treatment," starting all those years ago.

The door to the nicely appointed, carpeted family conference room opened, and Dr. Sasha Mehta, the child psychologist, entered. She sat in a chair across the small table from Rachelle.

Dark-haired and short, with half-moon glasses, the fifty-something woman always had a smile ready. Rachelle had initially thought her an unlikely person to specialize in caring for children who'd suffered severe emotional or physical trauma, but she'd learned otherwise.

"I spoke with both Shane and Kristin, and I have the same feeling you shared. They are doing much better." Her smile flashed.

"Thank you." Rachelle's hopes surged. "Can you tell if they'll get over this completely? I've read that childhood trauma can damage people for life." She hadn't read it, she'd lived it. But after what had happened to her, she'd had no one. Shane and Kristin had her and Drake. Nothing meant more to them than their children.

"Every child and situation is different, but Shane and Kristin are resilient. Plus they have the most important medicine—loving parents." She smiled again. "I think they'll recover completely."

Relief coursed though Rachelle as if pumped through her veins. *Thank you, Jesus!*

"You're smiling and crying," Dr. Mehta nodded. "It has been terribly hard for you." She leaned forward and put her hand over Rachelle's.

"I'm so relieved." Rachelle's voice broke.

"How are you doing?" Dr. Mehta peered over the tops of her glasses. "You went through a horrendous ordeal. Have you had anxiety, nightmares, flashbacks, sweats?"

"I'm fine." *Not really.* Post-traumatic troubles had been part of Rachelle's life since her childhood. Now, still living in the place where she and the kids had been abducted triggered flashbacks daily. It was a struggle, but she'd committed to getting by without more doctors or medication. The kids were doing better, and nothing else mattered.

"I was hospitalized for an infection, but I'm good now."

The infection that had taken hold following the burns she'd suffered trying to protect Shane and Kristin had almost killed her.

That and the other disturbing parts of her past needed to remain behind her.

"Drake is working at the ER?"

"Almost always." Rachelle shrugged.

"That's hard on both of you. Please give him my regards, and let's see the kids back in two weeks," Dr. Mehta said. "Call if you have any issues. Take care of yourself, and if you want to see someone, I can recommend a 'big people' doctor."

No doctor for her. No more medications. She'd just received the best possible medicine—the children would be okay!

"You're very kind," Rachelle said. "Thank you so much for all you've done."

***

Drake entered a final note on a patient he'd seen earlier. The chore of documentation never ended, among the reasons being that malpractice courts declared, "If it isn't documented, it didn't happen."

In the hours since the Crash Room baby's delivery, Drake had been on the run. He, along with one staff partner, three resident doctors, and nursing staff, had treated a flood of patients. They'd made a big dent in the waiting room crowd and handled all the true emergencies. A cardiac arrest, a stroke, two major trauma cases from a car wreck, and other life-or-death patients had been cared for. All had done as well as could be expected. In the end, that determined a good shift from otherwise.

Drake was now caring for yet another narcotic overdose. In earlier years, narcotic ODs were rare. Now he'd seen four in a few hours.

"Hey, Doc. Have you signed on here full-time yet?"

Drake turned to find Michael, a buddy of his who worked in housekeeping, standing behind him with a mop in hand. Michael worked all over the hospital, but most often he kept the emergency department clean and ready. Years back, they'd found they shared an interest in basketball, and that had grown into a friendship. Michael was a class act, and often he worked so hard he broke a sweat.

"Hi, Michael. I'm working more than full-time hours, but I'm still temporary. I'm hoping I can get signed on for good."

"It'll happen." Michael smiled, put the mop in the bucket on wheels, and moved on with his chores.

Drake hadn't been accepted as permanent staff at Memorial and couldn't be until the state Medical Board ended his disciplinary probation. If that happened, it wouldn't guarantee his acceptance, but he had high hopes. He also had doubts. Some people at Memorial would always see him as a criminal.

Drake checked the time, then picked up the phone. He felt bad missing the kids' clinic appointment. Dr. Mehta's evening hours were convenient for most parents, but Drake's job involved round-the-clock shift assignments that changed rapidly. He dialed Rachelle.

"Hello."

"Hi, it's Drake. How'd the visit go?"

"We just got home. The kids are upstairs getting ready for bed. I wish you were here. I'm so excited, I feel like dancing. Dr. Mehta says the kids are doing fantastic, and she thinks they'll recover completely."

"That's wonderful news. I wish I was there, too. You're a great mom." She doubted herself, but it was absolutely true.

Jim Torrins, the president of medical affairs, approached in the corridor. He signaled he needed to speak with Drake. Drake lifted a "one minute" finger.

"I know it's not over, but I'm so relieved, Drake. I felt they were doing a lot better, and it's such a gigantic relief to have Dr. Mehta be so positive. She has really helped the kids."

"And so have you. You're a star." Her first and last thought was always what was best for their children.

"You're full of it, but hearing that makes me feel better." She paused. "Get back to your work. I know somebody needs you—they always do. I love you. I can't wait to see you."

"I'll be late and you'll be asleep, but we should have some time in the morning. Hug the kids for me. Awesome news. I'm hugging you through the phone."

They disconnected. Torrins stepped forward. The amiable doctor-turned-administrator was not smiling.

"We need to talk." He avoided eye contact, his posture stiff. "Privately."

***

Drake held the Crash Room door open, then followed Jim Torrins in. There'd been five different Crash Room cases so far this shift, but no patients were unstable enough to need it now.

Drake faced the president of medical affairs over the bed in bay three. Torrins' suit and tie looked out of place in the setting. The usually mellow physician-administrator seemed on edge.

"Do you want to sit down?" Drake said.

"I'll be quick." Torrins' brow creased. "As you may know, there've been a number of malpractice suits and settlements in the past months. Bad outcomes including three deaths—it's been tragic. Much worse than we've ever had at Memorial Hospital." He glanced at the darkened monitors. "I've studied the cases and I didn't see evidence of physician or nurse malpractice, but the risk management lawyers recommended settling several, and we lost some in court. It's tragic but also costly. Payments have totaled in the millions, and a couple of cases are still pending. The hospital's malpractice carrier is threatening to drop us."

Drake's mouth went dry. Malpractice—*why is he telling me this?*

Malpractice was every doctor's nightmare. If Drake had made an error that harmed or killed someone, it would rip his heart out.

"Kline has the hospital board demanding action," Torrins said. "Being the political animal that he is, he's positioning himself for survival."

"So this isn't about any of my patients?"

Torrins shook his head. Relief flooded Drake.

"Sorry," Torrins said. "I forgot about our MD paranoia."

It was true. Every time someone mentioned malpractice or approached an emergency doctor and opened with "Remember that patient you saw the other day?" the physician would hold their breath. Drake was with his colleagues in this. Unpredictability was always a component of disease and treatment. Bad things happen. People die unexpectedly. It sucked but was all too true.

And though malpractice happened, the legal system was a poor judge. Drake had seen an innocent doctor destroyed by the money-motivated, win-at-all-costs ugliness of a malpractice claim. She was found innocent, but the years-long process had devastated her. Meanwhile, no attorneys went after the few crooked "pill-mill" doctors who made a fortune bilking insurance and Medicare while cranking out narcotic prescriptions for personal gain.

For attorneys, malpractice was business-as-usual, and they took cases based on the possibility of a big paycheck. For caring doctors and nurses, being charged with malpractice crushed their soul.

"You had me worried." Drake's nightmarish experience with the criminal justice arm of the legal system did not inspire confidence in its malpractice branch.

"This isn't about you," Torrins said. "Well, actually, it is. I'm dragging you into it."

"Now I'm really confused," Drake said. "Dragging me into what?"

"Kline believes the hospital's doctors and nurses are incompetent. He sold the board on an emergency committee to address the crisis. As president of medical affairs, he assigned me as chairman of the task force. I have one month to show results or I'll be fired."

"How do you show results?" Drake said.

"Exactly." Torrins shook his head. "The task force idea is classic Kline. It's a no-lose for him. If the committee is successful—however that's defined—he's out of the woods. If it's unsuccessful, I'll be the fall guy. Either way, he keeps his job and big-time CEO income."

"So what does this have to do with me?" Drake asked. This sounded radioactive and he needed to stay well clear of it. Kline already hated him for dodging the get-rich-quick scheme the CEO had engineered to try to steal the rights to D-44, Drake's experimental drug.

Drake's plan was to work hard in the ER, keep a low profile, have his probation ended, and hopefully be accepted as a permanent member of the Memorial Hospital staff.

"Yeah, I feel bad about what I'm doing to you." Torrins grimaced. "I'm appointing you as the primary investigator for the committee. You're—"

"Please," Drake said, "don't do that. You have to keep me out of this. You know what it could mean."

Torrins had been part of the discovery of Drake's past criminal conviction and cover-up. Only the carrot of Drake's breakthrough research, the involvement of an appreciative news anchorwoman patient, and the attorney Rizz had found had prevented the Medical Board from permanently ending his medical career.

"Sorry," Torrins said. "Though you're young, you're the most solid clinician I know. Second, if we do identify problems, we may have to confront other doctors. As an ER physician, you've dealt with almost all of them. Despite your past, um, issues, the staff doctors respect you." Torrins looked toward the Life Clock above the bed, then back at Drake. "Additionally, if somehow we succeed, it might increase the likelihood of ending your probation, and me getting you promoted to a permanent ER staff position."

Downside a certainty, positives nebulous at best. *Not good!*

"Most important is that Kline is right about one thing," Jim said. "There has been an unprecedented number of tragic deaths and bad patient outcomes. I don't have an explanation. I need someone who's good at sniffing out medical mysteries."

A cluster of malpractice or a wave of freakish deaths and injury? It didn't sound like there'd be any easy answers. Perhaps no answers at all.

"What if we don't find anything?" Drake said.

"Kline hates you for having blocked his attempt to get rich off your drug research, and he wants me gone. We need to find some kind of answer or we're likely both history. Consider it either a compliment or a curse, but you're the guy I want with me in this battle."

The bustle and hum of the ER penetrated the Crash Room doors, the chrome of the hanging medical instruments glistened in the light, and a Lysol-like chemical scent tinged the air. Compliment or curse? Jim Torrins was a first-class guy, but this was a giant pain-in-the-ass that Drake did not need. *Damn!*

The darkened Life Clock hung above the empty patient bed. Was it already invisibly ticking off the time Drake had remaining as a physician at Memorial Hospital?

Chapter 8

ICU

Blood jetted through the needle into the tube. Clara prided herself on her ability to stick a vein on the first poke on anyone. Her never-miss skills impressed her subordinates and meant less discomfort for the patients. But Clara was not concerned about the comfort of the woman whose blood flowed into the tube. The patient in ICU bed three had cared more about getting high than the life of the baby she'd been carrying.

Clara deftly switched each of several collection tubes onto the needle, filling each in turn. She then double-checked the patient's ID bracelet and applied the sticky-backed labels to the tubes. The physicians and nurses of the ICU were familiar with her drawing blood. Her staff appreciated their boss lending a hand with this challenging but thankless task.

They didn't like her, but she knew her helping out drew solid, if grudging, respect.

In truth, Clara craved the hands-on encounters with patients. It was the closest she came to her dream. She'd been born to be a physician. It had taken the corrupt medical school admissions process, her toxic parents, and lying applicants like Drake Cody to steal that from her. Heat rushed through her body and she clenched her teeth. Her anger surged.

She closed her eyes, took a deep breath, then let it out slowly. Now more than ever she needed to be cool and together.

She glanced around. The short blonde nurse was busy at the unit station. She was the one who'd taken care of Dan when he was shot and dying. The one who'd been allowed to touch him, to speak to him, to be with him as he died.

Clara had only been able to look on from a distance. So wrong.

She stuffed her resentment and focused. Now is what mattered.

She looked around once more, then quickly accessed the control panel to the IV pump. The pumps—mini computer-controlled delivery systems—were to be accessed by the nurses only. Clara finished her program entries in seconds. She then slipped two loaded syringes from the pocket of her white coat. Her breath came fast. *No mistakes!*

31

She kept the syringes palmed. Scanning with her peripheral vision, she sensed it was safe. She inserted the needle of the first syringe into the primary IV port and placed her thumb over the plunger. Her heart threatened to jump out of her chest.

She drove home the plunger, launching the biologic torpedo into the patient.

She swallowed, her mouth as dry as dust. She'd expected to be nervous, but the excitement surprised her.

Standing, she gripped the second syringe, then made another surreptitious scan. This was the most vulnerable point. Her throat tightened and she felt light-headed but did not hesitate.

She inserted the needle and drove home the plunger, delivering the second devastating drug into the small fluid bag connected piggy-back near the top of the main IV line. Before the substance could enter the patient's vein, Clara removed a small can of liquid nitrogen and sprayed the secondary IV line, freezing the fluid and stopping flow.

As she sat back down, her scalp tingled, and she felt a rush unlike any she'd experienced since the times Dan had driven her to bliss.

He would have appreciated her cleverness. The second drug would not enter the patient's body until the IV line thawed. The delay and the distraction she had planned would help eliminate any suspicion that might arise. If all went as it should, there'd never be a question—she'd considered every step.

Clara bent, collected the blood-filled tubes, picked up her tray, then stepped out of ICU bay three as she'd done many times in the past. But this was unlike any time before.

She took the blood specimens she'd collected, placed them in the pneumatic tube delivery canister, and entered the lab designation. The canister disappeared in a whoosh.

Clara sat at one of the computer terminals in the nurses' station.

Her heart raced, each breath feeling as if she had a steel band around her chest.

The blond nurse entered ICU three. Would she notice anything? The nurse pulled the curtain, but Clara could see though the gap. The nurse pulled back the sheet. Clara almost jumped to her feet.

The nurse laid hands on the patient's abdomen.

She was performing the uterine massage that helped post-partum bleeding stop. *Relax, Clara! Quit staring.*

She turned her eyes to the keyboard, working to hide what she felt. The seconds couldn't go fast enough, yet she relished each moment. Like sex with Dan had been, it was pain and pleasure and she couldn't tell where one began and the other ended. Her hands trembled.

After a moment, she looked. The nurse was tucking the sheet around the woman.

She hadn't noticed anything.

Clara wanted to shout and pump her fist.

The science, the wonder, her mastery—each instant now, the diabolically powerful drugs she'd injected were chewing holes in the cellular structures and biochemical systems holding the unconscious mother together. Clara was outsmarting them all, her medical knowledge refuting every rejection, every humiliation, every injustice. Step one of payback and a payday all in one.

A grim surgical saying about bleeding and death came to mind. "All bleeding stops—eventually."

Her fingers keyed in her administrator's password, then typed the command that would trigger the distraction. She took a deep breath and prepared to hit "enter".

"Hey, it's test tube lady." The braying baritone made her jump. "Slumming where the real patient care happens, huh?"

Her heart jumped to her throat. Unbelievable. How had she missed Dr. Bart Rainey's massive carcass arriving on the unit?

"Nothing to say, *Doctor*?" His broadcast-loud voice oozed with derision. The nearly seven-foot tall surgeon was, in every way, the biggest asshole on the medical staff. "Playing with test-tubes today?" he said.

She knew better than to respond, but the words were already exiting her mouth.

"I'm chief of health information management as well as laboratory services—

two of the most essential functions in the hospital. Functions without which you wouldn't be able to do your job at all."

Dr. Bart Rainey raised his arms above his head, nearly reaching the ceiling, then bent at the waist, keeping his arms extended in a parody of a worshipful bow.

"Thank you for honoring us, oh *doctor* of petri dishes and passwords. Our lowly patient care efforts pale in comparison to your PhD knowledge of chemistry, microscopes, and computers."

Everyone in the unit now watched her and the colossal asshole of a doctor. So many times he'd humiliated her.

God, how she hated him.

Someday there'd be a payoff. She hit the "enter" key.

***

Five minutes earlier

Eighteen years as a nurse, and every ICU shift still taught Tracy something. Sometimes that something was not pleasant.

Her new patient—the drug-overdosed new mother—was, in some ways, beyond anything Tracy could understand. How could a woman's compulsion to get high override the well-being of her unborn child?

Her patient's life and addiction must be brutal. A brother in Gary, Indiana, was reportedly the only family. The nurse administrator had reached him by phone. He'd been unsurprised by her overdose. He had no idea who the father of her child might be. He'd said she put their family though hell for years and asked to be notified if she died, but otherwise she was on her own.

How terribly alone this poor woman must have been.

For the umpteenth time, Tracy recognized her own good fortune. Her heart ached for people who suffered as her patient must.

The ICU was laid out with the nurses' station at the center and the fifteen ICU rooms positioned around it like the spokes of a wheel. Tracy sat at one of the computer terminals among the desks behind the circular counter that separated the station from the rest of the unit. She accessed her patient's most recent lab results.

The remote vital signs monitor showed that her patient's blood pressure and pulse had improved. She looked into ICU three and saw that that Clara

Zeitman, the lab and IT chief who preferred to be called 'doctor,' was at the patient's bedside. Though she was head of both laboratory services and medical records, she regularly drew blood on ICU patients. She seemed to always be in the hospital. Tracy felt sympathy for the woman. Stiff, never friendly, and socially awkward, perhaps she had nothing else in her life?

Tracy scanned the unit. One of Dr. Bart Rainey's post-operative patients was in room nine. The nurses called the massive surgeon "Black Bart" behind his back because he cast a dark shadow over everything. He'd been an unprofessional ass to Tracy some months back, for which Drake Cody had gotten him in front of the review board. He stayed away from her now and she avoided him. She'd seen him bully and verbally harass Clara Zeitman on more than one occasion. Tracy was sure they both hoped to avoid the colossal jerk when he showed up on his rounds,

The overdosed mother's hemoglobin had stabilized. Additionally, Tracy's latest exam showed that the vaginal bleeding had slowed to a trace. Things were looking up.

Nonetheless, the bleeding was nothing to take lightly. Disastrous in undeveloped countries, postpartum bleeding remained a major cause of maternal death in the US. After delivery, the uterus bleeds until its muscular walls contract.

The meds her patient received had helped, as had the uterine massage Tracy had performed. The clock showed it to be almost time to consider a repeat massage. The bleeding seemed controlled, but cutting corners never made good things happen.

The patient's urine toxicology screen appeared on the computer screen: methamphetamines, opiates, cocaine, THC. Meth, narcotics, cocaine, and marijuana—Tracy sighed, thinking about what those drugs meant for the struggling newborn in the NICU.

She looked up and saw that the Clara Zeitman had exited the patient's room and was in the process of shipping the blood specimens to the laboratory.

Tracy entered the room, then checked the patient—the flow of blood had virtually stopped. She began to massage the patient's uterus. This would be the last massage her patient would need.

Dr. Stone had been confident the bleeding would stop. She'd asked Tracy to page her immediately if the bleeding increased. The overdose was no longer a threat and the bleeding was in hand.

Maybe today was the day this patient's life would turn around. There was always hope. That was something else Tracy's years as a nurse had taught her—never write anybody off.

She completed the massage and tucked the sheet around her patient. Tracy froze as she heard the only voice that could boom from the nurses' station all the way to every patient's bedside. Dr. Rainey was on the unit.

She saw him make an exaggerated bow towards Clara Zeitman and the insulting tone of his words registered clearly. She sighed. Why was he such a jerk, and why pick on the friendless Clara? *Enough!*

If he carried on one more second, she was going to confront him.

She flinched as at that moment a clarion alarm erupted, and wall-mounted high-intensity strobe lights flashed. A mechanized voice sounded overhead, "Code red ICU, Code red ICU."

Tracy first scanned her patient's room—no fire, no smoke. She stepped out of the room and grabbed the fire extinguisher from its wall nook.

"It smells like it's from the utility room," one of the nurses said.

"Correct." It was Clara Zeitman calling out from in front of a computer. "System report shows the alarm source as utility room B-677."

Tracy ran to the utility room. The alarm and flashing lights continued as she put her hand against the door. It felt cool. She readied the extinguisher, her hand on the trigger.

One deep breath, and she pushed the door open. A burning electrical smell hit strong, but there was no smoke, heat, or flame. The stink led her to the counter against the opposite wall. A battery charger sat plugged into a wall outlet. A sniff confirmed it as the source. She set down the extinguisher, then took a towel from a stack of linen and used it to grab the charger's cord and yank it out of the outlet.

"All clear," she called out as she backed out of the room. "No danger."

Protocol called for security to check and clear any site triggering an alarm, and at that moment two security personnel entered the unit.

Within thirty seconds the alarm, mechanized overhead message, and flashing lights ceased.

The entire event had taken only two or three minutes. Unease gripped Tracy. Had the screeching alarm and lights jangled her nerves? Her ICU co-workers kidded her about being obsessive—she worried too much. They were right, but her edginess did not ease.

She hurried back to ICU room three, her eyes jumping ahead to the monitors. Pulse rate 133—too high. Blood pressure 70/30—too low. *What's happening?*

Her patient remained motionless with eyes closed. Had her color worsened? Tracy rested a hand on the patient's wrist. The pulse thready. The skin cool. Her tension ratcheted higher.

A spray of pinpoint bruises speckled the woman's face like freckles. Trickles of fresh blood seeped from under the transparent dressings overlying the IVs in her arm. She'd only been away from the bedside for minutes. *What the—?*

Her nurse's intuition flooded her with dread.

She drew back the sheet as her fear crested.

Oh my God!

Chapter 9

"This is Dr. Cody—over." Drake released the radio transmit key.

"Ambulance 831 on scene with an overdose. 911 call per roommate, who reported the patient is a narcotic user and injected drugs earlier. She found the patient unresponsive after not seeing her for at least a half hour. Upon arrival, twenties-year-old white female with needle and drug paraphernalia present. No pulse, no cardiac rhythm. Performed assessment and basic resuscitation. No response. There are no signs of life. Request pronounce 10-7."

Drake hung his head. It was not rare that paramedics were called to a scene to find their patient had already died. Drake's responsibility in these cases was to formally pronounce the patient dead and declare a time of death. He needed to make certain this was not done prematurely. Drake knew this medic and the grim certainty her report assured—another life lost. What was happening out there?

"Are police on scene?" Drake asked.

"A squad arrived at the same time we did. It's a medical examiner's case."

"Okay. Avoid any possible exposure to drugs and warn the police as well."

"10-4," the medic said.

"I have 2114 hours as time of death."

"2114 hours. Thanks. Ambulance 831 out."

Drake clicked off, then leaned on his elbows, head in hands.

A woman in her twenties—gone. Somebody's daughter, sister, friend, loved one—her life and future erased as of 2114 hours. Only a flood of anguish and regret left behind.

With this death, the earlier overdosed mother, and those that had been successfully resuscitated by the paramedics, the total so far this shift was seven. Crazy!

He thought of those who supplied the drugs for profit, and a dark part of him stirred. He pictured the overdosed mother in the ICU, heard again the shrill cry of her jittery, drug-toxic, premature infant.

Drug dealers were getting rich selling misery and death.

The muscles in his neck and shoulders tightened. The banked embers of rage that he worked to control flared. Those who preyed on the vulnerable and addicted needed to be dealt with. The deaths had to stop.

Drake swiveled his neck, trying to loosen his muscles. He left the radio room and moved to pick up another patient chart from the rack. People who needed the ER never stopped coming. How many narcotic ODs never arrived? How many were found too late for a 911 call and went straight to the morgue?

He checked the time—more than two hours to go in his shift. He wanted to be home. Exhaustion had struck as if someone had flipped his "off" switch. Sometimes it seemed hopeless.

I'll give all I've got and care for every person the best that I can.

His ER mantra was hokey, but he went to it often. He sighed, then picked up a new chart.

"CODE BLUE, ICU. CODE BLUE, ICU."

Drake slammed the chart back into the rack and was moving before the page ended. An ER physician needed to respond to every code blue at Memorial Hospital. No matter where or when, one of the ER docs needed to get free and respond. Drake caught the charge nurse's eye as he took off. He nodded. She gave a thumbs-up. That exchange communicated that Drake had the ICU code blue covered and assured that the nurses and other doctors would cover his patients in his absence. He slapped the wall plate, burst through the automated ER doors, and sprinted down the corridor.

"CODE BLUE, ICU." The overhead voice sounded calm. Good. Code Blues were triggered when a patient's heart stopped or was otherwise crashing. Any chance of saving such patients required clear-thinking—panic by any in the resuscitation team virtually guaranteed a bad ending. The tongue-in-cheek instruction for young doctors was "When you get to the patient, first take your own pulse."

Drake raced past Michael, a housekeeping worker and friend who had moved himself and his floor buffer to the side of the corridor. He gave Drake a nod.

"Save 'em, Doc," he said.

Everyone in the hospital understood what Code Blue meant.

Drake ripped open the door to the stairwell and powered upward. The ICU was on the sixth floor. After more than four years of responding to codes, he knew the fastest and best way to everywhere. He paced himself as he took the stairs two at a time. He'd been training lately and was in good shape, but he needed to be steady if called upon to perform critical procedures in the ICU.

"CODE BLUE, ICU."

When a code blue triggered in the ICU, the highly skilled ICU nurses were at the bedside immediately. They would initiate resuscitation efforts. Additionally, intensive care or other physicians might be present. Sometimes, when Drake arrived there was nothing for him to contribute—a good thing when the patient had already stabilized, but bad news other times.

He passed the fourth-floor landing. A memory of near-terror from a previous Code Blue flashed. He'd raced up these same stairs believing that Rachelle's infection had caused her to crash—that he would lose her. He remembered his profound and guilt-free relief at finding it was the abusive Dan Ogren who was dying.

Drake burst out of the sixth-floor stairwell and banked toward the ICU. The automatic doors were open and he entered the unit. A small crowd of nurses, techs, and orderlies hovered around ICU bay three.

The caregivers parted as Drake entered the room. A tall male nurse was performing chest compressions, while a respiratory tech ventilated the patient.

Drake's next and overwhelming impression was blood.

Splattered, shoe-tracked, and horrifically voluminous blood had filled the bed and flooded onto the sheets and floor.

His nurse friend, Tracy, sat in the corner staring blank-faced at her blood-covered, gloved hands. The other faces in the room bore the stunned bleakness that accompanies being witness to tragedy. It was a look Drake knew too well.

As the respiratory tech repositioned the airway bag, Drake's eyes tracked to the patient's face. His breath caught. *No!*

Barely recognizable due to blackened eyes and grotesque purplish bruising was the face of the mother whose baby he had delivered.

Her eyes were fixed and glazed in an unseeing stare.

The EKG monitor showed the flat line of a lifeless heart. Dr. Gupta stood near the head of the bed. His face was drawn. He met Drake's eyes and shook his head in a barely perceptible "no."

Drake's throat knotted. *She's gone.*

He took in the widespread bruising, the rivulets of red from the IV and blood draw sites on her arms, and the pool of crimson that saturated the bed and dripped to the floor. The units of blood hanging from the IV pole and the pile of empty transfusion bags showed that the ICU team had attempted to keep up with the runaway bleeding.

Dr. Gupta put a hand on the shoulder of the nurse doing CPR.

"If no one has an objection, I'm going to call it." Silence. The smell of blood hung. "Okay. Good effort. Thank you all. I'm calling it at 2150 hours."

Tracy raised her head over quaking hands. Her eyes were empty and her skin pale. Did she believe she'd overlooked something? Might the death have been prevented? Doubt could haunt those who had patients die on their watch.

Those were the worst doubts that any who worked saving lives had to face. It looked as if such doubts were clutching at Tracy.

They reached out for Drake, too.

Chapter 10

Q turned onto Thirty-SecondStreet, his headlights showing end-to-end parked cars.

The art support charity party he'd attended had been all right. He played the articulate black guy the rich-folk charity crowd loved to have at events. He represented himself as a businessman and citizen supporting his community. It was true, except he told people he was in real estate—not drug sales.

He'd only had one beer because being black, he could get pulled over just for breathing, but he was cruising a cocaine high primed with some of his high-test "Purple Haze" cannabis. He could pass any sobriety test. He played it safe. Job one at all times was keeping his ass out of jail.

A rare open parking spot sat in front of his Colfax Ave and Thirty-Second Street address. Q pulled his showroom-clean Lexus SUV into the spot.

As he climbed the steps to the front porch, the motion-activated light clicked on, lighting up the front of his new place. The big two-story Victorian on the corner lot was perfect. Already it felt like home.

He keyed the locks to the front door, went in, then entered the code into his state-of-the-art security system. The house was his sanctuary, his vault, and housed the laboratory where he worked his magic. He planned to buy it soon—with cash. His first real estate purchase—a good place to invest cash. He smiled—there'd be many more.

He relocked the door behind him, then reset the alarm.

The scent of wood oil and cedar greeted him. He kept the house as clean and stowed away as his lab.

Ten-foot ceilings, hand-crafted woodwork—it was far beyond the little rambler his mother had raised him in. He'd blown past everything she'd achieved in her play-by-the-rules life. To her credit she'd rode him hard through his early schooling and introduced him to chemistry. He owed her for that.

He'd rebelled as a teen, found drugs, and gone to the streets. As a teacher in the community, his mother had been ashamed of him, as she was every other black person she identified as a criminal. Beyond that, she'd railed against all who spoke poorly, cussed, dressed shoddily, talked loud, drank, or any of an endless number of behaviors that she identified as ignorant and bringing shame to black people.

After his conviction, she'd disowned him as a disgrace. No doubt she was still out there passing judgment on any who didn't behave like she thought they should.

Her chemistry-teacher influence was the key to his success. If she knew where the junior scientist chemistry sets and experiments she'd walked him through had led, she'd want to take her switch to him and whip him good.

He climbed the steps to the third floor, then unlocked the reinforced door. Before opening it, he turned to his safety table and the safety gear there. He slipped on an airway mask, a lab coat, and a pair of nitrile gloves. He opened the door and entered. He looked over the white, twenty-by-twenty-foot room and the tools of his trade.

Two slate-topped lab benches, a desk with computer, and an array of new equipment: a pharmacy-grade compounding processor, a tablet press machine, several digital micro-processor scales, packaging materials, multiple beakers, and his stores of quinine, and other cutting/buffering components.

Every time he entered the lab, he scored a hit of pride. It was the work-place of a professional. Mistakes or carelessness with product could kill, but he was its master. He'd come a long way and was making it big time.

He opened his storage safe and removed one of the vials filled with the miraculous crystalline powder. He smiled. What he held in his hands was worth thousands of times its weight in gold.

A "bump" was the amount of narcotic effect needed to get Q's users off. The amount of drug required for a bump differed for each narcotic drug and its purity. Measuring and blending together the right amount of drugs of differing potency and purity was far beyond junior chemistry stuff. It took an art-and-science juggling act to create a product that allowed users to "get right."

Q loved the challenge.

Today the narcotics that came into users' hands were an unknown. In the old days, it was always heroin—the only question was how pure.

Now the stuff being sold as heroin was likely a heroin-synthetic mix or contained no heroin at all. The new, synthetic narcotics were cheaper, easier to smuggle, and with a never-before-seen potency.

Fentanyl had been the first synthetic on the street. It was now cheaper and easier to get a hold of than heroin—partly because it came from laboratories rather than poppy fields. Little dudes created most of the synthetics in China, where they faced zero pressure from authorities and shipped drugs all over the world, often using the mail.

The highly potent, concentrated drugs were easy to transport. Each pound of fentanyl the Mexican cartels could smuggle in provided the same number of bumps as more than forty pounds of heroin.

Suppliers everywhere were using fentanyl alone or mixed with heroin, getting many more highs out of a smaller amount of drug and making more money.

Fentanyl had killed Prince. Q couldn't believe the musician hadn't had his head together enough to keep from overdosing. Using drugs was an individual's right, but they had to be careful—ignorant and unskilled suppliers were everywhere. The synthetics were not for amateurs. Q knew that most of his competitors were dumbasses, with none of the skills needed to deliver a professional product.

Q prided himself on his professionalism.

He held the vial up and admired the crystalline powder. It was one hundred times as potent as fentanyl, which itself was administered in millionths of a gram doses. Carfentanil was the most powerful narcotic in existence. He'd discovered it months before it made the mainstream media.

He'd been watching an Animal Planet TV program and researchers were using hypodermic darts shot from rifles to drug and examine hippos. The drugged animals had reminded Q of heroin users nodding off in shooting dens. When the program said the drug was a narcotic he'd been instantly interested. He'd gone online and tracked down the name of the animal tranquilizing narcotic—carfentanil.

Later, he web-searched articles. Twelve-hundred-pound polar bears could be dropped with a dose of less than 500 micrograms. It seemed impossible. The doses were measured in millionths of a gram! Dust-particle-sized doses took down moose, hippos, even elephants.

The drug had never been tested or used in humans due to its insane potency.

The business potential of such a drug blew his mind. Even a tiny amount of the pure drug would provide thousands of "bumps."

He'd used a dark-web access he'd learned about in prison to find a Chinese supplier and made a transaction. The dark web was full of scammers and cheats, but Q had risked his money. The online business courses he'd taken taught "you have to spend money to make money" and "high risk equals high reward." The possible rewards were off the chart, and he'd risked less than he spent for a kilogram of good weed.

A small brown packet from Shanghai with China Post and US Postal Service labels had arrived at his P.O. box. Inside were the plastic vials containing white powder. The vials contained a total of fifty grams.

It was too good to believe. His future delivered in the mail for a few thousand bucks? Had he been scammed?

Q had put on gloves and mask, then used the tip of a hypodermic needle to transfer one granule of the powder, smaller than a grain of salt, into a liter of water. He stirred it up and added just two drops of the solution to a tablespoon of peanut butter. He smeared the peanut butter on an oak tree in his north Minneapolis yard before he left for the day.

When he returned, there were three dead squirrels at the base of the tree. His heart raced and his scalp tingled.

It was real and as mind-blowingly potent as the science journals had said.

He did the math. Each gram of carfentanil contained the narcotic power to make over 3000 hits. When diluted and processed, his tiny vials contained enough drug for over 150,000 bumps.

The calculator had shaken in his hands. Each time he ran the numbers, it came out the same blow-your-mind result. The miracle in the mail could make him over six million dollars.

And it was happening. His operation had become a money factory.

He took out one of the vials, then double-checked his mask and gloves. Breathing in or touching the pure drug could kill.

He'd been selling most of the drug in packets as heroin, but had also compounded it into counterfeit Oxycontin pills. Dealers and users couldn't tell and didn't care—as long as they got a good high. With Q's product they did.

Microscopic mistakes in handling, diluting, cutting, or processing would result in product that killed. Worse, handling the drug without skill and caution could kill him. It required all his expertise. Q held the vial up to the light.

The drug had transformed his life.

His business had taken off. No more street punk. No more scamming ERs and doctors' offices for nickel-and-dime product. He was big time. Only the law could mess things up.

He'd gone clean-cut and worked at looking like a stand-up citizen. He didn't mind posing at the charity and social events—it was business.

His mom would have approved of his new style. A well-dressed, well-groomed, articulate black man. "Now there's a real man," she would have said.

She'd been right about some things. The years he'd spent being a punk, scraping by, and taking shit on the street were lame. No more.

He was a scientist and a businessman, on his way to crazy rich.

He opened the safe and pulled out his personal stash. He laid out three lines of high-grade coke. No narcotics for him—he didn't roll that way. Opioids took you down, and he had too much good going on.

He snorted the powder. The rush blew through him like a cool breeze. It targeted neurotransmitters and hot-wired pathways in his brain. His energy surged and his good mood elevated. The law said it was criminal to feel this good. He smiled. *Kiss my ass!*

It was time for work. He took out the quinine he used to cut the drug with and turned to the micro-balance. He turned on his sound system.

Working with carfentanil fully challenged his skills, and every hour he worked meant more product, more business, and more money. Not only was he getting big-time rich, but he'd never felt better about himself.

For an instant, he remembered prison and the world he'd been a part of, but the bad vibe was no more than a flicker. The lead-in words of Prince's "Let's Go Crazy" came from the remote speakers.

"Dearly beloved, we are gathered here today
To get through this thing called life"

Q laughed out loud.

He had his head on right and was never going back.

Chapter 11

Drake woke to thunder so powerful its rumble vibrated in his chest. He checked the bedside clock—7:38 AM. A flash of lightning penetrated the predawn dimness and another boom of thunder closely followed. Rain drummed the roof.

Rachelle shifted from her side to her back but remained asleep. Some nights she cried out, writhing with nightmares Drake wished he could will away. Even then, she rarely wakened. It had been after two when he'd climbed into bed. She'd not stirred.

Now she slept through the storm, her lithe dancer's body draped in one of his V-necked tee shirts.

He turned on his side, moving closer. He reveled in her warmth, the softness of her body, and the sound of her easy breathing. Her delicate features showed none of the worry that visited her so often when awake. The scar started below her ear and extended down her neck. It spread, twisted and irregular like melted wax, to the point of her shoulder. This was the oldest of her wounds. She'd never talked about it and deflected any questions. Drake knew the burn was from her childhood and nothing more.

Her right hand lay palm up and the healed grafts of her wrist and palm looked dark in the suffused light. She was self-conscious about her neck and these recent wounds. She worked to keep them hidden with long sleeves, her hair, scarves, or collars. When around strangers, she stayed on the periphery and did her best to avoid attention. Only he ever saw her so exposed.

For him, the scars highlighted her beauty and reminded him of her courage and all she'd overcome.

Olive-skinned, with eyes a depth of brown he'd seen nowhere else, he'd been transfixed from his first glimpse. He feathered a finger over her silken cheek, down her damaged skin, to the soft rise at the top of her breasts. The first time they'd touched it was as if the world had fallen away.

Their first kiss had taken him to a place he'd never been.

They both had pain in their pasts. They'd been hurt and many of the scars did not show.

He hadn't fully shared his past and neither had she, but their secrets never dimmed their passion. His senses registered only the wonder of her. The children made their bond immeasurably stronger.

Lightning flashed and the roof and furniture shook. Drake listened for the kids over the audio monitor. He hoped they'd come scrambling in seeking comfort and snuggles. He heard nothing. The children slept deeply like their mother. He stood and left the bedroom.

Standing outside his children's door his thoughts flashed to Bryce, the lost and struggling mentally ill boy. His parents had clutched each other and looked to Drake. He'd been unable to provide the "this will go away" reassurance they desperately sought.

He cracked the door to the kids' room and peeked in. Shane and Kristin slept in twin beds. Shane's hockey stick leaned against his headboard, and little Kristin's blanket lay covered with stuffed animals. At six and four years old, they'd already experienced ugliness no one ever should.

They rested, innocent and beautiful. The thought of losing the kids and Rachelle lurked in his mind like a dreaded beast. It had almost happened.

He'd killed to protect them. Savage thoughts flashed, and his jaw clenched. No one would ever hurt them again.

He stood in the hallway listening to the rain pound the roof. Their rental unit—this structure that had housed them for the past four years—had never felt like a home. For Drake, the time demands of his training and his spinal cord research had made the townhouse more of a way station.

Rachelle generally suffered in silence, but he knew she desperately wanted to get out of this place. This was where for years she'd been doing the work of two parents—with no one to help and not enough money to pay the bills. Worst of all, this had been where her and the children's kidnapping nightmare had begun.

He'd been in the ER that night, once again leaving her and the children on their own.

Later, the rental unit had been the site of Rachelle's recovery. She'd endured bandage changes and pain as the burns and skin grafts of her hands and wrists healed—then the development of an infection that had almost killed her. How could she not hate this place?

With the completion of his residency training, he'd expected to have more time. It had not worked that way.

He still worked too much, and they were still in this lousy rental. The ER was short of doctors. Rizz and John had not recovered from their gunshot wounds and might not ever.

Drake covered as many shifts as he could. Besides feeling it was his duty to help out, he wanted to make the best impression possible. He wanted to join the Memorial Hospital staff permanently. With his history, he had to do everything possible to improve his chances.

On the positive side, with his training complete, every hour he worked meant good money. He had a mountain of debt and needed to take care of Rachelle, the kids, and his mother. The advance payment he'd received from the pharmaceutical company for his breakthrough drug, D-44, had helped, but they still needed every dollar he could get his hands on.

With his improved wages, the D-44 money, and some luck, he hoped they could escape the townhouse soon.

Another lightning flash was followed by a more distant rumble of thunder. The storm would slow traffic. He had to shower and get moving.

***

In the shower, other issues facing him took their turn.

Thoughts of the hospital brought back the horror of the overdosed mother's death. As she'd been transferred to the ICU, all signs had pointed to her improvement. What had triggered the catastrophic bleeding?

His friend Tracy had looked devastated. Doctors and nurses couldn't react outwardly like others when their patients died, but they felt it. "Maybe if I'd..." second-guessing added to the pain the deaths caused.

Tracy was incredible, but it was the best nurses and doctors who judged themselves the harshest. The hot water was fading. Drake soaped his shoulders and arms.

Jim Torrins' forcing Drake to be a part of the hospital's malpractice committee stunk. The assignment was a personal and professional minefield. Jim's dumping the investigation of the mysterious deaths and bad outcomes on Drake was trouble he didn't need. *Thank you very little, Torrins.*

Drake tipped his face into the spray, then straightened as the now cool water pounded his chest.

Before sleep, the tragedy of the mother and baby had messed with his mind. He'd awakened with the narcotic epidemic on his mind. The threat level had changed—multiple fatal overdoses in the span of hours. Insane! How bad might it get? Greed-stoked predators were selling misery and death for money—big money. Could they be stopped?

Addicts and those who tried drugs were guilty of being flawed and human—just as Drake was—exactly as his beautiful Rachelle had been. Their addiction led to misery for them and all around them. The need for the drug eliminated reason and morality. But users did not deserve death. The drugs made them someone else. Something had to be done.

Was it his responsibility? Another emergency that demanded he take action?

When he'd defended his brother, he'd hurt people. It had meant a conviction and juvenile prison, but that did not burden his conscience. It was when he'd turned away from Kevin that haunted him.

He needed his probation ended and his medical license cleared. He wanted the life with Rachelle and the kids that they'd worked so hard for. Getting involved further with the drug threat would not help his chances. He took care of the users and overdoses that made it to the ER—wasn't that enough?

He grit his teeth as the water shifted to icy cold and stole his breath.

Damn! He knew what he must do. He had no choice.

Someone had to protect the victims.

He had to fight back, no matter what it cost him.

***

Rachelle awoke to thunder. She turned and saw the rumpled sheets, then heard the shower over the drumming of rain on the roof. She could tell by how she felt that Drake had slept beside her. His presence helped her sleep.

With Dr. Mehta's assurance about the children, everything looked brighter. Rachelle knew she worried excessively and complained to Drake about things he could not control, but it was guilt and her painful past that fueled much of her distress.

Drake had experienced hard times too, but he did not complain. He worked hard. He needed a wife, not a whiny, nut-job patient.

Now that the kids were doing better, she vowed to get stronger. They would get out of this place. She would do whatever she could to help him and the children.

Everything would get better.

***

Drake stepped out of the shower. He dried off, then wrapped the towel around his waist. Now that he'd committed to what he must do, some of his unrest had eased.

He moved quietly past the kid's room, stepped into the bedroom, and closed the door behind him. The curtains were open, but the light remained muted as the morning thunderstorm raged. The bed was empty.

Rachelle stepped out of the shadows. The oversized T-shirt she wore ended at the top of her thighs. The V-neck hung low. The white of the shirt accented her dark-toned skin. She was silent as she took another step forward and pressed herself against him.

He wrapped his arms around her and everywhere his skin touched hers was heat. She smelled of cinnamon and lilac—her scent unlike any other.

She looked up at him. In the subdued light, her eyes were glistening opals. His heart hammered, and where she leaned against him throbbed so powerfully he could not speak. She took his hands and stepped back, still looking into his face.

"I love you, Drake Cody," she said. "I'll always love you."

She let go of his hands, grasped the bottom of the T-shirt, and slipped it off over her head.

His breath caught, his body on fire. She rested her palms on his chest. He stood paralyzed in a sensual storm as lightning flashed, thunder pealed, and rain pounded the roof.

She dropped her hands and removed his towel.

He wanted nothing but her.

He needed nothing but her.

There was nothing but her... *Oh, God.*

Chapter 12

Clara toweled sweat off her face and hair. She'd just completed three circuits of stair climbs from the first to the eighth floor in the southwest stairwell. She ran them daily and always pushed herself to near vomiting before returning to her office. Punishing her body and burning fat were obligations she never skipped. She took off her sweaty scrubs and toweled dry. The feel of the doughy flab of her body disgusted her.

She'd been up at four a.m., to her office by five, and completed her stairs workout before six—a typical morning for her. A spray of deodorant under her arms, then she put on clean scrubs and a clean white coat. The worn scrubs went in a laundry bag in a lower drawer.

She sat at her desk and removed her personal laptop from her shoulder bag. Her fingers skipped over the keyboard as she logged on the private server that linked her to the dark web.

Virtually untraceable with access to almost anything—she loved the dark web. The media and others talked about it as if it was some supernatural or mystical portal. The dark web was basic. She'd downloaded the *.tor* software more than a year earlier, and the shadowy parallel internet had been a tool for her ever since.

The illicit services and products she'd discovered had been key to forming and executing her plans. She could track down restricted medications, toxins, and virtually anything she needed as easy as ordering a delivery pizza.

Her home site appeared. One code-protected message alert had arrived since she'd checked earlier. She entered her password, tensing in anticipation. The link opened. Her breath came quick as she recognized the source. This had to be it. She clicked the attachment.

The images filled her screen. She leaned close, examining them carefully. Perfect!

The diploma and license were flawless. Seeing her name and deserved title on the forged documents made her heart race—Clara Zeitman, MD.

With digital and hard copies of the forged medical degree and license in hand, she'd complete her legend by placing a false corroborating history online—easy for her.

The Guatemalan authorities would not rigorously investigate her credentials. Why challenge a U.S. doctor opening a charity clinic for the underserved of their country? Even though the odds of inspection were remote, she left no base uncovered. Her fund-generating scheme had honed her skills at avoiding discovery. No mistakes!

She slid opened a desk drawer, then removed the shallow box. She opened the box, removed the Littman Master Cardiology stethoscope, and placed it around her neck.

This tool signified the transformation that would happen. No longer simply a healthcare support worker, she'd finally be doing the job for which she'd been born. She flushed warm and her skin tingled.

She'd registered and equipped her clinic. Clinics in the third world were more like mini-hospitals. The location and building were ideal. She had a local administrator on site who was preparing the building and lining up personnel. Everything was ready to go.

She spoke the language and was more than prepared intellectually. Despite the flawed and corrupt system that had kept her out of medical school, she was more than "good enough" to be a doctor. The counterfeit credentials had been easy. All she needed now were more dollars in her offshore account.

Setting up in Guatemala would cost peanuts compared to the U.S., but it would still require a good deal of money. The untraceable payments she'd received had brought her close. The cut she expected from her most recent actions would assure she had enough. The phone on her desk trilled. She frowned at the interruption to her happy musing. She slipped on her headset and connected.

"Hello. Dr. Zeitman, lab medicine and information technology chief speaking."

"Where the hell are my culture results and sensitivities?" Damn, the asshole would not let her be. Even over the phone, Dr. Bart Rainey's voice boomed. "I ordered them stat on my ICU patient yesterday and I still don't have them."

"Did you call the lab desk?" Clara asked. "All ICU labs are stat and cultures can't be made to grow faster."

"No, missy, I didn't call the lab desk. I called you. And don't give me your 'stat' lecture, *doctor*. I'm a *real* doctor taking care of real patients. You know what patients are, right?" His voice grew even louder. "The results should be on the computer and they're not. You have five minutes to get me them. Do your damn job!" He gave the patient's name and disconnected before she could respond.

The asshole. Why did he hassle her? Was it all about her PhD and use of 'doctor'? Likely it was because he recognized she was so much smarter than he was.

One deep breath put her right. The oaf could not kill her mood.

She wasn't going to take any more abuse from Bart Rainey, nor anyone else who thought they were superior just because they had MD after their name.

His call reminded her there were critical actions she needed to complete before leaving Memorial Hospital. It was time to start collecting on other debts.

Debts that had nothing to do with money.

Chapter 13

Drake and Rachelle had tried to be quiet so as not to wake the kids. Their "stealth sex" efforts ended when they'd both burst out in bliss-inspired laughter under the pressure of trying to be quiet.

They'd heard the kids stir over the monitor. Drake had gotten up, thrown on scrubs, then taken them downstairs for breakfast while Rachelle got ready for the day. Now Drake roughhoused with them on the living room floor. The kids squealed and laughed.

His time with Rachelle and the kids was the best. The joy he felt with them pushed his problems out of mind.

Rachelle came down the stairs smiling.

"They chowed cereal and toast," Drake said as the kids played. "They're eager to get outside, but it's soaking wet."

"They'll have to stay inside for a while," she said.

He moved close and took her in his arms. "Playing inside can be fun," he whispered.

She smiled then rested her head on his chest. He spied the wall clock. "Man! Too little time. I really need to get going."

"How unusual," she said with a smile.

They kissed.

"Can you check with Kaye to see if she can watch the kids later? I might have someplace special to take you." His fingers were crossed—a very special place! "I'll see you all later."

He grabbed his work bag, hugged and kissed each of the kids, then was out the door. The rain had stopped, but puddles covered the parking lot under a dark sky. He got into his old Dodge. Every time he climbed in the car he felt unease. If not for the paramedics, he would've died in the vehicle.

"Call Detective Yamada," he said, using the hands-free function of his phone. The line connected as he exited the lot.

"Detective Yamada, Homicide."

"Aki, er, Detective Yamada, this is Drake Cody."

"Yeah, Doc. I hope this is a social call."

56

Drake remained unsure just what his relationship with the dogged homicide detective was. At times, there seemed to be a growing friendship, but other times the fortyish detective was an all-business hardass.

"Bad things are happening," Drake said. "I'm afraid we might be missing something big."

"Good morning to you, too, Doc. Did someone tell you I was having a good morning and ask you to make sure it didn't last?"

"We're seeing a flood of narcotic overdoses. People are dying. Something needs to be done. I want to help."

"Yeah, Prince's death, the opioid epidemic, more deaths from overdoses than car crashes or firearms. It's bad, but what's new about it?"

"It's worsened. Yesterday there were seven ODs during my shift alone. Two died in the field and one died in the ICU of complications, but that was just the ones at Memorial. It's happening throughout the cities. Wicked, tragic stuff. I think there's a new, super-deadly drug on the street."

"So what did the tests show?" Aki said.

"They haven't given the answer. I'm heading to the hospital to talk with our lab people. The newest and worst opioids don't always show up on initial screens."

"How about the medical examiners?" Aki asked. "Can't they tell what drugs are involved?"

"The medical examiners use the Memorial Hospital lab, so they're in the same boat at this point."

"Okay. How can you help?" Aki said.

"Selling drugs isn't as dramatic as shooting someone, but the victims end up just as dead," Drake said. "It's murder. If we can tie the dealers to the OD death, can they be convicted?"

"Yes, but it's tough," Aki said. "We got one on a third-degree murder conviction last month, but we were lucky. At a minimum, we need clear laboratory evidence and a link to the seller."

"I think the medics, ER staff, and medical examiners might be able to improve the odds. I'm heading to the lab now to see how we can coordinate things. I was hoping you might visit Dr. Dronen at the morgue and get his suggestions."

"Oh, goody," Aki said. "I get to visit Dr. Ego and be abused."

"Kip is different, but underneath it all he wants to do the right thing."

"Different?" Aki said. "Calling that guy different is like saying Attila the Hun was assertive."

"Don't let him get under your skin, Aki. People are dying and he can help. This problem is out of control. I'll learn what I can at the hospital and talk with you later. I'm not trying to dump on you."

"I'm just jerking your chain," Aki said. "We can use all the help we can get. By the way, the heroic, rookie detective Farley is with me today. We'll be expecting your call."

"Geez, don't call me that," sounded in the background as they disconnected.

Detective Farley—a modest guy who really had been a hero.

The Central Avenue Bridge loomed ahead. Drake slowed as he drove over the bridge. The Mississippi River flowed broad and fast, the water looking oil-dark on the overcast morning. Mist rose downstream from St. Anthony Falls and fogged the view of the Stone Arch Bridge.

Rizz's now-empty apartment looked over the falls. Drake wondered how his friend was doing. The bullet he'd taken for Drake and his family had left him wheelchair-bound, but lately there'd been positive signs.

Drake couldn't think of Rizz without thinking about FloJo and her ongoing veterinary workup. FloJo had been their breakthrough experimental spinal cord injury animal subject. The little cat now miraculously walked, but subsequently she'd developed seizures with the suspicion of a malignant brain tumor. She was undergoing a workup at the University's animal hospital.

Drake was convinced D-44 had helped her spinal cord heal but feared an adverse effect was now killing her. Rizz had convinced Drake to give the never-used-in-humans drug to him, and FloJo's illness left Drake fearful that D-44 would take down his friend next.

Drake turned onto Hennepin Avenue. He needed to get a grip on his runaway worries.

Just as in the ER, he had to address problems in order of their urgency, potential for disaster, and his ability to intervene. Some things needed to be addressed immediately. Others could be pushed to the waiting room. Some were beyond his ability to help.

Rizz, whom Drake envied for his unflappable outlook, often shrugged and said, "You can only do what you can do."

***

Drake entered the bustling Memorial Hospital lab.

He moved past multiple slate-topped lab tables and the white-coated technologists tending their complex devices. The work the laboratory technologists did was unseen by the rest of the hospital. The blood-draw personnel were visible in patient care areas, but otherwise the thousands of test results appeared as if by magic on computer screens or printers. Drake's background in biochemistry and drug research made him appreciate the complex, exacting work the technologists performed.

He spied an open door in the corner near what he recognized as a liquid chromatograph / mass spectrometer. A tiny plaque next to the door read "Fred Aplin, PhD – Toxicology." A lean man with thick salt-and-pepper hair, wire-rimmed glasses, and a walrus-like mustache sat in a closet-sized room at a desk surrounded by mountains of journals and textbooks. A computer screen and keyboard sat in the middle of the stacks on his desk.

Drake knocked on the door frame.

"Hi, Fred. I'm Drake Cody from the ER." Drake had attended a couple of lectures that Fred had given on poisons and laboratory assessment. The guy really knew his stuff.

"Oh sure, Dr. Drake Cody. I was quite interested in the toxicology aspects of some of the troubles you faced."

"Yeah, some wild stuff went down," Drake said. "Before we go further, I have to ask—Clara Zeitman is chief of laboratory services, so technically she's your boss. She seems tightly wound. Will she freak out if I talk to you without clearing it with her first?"

"You mean *Doctor* Zeitman." Fred winked. "No worries. Most of the staff are terrified of her, but she leaves me alone." He shrugged. "I've been here longer than she has, and she knows I do a good job. What can I help you with?"

"There were at least two narcotic overdose deaths yesterday and several others the paramedics saved. That was just during my shift. I think there's a new killer drug on the street."

"Could be. That's the way they show up," Fred said. "It used to be a cluster of ODs meant unusually pure heroin had arrived. Now it's cheaper, deadlier, synthetic stuff involved. We know nothing about the new drugs until people start dying."

"Then what?" Drake asked.

"Then people like me use all the tools we have to detect and identify what's killing people. I'll track down yesterday's specimens. All medical examiner cases come to me."

"I've talked with Aki Yamada of Homicide. I want to help the police and warn potential users. Dealers are selling death out there."

"I've been involved in virtually every prosecuted drug or poison homicide in Hennepin County for years. I'm aware of two sellers being convicted of homicide in the past year—two—and that was third degree. There were over four hundred opioid-overdose deaths. That's lousy arithmetic."

"I'm trying to coordinate with police, EMTs, paramedics, hospitals, media, and everyone else to keep people from dying and help nail the dealers," Drake said.

"That makes sense to me."

"I'm going to meet with the assistant medical examiner after my shift today."

"Dr. Kip Dronen? I don't know if I'd mention the 'assistant' part," Fred said. "It's a touchy subject."

"I'm aware."

"He freaks a lot of people out, but he and I get along," Fred said. "He's into the study of death and I'm into drugs and poisons. We teamed up on last year's overdose convictions. In this CSI day and age, the science testimony matters big time."

"Any ideas on how lab testing on OD cases from the ER might help track the drugs?"

"Let's set something up for both ER and morgue cases. The usual ER screens will miss newer synthetics. We have fentanyl on the panel, but carfentanil and the newer drugs need to be tested for specifically. I'll start by screening the specimens from your cases yesterday."

"Good." Drake said.

"I'll track down any and all the unknowns on the suspicious ER and all ME cases. I won't let anything slip by. Make sense?"

"Absolutely," Drake said. "You really are into this stuff, aren't you?"

"It keeps me off the street." Fred smiled. "And if a life or two gets saved, it makes it even better."

Chapter 14

The door to Clara Zeitman's office opened onto the hospital corridor just beyond the lab. Drake had walked past it hundreds of times but never knocked on the white, keycard-controlled door. He had about ten minutes before his shift began.

Drake knew Clara Zeitman by sight, but the recent awkward exchange in the Crash Room was one of few direct interactions they'd had. He hoped she'd be able to help him.

Next to the door was a placard:

Clara Zeitman, BSc, PhD, PhD
Director of Laboratory Services / Director of Healthcare Informatics

One person heading up both a hospital's information technology services and laboratory services departments was unprecedented. Any one person who could handle so much had to have incredible skills and energy.

He remembered her being present in the ICU when Rachelle was critically ill and Dan Ogren had coded and died. His fear that the code had been called for Rachelle had imprinted that night as if it was yesterday.

Laboratory results and medical records provided the evidence for malpractice litigation. Clara Zeitman's cooperation could make his dreaded malpractice committee investigation duties go much easier.

Today was not the day for him to discuss how her use of "doctor" in a patient care situation could make caregivers mistake her for a physician giving orders.

He knocked on the door. After a moment, the lock turned and the door opened a crack.

Clara Zeitman peered out.

Her eyes were prominent and a shade of gray so light as to be almost colorless. Her thin hair clung at her temples as if damp or sweaty.

"Yes?" She wore a frown. Her manner left him feeling like an unwanted door-to-door salesman.

"Good morning, Dr. Zeitman. I have an assignment where I need information from both lab and medical records. I'm hoping you might help me."

"I'm director of both laboratory services and healthcare informatics. I can answer any questions."

"Thank you," Drake said still feeling as if he were an intruder. "May I come in?"

She opened the door, then turned her back and moved toward the large metal desk. Her white-coated figure looked fuller than the gauntness of her face would suggest.

The room was chilly, with no carpet, a white floor, bare white walls, a faint chemical odor, and the soft whir of computer fans—more a sterile workroom than an office. Large computer consoles sat against each of the side walls. A keyboard and two jumbo display screens were positioned on a horseshoe-shaped desk. She took a seat at the chair behind the desk. There were no other chairs.

The wall behind her was bare, other than a slate counter and a door with a biohazard symbol and a sign reading:

Laboratory Access, No Unauthorized Personnel.

Drake stood in front of her desk.

"What is it you need?" she said.

"I'm working with Dr. Torrins on a hospital project." He smiled.

Her face was expressionless, but he sensed passive-aggressive waves bombarding him like radiation. Perhaps her attitude was based on his secret that was no longer secret—his previous assault conviction and time spent behind bars had been front page news.

"I need to review the hospital records on some patients. I thought you'd be knowledgeable on how to proceed."

"I'm the most knowledgeable person on everything related to our system." Her tone was icy.

Was this fallout from her knowing about his criminal record or had he somehow pissed her off?

"Okay, great. I need to review the records of these cases." He leaned forward and put a note card with the multiple patient ID numbers Dr. Torrins had given him in front of her. "Can you instruct me how and where to access these?"

Her eyes skipped over the numbers. Her eyebrows pinched. "You should leave. Right now."

"Excuse me?"

"I believe you heard me, *Doctor.*" Her tone had become even icier. She pushed back from the desk.

"I'm simply asking how I access the records."

"It's time for you to leave." Her pallid complexion flushed.

"Did I do something wrong?" *This is bizarre.*

"Besides being totally ignorant of basic HIPPA law?" she said. "You are an MD, aren't you? It's unbelievable to me how many physicians know nothing about patients' rights or so many other things necessary to do their job."

"Whoa," he said. Her imperious manner had him confused and annoyed. "How about lightening up a bit?"

"I do not 'lighten up' when it comes to my responsibilities." She glared at him. "And I would expect those selected to be medical doctors to be competent enough to meet theirs."

"I approached you to make sure I accessed the records appropriately. I informed you I'm working with Dr. Torrins on a hospital project."

"Leave now or I'll report you to the hospital, the state Medical Board, and the civil authorities. Your efforts to view the records of patients you did not treat are grossly inappropriate." She stood up and gestured toward the door. "Leave. Now."

"You can't be serious."

"You were not involved in the care of these patients and you will not have access to their records unless the families sign a release. I have nothing more to say." Her jaw muscles knotted and her eyes shot arrows. She marched to the door and held it open.

Drake's face burned. He'd heard her people skills were lacking, but this was nuts. "I'll go," Drake said, stepping into the doorway. "I'll have Dr. Torrins straighten out the medical records issue for you, Ms. Zeitman."

"It's *Doctor* Zeitman." Her words were clipped.

Drake turned and faced her. *It's not like she can get angrier.* "I'm fine with addressing you as doctor here, but wearing a white coat and using 'doctor' in patient care areas is confusing and inappropriate. Particularly as you're inclined to give orders." He exited.

The door closed hard behind him, followed by the sound of the lock being turned.

Drake mouthed a silent "Yikes!" Talk about hostile.

How not to win friends and influence people—get yourself stuck on a hospital's malpractice committee.

***

Clara twisted the lock.

Doctor Drake Cody—the bastard! Had he been playing her? All polite and "golly, can you help me?" Did he think she was stupid?

She paced in front of her desk, biting her knuckle. He'd asked to see medical records. What did he know?

Had she overreacted? She could barely contain her hatred. He'd killed Dan just as sure as if he'd pulled the trigger himself. She slowed her breathing and focused.

Control. I need to stay in control.

How much could he know? She'd been careful.

She reviewed all the steps she'd taken.

Drake Cody checking records—so what? It didn't mean anything. Her insecurity gave birth to these doubts.

But he'd said he was working with the president of medical affairs. If that were true, it could be trouble. She sighed.

How she missed Dan!

She went to the lower desk drawer and yanked it open. From under the folders she removed the family-sized, value-pack of Oreo cookies. She slid her chair forward until her abdomen touched the desk. The feel of the flab of her belly triggered disgust.

She found the seam of the package, pinched, and opened the wrapper. She slid the tray out, then ran a fingertip over the perfect rows of black-and-white disks. The aroma of chocolate and the cake-like wafers made her mouth water. The promise of the pure white sugary filling—so perfect...

She placed a whole cookie into her mouth, bit once, and let it rest motionless on her tongue. Her eyes closed as the sensory rush triggered a small moan. After a few glorious seconds, she began to chew.

It went as it always did with food. She was lost in the flavor and texture as she chewed, tongued, and then swallowed. She loaded another cookie, chewed, savored, and swallowed. Then another.

As the seconds and minutes passed, her awareness of the taste, smell, and consistency faded, but the repetitive actions were hypnotic and soothing. Her mind settled as she ate with effortless efficiency.

Dr. Drake Cody's visit raised doubts—the bastard. Could he or someone else ruin her dream?

Drake Cody was one of the many who had cheated her out of what she deserved.

A faint but bitter chemical flavor soured her tongue, the cookies' smell now seemed cloyingly sweet, and the roof of her mouth was coated with lard. The sound of her chewing registered in her ears like the grinding of a horse eating grain.

The counseling she'd been subjected to as a teenager said the thing that gave her comfort was wrong. She'd seen the eating disorder treatment center propaganda as simply more of her parents' control-freak manipulation.

The ember fanned into flames in an instant. Her neck stiffened. *She hated them all.*

They'd made her believe she wasn't good enough.

Drake Cody—a convicted criminal, an illegitimate, undeserving MD who'd lied his way into medical school. He, others like him, and the medical establishment had cheated her before. Would it happen again?

She's been careful, but fear edged her mind.

She looked down at the litter of black crumbs on her white coat and desktop. She wiped her mouth, sickened by the fleshiness of her face.

You're a fat failure!

A kaleidoscope of resentments wheeled in her head. They'd done this to her. Her parents, the medical establishment, Drake Cody, and so many others—they'd taken everything from her. *Damn them!*

Trembling, with her vision going red, she raised the half-filled tray of cookies above her head and smashed them onto the desktop with both hands.

The fragments exploded throughout the office.

***

Years earlier

Abba's "Dancing Queen" soared from the speakers and Clara soared with it. She and her fellow fourth grade dance-line teammates glittered in their purple sequined costumes. Learning the Jazzers' performance dance moves hadn't been easy, but tonight she felt magic. The crowd's shrill screams and cheers competed with the music. She'd never felt so special.

They nailed their ending. The auditorium full of other dance school members and their families roared. *Wow!*

And Father had seen her! Unbelievably, he'd come to see her. And she had soared.

Her face felt stretched in the biggest smile of her life. She giggled as she and her teammates bounded off the stage.

Mother and Father's work always came first. That's what being a doctor meant. They couldn't be with her for things. The other kids' moms and dads showed up, but a nanny would bring Clara. But tonight, somehow, both her parents had made it!

She went out to the lobby and spied them near the coat racks. The music for the next team's performance sounded from behind the auditorium doors. Dr. Carl Zeitman and Dr. Freida Zeitman—Mother and Father. They turned as she shrieked and ran toward them.

Father did not quite get his arms around her. He glanced at her, then looked around the lounge.

"Oh, Father. Did you like it?" Clara bounced in her dance shoes.

He adjusted her bangs, then straightened her shoulder strap. "It was a very good effort."

"Really?" Clara said.

"Yes. A very good effort."

"A very good effort." This is a dream!

"Mother, did I do good?" Clara grasped her mother's hand, hopping in excitement.

"It's did I do 'well', Clara." Her mother removed Clara's hand from hers. "It was the best you've ever danced."

Clara tingled. She was a balloon floating in the clouds!

"I could feel the music."

"All right, daughter." Father looked at his watch. "I have a full OR schedule tomorrow. Time for me to get moving." He reached for his coat.

"Go get your things," her mother said. "Meet me by the door. Father has his car. You'll ride with me."

Clara slipped around the loaded coat rack. Before heading to the dressing area, she stopped and turned back. She wanted to catch her father and try to give him a hug. *"A very good effort," he'd said!*

The music of the next team's routine eased, and her father's voice carried over the coat rack. "Brutal. The poor child has the grace of a toad," he said. "It would be funny if it weren't so pathetic. Embarrassing, to say the least."

"The best she's ever danced," said her mother, "and it was dreadful."

Pain gripped Clara's stomach. Her heart cramped. A high ringing filled her ears and she felt sick. *No!*

"No rhythm, and her legs and butt are three times the size of the other girls," her father said. "What is that nanny feeding her? Thank goodness the child's too clueless to know what she looks like."

A moan sounded in Clara's head. The floor opened up, and she plunged into blackness...

...a hand grasped hers. She lay on a pile of coats, her face and hair clammy with sweat. Confusion.

"Are you okay?" A man's face loomed above her.

"What happened?" A blond lady looked concerned.

"I heard her moan, then she went down," the man said.

Clara's mother's face appeared. She wore a frown.

"I'm sure she just fainted," she said to the other parents. "She was overly excited."

Clara's memory clicked. Her parents' words replayed. *No! No! No!*

Her mother pulled her to her feet. Clara felt like throwing up. Next thing her coat was on and they were walking to the car.

Her insides were hollow. They drove home in silence.

She never soared again.

Chapter 15

Farley followed detective sergeant Aki Yamada down the terrazzo hallway of the county morgue. Their footsteps echoed and the sickly sweet tinge of formalin strengthened as they neared the autopsy theater doors. Farley's discomfort grew with each step. Death and dead bodies freaked him out. It was one of many reasons he worried that as a rookie homicide detective he was a very round peg trying to fit into a square hole.

Aki stopped at the door to the examination chambers. His pause and deep breath showed he was on edge. Farley knew it wasn't death or dead bodies that bothered Aki. Generally, the homicide veteran didn't take crap from anyone, but Farley had seen the assistant medical examiner, Dr. Kip Dronen, make Aki look like an embarrassed schoolboy at the chalkboard.

"Here we go," Aki said. "Let's hope he's not in a pissy mood."

As Aki pushed the door open, the screaming vocals and driving rhythm of Queen's "Another One Bites the Dust" blasted them at high volume. Two naked, elderly corpses lay stretched out on stainless steel exam tables under surgical lights. The room was cold and the faint odor of dead flesh and putrefaction penetrated the blanket of formalin. Farley's stomach did a flip—the two Egg McMuffins and three potato cakes he'd had for breakfast were not sitting well.

Dr. Kip Dronen's gaunt, scrubs-clad body was hunched in front of a personal computer at a desk adjacent to the exam tables. His wire-rimmed glasses were perched in his Einstein-wild hair, and a surgical mask dangled from his neck. A coffee mug and half-eaten sandwich sat on a paper towel alongside the computer. The forty-something pathologist's fingers pounded the computer keyboard.

"Excuse us, Dr. Dronen," Aki yelled over the music.

The pathologist's head jerked. He turned, his eyes scanned Aki. He looked as if he'd found a dead bug floating in his coffee. He reached for his cell phone and the music died an echoing death.

"Good morning," Aki said.

"Not hardly," the doctor answered in his high-pitched voice. "Why are you here?"

The ME didn't acknowledge Farley. His focus on Aki was not friendly.

"Dr. Cody suggested we should talk."

"Talk to me? Hell, I'm only the *assistant* medical examiner. Perhaps you should talk to the chief." The ME's words were a mix of irritation and whine.

As a newer homicide cop, Farley had already seen the forensic pathologist play a key role in solving several cases. Dr. Cody had said Kip Dronen was the brightest ME ever, but he remained forever "assistant" chief because the "chief" position was a political appointment and involved tactful communication to media and the public. Tact was not part of his makeup.

"Dr. Cody thinks there's a new killer narcotic on the streets," Aki said. "He suggested we talk to you."

"So ER guy has sent you to me, the *assistant* ME, to once again help you do your job."

Aki frowned, took a deep breath, and folded his arms across his chest. Farley recognized his partner was working hard to keep his cool.

"Yeah, that's pretty much it," Aki said. "People are dying. You're the medical examiner. We're looking for your help."

"Yeah, I heard about the OD-related deaths. Someone got the *chief* medical examiner to do a rush post-mortem on the hospital's ICU death early this morning. It's probably the first off-hours work he's done in years. Actually, it sounded like a case worthy of my skills. Not sure why they wanted him." He shook his head. "But what do I know? I'm only the assistant medical examiner." The look that the doctor shot Aki left no doubt that the scrawny pathologist was on edge.

"Assistant ME makes no difference to me," Aki said. "Dr. Cody says you're the best and recommended we talk with you."

Kip stood and began pacing. The guy always had a wired energy but today he was sizzling.

"Drake said you might be able to help us nail the suppliers who are responsible for overdose deaths. That's why we're here." Aki nodded toward the dead bodies. "Sorry to interrupt."

The ME gave the bodies a dismissive wave.

"A trained chimp could handle these autopsies," he said. "I know their cause of death in a glance. I'll get you up to speed on opioids and ODs, but after that," the ME's focus remained on Aki and the hostility made Farley wish he were elsewhere, "I have a serious question for you."

"I'll answer now if it will help you end the pissed-off jerk act," Aki said.

"You may have just answered it," the ME said.

"Huh?" Aki said.

"The 'pissed-off jerk' comment." He moved nose-to-nose with Aki, leaning forward like a dog pulling at his leash. "Someone's been complaining about me to the powers-that-be. I think you know what I'm saying."

"What the hell are you talking about?" Aki said.

Farley stepped between the men and put a restraining hand on the doctor's chest.

"Seventeen effing years as assistant medical examiner. Seventeen years!" The doctor's voice hit screech levels. "There isn't a forensic pathologist in the country as good as I am. Check my publications. Look at who addresses the top national conferences, and still I'm the *assistant* medical examiner. It's humiliating."

"Too bad, but what does that have to do with me?" Aki said.

"I was refused the Chief appointment again. I just got word this morning," The ME's lip curled. "They said there'd been 'substantial' complaints. Some crap about inappropriate comments and behavior. What a crock of BS." He jabbed a finger towards Aki. "It was you, wasn't it?"

"Okay, sunshine," Aki said. "How about for one minute we forget you're a big-shot doctor and I'm only a middle pay-grade civil servant. Can you handle some bare-knuckles truth?"

"Do it," the ME said. His posture had not changed.

"You're an asshole," Aki said. "You treat me and others like shit. You act like I'm an idiot. Well, news flash—not everyone has studied for decades and lives and breathes death and its causes. Drake Cody says you're a genius and that may be true, but you're also off-the-charts weird and a prick. Your ego blocks out the sun. If it weren't for your position as a doctor, somebody would have already stuffed you head-first in the trash—I've sure as hell considered it."

Kip Dronen remained still.

Aki took a breath and continued. "All that said, you're damn good at what you do. You've helped us solve cases we couldn't have otherwise, and

I appreciate that. Regarding me running to higher-ups and whining about you—never happened. I'd go with the trash-can option before that."

He pointed a finger at Kip. "So now you know where I'm at. I'll put the gloves back on, big-shot doctor guy, but remember what's real. Now how about you quit whining and help us save lives and put away those doing the killing?"

Kip Dronen's posture eased. No discomfort had shown on his face and he'd nodded with the mention of "damn good" and "genius."

The pathologist didn't show any discomfort at having been verbally shredded.

"I thought for sure it was you," he said. "By the way, you're right about the genius part." His expression showed he wasn't kidding. He rubbed his chin and stared off. "So who the hell is bitching about me?"

Farley met Aki's eyes. They shared shrugs. Most anyone who dealt with the social misfit was a candidate.

"I have no idea, but maybe now you can help us get up to speed on these new killer drugs?" Aki said.

"Huh?" The ME cocked his head. "Oh yeah. I'll give you the 'Narcotics for Dummies' version. First off—narcotics and opioids are synonyms. They mean the same thing. A narcotic is an opioid, an opioid is a narcotic. Get it?"

Farley nodded. His partner had shaken his head at the "dummies" line.

"Here's something you can probably follow regarding the strength of the synthetics. Think about how much alcohol someone needs to get drunk. Now consider how much narcotic effect someone needs to get high. I'm going to compare the different narcotics to alcohol. Just as different alcohol products have differing strengths, so do the different opioids.

"An average guy takes about seventy-two ounces of beer to get drunk. It takes about twenty-four ounces of wine, but only six ounces of ninety-proof vodka. A differing amount of each source of alcohol does the job."

"Right," Aki said.

"Narcotic drugs have a much greater range of potencies. Codeine can give you a ride. Hydrocodone will do it. Morphine is killer strong, and heroin is about twice as strong as that. Heroin is made from poppies. The synthetic opioids are new. They're made in laboratories, and here's where things get crazy. Fentanyl is a synthetic, and it's fifty times as potent as heroin, so one fiftieth of the dose will get you high. That is like measuring dust. In our alcohol comparison, fentanyl-strength compared to heroin-strength vodka would require only," he paused with eyes closed for an instant, "six one-hundredths of an ounce rather than six ounces to make someone drunk. That's less than a tenth of a drop. If the bartender added a full drop, the drink would be strong enough to kill several people.

"Now try to wrap your head around the strength of carfentanil. It's the most potent opioid on the planet. It's never had any human use but has been used, hugely diluted, to tranquilize elephants and other big animals. It's a hundred times as potent as fentanyl, which means, in our alcohol comparison, one would only need," he cocked his head, "six ten-thousandths of an ounce of carfentanil-vodka to get drunk. That's," another brief pause, "only .02 milliliters. A one-ounce shot of carfentanil-strength vodka could get 1500 people blasted or would kill a few hundred. You want a bartender mixing you a drink with that stuff?"

"So how do dealers measure amounts of drug that small and be accurate?" Aki said.

"That's the point, Sherlock," the ME said. "They can't—not reliably. Measurements that precise require a skilled lab person using sophisticated equipment. The Chinese and cartel chemists know what they're doing, but the lower-level dealers are greedy amateurs or addicts themselves. Get it?"

Aki and Farley nodded.

"Sniffing, swallowing, or shooting drugs these days is like Russian roulette. There is no way to know what you are getting, and the next high could kill you." He spread his hands. "That's my 'Opioids for Dummies' lecture. You understand?"

"How many are at risk?" Farley asked.

"Some estimate there are five million opioid users in the US, but no one knows." Kip shrugged. "The idea that someone takes opioids once and goes straight to being a junkie is off target. That happens for some, but there are hundreds of thousands who use narcotics regularly and they are able to function. Their use is invisible to most others, but opioids slowly become what they center their life around. Often in the beginning it's pills, but then it becomes whatever narcotics they can find—the stronger, the better. Opioids are not a party or social drug. Most ODs are found dead and alone. At least sixty thousand will die of overdoses this year."

"Ugly," Aki said.

"Morgues are being swamped. Every overdose death is a medical examiner's case. I may be just the 'assistant' ME, but job security is a lock." His inappropriate yip of a laugh echoed in the cold vault of the morgue. It was followed by silence.

"This is truly scary," Aki said.

"There's something about it that might make you feel worse," Kip said.

"What's that?" Farley asked.

"Drake Cody is right. We haven't seen anything yet."

Chapter 16

Drake slipped into the administrative offices wing like a tardy kid sneaking into school. Jim Torrins' office shared the same large, carpeted lobby as CEO Stuart Kline's.

Drake, with others' help, had defeated the CEO's scheme to rip off his, Rizz, and Jon's D-44 research and the big dollars it might eventually yield. Kline hated Drake's guts. The hospital's head administrator remained an obstacle to Drake's dreams.

Hopefully the hospital board would recognize the CEO for the weasel he was and remove him soon.

Drake's shortened ER fill-in shift had been busy, and the time had flown by. The opioid disaster continued—more overdoses, but the ones he'd cared for had survived. He'd learned many others had been found too late.

The desperate need for action remained clear. Drake knocked on the partially open door to Jim Torrins' office.

"Come in, Drake," Torrins said. "What do you need?"

Drake closed the door and sat in the chair facing the president of medical affairs.

"I asked Clara Zeitman for help with the medical records on the malpractice cases you gave me," Drake said. "She almost tore my head off and threatened to report me to the board."

"Sorry," Torrins said. "I should have spoken with her. She considers medical records a sacred trust and she's ultra-conscientious."

"She's ultra-something," Drake said, then paused. "Jim, I'm really disturbed about you having 'volunteered' me for this malpractice thing. I'm already on probation with the state Medical Board, and the CEO hates me. I'm hoping to be accepted as a full-time staff member at this hospital. Being assigned to your committee is a suicide mission for me."

"If all you wanted to do was whine, you could have done that by phone. Is there a legitimate reason you wanted to meet?" Torrins said.

Drake's temperature rose. *What the hell?*

"My life and future aren't legitimate?" Drake said. The president of medical affairs had been a standup guy in helping to stop the theft of the D-44 research and other issues. But those situations had not been of Drake's making, and Torrins' responses had been the only path for someone with integrity. "I'm a physician—not an administrator," Drake said. "I take care of patients. Excuse me if I'm not thrilled about being threatened professionally by a rabid wolverine doing a job I never asked for."

Torrins took off his glasses and rubbed the bridge of his nose. He put his glasses back on then folded his hands on his desk in front of him. The graying physician-administrator looked tired.

"Oh no, Drake, golly, excuse me. I didn't realize how I was imposing on the individual who would have lost his research, medical license, and career if I had not leveraged my reputation and risked my job to support him. And excuse me if I think you're the best doctor I know to get to the bottom of patients dying unexpectedly. I can see where it must be annoying to be asked to help out. As for the malpractice committee burden—it's nothing I asked for either. Life is rough."

They stared hard-eyed at each other for several seconds. Drake thought of his time behind bars. He'd been in stare-downs with sociopathic criminals. But Torrins was not his enemy. He really had gone to bat for him. Drake did owe him. Being pissed at each other made no sense. As if out of his control, first a smile formed and then Drake laughed.

Torrins looked puzzled, then he smiled, and a chuckle followed.

Drake waved a finger and said with forced drama, "And let me tell you another thing!"

They laughed more, Torrins holding a hand over his mouth.

In a few seconds they gained control, but the tension had eased.

"Sorry about Clara Zeitman," Jim said. "She can be difficult. I'll make sure you have the access you need set up at a terminal in Medical Records."

"Thanks," Drake said. "I guess."

"I'm not happy about any of it either, but tough horse apples, cowboy. It ain't my rodeo, and it looks like you and I are the clowns."

"No worries," Drake said, smiling at the messed-up absurdity of it all. "It's just my career."

"There's more," Torrins said. "I sent you an email and was about to call you. A meeting has been scheduled for tomorrow with the lawyers. Ten a.m.

in the surgery conference room. Clete Venjer's firm has handled all the major cases against Memorial. Are you familiar with him?"

"I see the billboards, TV commercials, and ads all over, like everyone else in the Twin Cities. Beyond that I know nothing."

"He's good at what he does. There's a reason his firm gets ninety-plus percent of the personal injury business in the cities. He'll be deposing a couple of our doctors, but I get the feeling there is something else up." He sighed. "Kline is calling the shots. I'm not expecting anything good."

Drake's smile had left. Anything involving Kline meant trouble.

"I've got an afternoon shift tomorrow, so I can make it," Drake said. "I wanted to let you know I'm going on TV today to get a warning out on a worsening turn in the opioid epidemic."

"What?" Torrins blinked. "We need to talk about this. Kline will go nuts. He hates mention of violence or drugs linked to Memorial Hospital. It's bad for marketing."

"Probably true, but I need to do this." Drake stood and looked at the clock. He'd made up his mind he'd do all he could. "I meet the news crew in ten minutes."

"Hold off for a bit and let me see if I can run some interference first."

"Thanks, but it can't wait. People are dying. I just hope the message can make a difference. I also promised Rachelle I'd be home early, and for once I'm going to be there. See you tomorrow. I can't say I'm looking forward to it."

Among all the trouble today, he'd had some good, possibly great news. The call he'd received during his ER shift from attorney Lloyd Anderson had him eager to see Rachelle.

This would be the closest thing they'd had to a date in a long time.

He hoped it would be lifetime memorable.

Chapter 17

Q turned off the vacuum. As the motor died, a voice he recognized came from his TV. He glanced over. Oh, hell yeah. It was Tina Watt, the anchorwoman. Damn, she was fine.

Q didn't think much of relationships—he took care of his sexual needs with women that money or drugs made easy. But he had a wishful thing for this newswoman. He watched her broadcasts all the time, sometimes even recording them if he couldn't watch her live.

He grabbed the remote and turned up the volume. He checked the time. The station had interrupted its afternoon program.

"...a special report we present to you as a public service. We are coming to you from outside of Memorial Hospital." She held a microphone and looked killer-hot in a simple red dress. The arch of the ambulance bay with "Emergency" in big red letters stood above and behind her. "There is evidence of a deadly new narcotic killing Twin Cities drug users. The epidemic of opioid addiction and overdose deaths has been national and local headlines for months. Today we report a deadly escalation in this tragic story.

"Within the past few days, Twin Cities hospitals and emergency medical services have responded to a shocking surge in narcotic overdoses and deaths. Calls to 911 and use of the reversal drug, Narcan, saved dozens, but for many others, it was too late. In the last three days in Minneapolis alone, eighteen lives have been lost to narcotic overdose. St. Paul, rural areas and outstate communities have reported a similar spike."

"Amateurs." Q shook his head. His eyes locked on the screen as the camera moved to a close-up of Tina.

"This dramatic upturn has triggered a crisis response from emergency responders, hospitals, law enforcement, fire/rescue, the Minnesota Poison Center, and others. Among those concerned and the person who suggested this message be aired is emergency physician Dr. Drake Cody, who has been on the front lines battling this deadly scourge."

Q stiffened as the screen filled with the image of the doctor who had kicked his ass and gotten him arrested at Memorial months back. The sturdy-looking bastard wore scrubs and looked just as he had that day in the ER.

Tina held the microphone in front of the man whose face Q would love to stomp into the ground.

"Thank you. Our community is facing a matter of life and death."

The asshole looked serious, and even Q found himself leaning forward to listen.

"For those who use narcotics and for the friends, family members, and loved ones of those who might consider taking drugs, please take this message to heart and share it with everyone you care about."

The doctor stared into the camera.

The blue-eyed bastard had sucker-punched Q in the ER. He must have. No other way the dude could've handled Q like he did.

"Whatever drug you think you are buying, please believe me that you can't know what you're getting. It's likely even the person selling the drugs doesn't know.

"New, ultra-powerful, ultra-deadly synthetic narcotics are being sold as prescription opioids, heroin, and other drugs. These cheaper, easy-to-smuggle synthetic opioids are often packaged into pills that are identical in appearance to those that come from the pharmacy, but they are many times deadlier.

"Ingestion of as little as little as two sand-sized granules of these drugs will kill. Contact or breathing the dust of this drug can kill. The suppliers selling these drugs are not concerned about you or your safety. Their lack of laboratory and pharmaceutical skills multiply the already off-the-charts risk."

Q thought of his lab, his high-tech equipment, and his skills. The ER bastard was right. Most dealers were nothing like him. They were punks and losers, often addicted themselves. They didn't know shit about science.

"The drug you buy on the street, independent of its prescription-drug appearance or any assurances from the seller, may be your death."

The doctor paused. He looked choked up.

"We've all been touched by addiction and substance abuse. Tina and the station are going to show you a phone number and a website where users or their friends and family can get help. Please reach out.

"And please help stop the people selling misery and death—drug suppliers are killing your friends and loved ones. This is a drug crisis unlike any in history. These drugs will kill you and those you care about. Get help. Do not use."

The camera swung from the asshole doctor to the incredibly prime Tina.

A number and website appeared at the bottom of the screen.

The ER bastard!

Q's anger spiked. He'd dodged prosecution for pushing the ER bitch of a nurse, but the beatdown the ER doctor had dealt him had humiliated Q on the street. Later, he learned the supposed straight-arrow doc had done time for assault. That explained some things. Now the dude was messing with him again.

Heat washed over him. He clenched and unclenched his fists. He took a big breath and his business mind kicked in. He downshifted into a gear that he didn't used to have.

Be smart. Go easy, man. He was done with being a punk. Going primal did not pay. A good businessman does not react with anger.

It was all about business and dollars.

Preach all you want, doctor-boy. I've got the supply, and the demand ain't going anywhere but up.

Chapter 18

Rachelle had put on the red, scoop-necked sweater that Drake loved.

Kaye had picked up the kids and would watch them this evening.

Drake would be by shortly for a rare event. Just she and him going somewhere he'd said was casual but "very special"! Last evening the thrilling news from Dr. Mehta, and tonight a date.

But now she stood in front of the garbage disposal braced for an important task. A task that had taken her a lifetime to be ready to handle.

She opened the childproof cap on the first of her two prescription bottles. The Xanax tablets were a sedative prescribed for her post-traumatic stress and panic attacks. Rachelle had used them and drugs like them since the death of her mother and brother. In the past she'd used them too much. What had been a help had become a problem.

She flipped the switch and the garbage disposal motor roared. She dumped the medication. The blades chattered, and the pills were gone.

The second bottle contained Percocet. Opioids were the worst—and the best. Nothing felt better. The bottle was full. The medication had been given to her when she was discharged from the burn unit, but she had not taken a single one. She felt good about that.

She hadn't felt good about being aware of exactly where the pills were at every moment of each day. The thoughts of the bliss they could bring intruded frequently. That was their power. Having the drugs on hand but not taking them had been a test. She was ready.

The garbage disposal motor continued its electric whine as she twisted open the childproof cap.

Her hands trembled as she held the open bottle above the sink.

The drug pulled hard. No worry, no pain, and escape from the memories that haunted her. The craving was strong and would never disappear, but she would not give in. She dumped the bottle, and the garbage disposal roared as the blades chewed up the tablets. They were no more.

She would be strong for Drake and the kids, for herself. She was not her mother. She tossed the empty bottles in the recycling, then washed her hands.

The children were happy and safe. She was going on a date with her guy. What could be better?

***

Drake turned into the rental townhouse parking lot. Rachelle stood by the front stoop dressed in red and glowing in the late afternoon sunlight. So beautiful. His chest tightened, and his breath caught just as he had when he'd seen her the first time.

He couldn't wait to see how she would react to his surprise. He pulled to the curb in front of the townhouse, put the car in park, then hopped out to get the door for her.

Rachelle stood motionless, a huge smile on her face. "Going out on a date. Wow! I'm going to move slowly, so I can stretch it out as long as possible."

Drake laughed. He opened the passenger door and bowed deeply while extending an arm toward the old Dodge.

"Your limousine, madam."

Chapter 19

Drake pulled away from the curb with Rachelle wearing a big smile and her killer red sweater.

"You not only look incredible, but you're glowing. What's going on in that head of yours?" Drake asked.

"Take me on a few more dates, and maybe you'll find out."

He laughed.

"Truly Drake, I'm just really enjoying this." She sat back and looked as if she were.

She deserved to have more fun times. He liked to think he appreciated all she did, but in the day-to-day of the ER, his research, and his other responsibilities, he knew he'd come up short.

Theirs was a life of deferred gratification. They were always waiting: after I get into medical school things will be easier...when I graduate from medical school we'll be on our way...when I get done with residency everything will be better.

Now here they were and things were getting better, but things were still hard, and she was the one who bore the brunt of it.

It had been so lucky that he'd found her those years back. He'd been so lost and messed up that the pregnancy and Rachelle's wanting him had saved him.

There were things he'd done, something in him, an instinct and more that even today made him wonder if he was a fake—an impostor. He feared a part of him belonged in the high-security lockdown of the Furnace Correctional Facility. He'd been guilty of savagery behind bars. When released, he'd failed his brother and mother—the people he'd loved most.

He doubted he'd ever have felt worthy to handle the responsibility of a family. Rachelle had been a gift. Her love and support had helped him to endure.

What he'd done to the woman who hurt Rachelle and the children had showed that the beast still lurked within him. Without Rachelle by his side he'd never have made it through all it had taken to become a physician. He never would've experienced the wonders of the children.

The miles rolled by, Rachelle quiet and wearing a smile. Their destination wasn't far. His excitement grew. He wanted everything to be perfect.

"Where are we going?" she asked. "I don't know this area. What is this special place you're taking me to?"

"You'll see. It's a magical place," he said. "This might seem silly but please put this over your eyes." He held out a red neckerchief — one of the many she used to hide her scar. "This will be a special dinner. I want to surprise you."

"Drake this is very romantic. Who are you and what have you done with my work-obsessed husband?" She giggled.

God almighty, he loved nothing more than seeing her happy. He found her hand and squeezed it as he turned into the driveway. He pulled up to a gate in a wooden fence.

He got out, then moved to her door and helped her out. He held her hand and guided her through the gate. They walked on soft ground a short distance.

"It's not a parking lot," she said. "Grass under my feet, and wherever we are, it smells wonderful, but not like food."

He led her up five steps to a deck.

"Okay, you can take the blindfold off."

She moved in and looked around, her huge brown eyes widened.

"Oh my, Drake! It's beautiful."

And it was. He'd had the same awestruck reaction the first time he'd seen it.

They stood on an expansive deck at the back of a split-level, cedar-sided house with massive windows. The deck was surrounded by mature oaks, birch, and emerging spring flowers. In front of them, separated by a gentle slope of grass and trees stood the mirror-perfect surface of the lake. A small island was visible several hundred yards offshore. A blue heron stood at the shoreline alongside a wooden dock. A hint of lilacs was in the air. The sun was low and orange-tinged above the tree-lined western shore

"Drake, what is this? Why are we here?"

"I told you I had a special dinner plan for you at a special place."

"But what? Why? I—"

"I'll explain, but first I need to tell you something very important." He took both of her hands in his and stared into her eyes. "If not for you, and all we've shared, my life would have been so much less. You're the most amazing thing that has ever happened to me."

He stepped behind her and wrapped his arms around her so that they were both looking out over the lake.

"Tonight, we'll have a picnic on the deck of what, if everything works out, will become our new home. The owners accepted my offer today. It's not a done deal and things could go wrong, but they've already moved, and I couldn't wait to show you." His emotions surged as he held her tight. "This is where we will raise our children." She trembled in his arms and began to cry. It was not from sadness.

His heart soared.

Chapter 20

Drake awoke in a blink.

He checked the clock—almost nine a.m. He'd slept almost nine hours. Wow. He couldn't remember when he'd last slept that long. He felt spectacular.

After the thrill of showing Rachelle the house, he'd retrieved the takeout dinner and bottle of wine from the trunk of the Dodge. They'd eaten on the deck with blankets laid out like a picnic as the sun set and twilight faded.

The lake lay like glass as darkness settled. The smell of wood smoke from someone's bonfire drifted. Loons called as the moon rose. It made Drake's scalp tingle.

He and Rachelle celebrated the new place in the darkness and the privacy of the surrounding trees. After that, they lay side by side, wrapped in the blanket, and watching the stars appear.

When they got back to the townhouse, Kaye already had the kids in bed, asleep. After she left, Drake opened a second bottle of wine and he and Rachelle stayed up late sharing plans for their future. Finally, they could get a dog. Rachelle would have space to paint, with incredible scenes right out their door. The kids would be able to swim, fish, and boat. They talked for hours.

With the excitement they shared about their possible new home, she'd seemed as happy as he'd ever seen her.

It had been a wondrous night.

The door to the bedroom opened and Rachelle entered. She was fully dressed, in contrast to his memories of parts of their magical lakeside evening. He smiled and reached for her.

"Drake," she gestured with his cell phone, "it's Patti."

Drake took the phone and sat up. The ER charge nurse was one of the few people who had his number.

"Hi, Patti. What's up?"

Rachelle signaled that she needed to get downstairs and left.

"Oh, geez, Drake," Patti said. "I hope Rachelle didn't wake you for me."

"I'm up." Patti rarely called him. Usually she was the one answering the call. She'd saved his, Rizz's, and Jon's butts more than once.

"Do you remember the seventeen-year-old boy you admitted a couple of days back? A transfer to adolescent psych at Abbott."

His throat tightened. Dread imaginings flashed.

"Of course—Bryce. Please tell me he's okay."

"He's okay," she said. "Sorry. I didn't mean to alarm you. Bryce's mother is my cousin. I was out of reach up north until yesterday afternoon. I talked to her last night. I called you because, well, you know how it is. She's asking me questions, but it's all so foreign to her she can't tell me much. Bryce was released from Abbott last evening. She's scared and trying to figure out which way is up."

"He was discharged already?"

"She said the doctors told her he responded well to the medication," Patti said. "They felt getting him home and keeping things as normal as possible was best. My cousin was eager to get him home, but they're petrified. He's a wonderful kid. I'm worried sick."

"He was really scared and lost," Drake said. "He's been hearing voices for weeks and it's been worsening. My impression is schizophrenia. I truly hope I'm wrong."

"Should he be out of the hospital so soon?" Patti asked.

"That's a tough call," Drake said. "Bryce was terrified in the ER. The psych unit had to be a nightmare for him. I can't pretend to know what is best."

"What should I tell his parents?" Patti asked.

"Maybe you can just tell them you're there for them if they want to talk. I'm sure they know to follow the instructions, make sure he takes his meds, and seek help if they need it." His words felt inadequate.

"I feel helpless," she said. Her sadness carried over the line.

More than ten percent of ER visits were mental-health related. The mentally ill patients he and Patti saw were typically failing treatment and in crisis. It was a skewed view. No one came to the ER because they were doing well.

"I've thought of him and his parents a bunch."

"It just sucks," Patti said. "They're the nicest people."

"You being there for them means a lot." Drake said. "I'm in the ER this afternoon. You?"

"I'll be there." Patti's endless energy was missing from her voice.

"Hang in there, friend. See you soon."

They disconnected.

He'd awakened after one of the best evenings of his life. They were on the cusp of getting a real home, and dreams that had seemed impossible now appeared within reach.

He still glowed in anticipation, but the thought of what Bryce and his loved ones faced made his happiness seem somehow unfair.

Was it wrong to put aside the suffering of others? How else could anyone ever feel happy?

He stood up and stretched. His philosophical pondering created more questions than answers. The extended sleep had been great, but he needed to get moving. He'd have to hurry to be on time for the meeting with Kline, Torrins, and the malpractice lawyers. After that, he hoped to fit in a visit to Kip before reporting for his afternoon ER shift.

He wasn't sure which he looked forward to less—the malpractice meeting or the morgue.

***

Drake used his hands-free phone as he drove towards the hospital. "Call Rizz." He'd not heard from his friend for a while. The Mayo spinal cord injury rehabilitation unit pushed their patients hard.

"Michael Rizzini here."

"Rizz, it's Drake. Can you talk?"

"Yeah, I just did a three-mile run and some stair climbs, so I'm taking a break."

Rizz was paralyzed and wheelchair-bound due to the bullet he'd taken to protect Drake and his family. After a second illicit infusion of Drake's experimental drug D-44, he'd shown hints of recovery and was weeks into an intense inpatient rehab effort.

His smart-ass response was typical and reassuring.

"I'm glad I caught you before you got on the trampoline," Drake said. "Seriously—how are you doing?"

Rizz was rarely serious.

"Lots of spasms, which I'm seeing as positive. Best of all, I had a smoking-hot dream last night, and I woke up with a hard-on. And I swear I could feel it."

Rizz's complex makeup included an obsession with women and sex that he'd historically appeared to handle without victimizing or being victim.

"Too much info but great, Rizz. What are you doing in therapy?"

"Daily electrostimulation of my paralyzed muscles, stretching, working in the pool, and more. We're pushing hard. No spectacular gains, but it's coming back. I know it." Two or three sentences in a row where Rizz had been serious. Had to be a record.

"What have you heard from the veterinarians about FloJo?" Drake asked.

"I just got a final report from them this morning. I was going to spring it on you this afternoon. Her little kitty brain is cancer-free. They sent the brain MRI to a top specialist in feline medicine. She said FloJo's findings are secondary to trauma—what they saw on the image was scar tissue. Some time before she ended up in the pound and came to us, FloJo survived a head injury. They are convinced the scar triggered her seizures. They put her on low-dose phenobarbital and no seizures." Rizz spoke fast.

"Bottom line, my mad scientist, drug-creating friend, is that FloJo does not have cancer. And they've found nothing else wrong with her. Are you reading me? She got the zillion-dollar workup and she's golden. There's no evidence of adverse effects from the D-44 that she and I took. We're cruising, brother." Rizz's voice cracked. Drake's titanium-tough friend was choked up.

"Hot damn, Rizz. Absolutely fantastic." Drake smiled, and for a moment he couldn't speak. If his experimental drug were to have harmed or killed Rizz...

A rush of long-held tension drained from his body.

God, Karma, fate, whatever the cause, both the dream house with Rachelle last night and Rizz's reports today seemed too good to be true.

Chapter 21

Edison High School

Bryce sat alone in his second-hour study hall. Jimmy usually sat with him, but he was late—he was always late. The other kids gave Bryce looks and stayed clear, leaving him seated by himself. He heard murmuring voices, but this time he knew it was the kids who were talking.

Talking about him.

The voices in his head had quieted since the first of the pills in the emergency room.

He was glad to be out of the hospital. It had seemed like forever. The Adolescent Psychiatry Unit, they'd called it. A few nurses, a bunch of messed-up kids, and lots of questions from two different doctors. He'd never been more alone.

Everyone asked if he'd been taking drugs—it seemed like they wished he had.

After all the blood tests and questions, one of the nurses and the lady psychiatrist had a meeting with his mom and dad. What did they talk about?

Afterward, they brought Bryce in. The doctor told him he had an illness, but he was "responding" to medication. What did that mean? They said they had a plan. She and his parents thought he could go home. They felt school and his usual activities would be good for him. Did he agree?

Why wouldn't he want to go home?

His parents looked nervous.

The doctor said they had a "treatment plan" for him.

Treatment plan? He wasn't sure what any of it meant.

The lady doctor said it was too early to put a name on his sickness, but it was a type of mental illness. She didn't say he was crazy, but she didn't say he wasn't.

Nothing made sense. All he wanted was to go home and not be afraid and not hear the voices.

And somehow forget what the voices had told him.

He hadn't let on that the nurses and doctors hadn't fooled him.

Before they let him go home, they asked him if he thought about hurting himself. Then they asked if he thought of hurting someone else. He'd been asked that over and over.

Why did they keep asking that?

What he wanted was to get out of there and go home. He wanted to go to school, see his friend Jimmy, and not hear the voices or be afraid.

They said he could go as long as he took the pills. Everyone said he had to take the pills. His parents were serious about the pills. They kept the bottles and told him when to take them. They watched him swallow them last night and this morning.

Why was everyone pushing so hard for the pills?

The study hall door opened, and everyone turned and looked. Jimmy slipped in.

"So glad you could grace us with your presence, James," the monitoring teacher said.

"Sorry." Jimmy smiled and shrugged. The teacher shook his head and went back to his paperwork.

Jimmy winked at Bryce. He swung his backpack onto the table and slid into the chair next to him. Jimmy pulled out a book then leaned close, whispering.

"Jeez, dude, you look like crap. What the hell did they do to you?"

What did they do to me? It seemed like Jimmy spoke in high speed while his own thoughts were moving through Jello.

"They have me taking pills. I think they kind of helped."

"They kind of helped?" Jimmy frowned. "You look zonked. Do they make you feel good? Do they get you off?"

How could Bryce explain? He didn't understand it himself.

"They're not that kind of pills," he said. The pills didn't make him feel good, but whenever the fog of the pills started to lift, other things returned. None of it was good.

"I'll tell you what, dude," Jimmy said. "Same thing I've been telling you for weeks. You need to try some of the killer pills I scored. It's the best stuff ever. I take one and I'm floating on a cloud. Never felt anything better!"

Floating on a cloud? That sounded good. Bryce had gotten brave once and smoked weed, but all it did was make him cough and feel nervous. He was afraid of pills and stronger stuff. Jimmy wasn't. The DARE program and other warnings hadn't scared him.

Nothing scared Jimmy.

Bryce couldn't put his fear into words. How could he explain? He was fading away. Jimmy wouldn't understand. He'd acted mad after Bruce told him about the voices and hadn't mentioned it since. If Bryce told Jimmy what was really happening, he'd freak out. The only friend Bryce had left would dump him.

"Hey, Earth to Bryce." Jimmy elbowed Bryce's shoulder. "Don't space out on me, man. That's what I'm talking about. Whatever they have you taking has you totally messed up."

"The doctors say it's the right kind of medicine for me."

"Think about it, dude. If it doesn't make you feel good, how can it be right?"

Did that make sense? Everyone told him something different. Maybe Jimmy was right? Bryce's thoughts wouldn't come together. Each day he was becoming more mixed up, and the pills made his head feel like it was filled with cement.

And there was the other thing. The scariest thing of all. The thing he hadn't told the doctor in the ER or anyone else. Not even his parents. Especially not his parents. They had to have noticed it, but they hadn't said anything. They knew. Why didn't they say anything?

Every day he was getting smaller.

He'd noticed it for weeks. He was shrinking so fast that if it didn't stop soon he'd disappear. Each day he came closer to being gone forever.

The voices told him why his parents pretended not to notice. The voices were quiet now, but the words had burned into his mind. *Your parents want you to disappear.*

Fear flooded his veins like acid.

Would he still be afraid if he floated on a cloud?

Chapter 22

Memorial Hospital – administrative conference room

Kline, two hospital risk-management attorneys, Jim Torrins, and Drake sat at one table of the four that were positioned in a square with an empty space in the middle.

A stenographer sat at the table to Drake's left. She keyed silently while a red monitor light glowed from the audio recorder next to her.

The two Memorial Hospital staff physicians being deposed, one an anesthesiologist and the other a surgeon, sat at the table on Drake's right.

Personal injury attorney, Clete Venjer, sat alone on the table opposite Drake. Venjer looked to be around forty years old, a small man with a baby face and a chubby build. He wore an off-the-rack black suit.

If you put a white collar on him, the Twin Cities leading malpractice attorney could be the twin of the parish priest that Drake's mother idolized in Ohio.

"This concludes the initial depositions of the physicians named in the malpractice motion," the malpractice attorney said. A patient had died abruptly following a surgery. The cause of death was a mystery, and the malpractice claim alleged it was due to negligence.

Through his more than forty minutes of questioning the surgeon and anesthesiologist, Venjer had never raised his voice or been less than polite.

In spite of that, the two doctors looked like they had just completed a punishing multi-hour surgical case. Venjer's soft voice and seemingly earnest pursuit of understanding had the doctors stuttering, repeating themselves, and more on edge than Drake had ever seen either of them.

The attorney gathered papers and closed the folder.

Drake had not seen the records on this case, but he had not heard anything that suggested negligence. The deposition had not confirmed guilt or innocence, but just being in the room had made it hard for Drake to swallow.

Lives, careers, mental health, big money, and the hospital's ability to remain insured were at stake.

The surgeon and anesthesiologist rose. Venjer stood and gave a slight bow. "Doctors, thank you for your time, courtesy, and responsiveness."

The physicians left, looking drawn and unsure.

The deposition involved a case that had been initiated a month back on a death two months previous. The hospital and both physicians had been named in the suit.

Drake was learning of the grim realities of the malpractice litigation. More than half of all doctors were sued at some time—more than 80% within some specialties. The process often took years and involved huge financial and personal costs. Symptoms of clinical depression among physicians charged were common.

Attorneys understood that it was quicker and easier to settle malpractice suits than fight it out in court. A quick settlement put money in the attorney's pocket without the investment of time and dollars that a trial would require.

Hospitals, HMOs, and institutions that employed physicians also leaned toward the limited expense and known cost of a settlement. No one could predict what a trial jury might find—errant verdicts in both directions occurred, and multi-million-dollar awards were not rare.

Innocent physicians always chose the pain of a trial, as a settlement counted against them the same as a guilty jury verdict in their professional and public record.

Depositions were theoretically for the finding of facts. A number of nurses and other staff had already been questioned by members of Venjer's firm.

Jim Torrins said Kline had specifically asked for Drake to be present to "get a taste" of what Memorial Hospital was facing. It was Drake's first direct exposure to the process, and the Memorial Hospital legal team had worked to educate him.

The hospital's attorneys had told Drake that the depositions were, in part, fishing expeditions. The malpractice attorneys looked for anything that could be used to advance their claim of malpractice or sound damning to a jury of the medically naive.

The attorneys had advised the two physicians to answer all questions, but volunteer nothing more. It was best to answer with "yes," "no," or "I don't know," and little else. They stressed that the malpractice attorneys had an incentive to twist and distort answers in a system where "winning" meant huge monetary payoffs for them.

So far Clete Venjer, while making the doctors sweat, did not appear to have the horns and tail that the risk management attorneys' comments had led Drake to expect.

"Would you like to take a break before we continue?" asked Venjer. He reached into his briefcase.

"Continue?" Jim Torrins said. "That's everyone involved in the case. There's no one left to deposition."

"Perhaps I'm mistaken," Clete had a new file in his hand, "but CEO Kline contacted me and—"

"Yes. That's correct, counselor," Kline said. "I'd yet to mention my proposal to our president of Medical Affairs."

"Proposal?" Torrins looked at the hospital attorneys. They kept their eyes down. Drake sensed things had gone off script.

"I asked Clete if we might attempt to streamline the process," Kline said. "I became aware of a new potential action and thought we might expedite things. Clete agreed to update us on where his newest client stood. We may be able to take care of things quickly."

Torrins was open-mouthed, and the risk management duo remained with eyes averted.

"This is unusually quick, but when CEO Kline asked, I agreed," Venjer said. "This is all preliminary, and nothing I say now binds me or my client, or any future clients. If that's understood, I'm comfortable with sharing where our newest potential litigation stands."

"Understood." Kline said. "Please go ahead."

Venjer's dark eyes flickered between Kline and Torrins. The attorney had picked up the friction. Clearly, the guy didn't miss much.

"While this is friendly and informal, I'm asking that we keep the recorder running—a professional habit." Clete smiled and opened his file.

"Yesterday, I entered into an attorney-client relationship with Marcus Jackson. He lives in Gary, Indiana and is the brother and only living relative of Ivy Jackson."

What? No! Drake hadn't learned the overdosed, new mother's name until after she'd died in the ICU. They were going to sue? No way. It didn't make sense.

"As some of you know," the attorney continued, "Ms. Jackson expired in the ICU of Memorial Hospital just days ago. I've been retained to file a wrongful death action against the hospital, the physicians, and other staff who were caring for her in the intensive care unit."

"Excuse me," Jim Torrins spoke, his face a frown. "The young woman has barely been pronounced dead. This discussion is not only premature, but borderline ridiculous. Let's at least wait for the post mortem findings and—"

"Actually," Venjer said, "we have that report." He held up a sheet of paper.

"That usually takes at least a week." Torrins looked surprised but recovered. "Regardless, this is still too fast. How can we respond when we haven't even spoken with the physicians involved?"

"Dr. Torrins," Kline said, "Nothing being discussed here today will harm anyone. Clete is indulging my request. It's possible that we can head off a malpractice action and avoid the bad publicity and, er, distress it would cause. It could end up best for everyone."

"I understand Dr. Torrins' unease," Clete Venjer said. "This is very unusual. Perhaps the President of Medical Affairs is correct. I can—"

"Thank you, Clete," Kline said, "but please continue. I've thought it through. I'm comfortable it is in Memorial Hospital's interest."

Torrins looked at Kline in disbelief. He dropped his hands to the table.

"I'll keep it brief," Venjer said. "I'll state for the record that my client and I reserve the right to change any and all elements of the malpractice actions we are bringing against Memorial Hospital and the nurses and doctors involved." He paused and met eyes about the table. All were leaning forward. Drake held his breath.

"We will name Memorial Hospital, Dr. Julie Stone, Dr. Vijay Gupta, and ICU nurse Tracy Miller in a malpractice suit involving the wrongful death of Ivy Jackson." Venjer appeared apologetic. "But Dr. Torrins is correct. It is early, and we will pursue all the facts and revisit our plans in due course." He closed his file. "That's all I have for now."

He put the file in his briefcase. He began to stand, then sat back and raised a finger.

"Excuse me, one last thing if I may. Dr. Cody, I recall that you saw the deceased before she was admitted to the ICU, correct?"

"Yes." Drake's first view of the mother and the infant's protruding legs flashed.

"When you cared for her in the ER, it was hours before she passed away. I imagine when you learned of her death, it saddened you." His tone and manner broadcast sympathy. "I've been around enough to know that a patient's death, especially a young patient in tragic circumstances, devastates caregivers. It had to be rough." He seemed to genuinely empathize. What he'd said was true.

Clete Venjer was an attorney. He was doing his job. He was not responsible for the messed-up malpractice system. He'd been nothing but respectful and classy.

"Actually, Dr. Cody," Venjer said, "I understand you saved her life and that of her baby."

"The paramedics saved her," Drake said. "I was part of the team that cared for her when they brought her to the ER."

"You're being modest." The attorney smiled. "You managed the complicated delivery of her premature baby and got him safely to the neonatal intensive care unit. Then you stabilized her multiple problems and transferred her to the ICU. That's true, isn't it?"

He glanced at Torrins, whose eyes flashed a warning. Drake remembered the hospital risk management attorney's cautions to the earlier doctors. *Answer the questions but volunteer nothing more.*

"Yes. We delivered the infant and transferred the mother to the ICU."

"The record shows that you administered drugs to manage the overdose, delivered the baby and the placenta, gave fluids, and began to transfuse blood, all within fifteen minutes."

"Yes. The ER team accomplished those things." *If it's in the record, why is he asking me?*

"The documents show the baby was successfully transferred to the neonatal care unit and the placenta was delivered. The mother responded to your treatment of her overdose, and her vital signs and bleeding greatly improved before she was transferred to the ICU. I suspect you, er, your team felt good about the care provided."

They had felt good. Damn good. It was what they were all about. Paramedics, nurses, techs, doctors and the other members of the emergency care team had worked together to save lives. *Why is he asking this?*

Venjer waited several seconds, but Drake remained silent.

"Personally, I'm very impressed with what you did." Venjer paused, then shook his head. "But hours later, something went horribly wrong." His voice quavered. "A young mother lost her life."

The hollowness of the tragedy gripped Drake.

It seemed Venjer also cared. He definitely did not fit the stereotype of a greedy ambulance chaser.

"One last thing, Dr. Cody. Thanks for bearing with me. You got the baby delivered, the afterbirth followed, and then your obstetrical colleague arrived in the ER." He paused. "Is that what happened?"

Was that one question or three? Is he trying to get me to support his claim against Julie?

"The placenta delivered before Dr. Stone arrived," Drake said.

"I see." Venjer's brows knitted. He paused, then gently shook his head. He turned to the CEO, the attorneys, and Jim Torrins. Last, he looked at Drake, his expression sad.

"I apologize to all, but I must amend my earlier statement." He nodded to the stenographer. "In the spirit of transparency and cooperation initiated by CEO Kline, I have to make a correction. Within the last several hours, I received confirmation of a pertinent medical finding." He shook his head. "One might say a most unfortunate finding." His hound dog eyes scanned the group, then rested on Drake.

"I regret to inform you that we will be adding Dr. Drake Cody to the malpractice suit involving the wrongful case death of Ivy Jackson.

The floor gave way under Drake. What? Had he misheard?

"Dr. Cody acknowledges he oversaw delivery of the placenta and, per the record, he examined it."

The attorney gave a big sigh, then opened his briefcase and took out a single sheet of paper.

"This is pathology report on specimen C2984, identified as the placental tissue of the birth-mother Ivy Jackson. I'll quote the significant element: "Placental tissue weighs 0.46 kilograms. The specimen is not intact. Examination confirms disruption and separation of tissue, with an unknown amount of placental tissue absent. Clinical correlation advised—retained placental tissue is a known risk for disseminated intravascular coagulation and other pathologic processes."

Venjer set the report down. The room was silent.

"As the physicians here know," Venjer said in a voice just above a whisper, "retained placental material is a well-documented possible trigger for runaway bleeding. If the incomplete placenta had been recognized in the ER or thereafter, steps could have been taken to address the retained placenta, and Ms. Jackson would be alive today." He paused, his head bent.

"Id ergo est. The thing explains itself," he said. "Dr. Drake Cody's failure to recognize the possible presence of retained placenta was negligent and a proximate cause of Ivy Jackson's wrongful death. His treatment of her did not meet the standard of care and she suffered damages, in fact the ultimate damage, because of his failure. This is the definition of malpractice." Venjer raised his head, looked at Drake, and laid his hands flat on the table. "I am truly sorry, Dr. Cody."

A high-pitched keening filled Drake's ears. He fought for air, feeling as if he'd been kicked in the head. He tried to maintain his outward appearance while inside he collapsed like the walls of a dynamited building.

Lord, no!

Chapter 23

Drake made his way out of the conference room, unsure of how he remained upright. His insides were hollow and his mind thrashed. He said something to Jim Torrins, then turned down the nearest hall alone. Whatever he'd said to Torrins could not have reflected what was inside him.

He wanted to run to the hospital exit and explode onto Chicago Avenue screaming.

Accused of malpractice. *What could be worse?*

Clete Venjer and his legal team would work to have him declared guilty. They would do or say anything necessary to persuade a jury he was a negligent and incompetent physician. Their careers and income depended on it. It was their job.

They'd enlist medical "experts," physicians who testified in malpractice trials for pay, to paint Drake as guilty of causing his patient's death.

He was already on disciplinary probation. The impact of a verdict or settlement for a charge of malpractice in the wrongful death claim was clear. The state Medical Board would yank his medical license in a heartbeat. His dreams would come to an end.

The charge wasn't true. It wasn't right. It wasn't just.

Goddamn it—not again.

***

Cincinnati, Ohio

Drake's childhood

Drake's younger brother Kevin's mind was good, but his brain's control center for movement had been damaged at birth. Cerebral palsy.

Kevin's body defied control. Few could understand his speech, and only through iron resolve and exhausting effort did he eventually walk with special crutches. Kids made fun of him and adults looked away.

Drake's mother said to Drake, "God made you brave and strong so you can watch over your special brother."

And he did.

Kevin never quit. He never cried. He and Drake communicated without effort, sharing laughing fits or pain, often without exchanging a word.

Kevin was the largest and best part of Drake's world.

Kevin entered seventh grade at the same public junior/senior high where Drake was starting the tenth grade. On their third day, they waited next to the auxiliary parking lot of the main school building. Their mom would pick them up any minute.

Three slouching twelfth graders with shaved heads stood by a trash dumpster smoking cigarettes and talking loud. Kids called them skinheads and stayed clear.

"C'mon Kevin, let's wait over there." Drake pointed farther down the lot.

"O-ho-KAY d-DRAKE." Kevin started his flailing crutches movement away from the dumpster.

"Hey! What the hell is that?" came the shout. Coarse, biting laughter followed.

The three skinheads advanced. "Hey, wait up, retard," one yelled. They all laughed.

Drake's face flushed hot.

"I-it's o-kay D-Drake! C-c'mon!" Kevin worked his crutches, struggling to stay ahead of the hyenas.

The largest and loudest of the three caught up and stepped in front of Kevin, causing them to stop. "ARYAN" was tattooed on his forearm. He finger-flicked his cigarette, bouncing it with a burst of spark at Drake's feet.

A drumming started inside Drake's head. He stood on the sidewalk where a tree root had caused a jagged crack and an uneven step-off under his feet. The smell of cigarettes grew stronger.

"I think I'll try out those sticks, spaz boy," said Aryan tattoo, pointing at Kevin's crutches.

Kevin stood, crutch-propped and weaving, the skinheads laughing at him.

Time stretched. Drake's vision tunneled, and edges sharpened. The drumming in his head intensified. His face burned as though he was standing too close to an open fire. His reflexes were trip-wired.

Aryan stepped forward, grabbed Kevin's right crutch, and yanked. Kevin lurched and almost fell. The skinheads howled.

Drake grasped Kevin's shoulders and smoothly lowered him to the curb. He took the left crutch, slipping the aluminum forearm ring free of Kevin's arm.

Aryan jerked harder on the right crutch, dragging Kevin.

Kevin's eyes pinwheeled. He held on. "Nuh-nuh-NO!"

Aryan raised his leg and launched his foot, the sole of his boot driving towards Kevin's face.

The crutch whistled as it sliced through the air. It struck Aryan's face, feeling in Drake's hands like an ax biting into a log. The skinhead pitched onto his back, his face a volcano of erupting blood.

Out of the corner of his eye, Drake saw a second skinhead advancing. Drake pivoted, shifted his grip, and drove the tip of the crutch into the attacker's belly. The skinhead jackknifed to the ground, arms hugging gut.

Drake glimpsed, too late, the third skinhead's swinging fist. A bolt of pain lanced his jaw and the taste of pennies filled his mouth.

He was on his back, the puncher straddling his chest and pounding his face.

Drake drove his hand through the punches and found the attacker's throat. His fingers closed. As the blows rained down, he squeezed.

Rage fueled his grip, his fingers hydraulic. A strangled yelp. The punches stopped. The drumming in his head thundered on.

And still he squeezed.

Fingers clutched Drake's arms, and Kevin's voice cut through the drumming. "N-NO! D-draAKE! N-noO!"

Drake pushed aside the gurgling body. Turning, he saw the other skinheads on the ground. He met his brother's wild eyes and wrapped him in a hug as they lay on the cracked sidewalk. Kevin's body quaked with sobs.

The criminal charges read "felony assault with weapon, resulting in grievous bodily injury." The father of the assailant whose face Drake had crushed was the largest highway construction contractor in the state. Drake's "victims" wore sport coats and ties in court. Their hair had grown to crewcut length.

In the trial that had swung a wrecking ball into Drake's life, the truth had not mattered. It had come down to the story the prosecutor and paid-to-testify "experts" sold to the jury.

Drake's attorney was a public defender in his first significant trial.

Drake was sentenced to the Scioto Facility for Juvenile Violent Offenders in Furnace, Ohio. The "Furnace" had six times the frequency of violent events as the worst of Ohio's adult maximum-security prisons.

When a pro bono criminal justice oversight group secured Drake's early release, it had been too late to put his life back together.

***

Drake's shoes squeaked as he walked down the empty, white hospital corridor. His assault conviction was now known, but the lies he'd told in hiding it had jeopardized his medical license and left him on probation.

No one close to him knew what he'd had to do to survive in the Furnace. It had changed forever the architecture of his mind. There were places in his head he wanted to keep closed forever. He was still serving the sentence his conviction had wrought.

He stopped and leaned against the wall. *Malpractice.* Once more, he would have the course of his life decided by the legal system. It was called the "justice" system, but for Drake that name had not applied.

He took deep breaths, trying to focus the frenzied energy within his mind.

He was no longer a naive juvenile with a low-income mother and a vulnerable younger brother. Back then, his fate had been solely in the hands of an inexperienced, outclassed public defender. Now was different.

His assignment to investigate Memorial Hospital's malpractice cases was no longer just a troublesome chore. Clete Venjer's lightning bolt had changed that.

The malpractice attorney said the woman had died because of Drake's incompetence.

It wasn't true. Drake would defend himself.

He made his way to the medical records office and signed in on the dedicated computer that Torrins had arranged. He accessed the records of the overdosed mother. Could he find the explanation for her freakish, mysterious death?

Sweat beaded his brow as he reviewed every word and lab result in the record. He found nothing that confirmed the overwhelming likelihood that her bleeding and death had resulted from her overdose and shock rather than the retained placenta claim.

Next, he went through each of the earlier malpractice cases and took four pages of notes.

He tracked patient identification numbers and examined unending laboratory results and hundreds of detailed doctors' and nurses' notes—his head ached. Had he discovered anything meaningful? Something that might link the mysterious deaths?

At times, he'd sensed something, but it slipped away.

Or was he just hoping to find something that wasn't there? Had he failed his patient?

No, damn it. I did not fail her.

He rubbed his temples. It was time to head to the ER to start the partial shift he'd volunteered to cover. Before the meeting with Clete Venjer, Drake had planned on using these past hours to visit Kip Dronen and seek his help with the malpractice committee investigation.

Kip Dronen knew more about death—mysterious, tragic, or otherwise—than anyone. Would Kip help? Drake never knew what went through the man's mind.

Earlier, his desire for Kip's help had been in the "would be nice" zone. Now, after Clete Venjer's revelation, Drake's need was hanging-from-a-cliff's-edge desperate.

Chapter 24

Surgeon Bart Rainey swallowed the last sip of coffee from his oversized mug. As he refilled the mug, he noticed a dirty brown stain and a collection of dust between the coffee machine and the wall. His height gave him a view on things that no one else had. He shook his head. Who the hell was doing the cleaning around here?

If he was running the hospital, he'd find the maintenance person responsible and fire their ass.

Free coffee in the doctors' lounge was one of the few perks that remained, and if he didn't need the caffeine boost, the filth behind the machine would have made him dump it. He'd heard about past days when physicians had free parking spaces and free meals, and the lounge was filled with treats and beverages of all sorts. Those days, doctors were actually appreciated, and administration and everyone else knew who was in charge.

In the New Age of medicine, they were lucky to get coffee, and every day countless people tried to tell Bart what to do.

He paced while sipping the coffee. An orthopedic surgeon, a plastic surgeon, and one other general surgeon were, like him, impatiently waiting for operating rooms to open up for their next scheduled cases.

Two internists and a hospitalist were sitting in the computer bay, checking labs. Rainey felt their glances. Even on his college basketball team, he'd stood out due to his size. It had embarrassed him as a kid, and even today the "What's the weather like up there?" comic geniuses pissed him off, but he no longer cared what others thought.

He'd completed four major cases since starting at six a.m.

There was nothing better than operating. Taking patients to the OR and opening them up was the ultimate challenge. You never knew exactly what you'd find, yet you had to execute flawlessly every time. There were no "time-outs," there were no "do-overs." The patients had critical problems and it was up to him, Bart Rainey, to do the right thing and do it perfectly.

He loved it. He'd work as a surgeon for free.

Clinic hours were time-pressed and sometimes boring, but it was there he got to follow up on the patients he'd helped. His patients loved him.

They appreciated that he'd saved their lives or cured their suffering. It made putting up with all the other annoyances tolerable.

Dealing with administrators, nurses, techs, insurance companies, IT nerds, and everyone else who tried to tell him what to do pissed him off. Lots of people thought they knew how he should do his job. Screw them. His job was not about making them happy. They were around to do what he ordered—not the other way around.

His responsibility was to make sure his patients got the best care possible, and he'd never been afraid to get in people's faces to make that happen. Being a nice-guy doctor might make nurses and other hospital workers like you, but it didn't ensure your orders would be followed.

He could guarantee that when he gave an order, it got done—or else.

He was in deep shit with the hospital for how he'd treated some staff, but he could handle that. No one could suggest he didn't treat his patients well. Hell, he had the highest patient recommendation marks of any surgeon in his group.

Would his latest exchange with that weirdo Clara chick who was head of lab and IT bite him in the ass? Everything about her irritated him.

She insisted on being called "doctor" because she had a couple of bullshit degrees. She knew all about the test tube world, computers, and the damn electronic medical record. She hung around the ICU in a white coat like she was some kind of clinical supervisor. She got off telling doctors and nurses what hoops they had to jump through to order tests, and what they had to document in the soul-sucking, pain-in-the-ass computer. The only real thing he'd ever seen her do was draw blood.

She sure as hell wasn't a real doctor. She didn't take patients to the OR, save lives, or do any of the things that real doctors do. Yet somehow, she thought herself above him. Her sense of superiority came off her like a bad smell. She was the most annoying of the many clueless people who presumed to tell him how to do his job.

He had to acknowledge one thing. For all the times he'd put her in her place, she'd never filed a complaint.

That was better than the nurses, anesthesiologists, and other staff who had written him up.

The automated doors to the OR corridor swung open, and the ENT who'd been operating in OR six exited with her scrub mask hanging loose around her neck. Good. Bart's case should be able to go as soon as they turned the room over. He'd already talked with the patient who was waiting to be rolled in and put on the table.

Today the OR had been good. None of the hang-ups, staff shortages, or unscheduled cases that often jammed up the schedule. He had two more cases—the last a complex tumor resection in a young guy. Hopefully the patient would be another he'd see in his clinic for years to come.

He exited the doctor's lounge, went down the hall, and keyed in his entry code to the doctors' locker room. He ducked his head as he went through the door.

Locker rooms had been a part of his life forever. His time in college playing division one basketball had been among the best years of his life. But the pressure and rush of a really big game didn't compare to the challenge of performing major surgery.

He worked the combination to his locker. He reached onto the top shelf and pulled out his tin of tobacco. He took the last remaining pouch of Copenhagen and put it between his cheek and gum. He'd have to remember to buy more.

One of the country boys who'd played basketball with him had turned him on to smokeless tobacco. Bart had used it and caffeine to help him through medical school, residency, and his years as a staff surgeon. When people learned he used chew, some asked how he could get away with spitting. He didn't spit. He swallowed the saliva and it never bothered him a bit.

Few understood what it took to be a surgeon. He hated the comments like "amazing for a big man." As if his size would make him deficient in any way.

That sure as hell wasn't true. He was almost seven feet tall, strong and coordinated, smart and fit—he'd given up apologizing for being special a long time ago.

He had something of a ritual before and between cases—coffee, then tobacco. He closed his locker and went into the bathroom and took a piss. He ran cold water over his hands and forearms, then splashed it on his face. He took a towel and patted himself dry.

He exited the locker room, made his way past the doctors' lounge, and hit the metal plate that opened the door into the operating room. As he stepped into the bustle of nurses, techs, anesthetists and others, he felt as comfortable as he did anyplace on the planet.

He stopped and slipped a new pair of paper surgical booties over his shoes. His were in the box marked "Dr. Rainey." There was only one person on the hospital staff who had size 19 shoes. He leaned over the counter to the OR charge nurse.

"Hey, Gwen, is room six good to go?"

"Let me double-check." She scrolled the computer screen. "Yep, all good, Dr. Rainey."

"Clear the way. It's time for me to work my magic," he said.

She shook her head. "You singlehandedly keep the stereotype of the arrogant doctor alive around here."

"I only speak the truth," he said. And hell if it wasn't true.

He walked to the scrub area for OR six. From his height, he could see the whole room through the plate glass. His patient was being placed on the table.

He used a finger to fish the plug of tobacco out of his mouth and tossed it into the waste receptacle.

He faced the basin, then stepped on the foot pedals and began his pre-surgical scrub.

Game on!

Damn, he loved his work.

Chapter 25

The ER was dead.

On a day when Drake longed for the distraction that taking care of emergency patients provided, the impossible had happened. In the middle of the afternoon, Memorial Hospital's emergency department's waiting room was empty and there were several open beds. He hadn't seen the department this empty other than a few times in the middle of the graveyard shift during a blizzard or thirty-below temperatures.

He wanted to work. He wanted to help others with their emergencies rather than face his own.

Instead, grim thoughts were smashing around in his head like a pinball. Accused of malpractice—would he lose his license? Would the dreams that had seemed so close disappear? The narcotic overdoses—what could he do? Was he responsible for the death of the addicted mother? Rizz was doing better but—

Damn, Drake Get a grip! Worrying accomplished nothing. His life was a multiple car pile-up and he needed to perform triage.

Figure out what needs to be done and do it.

The ER was quiet. There were no charts of patients waiting to be seen. Unbelievable.

He picked up the phone and dialed. He got a pickup on the first ring.

"Hello, Lloyd Anderson, attorney speaking. How can I help?" The seasoned lawyer's baritone fit him. The burly fifty-something-year-old never seemed shaken or out of his element. Without his wiles, Drake's license to practice medicine would not be on disciplinary probation—it would be long gone.

"Drake Cody here. Lloyd, I need your advice."

"Of course. I've done an assessment of the lakeshore property. No liens. The title is clean. Unless the bank gets weird on the mortgage, everything looks good to go. It's a beautiful place. I think you're getting a great deal," Lloyd said.

"This isn't about the house." Drake looked around and cupped his hand over the phone. "I just learned I'm to be named to a malpractice suit."

"Oh man. I'm really sorry to hear that."

"I'm in the ER. I don't know how much time I have to talk," Drake said. "The hospital, two other physicians, and a nurse are also being accused."

"Yeah," Lloyd said. "That's how they always play it. Toss a large net and see what you catch. It's unfortunate but the system rewards that. The plaintiffs and malpractice attorneys pay no penalty for accusing people falsely, and it works to their advantage. More pockets to seek money from, and sometimes the defendants start turning on each other. It's not a good system. Can I ask what damages they say their client suffered?"

"It's a wrongful death suit, Lloyd. The woman died," Drake said.

The woman died. Drake's gut clenched.

"We'll need to meet. Do they have a deposition scheduled? When will you face the attorney who filed?"

"I already did. I met him this morning."

"You met the prosecuting attorney? Geez, Drake. I wish you'd contacted me sooner. You shouldn't have talked to anyone without me being there. Especially the plaintiff attorney."

"I was blindsided," Drake said. "It came out in a meeting on something else. I had no idea."

"Something is not right. From now on, do not talk to anyone about this case without me present—okay?" Lloyd paused. "So who's the attorney?"

"Clete Venjer."

There was silence. "That's really not good." Lloyd paused again. "I'll get on this."

"I was told the hospital attorneys would represent me, but I wanted your opinion," Drake said.

"Hell in a handbasket, Drake. Whatever you do, you must have your own attorney. If not me, then someone else. The hospital attorneys are paid to look out for the hospital's interests, not yours. The hospital will make decisions based on their bottom line—nothing else. And I guarantee the hospital's CEO would toss you under the bus for a nickel."

Drake's stomach gnawed. He'd heard that any time a physician was named in a malpractice suit, no matter if there was zero guilt, they'd already lost. A subsequent finding of innocence did nothing to erase the time, pain, professional damage, and emotional anguish caused by the false accusation.

He believed it.

"Lloyd, if I need an attorney, you're who I want. But I'm sure it's expensive. I don't—"

"Stop right there. Hell, yes, I'm expensive, but I know you're good for it. We'll figure something out. You need me." Lloyd was silent for a moment. "Clete Venjer is no hack. He wins because he's clever and can handle juries like a hypnotist. I'm hoping you were only named as part of that wide net I mentioned. It's possible you could be dropped before this goes too far. I'll see what I can find out and contact you. Sound good?"

Sound good? It sounded like a nightmare.

"Thanks, Lloyd. I appreciate your help."

They disconnected.

Several hours earlier, Drake had awoken after one of the best nights of his life. Rachelle was at ease and as happy he'd ever seen her. They were on track to move into a beautiful new home. He'd spoken with Rizz and got the most hopeful news he could have heard.

Now it seemed like that had been someone else's life.

***

The afternoon remained slow. Patients were showing up to the ER almost as if they had scheduled appointments.

Drake didn't have to rush, as was routine for virtually every shift. He'd taken care of a dislocated shoulder, a broken wrist, and a complex laceration—relatively few patients, with problems he'd been able to address.

The glaring, ugly exceptions had been several overdose patient resuscitations and three he'd had to pronounce dead over the radio. The disaster continued to worsen.

Drake had just got off the radio following one of the fatalities when Patti had arrived to start her shift as charge nurse.

"They sent Bryce to school today." She clutched his arm. "I'm worried sick about him." She appeared on the verge of tears. They hugged. So sad.

After the hug, she avoided eye contact and hurried off. Her charge nurse phone trilled, and she answered as she moved away.

A thousand pounds weighed on Drake's shoulders. This day had become a plague.

He moved to take the lone chart from the patient-to-be-seen rack.

"Drake!" Patti was running toward him, her expression grim. "The OR called. Dr. Bart Rainey collapsed. He flipped out and is having some kind of spasms. They had to force him to stop operating. He tossed some people around and security is trying to control him. He looks bad. They're trying to get him down here. They think he's dying."

"Use Crash Room bay three," Drake said. He'd butted heads with the giant of a man in the past—stubborn and rude, but underneath that he was a dedicated surgeon. A bulldozer couldn't drag Bart Rainey away from one of his patients in the OR. What could be going on?

The secretary had overheard, and Drake nodded to her. Her call for a resuscitation team to Crash Room three sounded overhead.

He entered the Crash Room as resuscitation team members scrambled. Someone had triggered the Life Clock. Big red numerals flashed the seconds since the OR call. Drake had no doubt that whatever had taken Bart Rainey down was capable of ending the big man's life.

The hair on Drake's neck stood on end as his gut told him something wicked bad was heading his way.

Chapter 26

Drake stood at the head of the bed in Crash Room bay three, his heart lodged in his throat. The hospital's harshest physician, the one Drake had brought up on charges before the physician review committee, had coded and was seconds away.

Two nurses, a respiratory therapist, a lab person, a radiology tech, and an EMT readied monitors and equipment. Patti stood at the foot of the bed, holding an oversized clipboard.

Drake checked the airway and vascular access instruments. The Life Clock flashed 3 min 14 secs.

He factored what was known about the giant patient being rushed to him—rapid onset of agitation, pain, spasms, and combativeness, followed by collapse. Dozens of possible explanations riffled through his mind—all were grim.

He hadn't yet laid eyes on Bart and didn't even know the vital signs, but experience told him that whatever had struck this hard and fast was deadly.

"We don't know much," Drake said. "Our patient is agitated and combative and he's twice the size of a normal person. Be careful. I'll be—"

A thunderous impact shook the wall and shouting sounded from outside the Crash Room.

A scrub nurse with her surgical cap and mask hanging loose jammed her head into the room and screamed, "Please! We need help."

Drake burst through the doors.

An overturned hospital transport bed blocked the corridor. Four security guards, an anesthesiologist, and the scrub nurse surrounded Bart Rainey, who was sprawled on the floor. Sweat drenched his scrubs and his eyes darted wildly. "Get away from me!" he yelled. He flailed an arm, knocking one of the security guards aside as if he were a child.

"Patti, get me a syringe with ten milligrams of Ativan," Drake said, as she arrived at his side.

"He was fine," the anesthesiologist said, "but about ten minutes into the case, he started getting pissed off and yelling. I thought it was just his usual bad temper, but then he started twitching and jerking. Obviously in a lot of pain. I had to get security in to get him to stop operating. We somehow got him on a cart and rolled him this far, but he flipped the cart. We haven't been able to do anything for him. Something really bad is going down."

Bart Rainey groaned and raised himself to a semi-sitting position, his back against the overturned bed. He made a tortured sound as the muscles in his neck stretched tendon taut and his mouth opened so wide Drake feared the jaw would dislocate. Bart's horrified eyes met Drake's. Recognition flashed and then a wordless desperate plea. Drake had seen that look in the eyes of others before.

He knows he's dying.

Bart's gaping jaw snapped shut like a sprung trap and his body went rigid. A low animal moan came from him. His eyes rolled back, and his body began to jerk in a bone-snapping violent seizure. Harsh, spastic, snorting gasps sounded. Snot and spittle flew. His face went blue. The veins in his neck bulged. The back of his head hammered the floor with sickening thuds as his body bucked. A quick-thinking tech slipped a folded blanket under his head to buffer the blows. The smell of urine rose, and fluid wet the floor.

Getting the needle of a syringe into the thigh or buttock of an out-of-control, combative, insane, or seizing patient was like trying to inject a bucking bull. Stabbing a needle into the muscle was far easier than getting an IV, but the intramuscular injections took minutes to work.

Bart Rainey did not have minutes.

His body thrashed viciously, the sounds ugly. His color worsened by the second. The softened but brutal hammering of his head on the floor continued. Drake had not been able to do a thing to help. Untreated, the surgeon would die.

Bart needed medication and he needed it now.

"You two and you two," Drake pointed to the strongest-looking of the people poised to help. "If I ask you to grab his arms and hold him, will you try?" Bart Rainey was the largest human Drake had ever been around.

They nodded.

"Patti, when I hold my hand out, take the cap off the needle, hand me the syringe, and then stand clear." The massive dose of Ativan he'd asked her to draw up was both a sedative and seizure control medicine.

Independent of what had triggered the seizure, its intensity and duration threatened brain damage or death.

"When I give the word, you guys grab him, and stay clear of me. I'm going to try to control his head without him breaking his own neck. I'm going to go for a direct injection into his external jugular. He's dying on us." He held out his hand and Patti placed the syringe in it.

"Ativan ten milligrams," she said. "A huge dose."

He nodded. She was right to point it out. It was more than triple the largest single dose he'd ever given. The group surrounded the convulsing physician, his face now a deathly purple. "Ready?" Drake said.

They leaned forward as one, then froze.

Bart's violent quaking eased. His body had begun to rise from the floor like something from a Zombie flick as his back and neck bowed backward. His spine arched impossibly far, raising his body like a grotesque bridge. His eyes were rolled back, his teeth bared, the veins of his neck standing out.

The distorted body and movement looked hideous and surreal. Drake dove forward onto the floor. He stabbed the needle into Bart's neck, aiming for the surgeon's bulging external jugular vein. He slammed the plunger home, then ripped the syringe free, throwing it clear.

At that moment, the grotesque bridge collapsed, and Bart's body began to flop like a fish on a dock.

"Just try to keep him from hurting himself," Drake said, hoping the massive dose of medication would work quickly.

Bart Rainey continued to thrash in what Drake feared was a death roll of convulsions.

"Flip that cart upright and be ready to move him," he said. "Get oxygen to him and be ready to lift. We need to get him into the Crash Room." Were the convulsions slowing? *Please!*

"Patti, I need succinylcholine 200 mg IV ready. Lab, we need an immediate glucose check. Respiratory, be ready to bag him, and I'll be intubating him immediately."

Drake looked around—everyone was with him and ready to go. The sick sound of body parts striking the stone floor still sounded. But, yes. The rate had slowed. The convulsions were lessening. The Ativan was taking effect.

The massive man no longer jerked as if connected to a high-voltage line. Every diagnosis Drake considered as causing Bart's condition was likely to kill him—at least now they had a chance to fight back.

Chapter 27

Clara heard the code-orange call for security to the operating room. Her breath caught. *Could it be?*

Security emergencies were common in the hospital, but she'd never heard of one within the controlled environment of the OR. Had the rat taken the bait?

She left the lab and ran to her office and computer console. Her fingers flew as she accessed the closed-circuit security camera view of the anterooms, scrub basins, and staging area leading to the operating rooms.

It was chaos.

A throng of staff milled about, craning their necks and looking into operating room six. Two orderlies rolled a hospital transport bed to a spot just outside the door.

Then the people in the hallway backed away with looks of fright. One ran. The monitor images were soundless, so she had to imagine the distressed voices.

The bear-sized hulk of Dr. Bart Rainey filled the OR six doorway. His gloves were still on, his surgical gown was torn, his mask hung loose. A security guard hung from each arm. He was red-faced and snarling. He struggled, yanking the guards about as if they were nothing.

An anesthesiologist moved in front of the huge surgeon and pointed toward the waiting transport bed.

Dr. Bart Rainey, the surgeon she hated, doubled over, his face spasmed, and he fell. The guards, anesthesiologist, and several staff moved forward and struggled to lift his mass onto the transport bed.

The camera caught the stricken surgeon's face. His lips were drawn back, and his teeth were exposed in a freakish grimace. He was a portrait of agony.

The abusive doctor epitomized so much of what she hated about the medical establishment.

His arrogance, his sense of entitlement, and the way he wore the MD degree as a mantle of superiority repulsed her. Even if he hadn't taken every opportunity to insult and demean her, she would've despised him.

She punched keys and backed up the image of his face, then replayed it.

She skipped back to the live view.

The frantic action in the OR corridor continued. Dr. Kelly, another general surgeon, was completing what must have been the shortest surgical scrub in history. A nurse helped him throw on a surgical gown and gloves and they ran into OR six.

Had Bart Rainey left his patient open on the table?

The anesthesiologist, security guards, scrub nurse, and techs raced the transport bed and its massive cargo down the hall and out of the OR anteroom.

Clara accessed the security camera covering the hallway. They were rushing him to the ER.

She knew who was working. How perfect would it be if Bart Rainey died with Drake Cody trying to save him?

Clara accessed the emergency room security camera as the transport team rolled through the automatic doors. She saw a massive arm reach out and catch the corner, stopping the cart. Then a huge leg rose and a foot hit the wall. The transport bed teetered, then flipped, and Rainey crashed to the floor.

His eyes bulged, his arms jerked, and his contorted face showed panic. He looked like a wounded animal trying to escape.

His agitation, apprehension, spasms, and rigidity confirmed profound neurologic toxicity. Seizure activity would likely develop next. It looked to her that the arrogant prick did not have much time left. She smiled.

But what could I know? I don't have MD after my name. I wasn't good enough.

Chapter 28

Rachelle leaned forward and feathered cadmium yellow onto the canvas.

The afternoon sun lit up the lone, early spring tulip that had popped up beside the concrete slab out the back door of the townhouse.

She'd woken up this morning feeling like she was about to be released from jail.

This afternoon the sun shone brighter, the air smelled fresher, and the colors glowed more intensely. The hardy yellow flower had caught her eye and it mirrored the hope she felt.

The kids were playing on the rusted swing set on the other side of the alley.

For the first time since the kidnapping and tragedy, she'd set up her easel, canvas, and paints. The challenge of capturing the beauty of light, form, and color never failed to engage her. *Why have I avoided it all these months?*

The painting flowed fast and effortless.

For the first time, standing in this spot did not make her stomach tense and her breath come hard. Today the memory of when she and the kids had been dragged, gagged and bound, into the alley and thrown into a van did not smother her.

At long last they were going to escape this place. *Thank you, God!*

Drake had said it was too early to tell the kids about the lake house. It was possible something could go wrong, but she ached to tell them.

The evening she and Drake had shared seemed too wondrous to be real. His excitement, the magic of the lake, and the fun they'd shared imagining a life in that beautiful home gave her goosebumps.

She pictured Shane and Kristin playing with neighborhood friends, imagined them swimming, fishing, and playing with a dog as they'd always dreamed of—so wonderful.

It would be a place free of nightmare memories. A place where she could feel safe and leave some of the scars and worries of her past behind. A place where she could paint. She could be Rachelle Cody, a healthy person and a good wife and mother—not someone gripped by doubts and fears.

Was it unrealistic to imagine her life could change so radically?

She executed another brush stroke. The flower's fragile beauty was alive on the canvas. She closed her eyes and listened to the children laughing at play.

The life they'd dreamed of was within reach. The place Drake had shown her was so much more than a house.

The high of hope and anticipation surpassed any drug rush she'd ever experienced. *Please, Lord, make it happen.*

Chapter 29

The huge dose of Ativan stopped the whipsaw thrashing of Bart's body.

They wrestled the stricken surgeon, impossibly heavy, damp and smelling of urine, into the Crash Room.

As the respiratory therapist supported Bart's breathing with a mask and ventilator bag, Drake ordered the largest dose of paralyzing drug he'd ever given. The drug eliminated all possibility of movement. Bart's body briefly quivered, then went limp as the drug took effect.

Drake used a laryngyscope to visualize Bart's airway and inserted the largest-sized airway tube into his mouth, between his vocal chords, and into his trachea. The respiratory therapist connected the tube to a ventilator. As the ventilator breathed for him, Bart's color improved.

Next, Drake inserted a four-inch needle attached to a syringe into Bart's upper chest. He advanced the needle blindly, using surface landmarks as guides to avoid puncturing the lung or the major artery lying alongside his target. A rush of dark blood into the syringe confirmed he'd entered the large subclavian vein in Bart's chest. He threaded a large-bore IV over a wire and into the central vein, providing access for delivering fluids or medications into Bart's circulation.

The surgeon's dimensions dwarfed those of a normal person. It was like working on a Grizzly bear. Drake's thoughts went to his similar procedures for the premature infant just days before. Bart's baby finger was larger than the neonate's leg.

With airway and access secured, Drake's mind revved in the furious drive to diagnose and treat whatever had triggered Bart's catastrophic condition. What was killing the huge man and how could it be stopped?

Bart's temperature was 101.4° F. Was infection causing the temperature, or was it due to the prolonged and violent seizing? Meningitis or encephalitis could account for the fever, agitation, and seizures, but the onset was unusually rapid for that.

Likewise for a noninfectious inflammation—there was no history of systemic illness.

A brain tumor, bleed, or stroke?

A metabolic condition? It was not diabetes-related. The quick-test blood sugar was normal. Thyroid storm?

Dozens of possible diagnoses ripped through Drake's head, but none clicked.

Drugs or toxins? Drake couldn't imagine Bart as a drug user, but could he have been exposed to a medication or poison in the hospital?

Unlikely, but in many ways this fit the picture best.

The possible causes were many, and missing a treatable diagnosis could mean the difference between Bart Rainey surviving intact versus irreversible damage or death.

Drake's throat tightened. Bizarre, mysterious, and deadly—a riddle that needed to be solved. If Drake could find an answer, Bart Rainey might continue his career of pissing off coworkers and helping patients.

If he failed, Bart's death would join with the others that lurked in the dark places within Drake's mind.

***

"Be ready to transfer him as soon as the ICU is ready," Drake said.

The CT of the head had not revealed a bleed, tumor, or other abnormality.

Drake had performed a lumbar puncture. The spinal tap had yielded clear cerebrospinal fluid that showed no evidence of meningitis or encephalitis, although they remained a distant possibility.

Lab work showed significant abnormalities, but none were unexpected for someone who had suffered such a prolonged and violent seizure.

Drake had paged intensive care specialist Dr. Vijay Gupta and asked him to accept Bart Rainey as his patient. It was a huge responsibility, but Vijay accepted without a ripple. He was wicked smart and unflappable. A totally different kind of guy than Rizz, but they were similar in clinical cool. They were born to take care of critically ill people.

He and Drake had agreed to cover Bart with antibiotics and antivirals for the small but deadly possibility of meningitis or encephalitis. No clear-cut explanation for Bart's collapse had been found.

Drake hated sending a patient out of the ER without a confirmed diagnosis, but it happened. Some patients were discharged from hospitals after days or weeks, with the exact nature of their illness still uncertain.

Drake focused on the rapid onset of symptoms, the fierce spasms, seizure, and, in particular, the grotesque arching and total muscle contraction that Bart had displayed. He'd never seen anything as freakish except in textbooks.

It had been more suggestive of tetanus than any other condition Drake had seen or studied. Tetanus results from a neurotoxin made by bacteria that causes every muscle in the body to contract continuously with a force that could snap bones.

Drake had seen pictures of the tortured arching that people had suffered before immunization made tetanus in developed countries exceedingly rare. But Bart did not have tetanus. The records showed he was immunized, and the onset did not fit. It was not tetanus, but the rigid, arching bridge his body had formed was a rare and distinctive phenomenon.

It pointed Drake toward a diagnosis—a neurotoxin.

The initial toxicology screens did not reveal anything, but those screens were limited. They could only detect the relatively few substances they were designed to detect.

Drake had an idea that fit, but it was outrageous. He flashed back to the diabolical death of his friend Jon's wife and his discovery of its cause. Regardless of how shocking the diagnosis seemed and what it would mean if he were right, Drake had to trust his physician instinct.

If he was correct, things were even uglier than they looked.

The ER remained slow and Drake's colleagues were able to manage as he picked up the phone to seek help.

Fred Aplin, head of laboratory toxicology, answered on the first ring.

Chapter 30

"Here you go, Smurf," Q said. He punched in Disney Children's Radio on his Pandora and "Lion King" sounded from the deluxe speaker system of his car.

Smurf, the seventeen-year-old daughter of one of one of his longtime customers, clapped and smiled. She had Down syndrome but was a happy kid, despite being saddled with a strung-out mother.

Q liked having Smurf around. She used to do housework for him when he rented next door to their North Minneapolis apartment building. If her mother scored a run of crack or other shit, she sometimes disappeared for days. He looked out for the girl.

Her name was Tonya, but he'd given her the "Smurf" nickname because she was in heaven when she was watching cartoons. Every time he said it she smiled.

Now that he'd moved to the house in Uptown, he only saw her when he needed to deliver product. Earlier he'd picked her up at the apartment, given her mother some product in payment, and now his smiling helper was on the job.

Q turned into the parking lot of the Target store on Lake Street. A black Ranger-450 pickup truck with oversized tires was parked near the Hiawatha Avenue bus stop adjacent to the lot. They'd used this spot before.

Q pulled up behind the truck, blocking it. The dude at the wheel put his arm out the window and swiped it horizontally in a gesture for "safe."

"Okay, Smurf, give the man the present and he'll give you one back," Q said.

"Okay, Mr. Q." She hopped out of the car, went to the truck's door, took the wrapped package out of her shoulder bag, and handed it to the man. After a few seconds, the driver handed a shoebox-sized package to her.

"Thank you. Mister!" she said cheerily and returned to the car.

Q cracked the lid to the box, did a quick scan, and smiled. Ka-ching! Another major contribution to the Q enterprises revenue stream.

He pulled away, both jazzed and relieved.

Delivering product and collecting money was the part of Q's business model that left him the most vulnerable. It put him in the law's crosshairs because the gang members, felons/ex-cons, minority crime families, bikers, and others that formed his network were regularly targeted by the local cops and DEA.

He had no choice but to use these high-risk groups. Most were losers, but only they had the contacts, fear-based loyalty, and know-how to reliably move the amount of product he produced. He'd been charting his revenues on an Excel spreadsheet and the numbers blew his mind.

He would've preferred to exchange the drugs via a bus locker drop and receive payment over the dark web, but the people he had to deal with were not trustworthy or sophisticated enough for that. The drug and money exchange had to be done in person. Rip-offs were possible, but the biggest business risk was the law.

Smurf was his executive assistant for distribution and revenues. She was the key to his risk-reduction strategy and she didn't even know it

Different groups favored different product—his online business classes talked about "product mix" and "targeted marketing." Today's delivery was primarily his special-blend packets. He called it heroin, but it was carfentanil, with quinine powder as the cutting agent. Each of his custom packets was marked with his glyph—his custom symbol. Brand recognition was another thing he'd learned from his online studies. The packet buyers either shot the drugs or snorted them. He pushed to the upper edge of potency for these users and charged in line with that.

He never laid hands on product when out of his house. Smurf carried the drugs in either a shoulder bag or a special coat he'd bought her. Being a minor and mentally challenged, she could be caught with a kilo of smack and an AK-47, and the courts wouldn't touch her.

Q, having neither drugs nor a weapon on his person, could not be prosecuted.

On delivery days, he brought Smurf to his house and loaded her with the drugs to be delivered. He also had her carry the closed leather pouch that held his pistol.

He had her convinced he and she were engaged in gift exchanges. She thought it great fun and couldn't testify about what she did not understand.

In addition to the risk of arrest, there was the threat of his "business associates" taking him down. He gave them no incentive. He made their business with him a win-win of mutual moneymaking.

He also had the reputation he'd earned during his earlier years and while in Stillwater State Prison. He'd dished out some serious hurt back then. No one saw him as an easy mark.

It had taken him a long time to see that his earlier gangster life would either get him killed or locked away forever. His turnaround had started after he'd stomped the face of an inmate in Stillwater. They'd made him see the prison psychologist.

The lean, sharp-dressed man with the wire-rim glasses had been unlike anyone Q had ever met. He'd never have achieved all that he had if not for Yusuf Shabazz.

***

Within two prison counseling sessions with the fifty-year-old ex-con, now clinical psychologist, Q was beginning to question almost everything he'd thought mattered. No one else had ever challenged Q's head like Yusuf Shabazz. Q had believed that his "rep" as a gangster and a badass meant everything.

The psychologist understood that violence had value in the predator-prey world of prison. Q's readiness to destroy anyone who messed with him made him safer. Dr. Shabazz said fierceness and a reputation for violence "conferred survival fitness in the unique ecology of prison."

What he got Q to consider was what this inclination for violence and in-your-face attitude did for him out in the "real world."

Dr. Shabazz suggested that Q's and other young men's pursuit of the rap-glorified lifestyle of bitches, drugs, and criminality virtually guaranteed admission to prison.

"The winners of the world are not locked up in here," Dr. Shabazz said. "The men in this prison with the biggest reps will never take another free breath. The gangster fiction is laying waste to too many black men."

The psychologist didn't preach at Q but treated him as if he had a brain. Q looked forward to the three-times-a-week sessions.

He shared his memories. His mother's fire-and-brimstone religious rigidity and her scorn for those she identified as "bad black people" had been the backbone of his upbringing.

When a crime was reported on the TV news, she would start chanting, "Don't be black, don't be black, don't be black." If the image of a black man then appeared on the screen, she'd scream, "Lord, no! You ignorant excuse for a human. May the devil take you!"

She'd then lecture Q. "You're not just a person. You're a black person. You can't be like those others. You have a responsibility."

In his house it was not black pride but black shame. At home, just as elsewhere, his behavior wasn't judged as that of a person, but as a black person.

The race-based burden she and the world at large placed on him was messed up. He rejected most of what she believed. He embraced rap. He embraced drugs. He embraced the myth of gangster cool.

Dr. Shabazz wondered if Q had rebelled against his mother's shame for their race by embracing the things she hated.

"Being black has absolutely nothing to do with being a badass or pursuing a criminal lifestyle," Dr. Shabazz said. "Buying into that is as sick and damaging as the bigotry of a Klansman. It's not too late for you, young brother."

The person Q had been working at being was not who he was meant to be. He was smarter than that.

Yusuf Shabazz would not approve of Q's current business, but he'd be glad to know he'd helped Q to find his way.

After a long time lost, Q felt good about himself. He'd become his own man.

Chapter 31

Drake's call connected.

"Hello. Fred Aplin, Toxicology."

"Fred, this is Drake Cody. I—"

"I just tried your cell phone," Fred said. "You were right—your pregnant patient had a synthetic opioid on board. The preliminary mass spectrometer signature looks like carfentanil. I then tested the ten most recent ME cases of suspected overdose. Only one involved heroin. Six tested positive for fentanyl and three look to be carfentanil. With your ICU patient, that's four known carfentanil deaths and who knows how many more have yet to be processed at the morgue. We're in trouble."

"Bad news," Drake said. "But I'm calling you now for help on an ER case. One of our surgeons is in critical condition. An abrupt onset of irritability, muscle twitches, spasms, then rigidity followed by generalized seizures. It feels like a toxin to me." Drake paused, dreading the implications of what he was suggesting.

"Initial toxicology screens are negative?" Fred asked.

"Yes. This isn't anything common. In the middle of seizing, his spine arched backwards and lifted his body like a bridge. The only thing I've seen like it are old images of tetanus patients, and it's not that," Drake said. "Poison fits best. I'm thinking strychnine."

"What? How would he come in contact with that?" Fred said. "In the past it was used to kill rats, but it's rarely used anymore. How could your doctor have been exposed?"

"Let's find out if it's there. How quick can you test for it?" Drake said. Strychnine struck in less than an hour. Bart would have had to come in contact while in the hospital. Fred's question loomed. How? "If he's got strychnine on board, it's not likely an accident."

"I was driving home, but I'm turning around," Fred said. "I should have an answer in less than an hour.

"Thanks, Fred. Dr. Gupta is taking care of Dr. Rainey in the ICU. As soon as you get a result, please get it to him immediately. Call me too, but please don't put in the medical record at all yet. I really appreciate your help."

As Fred hung up, Drake thought about calling Rachelle. What a monumentally bad day. He picked up the receiver.

When he'd left this morning, she'd been happier than he'd seen her in forever.

He set the receiver down.

Dr. Julie Stone entered the ER at the end of the corridor. As their eyes met, she signaled toward the minor trauma room in the back corner of the department. Drake nodded and headed down the hall.

They entered the minor procedures room and Drake pulled the curtain closed. She faced him, her expression a wince. "It's unreal, Drake. Have you heard?"

"Yes."

"The CEO told me we're both going to be named in a suit. He spoke to me as if my guilt was a certainty. He was talking about settling the suit. He's ready to sign off on me as having been responsible for the death of my patient."

The impact of the malpractice claim showed. She looked lost and her features were pained.

He and Julie had worked together on critical patients and shared agonizing uncertainty. Outcomes were never a sure thing.

Those they'd worked on together had survived—most recently, the anchorwoman, Tina Watt, who'd become a friend to both of them.

Few people ever had the opportunity to help save a life. As with the nurses and all the ER team members, it was special. Drake understood what it meant to Julie—it was why they did what they did.

Now they were to be publicly charged with the wrongful death of their patient due to negligence and medical incompetence.

Silence hung. The fluorescent light flickered and the yellow tile of the procedure room showed a greenish tint. The finger traps, weights, plaster, and support stands used for setting fractures lay in wait. The banana-like smell of benzoin adhesive tinged the air.

Julie looked up, her expression raw. "I didn't do anything wrong, Drake." She looked down, her head shaking. "I don't know what caused her to bleed out. My care was solid. There were no signs warning of what was going to happen. Placentas are often irregular. I don't believe that report." She raised her head again, her blue eyes tear-filled. "I didn't kill her, Drake."

"I know you didn't, Julie." He put a hand on her cheek and looked her straight in the eye. "You didn't kill her." He paused. "And neither did I."

He recognized the intimacy and removed his hand.

"She was getting better and then everything went to hell." Drake sighed. "Another mysterious and tragic death."

"Another?" Her eyes probed.

"There have been other unexpected and mysterious hospital deaths in the last several months," Drake said. "Each of them seemed to have been recovering before they crashed. No one knows what it means—if it means anything."

Perhaps it was ill fortune—an unfortunate cluster reflecting how little control even the best and most modern medicine had?

It was addiction and carfentanil that had started their patient on her way to death. Something had triggered her bleeding, most likely related to her overdose and shock, but they couldn't prove it.

Despite the report Clete Venjer had shared, the placenta was not likely the cause. In the remote possibility it had contributed, there was nothing that could have been done. There was no malpractice involved. Nonetheless, the attorney and the doctors he paid to testify would do everything they could to persuade jurors there was. And sometimes malpractice verdicts were influenced by good-hearted jurors wanting to help the victims of tragedy independent of its cause.

"I'm going to ask a forensic pathologist I know to review our patient's death. Maybe he'll find something." He took her hands. "Julie Stone, you're a skilled, caring physician and a wonderful person. Don't let this charge make you think anything else."

She wrapped her arms around him and held him tight with her head pressed against his chest.

"Thank you, Drake," she said, her voice husky.

She stepped back awkwardly, not looking at him. "I have patients I need to check." She pushed through the curtain.

Her pain, the memory of the softness of her body, and a faint flowery scent trailed after her.

They were accused of killing their patient due to negligence and ineptitude. Implicit in the charges was that they had not cared about the young mother's life.

It was not true. It was not right.

He felt sorry for Julie. He felt sorry for himself.

He looked at the clock. It was past the end of his shift. One last test result to check, a patient to discharge, and then he could escape. He could be on the way home in minutes. Thank God. This nuclear meltdown of a day had him beyond drained.

Did it make sense for him to continue to fight? From the start, becoming a physician had been nothing but obstacles. He'd hidden his past, lied, broken rules, and spent years pushing himself beyond physical and emotional exhaustion.

And what had it done to Rachelle? No money, alone and struggling for years as a single parent, while he pursued his research and ER obsessions.

The nightmare of his family's kidnapping and the tragedy of Rizz and Jon—it was all too much.

He hated to whine, but he couldn't stop.

Should he tell Rachelle about the malpractice threat? How would she face learning, once more, that his medical career—and their dreams—would likely end? What about the purchase of the lake home?

He had no answers, but the questions continued.

Wouldn't he and those he loved be better off if he had a different job and lived a more normal life? Was what he did worth it? People were dying because they took drugs—was there anything he could do that was really going to make a difference?

Did anything he did really matter?

People died every day because tragic, unpredictable things happened—that was the reality in the ER, in the hospital, and the world at large. Some people can be helped—some can't. We all die.

If he were not in the ER, someone else would be. He was not irreplaceable.

How many times did he need to be slapped down before he accepted he was not meant to be a physician?

Why keep fighting?

The last test was back. Drake completed his ER note. 8:20 p.m. His shift was over and he was ready to collapse.

If he were near the end of his trouble-plagued career, the memories of this day would help erase regret.

As he picked up his bag and checked for his car keys, the signal identifying a routine paramedic radio call sounded overhead.

Routine radio calls were different from Crash Room calls. Often, the patient might not even need to be transported. It would just take a minute.

Drake stepped into the radio cubby and set his bag on the counter. He hit the transmit button.

"Dr. Cody here, over."

"Ambulance 724 on the scene with ODs of two teenaged guys. We were able to resuscitate one. He's awake and alert after Narcan. The second is ten-seven." Static intervened. "The survivor says they each sniffed a packet of powder about thirty minutes ago. One kid lost consciousness right away, and before the friend could contact 911, he went down. When he came to, he couldn't wake his friend." There was a static-filled pause.

"He called 911.When we arrived, his friend was fixed and dilated. No respirations. No pulse or cardiac rhythm. No signs of life." More static sounded. "We ran a full resuscitation on him anyway, but he's gone. Requesting a field termination order. His friend is crying his eyes out. Seventeen-years-olds, and the dead kid was a first-timer." The veteran paramedic's voice broke. "Doc, this is a bad one."

"Make sure you avoid contact with any drug, okay?" The carfentanil that was on the street could kill by contact or inhalation. "Use full precautions. Are police there? Are they treating it as a crime scene?"

"Yes to all of that," the medic said.

Ragged cries in the background carried over the open radio line. The sound of agony—of a mistake that could never be undone. It rose to a tortured wail. Static interrupted, then anguished words sounded. "Bryce, oh God, Bryce."

Drake's breath left him. Time stopped. The temperature dropped twenty degrees before his next heartbeat. *No! Please, no.*

Patient names were forbidden by privacy law to be used over the radio.

"724, is the deceased wearing a ring?" Drake asked.

"Yes. A gold ring. How could you know that?"
Drake couldn't answer. He couldn't speak.
Most of all he couldn't understand.
Why?

Chapter 32

A black, moonless night and Drake drove too fast. He blocked out reason, denied the odds, and clung to the tiniest sliver of hope. *Don't let it be him!*

Cell phone in hand, he'd raced out of the ER while calling the dispatch operator.

Ambulance 724 was in a modest neighborhood less than ten minutes south of the hospital.

Drake kept to the center of Portland Avenue's three-lane one-way, driving fast, his eyes peeled for pedestrians. He banked hard on Minnehaha Parkway, slowed, then swung left on Oakland Avenue.

The ambulance and a police cruiser were parked in front of an old rambler with a drooping front porch. Drake braked hard and pulled to the curb. He was out of the car and headed for the front stoop before the engine died.

The front door sat open under the glare of a naked bulb. An officer stood alongside. Drake still wore his scrubs, and the officer nodded as Drake approached.

"Are you with the medical examiner?" the officer asked. "Detective Farley just got here. He's downstairs with the body." He paused. "The surviving kid's mom got home from work right after we got here. The medics say her boy looks okay, but he's really torn up about his friend." He grimaced. "It's not good."

Drake stepped into the small entryway. Moaning and soft voices came from within. He stepped in.

A woman wearing waitress garb sat on a worn living room couch. She cradled the head of a stricken long-haired boy in her lap as he moaned. His cries and whimpers were that of a grievously hurt animal.

Tears ran down the mother's face as she rocked forward and back, repeating, "It's okay, Jimmy. It's gonna be okay." Her expression and tone said she knew it wasn't true.

A Memorial paramedic knelt on one knee, her hand on the boy's shoulder, the medic bag on the floor next to her.

Agony and loss fogged the room like steam in a sauna. Drake's throat clutched.

The officer pointed down the hall. "Through the door on the left. Down the stairs."

A creaking floor, worn carpet, aged linoleum, and the smells of an old house. Drake ducked through the small basement doorway and went down wooden stairs that shook underfoot. The odor of mildew and an ancient furnace hung as Drake entered a low-ceilinged, shag-carpeted recreation room. A worn Foosball table, a TV, and an old stereo system with a turntable sat on one side of the room. A standing lamp on each side lit the room in yellowish light. Posters of Jimi Hendrix, Kurt Cobain, and Prince were taped to the walls.

Drake glimpsed the arms and legs of a body sprawled, as if shot, on a black vinyl couch. Detective Farley bent over the body, partially blocking Drake's view.

One hand lay stretched toward Drake, palm up, and frozen. The oversized ring glistened on one of the clawed blue fingers.

Lord, no.

Farley straightened, clearing Drake's view.

A silent scream filled his mind.

Bryce's head lay lolled back, his eyes open and unseeing. The cruelly fated boy's handsome face was grotesquely blue and as starkly dead as any Drake had ever seen.

Hope gone. Drake's soul writhed in pain. Somehow his body remained upright.

Why, God, why?

"Dr. Cody? Drake?" Detective Farley's voice penetrated. The beefy young detective came into focus. "Are you okay?" He wore gloves and a respiratory mask. His brow was furrowed. "You need to take precautions. You know that."

"Huh? Right," Drake said.

"What are you doing here, Doc?"

Drake stared at Bryce's sprawled, lifeless body. Words would not come. He swallowed.

"I knew him." He swallowed again. "He was my patient."

The words did nothing to describe the boy or what Drake felt.

"My sympathy, Drake," Farley said. "But do me a favor and wait outside, okay?"

"You're working this as a homicide, right?" Drake said. "That's what it is. They killed him with their poison."

"Absolutely. We're on the same page. Just like we talked about with Aki yesterday." Farley was looking at him strangely.

A tightness gripped Drake's shoulders and neck, and a pounding started in his head. The sadness that had threatened to overwhelm him hung as jagged rocks of rage rose from underneath. Damn. The desire to get his hands on those responsible pulled strong. His breath came hard.

"You sure you're okay?" Farley said.

"I'm okay." *Am I?*

He remembered saying "we'll be okay" to his brother Kevin as they lay on the broken concrete so many years ago. He'd been wrong.

"Please trace every detail you can," Drake said. "We need to get whoever supplied this."

"I've bagged the drug packets," Farley said. "They look empty, but there'll be enough for the lab to test, and there's a symbol printed on them."

"They're advertising their poison." Drake was unable to take his eyes off the lifeless body of the soft-spoken boy he'd tried to help.

"Go outside and I'll see you in a couple of minutes," Farley said. "So sorry. Try and take it easy."

Drake made his way up the stairs, through the house, and out onto the front yard, without saying a word. If a functional MRI were to show his brain, the primitive, most savage parts would be lit up and pulsing like molten lava.

He wasn't taking things easy.

Not easy at all...

Chapter 33

Clara closed her private laptop and slid it into the drawer in her office desk.

The email she'd just reviewed from the Guatemalan authorities confirmed acceptance of her as a medical provider and documented the "certificate of operation" for her clinic. Everything stood ready.

Her dream was within reach.

At long last she'd be assuming the role for which she'd been destined. She tingled in anticipation.

Earlier, she'd checked the balances in her offshore accounts. The latest totals assured she had enough to operate for at least the first six months. With her other anticipated deposits, including the largest of all, she'd be set.

She saw herself standing slim and straight in a white coat with a stethoscope draped around her neck, her clinical staff at her side. In front of her stood a throng of worshipful patients. She smiled.

But before that, she needed to collect from those who owed her.

She accessed the security cameras covering the ICU and viewed the images on her screens. The surgeon was in ICU bed seven. The camera did not allow her to see into that bay, but the documented orders and notes of the nurses, doctors, and others confirmed that he remained in critical condition on a ventilator.

Strychnine had earned the label as the least subtle poison. It caused its victims to suffer. The surgeon clearly had—and continued to. Strychnine's use as a rat poison had fallen out of favor, as it was considered too inhumane even for vermin. She'd chosen well.

The ICU did not look frenzied and she hadn't heard a "code blue" called. It appeared the arrogant jerk might survive, but that didn't bother her.

She'd evened the account with him.

Many others had wronged her—too many to ever fully close out the ledger. But the one who'd wounded her most grievously had not yet paid.

Dan had not been an abuser. His wife had only gotten what was coming to her. Drake Cody's sanctimonious ER meddling and police report had taken her man from her.

She opened her tracking program and entered the ER doctor's personal ID and password. The screen populated with every document viewed and every entry made by him in the past twenty-four hours.

As she scrolled through Drake Cody's activity, a cluster of his viewings caught her eye. Using a portal in the medical records office earlier today, he'd spent two hours and seventeen minutes viewing patient records.

She scanned the medical record numbers and patient names. Worry's icy fingers clutched her throat.

Damn him to hell.

Drake Cody was responsible for Dan's death, and now his poking around threatened her dreams.

Her plan had been to make him pay by taking from him what he cared about most and leaving him in pain forever. Everything was on track to make that happen, but now she wondered if that was a luxury she couldn't afford.

He might need to be taken out of the picture—and soon.

Chapter 34

Drake had kept away from Rachelle and the kids for their sake. He hadn't spoken with her since their giddy, everything-coming-up-roses morning.

In the hours since then, everything had crashed and burned.

He pushed the button for the sixth floor of Rizz's apartment building. The elevator door slid shut and began its ascent.

Should he tell Rachelle about everything? Even if he said nothing, one look in his eyes and she'd know they were in big trouble. He could keep some things from her, but this was too much. The elevator door pinged open.

The drive from the scene of Bryce's death had brought him past the hospital, through the evening's downtown traffic, and across Washington Avenue to the riverside complex.

He used the backup key he had for Rizz's apartment to open the door. He hoped things continued to progress well for Rizz in his rehab stay at Mayo. Drake needed to talk with his no-BS friend, but right now even that felt like too much to handle.

As usual, the apartment was operating-room clean. The furnishings were classy and high quality. Rizz had to have the best in all things. For a kid who'd grown up poor in a rundown section of St. Paul, Rizz's tastes were exclusively high end.

He found a bottle of tonic in the refrigerator and enough liquor in the cabinet to throw a party for fifty. The amount of alcohol on the premises suggested Rizz's rehab efforts did not involve tapering his consumption.

Drake poured himself a tall vodka and tonic that was mostly vodka.

He crossed the room and slid open the door to the balcony. The view included the spotlight-illuminated Stone Arch Bridge and the surging water of the Mississippi as it cascaded over Saint Anthony Falls. The temperature was in the 40s, and the night air hung heavy with the humidity of river mist and spring. Drake did not feel the cold.

The first drink went down fast. With all that had happened and all that threatened, the urge to escape grew. His mind scrambled from problem to problem like a trapped animal looking for a way out.

The desire to avoid facing painful realities was nothing new. After his arrest at sixteen years old, through his separation from his mother and brother, surviving the hell of incarceration in the Furnace, and worst of all, after the crash that killed Kevin and crippled his mother, Drake had wanted nothing more than to be numb. He'd barely survived the mix of anger, fear, grief, and guilt that had threatened to suffocate him.

He went inside to pour another drink. As the vodka splashed over the ice, Drake remembered the time before he'd found a better way. He'd tried to erase his pain and guilt with alcohol. For a long time after Kevin's death, Drake had tried to lose himself in drinking, fighting, and chasing meaningless sex. The label "party animal" some assigned him couldn't have been less accurate.

It had been no party. He'd been lost in a very dark place.

He understood the powerful appeal of blurred consciousness and altered perception. Alcohol and drugs were an attempt to escape—to avoid pain.

Drake dealt with drug seekers and users almost every day in the ER. They lied, stole, and prostituted themselves to get the drugs they were addicted to. They destroyed their families and hurt everyone around them. Addiction was identified as a disease, and that made the addicts victims, but it was difficult to embrace that when their addiction caused them to victimize everyone else. Those who saw the destruction they caused were challenged to feel sympathy.

Addiction and the effect of the drugs made the users someone else.

Opioids created a place where worries, doubts, and fears did not exist. Some users called it "seeking the nod." The drooping lids, breathy voice, and shuffling posture were accompanied by absence of fear and anxiety—the drug provided a sense of peace and contentment unlike anything ever—until the drug effect left.

Inexorably, the users' lives and the lives of those who cared about them spiraled into hell. The merciless physical and psychological claws of opioid addiction dug in, causing them to want more, to continuously need more, to be unable to get enough.

And now the newest drugs were helping to kill in numbers like wartime slaughter. Young, old, first-time pill poppers, or needle-scarred junkies—none were safe.

What had triggered Bryce's decision? In the ER, fear had radiated from him like heat from an oven—so hurting and vulnerable.

Greedy, heartless bastards had profited from his suffering by selling the drug that had killed him.

Drake's hands clenched and the urge to make someone pay surged. Underneath was his sadness and regret. Could he have done more? Phantom doubts and unknowable "what ifs" haunted him. Only those who made life-or-death decisions might understand, yet he'd never heard it discussed among his peers.

The starkest loneliness gripped him.

He carried his drink back to the balcony, then took a swallow of the high-test cocktail. The first traces of the alcohol's anesthetizing buzz nudged. It felt good.

What if someone had offered him opioids in the dark time following Kevin's death?

Drake looked at the nearly full glass in his hand. He wanted to slip away—to ease his troubles—if only for a while.

He thought of all the dying patients he'd cared for. Many, especially among the elderly, faced their plight with courage and sometimes even humor. What was their secret?

He shook his head. For one thing, they didn't whine and feel sorry for themselves.

If he could kick himself, he would. Life was a gift and you had to fight to make it as good as it could be. *Quit your whining!*

He cocked his arm back and hurled the drink off the balcony toward the river.

The faint crash of glass hitting asphalt sounded as he pulled out his phone.

Before he could call Rachelle, the phone rang. A Memorial Hospital number showed.

"Drake Cody here."

"Drake, it's Fred Aplin in the lab. Strychnine lit up big time...the surgeon had a boatload on board. I can't believe he's alive. Who is this guy? Rasputin? I just got off the phone from notifying Dr. Gupta in the ICU."

Rasputin? Fred had no idea how on target he was. Heck, Bart Rainey could probably whup Rasputin's ass. There was no antidote for strychnine, but with control of the seizures and the intensive support he was receiving, Bart had the potential to recover.

The big man might one day be back to helping patients and being a jerk to coworkers.

"Do me a favor and still don't put the strychnine order or result on the computer," Drake said. "I need to contact the police. I'm headed back to the hospital, so maybe I'll see you."

"I did an initial screen and a confirmation study is running. I'll keep both unreported except to the caregivers. And you will not see me. My work is done for tonight. Later." He hung up.

Drake's work should be done, but it wasn't. Now that he'd quit whining, he had much to do. First off, there was an attempted murder to report. He entered Detective Aki Hamada's number. Before the phone rang, another grim thought landed.

Each of the surprising and mysterious hospital deaths had occurred in critically ill patients who looked to be improving. Drake grabbed his stuff and hurried for the door.

The big surgeon fit the risk profile like a Rasputin-sized glove.

Chapter 35

The unmarked cruiser pulled into the reserved police/fire spot under the emergency department ambulance arch. Drake approached the car's passenger-side door. The lock clicked, and Drake opened the door. Detective Aki Hamada sat behind the wheel in sweatpants, white athletic shoes, a Minnesota Vikings T-shirt, and a windbreaker.

"Have a seat, Drake. What's with the secret hookup?"

"I ran it by Farley," Drake said as he got in and shut the door. "He thought it made sense. Where is he? "

"He's working the overdose death."

"Of course."

"Sorry to hear you knew the boy. A sad deal."

Drake nodded.

"Excuse the clothes," Aki said. "I was at the gym and missed Farley's first call. I made it to the overdose scene just after you left. You have a possible attempted murder to report?"

"I'd say overwhelmingly likely. One of our surgeons is in critical condition and we found he's got strychnine on board. "

"Strychnine?" Aki asked. "Isn't that like an old-time Agatha Christie poison?"

"It's been around for a long time," Drake said. "And it's deadly. The only legitimate use is in rat poison. The lab proved it's in his system and there's no way he could've come in contact with it accidentally."

"Suicide attempt?"Aki said.

"This guy would not kill himself and definitely not while he was operating."

"Stranger things have happened—"

"I don't want to tell you your business, but it's not suicide," Drake said. "I suggested meeting you out here to give you the lay of the land without drawing attention. So far, the only people who know about the strychnine are those caring for him, Farley, and now you. And of course, whoever poisoned him. I thought it might help if we kept the news undercover for as long as possible. If it is what it looks like, the killer is probably somebody in the hospital." That ugly thought nagged like a pebble in a shoe.

"How do you know that?"

"No matter what route it's delivered, and oral is the most common, strychnine strikes within fifteen minutes to an hour. The surgeon, Dr. Bart Rainey, had been in or near the operating room for several hours before he crashed."

"Is he a guy with enemies?" Aki asked.

Drake frowned and rubbed his chin.

"That looks like a yes," Aki said. "Spit it out, Drake. Loose talk and gossip have solved more murders than all the CSI gadgets combined. Don't sweat bad manners or hurting anyone's feelings. We're talking about attempted murder."

"Okay." Drake took a breath. "He's probably the biggest jerk on the medical staff. He's hated, er, strongly disliked by a number of nurses, doctors, and others. I should also tell you that when Jon Malar was shot, Dr. Rainey took care of him in the ICU. He and I almost came to blows. I put him up for disciplinary review for his behavior and his verbal abuse of a nurse."

"Of course," Aki shook his head. "You call to report an attempted murder at Memorial Hospital. What could I expect but that you're a suspect, and the victim is less popular than a baby seal hunter at a PETA conference?"

It felt good that the detective trusted him enough to joke with him.

"Keeping the poisoning aspect quiet is smart," Aki said. "So far, whoever did this may not know it's being investigated. That won't last long. I left my cloak of invisibility at the station."

"I can help you keep it low profile, but you're right. No way this will stay under wraps long."

"How safe is he now?"

"I called the ICU doctor and nurses on alert for the possibility of someone trying to finish the job. No visitors, and no one gets near him but select hospital staff."

"Good, but we can't let trying to keep a low profile increase his risk." Aki's brow furrowed. "I'm going to post an officer up there."

"I'm glad," Drake said. With what had gone on, aggressive safety precautions made sense. "Anything I can do?" Drake asked.

"Your input as a physician establishes probable cause that a crime has been committed. I can initiate a case number on that basis. Everything related to the investigation from there on is filed under that. I'll need written documentation and a formal report that confirms strychnine in the victim. The lab is going to need to provide chain-of-evidence specimens that can be secured for use in possible trial. Next, I need to see this doctor's hospital office, so—"

"Bart doesn't have an office in the hospital, Aki. Other than the hospital pathologists and radiology, virtually none of the staff physicians have anything more than a locker in the hospital."

"Okay, I need someone to show me his locker and get it opened. It and the OR needs to be examined and then locked down. I'm going to call in a crime scene investigator to help. I need to question the daytime OR staff and any others who know where the victim was and what he was doing for the two hours prior to him getting symptoms. If you can put me in touch with the administration and security people, I can get everything set up."

"I can do that," Drake said.

"Is two hours before he became sick long enough for this poison?" Aki asked.

"Strychnine hits within an hour at the outside. Two hours is reasonable." Drake's mind flashed to the murder of his friend Jon Malar's wife, Faith, whose diabolical death involved an initially mystifying mechanism. "Some folks from the second shift and nurses working doubles will still be here. They will have been around or heard about where and what Bart was up to."

"Good. I'll talk to them first. I also need to see the victim. All that should give me a good start. I'll get Farley over here when he's able."

"Just let me know what you need," Drake said. "With Bryce's death and now this, I wouldn't be any good at home right now. I'd like to be useful."

Aki reached a hand over and rested it on Drake's shoulder. The police radio screeched and an unintelligible, low volume transmission sounded.

"Bad stuff, Drake. We'll find whoever sold that shit." Aki looked less certain than his words. "And I appreciate your help on this. Maybe you can come up with some answers."

"The hospital seems to be cursed lately," Drake said. "It's crazy. Bart can be a real jerk, but murder? He's on a ventilator in critical condition. He's got great nurses and doctors, but he could die anytime." Drake shook his head. "As far as answers—who did this, how they got the strychnine into him, and why?" Drake met the detective's gaze. "I have absolutely no idea."

Chapter 36

The headlights of Clete Venjer's Audi A8 lit up the entrance to his Lake Harriet home.

He clicked the opener and the eight-foot-high ornate metal gate swung inward. Clete piloted the car up the drive to the estate his malpractice litigation career had built.

The 4000-square-foot, multi-level, stone mansion perched on a north-facing massive lot that rose to forty feet above lake level. Lake Harriet Parkway, bike and hiking trails, and the grassy, tree-studded shoreline separated his walled estate from the lake.

His was the most spectacular home on a lake surrounded by spectacular homes.

The elevated lot provided unimpeded views, while the eight-foot high stone wall, high-tech surveillance and alarm systems provided privacy and security. The grandeur of the estate made Clete uncomfortable.

He believed many people saw all lawyers as money-grubbing fat cats, and feared his displays of success fueled that view. The luxury Audi, his other cars, his home and vacation properties, all gave evidence of an income and net worth that others couldn't imagine.

His accountant and the business advisers that had helped make his malpractice firm the most successful in the Midwest had recommended the high-dollar purchases as tax-advantaged investments.

Clete appreciated the money and what it bought but considered his true objectives were on a higher plane.

He thought it ironic that he was a master in an industry that measured itself exclusively in dollars.

He felt disgust for many in the industry—and he acknowledged that the malpractice system and its big money rewards had spawned a grasping, unseemly industry.

There were many attorneys, insurance professionals, and disingenuous patients or family members who were motivated solely by the money involved. Even physicians bellied up to the trough, as many earned large sums giving "expert" testimony to whoever would pay,

An attorney's decision to pursue any individual case included considering the cost of bringing a suit and the likelihood of gaining a settlement or guilty verdict at trial. What tipped the balance was the most important aspect of all—how big a settlement or award might the case yield. Multi-million-dollar payouts were the Holy Grail of malpractice litigation.

It made sense to pursue a weak case with only an outside chance of winning if the potential settlement or award was huge.

On downcast days, and he had many, he considered his job as ninety percent salesman and ten percent poker player. His special skill was his ability to powerfully engage and persuade jurors.

In case after case, he'd convinced twelve medically uninformed people that a particular doctor, nurse, or other provider had been unlawfully careless and incompetent. Malpractice law had a lower burden of proof than criminal law. Clete did not have to prove guilt beyond a reasonable doubt, but only persuade that the "preponderance of evidence supported the possibility of his claim."

His courtroom words made the jurors feel the pain of the death or injury and made them recognize they had the opportunity to help offset the tragedy. Their verdict could provide large sums of money to those who had suffered injury or loss.

It was an imperfect system, but it was the only tool Clete had.

He pulled into the fourth stall of his garage and glanced at the new Cadillac Escalade, the Jaguar XKE, the 1970 Dodge Charger, and the 1960 Austin Healy. He considered his possessions more of a distraction than a passion.

It was his work that he lived for—and had for more than twenty-five years.

Hospitals, insurance companies, and administrators feared malpractice costs. Most doctors' and nurses' greatest fear was failing their patients and being declared uncaring and incompetent.

It was those awards and that fear that drove institutional change and changes in healthcare culture. That's how he made a difference.

The millions of dollars he'd won in settlements and trials showed that he'd made a big difference.

Clete had told an interviewer for a feature in *Midwest Magazine* several years past, "The money isn't what matters to me."

In the article they'd printed his quote in enlarged, bold print juxtaposed under a listing of his possessions and net worth as the key element of the feature.

Clete still flushed with embarrassment every time he thought of it.

He had a story to tell that would have shut down the cynical and unfair judgment by the magazine, but it was one too painful and private to share.

Counseling and medication had done little to salve his regret, guilt, and unrelenting, heart-squeezing loneliness.

It drove him to try and make a difference—to prevent others from suffering as he had...

***

Twenty-five years earlier

Clete's laziness had caused Anjanee's cut.

It was between her eyebrows, less than three-quarters of an inch in length but deep. The young doctor in the ER had called it a "superficial laceration." They'd lived in student housing near the University St. Paul campus back then. They'd been married just four years, with Clete attending law school at the U. Their beautiful Anjanee was just a toddler.

Clete had left the toolbox open on the floor in the tiny apartment. Careless.

Anjanee had fallen and struck the sharp metal edge of the toolbox lid. They were worried the cut would leave a scar.

It would mar their Anjanee's beauty. A flaw she would have forever.

They later learned the "ER doctor" was a first-year doctor doing a four-week training rotation in the ER. He had earlier experience with repairing wounds in the OR and had capably repaired wounds during his weeks in the ER.

They'd had to wait for over two hours to get Anjanee into the ER. His wife had become more agitated with each minute.

If Clete could do it over again—and God, how many thousands of times he'd thought of how it could have been done differently—he would have insisted his wife stay in the waiting room. Once in the ER, her hysteria grew and transmitted to Anjanee as if by touch.

The young doctor recommended they restrain Anjanee. They would wrap her in what he called a papoose. It would help hold her while he inject-ed the local anesthesia into and around the wound. He assured them there would be no pain after that.

The papoose and their restraining hands would protect against any sud-den movement.

Anjanee was crying. His wife clung to her.

His wife demanded Anjanee be "put out." The doctor said that was not necessary or safe. His wife escalated.

The doctor suggested that an intermediate step would be to sedate Anja-nee. It would require a shot and Anjanee would still need to be held but she would be sleepy and likely not remember the procedure.

"Yes. That is what you must do," his wife said.

The ER was hectic, every bed taken. A nurse came and gave Anjanee the injection. His wife moaned but Anjanee did not cry. As they completed the injection, a "trauma" announcement came overhead three times. The atmos-phere in the ER became charged, and bodies hurried towards the front of the ER.

The nurse attached a clothespin-like clip to Anjanee's finger. "Check that," she'd said to the doctor and pointed to the box connected by a thin ca-ble to the clip. "Make sure it's registering."

She and other staff moved toward the incoming ambulances and the flur-ry of action.

The shot worked. Anjanee calmed.

The doctor injected the local anesthetic around the wound, then care-fully cleaned it. Next, wearing special gloves, he draped blue cloths over and around Anjanee's cut. Only her wound and forehead were exposed in the middle of the field of blue fabric. The doctor directed a bright light there. He explained about keeping the site sterile and not touching anything. Infection could occur.

Infection was the big risk.

His wife held Anjanee's hand under the blue drape.

The doctor's use of the needle, suture, and instruments to repair the skin held them transfixed. For several minutes, the physician's attention was absolute. Clete's wife's posture eased for the first time in hours.

Anjanee remained quiet under the drapes.

The gaping wound edges were aligned, and as the doctor drew the last suture snug, the result looked almost magical.

"Wounds heal by forming scar but barring infection, I think hers will be minimal." The young doctor looked pleased.

He set the instruments aside and lifted the blue drapes.

Clete's heart convulsed. His mind writhed, the pain beyond imagination. *No!* He tried to stand but collapsed to his knees

Anjanee's eyes were open but unseeing. No blink. The minutes had rendered them dull.

A nightmare of panicked activity followed. Time slowed. His wife's screams, the young doctor's devastated disbelief, followed by his slow collapse to the floor with face in hands.

The frenzied efforts at saving her changed nothing.

Their Anjanee was gone.

Chapter 37

The rest of that day was an empty space in his memory. The agony and loss too overwhelming to process. In the days, weeks, months and years since, he'd filled in the blanks.

He learned that the clip on Anjanee's finger was part of an oximeter. The safety device checked if a patient was breathing adequately. Sedation medication can cause people to stop breathing, and every individual responds differently. Because of the risk, every patient receiving sedation needed to be monitored.

Anjanee had received a very small dose. It would have been okay for ninety-nine out of a hundred patients, but it was too much for her. The sensing clip on her finger had not been in the right position. A simple repositioning would have ensured a warning alarm.

Normally, the nurses would have checked and rechecked Anjanee several times, but the ER was packed, and the limited number of nurses were helping save the trauma victims.

A family struck by a semi truck had arrived just as Anjanee received the sedation. Two of that family had died, three survived in critical condition.

The doctor-in-training should have checked the oximeter and the patient.

Due to inexperience or fixation on the procedure or some other failing, he did not.

The staff ER doctor should have been told about Anjanee and overseen her repair.

The young doctor had overstepped in ordering the sedative without notifying the ER staff physician.

The staff physician had been taking care of the multiple trauma victims.

The multiple trauma patients had contributed to the string of failures, though Clete did not accept this as an excuse. Their Anjanee should not have died.

Clete's old life had ended on that day. In many ways, he had become someone else.

Their marriage did not withstand the torrent of guilt and recrimination. To his everlasting shame, Clete had once, in one of their arguments, blamed his wife for insisting on sedation.

In the months after their divorce, he heard that she was not doing well.

On a clear summer night shortly thereafter, her car struck a highway bridge support at high speed.

They ascribed the deadly crash to an elevated blood alcohol level. They were wrong.

Loss and guilt had killed her.

The open toolbox had been his responsibility. But his toolbox had not killed Anjanee, nor had his wife's anxiety.

The deadly power of modern medicine, misfortune, and human error had taken her life.

His life now revolved around this one thing. Each and every health provider needed to be constantly aware of the risk. It was Clete's duty, his sacred obligation, to make doctors, nurses, and hospital administrators conscious, each and every second, of the power and responsibility they wielded.

Was the malpractice system fair and just? Oftentimes it was not.

Did it unfairly damage or destroy some physicians and nurses who were caring and competent? Yes, it did.

That was the cost that needed to be paid.

There could be no more Anjanees.

Chapter 38

Drake walked Aki to the hospital security office on the basement level.

After introductions, Aki remained inside coordinating with the head of security while Drake stepped into the empty basement corridor. He pulled out his cell phone and dialed.

"Hello. Jim Torrins speaking."

"Dr. Torrins, this is Drake Cody. I've got bad news—"

"Please not another mysterious patient death." Torrins' voice sounded tight.

"No. I know you're aware that Bart Rainey collapsed in the OR today. I—"

"Did he die? Please, no."

"He's critical and still on the ventilator, but detective Aki Yamada of Homicide is with me. Bart Rainey was poisoned. Strychnine. He'd been in the OR since early morning, so his exposure looks to have occurred at the hospital. The police have opened an attempted murder investigation."

There was a pause so long Drake wondered whether the connection has been lost.

"Dr. Torrins?"

"What in the name of God is going on in our hospital?"

Drake had never known the veteran physician-administrator to get rattled—despite significant cause. He sounded more than rattled now.

"So far, we've kept the news under wraps," Drake said. "Given the circumstances, hospital personnel are suspects. Detective Yamada is talking to Security now, and I figured you'd know best how to deal with this. The detective needs help with his investigation. I suppose the CEO will need to be informed."

"Man, oh man. I can only imagine how Kline will react," Torrins said. "And the media will go nuts. But of course, we need to help the police in every way we can. I'm coming right in."

"Detective Yamada is cordoning off the OR Bart was operating in and freezing his locker, for starters. A crime scene technician is on the way."

"Okay. The most important thing is we keep Dr. Rainey alive and make sure Memorial Hospital is safe for everyone." Torrins paused. "I haven't spoken to you since Bart went down. I heard about the resuscitation in the ER. Well done. You saved his life."

"Me and many others," Drake said. "His resuscitation is one of the few things that went well today."

"I was going to text you about the malpractice suit, Drake. Kline contacted me a little while ago. He's called a meeting at ten o'clock tomorrow morning with me, you, and the others named in the suit. It has me worried. I don't trust him."

"Something tells me it won't be a pep talk," Drake said.

"Why don't you head for home? I'll be at the hospital in fifteen minutes to help the police," Torrins said. "You must feel like you've been run over."

Drake sighed. Torrins was right—he did feel like he'd been run over. The administrator knew nothing about Bryce or his death. Drake had been battered about so much that he didn't know if he was angry, sad, or numb.

"I'll take Detective Yamada to the OR and tell him you're on the way. I may see you later. I'm going to crash in one of the call rooms pretty soon. I'll be here early for the meeting."

He also needed to revisit Medical Records. His review of the malpractice cases had triggered something he couldn't put his finger on.

He'd give Rachelle a quick call and tell her he needed to stay at the hospital overnight. It was true in a sense, but mainly he was dodging her.

This morning the outlook for their lives had been sunshine and blue skies.

Tonight the elements forecast disaster.

Chapter 39

Drake looked up from the medical records computer. He only had a few minutes to get to the CEO's a.m. meeting. He could readily imagine Kline showing up late just to show them all that he was the boss. Drake didn't want to arrive early only to spend time waiting and worrying. He was doing more than enough of that already.

At least last night's call to Rachelle had gone well.

He'd kept it short and simply told her he had to stay overnight. He'd made so many similar calls that Rachelle hadn't asked any questions. She said she loved him and that she'd been painting. It was clear she was still in a good mood.

Last night Drake had helped Aki cordon off operating room six. Then, with security, they had secured Bart Rainey's locker in the physician dressing room.

When Jim Torrins had arrived, Drake had handed Aki off and gone to the on-call room. After his mind grappled with the disasters of his day, he'd dropped into a deep sleep.

He woke early and headed to the ICU to check on Bart Rainey. As expected, the huge surgeon was still heavily sedated and on a ventilator. On the positive side, he had good color and vital signs. It looked like he would survive.

He updated Detective Yamada and Farley by text from the ICU. They were to meet after Drake's meeting with the CEO.

Drake then dropped down from the ICU to the neonatal intensive care unit to visit his patient. He received an update from one of the NICU nurses while viewing the tiny, hard-luck infant in his warmer.

The three-day old preemie was being treated for opioid withdrawal, but his lungs, the most serious problem for premature infants, were holding strong. Drake left the NICU with sadness but also hope. He was pulling hard for the little guy.

He'd swung by the doctors' lounge where he'd scrounged a couple of bagels and peanut butter. He'd drank two cups of coffee and brought a third with him to the medical records office where he signed in on the computer.

As he'd started his review of the records, he'd sensed the same nebulous pull. From the first time he'd requested records from Clara Zeitman, he'd felt he was missing something. He couldn't grasp it—like the drawing that appears as a young woman, but, seen differently, becomes an image of an old lady.

Now, after more than an hour of intense focus, no answers had appeared.

True, a cluster of Memorial Hospital patients had died. It was mysterious and sad, but seriously ill patients often die unexpectedly—maybe there were no answers to find.

He'd put the other malpractice cases aside and focus solely on his overdosed young mother's death. The death he was accused of causing. Every aspect of the charge sickened him.

If he was found guilty of malpractice, he'd lose everything. Malpractice, Bryce's death, Bart, the mysterious hospital deaths—too much was going on. It was like being in the ER and having four critical patients arrive in the Crash Room at the same time. He needed help.

He'd reach out as soon as he could.

He signed off the computer and made for the door.

Kline's meeting was scheduled in the administrative conference room. Drake exited Medical Records and started through the nearly empty corridor, his shoes squeaking on the buffed white floor.

Drake had contemplated calling Lloyd Anderson but decided that talking after the meeting made more sense. Lloyd had dealt with Kline before and warned that he was "a well-dressed little rat." As Drake passed down the hallway, he reminded himself that if the meeting had anything to do with the malpractice charge, Lloyd had advised him to say nothing.

Drake pushed open the door to the administrative wing and approached the secretary's desk in front of Kline's office. She pointed a finger at the closed door to the administrative conference room.

"They're all in there already, Dr. Cody," she said.

"Thanks." Drake glanced at the clock, noting he was one minute early for the meeting. All in attendance already and the secretary's somber manner suggested everyone was feeling as pressured as he was. As he opened the conference room door, the sense of helplessness that he'd experienced as a sixteen-year-old kid awaiting the verdict in his felony assault trial returned. It appeared he had entered a tribunal.

Kline was at the head of the table in an oversized elevated chair. Seated along the sides of the table were Dr. Julie Stone, OB/GYN; Dr. Vijay Gupta, intensive care specialist; and Tracy Miller, ICU nurse, with Jim Torrins at the end. Drake took the last remaining seat alongside Tracy and farthest from Kline.

"Now that we're all here," Kline said with a tone suggesting Drake had been late, "I have an important announcement to make."

Kline wore a black suit and a white dress shirt with an oversized collar. The only thing lacking was a powdered wig such as worn by a British magistrate.

The feel of the gathering mirrored the wire-tense ambiance of the previous day's malpractice depositions. This time Kline had assigned himself as the lead figure.

"With the exception of the president of medical affairs, you are the physicians and nurse," he nodded towards Tracy, "that are to be charged with malpractice in the wrongful death of the young mother in the ICU."

Wrongful death. Drake's throat clutched.

Kline looked from one person to the next like a judge preparing to deliver a death sentence. He slid a leather-bound folder on the table and tapped his finger on it. "These are the articles establishing Memorial Hospital's charter. The emergency department physicians, the Memorial OB/GYN group, the intensive care physicians, and all Memorial nurses are hospital employees who serve at the behest of the hospital board. I, chief executive officer Stuart Kline, am the operational representative of the board."

Drake slipped a glance at Torrins and sensed he was as lost as Drake was. Whatever Kline was up to, he was playing the moment for all the ego-stoking drama possible.

The already smothering tension in the room surged as they awaited Kline's move.

Julie Stone sat rigid and white-faced. Tracy held a fist to her mouth with eyes on the table. Dr. Gupta frowned, his head cocked in obvious puzzlement.

Kline continued, "I remind everyone of their rank and the hospital's chain of command to avoid any subsequent difficulties." Again he looked at each member around the table.

No one moved, but Drake sensed his colleagues, like him, were writhing inside. Whatever the asshole was building up to had to be monumentally bad. Drake worked to avoid returning Kline's arrogant gaze with a Furnace Correctional Facility "mess with me and I'll snap your punk-ass spine" stare.

"Based solely on what is best for Memorial Hospital and its patients," Kline said, "I've made a decision." He raised his chin and posed as if a leader addressing the masses. "I will be pursuing an immediate settlement for the hospital and all involved medical providers with attorney Clete Venjer and the young mother's family. The assertion of malpractice and wrongful death will not be contested."

The air left Drake's lungs. His stomach plunged.

"You can't do that!" Torrins said.

"Quiet!" Kline slapped his hand on the table top. "I can and will do what I think is best for Memorial Hospital." He glared at Torrins, then looked around the table to see if any other dared challenge him.

Drake was too stunned to react. This was beyond his worst imagining. A settlement for a wrongful death while being on probation guaranteed he'd lose his license. *Please no!*

"The medical providers seated around this table are Memorial Hospital employees. All were part of a grievous error," Kline said. "The pathology finding of the incomplete placenta is in the medical record. I researched some online medical sites last night, and retained placenta is clearly identified as a clear risk for uncontrollable bleeding. My decision will save you the humiliation of a trial." Again, he looked around the table.

"Additionally, a quick settlement will limit the financial exposure of Memorial Hospital. Hopefully it may head off some of the destructive publicity that our hospital is receiving due to the incompetence of some of its doctors and nurses. That problem is something Dr. Torrins as head of Medical Affairs needs to address."

Torrins glared at Kline.

Kline picked up the leather folio and held it up in both hands like Moses holding the commandments. "The hospital charter establishes my authority to act. You are employees of Memorial Hospital and I am the chief executive officer." He paused. "My decision is not open to discussion. This meeting is adjourned."

The pompous ass would have liked to have a gavel to pound.

"I want our president of medical affairs and Drake Cody to remain. The rest of you are dismissed." He laid the folio flat.

Tracy looked almost as devastated as she had the day of their patient's death.

Dr. Julie Stone's earlier look of puzzlement was now stunned disbelief.

Dr. Gupta was open-mouthed.

Kline had delivered a death sentence.

He'd convicted them all without a trial.

Chapter 40

The conference room door closed behind the last of Drake's exiting colleagues.

The always restrained Jim Torrins had both hands on the table top as if to keep himself from leaping for the CEO's throat.

"This is the most outrageous behavior I've witnessed in my forty-two years of medical practice and administrative work," Torrins said. "What you just did—"

"Enough!" Kline shouted, red-faced, pointing his finger at the president of medical affairs. "I don't care what you think. Be quiet and listen." He lowered his hand, but kept his eyes locked on Torrins.

"I'm going to talk, and you and he," Kline nodded towards Drake while keeping his eyes on Torrins, "are going to listen and do what you're told. I'm the CEO of this hospital. I will no longer tolerate the arrogance of doctors who believe they're beyond everyone else. As has been shown once again, the physicians and nurses you have staffing this hospital are incompetent." He paused. "I presented the malpractice crisis to you several days ago and you wouldn't acknowledge it. This newest disaster has proven me one hundred percent correct." He shook his head. "And yet you still dare to challenge me."

Torrins leaned back in his chair. He gave a sad chuckle.

"You are even more of a fool then I thought, and believe me I considered you a grade A, colossal fool."

Kline's eyes bulged. "You're not long for your job, Dr. Torrins."

"I'll be talking to the board myself," Dr. Torrins said. "I don't know what you've told them, but most of them recognize that I'm the one who has kept the medical staff from running you out of the hospital tarred and feathered." Jim Torrins' famous restraint and tact had been put away.

"That's big talk, *Doctor*." Kline said the last word with disdain. "This hospital is in crisis. You're head of medical affairs. What the board members recognize is that your inept doctors and nurses are costing us millions. You know from the malpractice committee ultimatum where the board's support lies. The newspapers, TV, radio, and social media are all reporting on the hospital's malpractice issues or," he looked pointedly at Drake, "identifying it as the hospital for junkies. The board will back me doing what is necessary to remain open."

"There is no leader more dangerous or irresponsible than the one who knows little and believes he knows all," Torrins said.

Drake could not have imagined Dr. Torrins ever being involved is such a knock-down, no-holds-barred exchange.

"I deal with reality," Kline said. "This latest medical disaster, this wrongful death of a vulnerable, young, black mother, is the most egregious of all. We can only hope that Clete Venjer and the patient's brother will accept a settlement."

"Accept? You have no—"

"Torrins, stop and think for a moment. Picture the scene when the tiny black baby is brought into the courtroom and attorney Clete Venjer looks into the eyes of the jurors and talks about how the child's mother was stolen from him? If the kid has some kind of handicap or special needs, it will be even worse. If Venjer were allowed to have each juror hold the baby in their arms he'd do it."

"Our staff did not commit malpractice, Kline. There's—"

"Don't be naive, Torrins. It won't matter. With Clete Venjer's skill, the placenta pathology report, and that orphaned baby, there's no limit to the amount of money the jurors will award." He paused. "This hospital is already on the edge and the board is aware of that. If you want any chance to remain employed, you'd better figure out how to get the doctors and nurses at this hospital to raise their care to at least the minimum standard. And even that assumes they haven't already done enough to get us shut down."

Torrins opened his mouth to speak.

"Stop!" Kline said. "I'm done with you, but you can listen while I deal with another of your trouble-making staff." He turned to Drake.

Kline reminded Drake of the worst of the Furnace Correctional Facility gang leaders. Though Kline wore fancy suits, had a two-hundred dollar haircut, and had probably never had a physical confrontation his life, he shared the same self-absorbed lack of humanity and evident pleasure in using his power and position to threaten others.

"Drake Cody," Kline said with distaste, "I wanted you fired a long time ago. Powerful people in and out of the hospital have supported you. Including some," he glanced at Torrins, "whose judgment has been proved to be abysmal. I want you gone, but while you are still here you absolutely will not address the media again regarding the junkies, their drugs, or their overdose deaths. That is not the kind of marketing we want. Your little TV stunt has helped make the community believe we are the junkies' hospital."

Drake thought of Bryce—emptiness and anger swirled. He kept his face blank.

Kline continued. "Insured people and suburban families do not want to be around drug-using degenerates. Our trauma service already draws enough undesirables from the knife and gun club. By law, we take care of everyone, but there are certain marketing realities that must be acknowledged." He paused.

Drake burned hotter with each word from Kline's mouth. "We" take care of everyone. *Who the hell is "we," you bean-counting shill?* Realities? The only realities he's capable of understanding come with a dollar sign in front of them.

"You will make no more announcements or have any contact with media regarding addicts, drug use, or overdoses." Kline had drawn himself up on his oversized chair and looked down on Drake as if addressing a servant. "Is that understood?"

Drake didn't respond.

"I said, is that understood?" he repeated.

Drake just stared at him, keeping his face passive. The man was a punk.

Kline looked flustered by the lack of response to his effort at intimidation. Then he smiled. "I've recently heard you have an interest in lakeshore property." He looked smug.

What? How did he know? Of course, the mortgage application employment info. Damn!

"You need to understand that the hospital can't, in good faith, attest to your continued employment at Memorial Hospital. Your supporters somehow kept you on staff to this point, but your days are clearly numbered." He shrugged. "In what little time you have left, perhaps you can assist Dr. Torrins in helping Memorial Hospital nurses and physicians achieve some level of medical competence. Perhaps that experience might help you find some kind of job down the road. Until then, you'll find financial institutions will not expose themselves to the risk of your uncertain professional future."

Kline was now openly smirking. The message was clear. There would be no mortgage—no house.

Drake absorbed the sucker punch without giving the jerk the satisfaction of a wince. Rachelle would be crushed. Drake's heart ached.

In his two-part meeting, the CEO first looked to destroy three of Drake's colleagues—two physicians and a nurse, all of whom were dedicated, highly skilled, and deeply caring.

Next he identified his plans to ruin Drake and keep from him and Rachelle the house that was their dream.

Sickest of all, the man had taken pleasure in it.

Old pathways sparked through the wires of Drake's mind. The urge to destroy the ignorant asshole flared like a struck match.

Acting on his impulse was out of the question, though the desire was heartbeat strong. Holding back felt wrong. A further level of restraint involved doing what attorney Lloyd Anderson recommended.

Say nothing.

Inside, Drake boiled.

Chapter 41

Rachelle closed and locked the driver's side car door.

"We hold hands in the parking lot," Shane said, reaching toward his little sister. Kristin took his hand.

Rachelle took Shane's and they crossed the lot to the front of their rental townhouse.

"Mom, can we go play on the playground?" Shane asked as Rachelle unlocked the two separate locks. "Please," Kristin added.

The playground was a rusted swing set and monkey bars located across the alley and directly behind the townhouse.

"Okay," Rachelle said. "Don't wander off. I need to be able to see you from the window."

She opened the door and the kids ran in as she entered the security code.

The kids raced through the living room and kitchen. Rachelle followed and opened the back door, entering the security code there.

"I liked going to the lake, Mom. That was cool," Shane said.

"Yeah, me too," Kristin said.

They scampered off to play.

Rachelle agreed with Drake to not tell the kids about their dream house yet. But she'd been unable to think of anything else. She hadn't seen any harm in taking them to the park and nature area on the east side of the lake.

The morning had been wonderful. There were several other children at the little park and Shane and Kristin had great fun playing with them. Then they took a short hike down a gravel path to the park's undeveloped shoreline. They'd walked out on the small public dock and found they had the area all to themselves.

There was no wind and the lake's surface was glass. The kids had stood wide-eyed as six swans flew overhead, honking like trumpets, then circled back and made a long, low approach, skimming the mirror surface and landing no more than fifty yards from where they stood. New spring buds colored the trees, a cardinal trilled its song, and a great blue heron rose from near the shore, flying low over the water with great, lazy-appearing flaps of its wings.

Rachelle had been breathless with her arms around the kids. They'd been silent, the kids open-mouthed, and Rachelle so happy her eyes filled with tears.

This would be their home. The tingle of anticipation had penetrated to her core. Standing there, just as when she'd visited the incredible house on the south shore with Drake two evenings before, she knew this special place was meant for them.

Now, Rachelle glanced out the kitchen window, seeing Shane and Kristin at play. Unfortunately, there weren't many kids in the complex and the rundown play area was generally deserted.

It was one more thing about this place that Rachelle hated.

Like the trauma of her childhood, her memories of what had happened here could never be erased.

She rinsed the breakfast plates then wiped the counter clean.

She stepped into the living room and looked at the still life of the flower she'd painted the day before. She'd captured the special feel of the bright, hardy, little flower—that felt good. The thought of the painting she could do at the lake home made her smile.

Could she mirror the beauty and grace of the swans? She couldn't wait to try.

She turned back into the kitchen, glanced at the kids, opened the back door, and stepped out on the stoop. The sun was slipping behind a dark cloud. More clouds approached from the west.

She scanned the eight-by-eight-foot enclosure that formed their "yard." *Oh, no!*

The lone little flower lay on the dirt alongside the concrete walk with its stem broken. Some of the petals had separated and lay with the edges brown and curled.

Rachelle picked up the petals and damaged flower that had impacted her so strongly. She let the torn petals drop and took the flower and stem into the kitchen.

She put water in a paper cup and placed the flower in it on the window sill.

The flower had been the only thing she'd enjoyed about the townhouse for a long time.

Lord, please make this move happen fast.

She thought again of the lake, the swans, and the laughter of Shane and Kristin as they'd played with new friends on the playground. A new chapter in their life would open soon—in a home where she and the children would be safe. Where no one could be hurt.

The old wall-mounted phone jangled, startling her. She picked up the receiver.

"Hello, Cody residence," she said.

"Is Drake or Rachelle Cody available? This is the mortgage department of Equity Trust."

"Yes, this is Rachelle Cody speaking."

"I'm calling with disappointing news," the man said. "I regret to report that we will be unable to offer a mortgage loan on the lakeshore property at this time."

What? "My husband told me that the mortgage had been pre-approved," Rachelle said. *This has to be a mistake.*

"Yes, that was true. And I apologize, but we've received updated information from your husband's current employer. We have no choice but to reverse our decision. Without secure employment, your application is not sufficient to support the purchase of the home."

"I don't understand," Rachelle said. Her chest tightened. *It's going to be our home.*

"Our department has been informed that Dr. Cody's employment at Memorial Hospital is not anticipated to be long term."

"Drake is planning to work there for a very long time," Rachelle said. "There must be some sort of mix-up." *Drake would've told me if there was a problem.*

"There's no mistake. I received the call myself. It was from the administrative offices of the hospital, and the person identified himself as the CEO. Being that it was unusual, I called the hospital back afterwards and confirmed the origin of the call. I tried your husband's cell phone to update him on the application's changed status but did not get an answer. This was the other number listed."

"B-but..." Her breath came short. She raised a hand to the scarred tissue of her neck. *This can't be happening!*

"I understand how time-pressured buying a home can be, so I wanted to get the info to you quickly. Perhaps you and your husband will be able to work something out? Please let me know if I can help make that happen. Do you have any questions?"

Rachelle slumped with her back against the wall. "No questions," she said in a voice just above a whisper.

"Thank you. Goodbye."

This can't be.

She hung up the phone and slid down the wall, ending up sitting on the floor with her face in her hands.

Please, God. Haven't I paid enough?

***

Twenty-one years earlier, rural northern Kentucky

Since Joe had moved in, Rachelle's momma only laughed when she drank or they smoked the stinky pipe. Even then, Rachelle could see her sneak nervous looks at the huge man. Even Momma was afraid.

Rachelle hated Joe.

One day Joe couldn't find the TV remote. "Damn it!" His words made them jump.

They all scrambled to find the remote. Rachelle was scared-sick but then she found it. It was in her little brother's baseball glove sitting right there on the couch.

Billy had just turned six years old and was her best friend.

"Here it is, Joe. It was sitting right here all the time." She was so relieved she laughed.

Joe ripped it from her hand snarling like a dog. He looked at the glove, then down at her brother.

Billy flew through the air like a rag doll and smashed into the wall. He fell, screaming bad. Joe tore after Billy, standing over him all crazy-purple and yelling. He kicked Billy hard.

They left her in the farmhouse and took Billy to the far-away hospital in Oswalt.

Finally, way past dark, they came back. Billy had a cast on his arm and his face was swelled and cut—it hurt for him to move.

Hours later, in the shadowy moonlight coming through the bare and dirty windows of their room, Billy whispered, "Rae-Rae." He'd known she was awake.

Rachelle slipped out of her bed and cuddled next to her brother's skinny, quaking body. His sheets smelled of dried urine.

"Joe told them I fell down the stairs." Soft, moist sobs sounded. "He said unless I said it was true he was gonna hurt me real bad."

She laid a hand on his heaving chest. "Momma and I'll protect you, Billy."

"No." He moaned and a tear glinted in the moon's glow. He turned to her, his eyes huge. "Momma told them I fell, too."

Joe worked in the stinky shed some days. He put on a mask thing when he went in. He said it would "blow to hell" if there was "even a spark."

Rachelle had seen a table with boxes and bottles and lots of glass stuff in the shed.

On a day soon after Billy got out of his cast, Joe was working in the shed.

Rachelle took the jar candle from where she'd hidden it behind the building. She shook so hard, it took almost the whole book of matches before she got it lit. Rachelle shifted the loose board from the hole at the base of the wall. She slipped the lit candle inside onto the floor, crawled backwards, then stood and ran.

She got on her bike and bumped down the long dirt driveway. She stopped near the road and waited.

The back door to the house opened. Momma dragged Billy by the arm toward the shed.

"No, Momma!" Rachelle screamed. She jumped on her bike and pedaled harder than ever before.

Momma pulled Billy into the shed. The door closed behind them.

Rachelle threw her bike down and ran, screaming, "Billy, no! Please, Jesus, please!"

She grabbed the door and pulled.

And they all blew straight to Hell.

They'd found the charred bodies of Joe, her mother, and Billy in the rectangle of blackened rubble and smoking timbers.

Later, in the house that stunk of garbage, and had drug paraphernalia in plain sight they'd found her—a dark-haired girl laying curled on a filthy carpet. A severe burn extended over the left side of her neck.

She'd stared blankly during her ambulance trip to the tiny rural hospital and her subsequent transfer to the city. She did not speak for eighteen days. The specialists diagnosed her with post-traumatic shock. On the nineteenth day, she said, "Billy," and tears ran down her cheeks.

***

Her childhood home, like the townhouse, was a place Rachelle wanted to forget.

She'd felt so certain that the lake house would be theirs—as if it were destiny.

Now she was reeling and lost. It hurt too much.

Would she suffer forever for what she had done?

Chapter 42

Jim Torrins exited the conference room disaster ahead of Drake and gestured for him to follow him into his office. He closed the door behind them.

"Have you still got that big-gun attorney?" Torrins asked. "You'd better call him." He collapsed into his chair.

"You shot straight in there," Drake said as he sat in the chair facing Torrins' desk.

"He didn't hear a word of it," Torrins said. "He's clueless, but he thinks he has all the answers." He paused. "What worries me is that if he gets the board to follow his lead, this hospital is doomed. Between taking care of patients and heading medical affairs, I've been here for over four decades. I know every physician and most of the nurses. I've been a patient here myself. This place means something to me."

"You were looking out for us in there, and I appreciate it," Drake said. Even when they'd disagreed, he'd always had a lot of respect for the veteran physician and administrator. The exchange in the conference room had only increased that.

"I'm no hero," Torrins said. "The worst that can happen is I get fired. My direct patient care days are over, and this administrative stuff is becoming more distasteful every day."

"I hope you hang in there. The hospital needs administrators who understand what patient care is about." Drake looked at the clock. "I'm meeting with the homicide detectives in a little bit. They want a doctor's input on whatever they found in Bart's locker and the OR."

"There's no shortage of people around the hospital who dislike Bart Rainey." Torrins paused. "Kline's job threats to you were clear. What was with his lakeshore property comments?"

"We made an offer on a house and it was accepted. I had a mortgage preapproved. Kline was letting me know he shot down the mortgage approval. No way I qualify without secure employment." The loss hammered his insides.

"This would be your first house, right?"

"Yes. We married when I was a premed student working as an ER orderly and a research assistant for the dean of Pharmacology. Cool jobs where I learned a lot, but they paid next to nothing. Then medical school and residency, where we were scrambling for every dollar we could borrow to cover tuition and bills. We've always lived in bare-bones rentals."

"I remember how excited we were when we finally got a house," Torrins said.

"Excited is an understatement. We went nuts over the place. It's beautiful. I don't know if she's ever been happier than when I showed it to her. Ever since then, she's been flying. I can't bring myself to tell her about what's been going on. I didn't tell her about yesterday's malpractice threat and now this."

Drake leaned back, exhaling hard and running both hands over his scalp. "An uncontested wrongful death settlement with my license on probation will be the end for me. There's no court of appeals for malpractice." He sat forward, shaking his head. "I feel sick—and angry."

"Talk to your attorney today," Jim said.

"He's one of several calls I need to make. I've got a lot of issues hanging," Drake said. "Let me give you a heads-up on the media thing that Kline mentioned. He's going to be pissed."

"You already talked to the media again?" Torrins said.

"No, but late yesterday, the lab confirmed that carfentanil is what OD'd our pregnant patient. From what we've found, it looks like a flood of synthetic opioids has hit the streets." The image of Bryce's blue hand and clawed fingers flashed. "It's going to get worse."

"If you haven't talked to the media again, he can't go after you on that."

"Screw him. If his hating me was enough to get rid of me, I'd have been long gone." Drake stood. "Some powerful people have helped me. Tina Watt at WCCY is one of them. I'll be talking to her very soon. People are dying out there. We need to get the word out."

"Good luck." The graying physician extended his hand. "On everything." They shook hands.

Today's words were the most personal they'd ever shared. Drake wondered if he was making a good friend in a job he was not likely to have for long.

***

Drake found himself at the inner doors to the emergency department. He swiped his ID card and the doors swung open.

He was to meet the detectives in the OR in about ten minutes. While his mind thrashed like a blender full of ball bearings, his feet had led him to the place he knew best.

He faced a similar task to what the emergency department faced every day—too much to do and not enough time to do it.

Detectives Yamada and Farley wanted his help in finding who had tried to kill Bart Rainey.

He had to stop CEO Kline from accepting a wrongful death settlement assigning guilt to Drake and his colleagues in the bleeding death of the overdosed mother.

He had to do what he could to prevent more tragedies like Bryce. And help in any way he could to find the drug supplier who'd been responsible for the boy's death.

He needed to follow up on the cluster of mysterious deaths and malpractice suits at Memorial Hospital and determine if something other than the hand of fate was involved.

He had to follow up on Rizz's recovery and the future of their breakthrough drug D-44.

And underpinning all, he had to keep Rachelle from being crushed again. If he lost his career, as looked likely, he had to convince her he could make things work some other way—and then make that true.

Just as in the ER, every problem couldn't be treated at once, and no one could do it alone.

What needed to be done first? Who could best help?

Among the ball bearings clattering around in his head, Stuart Kline's intent to immediately accept a wrongful death settlement was the most urgent. Drake would reach out to his attorney Lloyd Anderson, Rizz, and his other friends. He had to let Rachelle know what they faced.

As he made his way through the ER, the people, noises, smells, and sounds were a blurred background. He entered the empty Crash Room and grabbed the wall phone to call one of the most brilliant people he knew.

"County Morgue. How can I direct your call?"

Drake asked to be connected. He'd planned to get there yesterday but with Bart and then Bryce...

"Dr. Kip Dronen, forensic pathologist to the stars speaking." The screechy voice and irreverence could be no one else.

"Kip, it's Drake Cody from the ER."

"Yeah, ER guy. You never call, you never write, but you send your flat-foot flunkies by so I can educate them. And I don't even get a thank-you. It looks to me like we've got a one-way deal going here. I help you and in exchange, I get to help you some more. Not a hell of a lot in it for me, though I admit you have hooked me up to some excellent deaths. What do you want now?"

Kip Dronen was the strangest person Drake had met in the medical profession. It was a wonder he'd gotten through the selection process—yet a good thing he had. And it probably was also a good thing that all of Kip's "patients" were beyond the need for caring. He had all the warmth of one of his stainless-steel autopsy tables.

Death and all its causes obsessed him. The scrawny, egotistical physician was a genius.

"Kip, you're right. I need your help. You're the best, and I can't give you anything in return but my appreciation. A tragic death occurred at the hospital, and I'm one of those charged with being responsible. The CEO is looking to make a quick malpractice settlement. A settlement or a loss at trial—either way, in the eyes of the state Medical Board, I'm guilty. My license will be gone forever."

"I decided I wasn't going to be a sucker and help anyone else out," Kip said. "It hasn't done squat for me so far. This 'help me or my career is dead' story is a new one. I probably should care about that, though I really don't." He paused. Drake sensed nothing to suggest Kip was joking.

"However, like I said earlier, you've plugged me into some pretty awesome deaths, and you know there's nothing I get off on more. And I did score a cover article in the *Journal of Pathology* for my analysis of your water-logged chick." His voice gave no hint of modesty. "I guess I can help you out, ER guy, but please tell me there's an interesting death in it."

"Thank you. It means a lot to have you in my corner. I have to run right now, but I'm going to come by later. How long will you be there?"

"I'll be here." Kip practically lived at the morgue.

"It was a death of an opioid-overdosed patient, who presented to the Crash Room in labor. She subsequently bled out in the ICU. Her name was Ivy Jackson and that's all I have time to tell you now."

"Hey, that sounds like a good one. Might be fun. Later, ER guy."

No, Kip, it's not a good one. And there isn't anything about it that's fun.

***

Drake waded through the packed ER hallway toward the OR.

"Drake."

He turned to see Dr. Laura Vonser, one of his emergency medicine partners, coming his way. Earlier this year, Laura's quick diagnosis and aggressive care of Rachelle's deadly infection had made her forever one of Drake's favorite people.

"Have you heard?" Laura looked uncharacteristically serious.

"What?"

"Overdoses," she said. "It's out of control. Between the medics and the ERs, there have been at least twelve deaths and no one knows how many overdoses in the metro area just since last night. I heard the lab confirmed carfentanil and you put out a warning on TV yesterday. It's deadly out there. Keep trying to spread the word, partner."

"I will." It was out of control. Where would it end?

Chapter 43

Stuart Kline leaned back in the chair at his massive mahogany desk.

The air smelled of fresh paint and new carpet. His office was silent but for the whisper of the ventilation system. Everything was so different from the noxious odors and noise that accosted him when he had to venture to the patient care areas of the hospital.

The morning's showdown meeting had gone well. It had been way past due.

He was the CEO of the hospital but to date, it had clearly been a case of the inmates running the asylum. These doctor and nurse types were smart, but they were too used to calling the shots. They understood all the complex medical stuff that was a foreign language to Stuart, but they had no business sense.

Beyond that, they presumed moral and ethical superiority. The mantra they used to justify anything and everything—*whatever is in the best interests of the patient*—eliminated all discussion.

What he needed to do was clear. Torrins had resisted every forward-thinking move that Stuart had advanced. He'd totally rejected cutting staff—not just physician staff, but the largest personnel cost of all, nursing staff. They acted like their cushy patient-to-nurse ratios were immutable laws.

And Torrins stubbornly continued to insist that the nurses and doctors of Memorial Hospital were clinically excellent. Stuart, on the other hand, understood that economics were the true measure of performance. The millions of dollars in settlements and malpractice verdicts proved the staff were incompetent.

Stuart was convinced that if they reduced staff, the remaining nurses and doctors would do more work in less time. When one is forced to work harder and expectations are raised, it consistently results in greater efficiency, as well as better focus, greater output, and improved performance. It worked that way for weightlifters, runners, sales people, and even accountants.

Every time Stuart advanced staff reduction plans or other fiscally sound initiatives, he was met by their knee-jerk mantra of "it's not in the best interests of the patients."

He'd had enough.

He wanted Jim Torrins and the other rigid thinkers like him gone.

Torrins and his ER supporter, Drake Cody, also supported a number of guaranteed-to-lose-money ideas.

Drake Cody had gone on TV and practically begged drug addicts to come to Memorial Hospital. Torrins supported similar efforts to roll out the red carpet for immigrants, minorities, drug-users, the mentally ill, street people, and other money-losing patients.

The trauma service and the helicopter air rescue branch brought in highly sought-after victims of car accidents, industrial injuries, and other good-paying patients. However, the level one trauma designation also made the hospital a revolving door for victims and perpetrators of gunshots, knife wounds, and other criminal violence. Financial compensation for the care of these patients, some of whom were hospitalized for months, was often little or nothing. They were consistently among the medical center's loss leaders.

The hospital was obligated to help the needy, but it had to be limited by the realities of operating a sustainable business.

Financially ruinous services and practices needed to be eliminated. Caring for addicts, criminals, and the mentally ill always lost money.

And now, the latest medical malpractice disaster had left a vulnerable young mother dead after delivery of her possible media darling of a child. The potential cost in dollars and bad publicity was inestimable. He'd been hired to put the hospital on track financially. A quick and quiet settlement was definitely the way to go.

Clete Venjer seemed like a guy who understood the bottom line. Stuart was impressed. The attorney's politeness and seeming respect for the doctors was a smokescreen as his apparently innocent questions set them up for the slaughter.

The soft-appearing little man knew he had a winner of a case. The only question was how big the payout would be.

The insurance company backed Stuart's plan for settlement. Clete Venjer rarely lost, and they understood the size of the award that might result if he got the case in front of a sympathetic trial jury. The company was ready to pay plenty to protect against an award so large it would make national news.

The doctors and nurse involved were all employees of the hospital and were all under the Memorial malpractice policy. A joint settlement with one single payment was clearly the best course.

Clete Venjer and the victim's family would make a big score and get paid quickly. The hospital would dodge the horrific publicity of the tragic death, drawn-out trials, and likely losing verdicts. The insurance company would limit their expenses and losses by avoiding a jury trial and a potentially mega-million-dollar award.

It was time for Stuart to take charge. Time to cut losses. Time to introduce a new and more profitable culture. That was Stuart's mandate. Change was hard, but perhaps there was a silver lining.

It wouldn't hurt to inquire if he might benefit financially from the settlement. It seemed appropriate. A reward for the person who was smart enough to help the process along.

He picked up his desk phone then stopped. He hung it up.

He pulled his cell phone out of his pocket. It would be best to keep this call confidential.

"Call Clete Venjer," he said into his smart phone.

This would be a private and hopefully profitable conversation.

Chapter 44

Q used the gloved, baby finger of his left hand to push the volume gain on his sound system. Grover Washington saxophone riffs filled the lab.

Q had been cranking through the night. He and Smurf's deliveries yesterday had brought in more money than his mother made in a year. When he dropped Smurf off, he'd tipped her momma with a couple of free hits of product. Business was booming and when he got home he felt like celebrating. He'd been riding a smooth blend of cocaine, Marley-strength weed, and Surly Furious beer all night.

He didn't drink as much as he used to, and with cocaine on board he never felt drunk. His blend of refreshments kept him mellow, focused, and on task. Momma would admire his work ethic. He smiled. He was one hell of a badass businessman.

He'd used his new pill-configuring device to create nearly 2000 pills identical in appearance to prescription Oxycontin. Oxys were very popular. Some still called it "hillbilly heroin" as its initial release by the drug companies had been followed by a stampede of redneck users and addicts in southern states. Highly potent and an all-world high, especially when crushed and snorted. He sold his knock-offs as fast as he could make them.

At this point he'd not yet juiced this batch with carfentanil. The pill material was starch, cellulose, and quinine. The last and critical step was delivery of carfentanil solution to each pill.

Carfentanil powder was too potent to handle in the microscopic amounts needed. The amount of carfentanil powder needed per pill was less than one grain of salt. In order to deliver that miniscule amount of drug, Q dissolved a small amount of the drug in a large volume of liquid. His approach allowed him to deliver a tiny but manageable amount of the diluted drug solution to each pill. His laboratory skills were improving each day.

His technique meant each pill received a precisely delivered volume of solution, assuring an opioid dose that delivered the high of an 80-milligram prescription Oxycontin. He used the same type of micropipettes used by university researchers and got off on the process. He was a scientist—a professional.

Oxys on the street were going from $80 per pill. Folks paid a premium for the pharmaceutical stuff. Q had established his price point between $35 and $45 each, in minimum orders of 200 or more. The larger the volume, the lower the price. The quantity discount was sound business. Larger volumes meant fewer person-to-person exchanges for him and less exposure. This production run alone would bring in between $70,000 and $90,000.

He was swimming in money.

He sniffed. The respiratory mask kept him from rubbing his nose. The clear glasses protected his eyes. The threat of airborne carfentanil was real, but rubbing his nose or eyes with drug-contaminated gloves was an easier mistake to make. Either type of exposure could drop him like a darted rhino.

He checked the clock. He'd been at it nonstop for hours. The cocaine kept his focus sharp and generally made him forget about food. He'd lost fifteen pounds in the last few months and was looking lean. He was still carrying the muscle he'd gained from weight lifting while in the penitentiary. He wondered if, with his serious money, cleaned-up act, and badass body, he might someday hook up with a woman as prime as Tina Watt. *Oh yeah!* He really did have a major thing going for her.

The reefer effect must have been kicking in because he was thinking about food. There was a live WCCY morning show he liked to watch. Tina Watt sometimes delivered news updates during the broadcast.

He carefully secured the vessel containing the carfentanil fluid. He would continue the carfentanil dosing of the Oxycontin look-alikes later. Maybe he'd try to sleep. As a self-employed entrepreneur, his time was his own. God bless capitalism and the free enterprise system.

After all the deliveries he and Smurf made yesterday, he had more product in distributors' hands than ever before. He didn't have to do much for marketing. The users couldn't get enough, and the quality and price of Q's carfentanil-based product brought the distributors back to him in a hurry. In the end it was all about money. Free enterprise had set him free. He smiled.

He moved to the lab door, stepped out, stripped off his gloves and respiratory mask, then tossed them in his plastic-lined wastebasket. He locked the door.

"Good Morning Minnesota" was on TV and Q was eating Frosted Flakes. The place smelled of toast that had burned black when he'd visited the bathroom.

The show's host and hostess were good-natured, and Q enjoyed most of the content. The forecast promised some sun with an outside chance of a storm late in the afternoon. He glanced out the back window. The buds on his oak tree were starting to leaf out. He enjoyed his new place more every day.

"We go now to Tina Watt for a special news update," the morning host said.

The image flipped to a remote shot with Tina White standing outside near a park bench with the calm waters of a lake in the background. Wow—even wearing a jacket she looked smoking hot.

"This is Tina Watt with grim news. Behind me is Lake Nokomis, and this bench is where three Minneapolis high school students experienced apparent drug overdoses hours ago. Paramedics arrived on the scene after a 911 call. Two of the students were resuscitated, but the report at this time is that one student expired."

Q left his spoon in the bowl and leaned forward. Punk kids don't know what they're doing. Damn, that woman looks fine even when she's sad.

"This tragedy is part of a wave that is sweeping the Twin Cities. On my way to this scene, I was contacted by Dr. Drake Cody, Emergency Medicine specialist at Memorial Hospital. Dr. Cody joined us two days ago and warned about a dramatic worsening of the opioid epidemic in our community. Today he reports laboratory confirmation that the powerful opioid drug fentanyl and the even more deadly drug carfentanil are involved in the rash of overdoses. The ultra-potent carfentanil has been confirmed to have caused at least eight of the more than thirty presumed overdose deaths in the past seventy-two hours. Both numbers are expected to grow as law enforcement and the medical examiner's office process the deaths."

Drake Cody again. Bastard!

A thought jumped to his mind. Is someone else in the cities moving carfentanil product?

"Dr. Cody shared that in the last several hours, emergency medical system responders have been deluged with never-before-seen numbers of drug overdoses. More than forty 911 overdose-triggered calls have occurred in the last twelve hours. We will be tracking all developments and following up with a special report on this exploding threat during the noon news broadcast." She paused and the camera panned closer.

"We repeat Dr. Cody's warning from two days ago. Anyone who might consider taking drugs must be aware that you cannot know what you are buying on the street. It will kill. Don't take chances, Twin Cities. Back to Sid and Sarah, where they'll share a website and phone number to help those with substance issues."

Q snapped the power button on the controller. The screen went black and the house silent. What in the hell was going down? They'd confirmed carfentanil. Damn! That was his special advantage. If others had scored as he had, the market could get flooded. Supply and demand—too much product on the street would drive his prices down.

And the deaths? High school kids at Lake Nokomis? Q had a distributor on the south side who went young. Q pushed his bowl of Frosted Flakes aside, his appetite gone. *How many of the overdoses and deaths were from my product?*

He got up, then hurried up the stairs. He put on a new mask and gloves, unlocked the door, entered the lab, and took a seat at his laptop. His uneasy wonderings grew.

None of his distributors had his phone number. None of them knew where he lived. He limited contact to the dark web, where drugs, prices, and deliveries were arranged. For his distributors, he'd built in a number of safeguards and communication tells to warn if their message was forced and police were involved.

He accessed his server site.

The first message, "Hell, man. Got word of several ODs."

His unease grew to icy fear.

The next, "Dude, I think a couple of my customers died."

There were more.

His insides churned. *Damn! Damn! Damn!*

Were the ODs all clueless rookies or could he have made a mistake in the lab? Was his product too jacked up?

He thought about how good things were going. He thought about all the money he was making. He thought about maybe someday a woman as classy as Tina Watt. Everything depended on his business.

And now he may have messed up. And that Drake Cody was making everything worse.

Son of a bitch.

***

Clara decided she'd help out with the current ICU blood draws.

She'd slept late. The last thing she'd done was review the labs and documentation on Bart Rainey. As of midnight, there was no evidence the strychnine had been discovered. She'd re-checked at 8:00 a.m. when she woke from the inflatable mattress she kept in her office. The doctors still hadn't tumbled to it.

She knew strychnine had been removed from general toxicology screens in the 1980s because its use had virtually disappeared. She figured it was still likely it would be tracked down eventually, but she'd set things up so well they'd never be able to connect her to it. And they hadn't even ordered a test to look for it yet.

After a brief meeting with her lab supervisors and her stair climb, she'd showered and was ready to help out in the ICU. Laying eyes on the massive jerk had great appeal. The only thing better would be letting him know she was responsible.

She entered the main lab, gathered the new ICU lab orders, picked up the collection tray of needles and tubes, and made her way to the elevators. She ignored the people in the hallways and on the elevator. When the doors opened to the sixth floor she exited, went down the hall, and made the turn toward the ICU. She slowed, controlling the urge to stop dead.

A uniformed police officer was seated at a small table at the ID-controlled doors to the unit.

"Good morning," the thick, balding officer said. "Can I see your ID and ask your business, please?"

"What's going on?" she asked, knowing the answer.

"Some heightened security. Nothing to be alarmed about." He looked at her ID, then her face.

"I'm here to draw blood." She held up the orders.

He looked at the printouts and scanned her blood-draw basket. "Thank you." He swiped her card through the reader and handed it back to her as the doors opened.

She entered the ICU.

A fleshy guy in his thirties in a sport coat stepped from behind the nurse's station counter. He looked hesitant and out of place.

"Excuse me," he said taking a step to the side, flushing slightly.

As she moved past, she spied a badge clipped on his belt below a belly ballooning his white shirt. She caught him looking at her again and he quickly redirected his eyes.

She steadied herself, ignoring the jump in her pulse. Her mouth had gone dry.

The doctors had not been as dumb as it appeared. There were no reports of poison in the lab reports, but it was clear they believed Bart Rainey's condition was not an accident or illness. Had they confirmed it was strychnine? Why was there nothing about him being at risk and needing protection in the doctor or nursing notes?

Her mouth went dry. The police knew—and they were on the hunt.

Calm down! She'd anticipated her intentions being discovered at some point, but the police presence this early surprised her. She needed to stay focused.

She took a deep breath and slipped into her work mode—total concentration.

She entered the first bay. The patients in the ICU were often sedated, comatose, or simply beyond noticing her and her chore. She carried on as usual—efficient, skilled, and mistake-free. She moved from bay to bay, a nurse occasionally giving her a nod or "hello."

She entered Bay seven—Dr. Bart Rainey.

The foot of the bed had been extended to support his height. He was intubated, deeply sedated, and motionless, except for the ventilator-driven rise and fall of his chest. A scan of the monitors showed his vitals were stable. Most disappointing of all, his face looked almost peaceful.

Unless there was hidden neurologic damage, it looked like the disgusting hulk of a man had absorbed the nuclear bomb of strychnine and would likely recover. Some men are hard to kill—her Dan had withstood more than anyone thought possible before he slipped away.

It was okay. The giant jerk would live, but his suffering had been profound. She'd settled her account with him and she'd be gone before he could ever insult her again.

She inserted the blood-draw needle, his veins like garden hoses. Her mind raced as she filled the tubes.

It was possible they knew the poison or soon would. Beyond that, they knew nothing. If the pudgy plainclothes guy was doing the investigation, she wasn't too worried. He didn't look dangerous.

Nonetheless, it was time to quit messing around. Everything was ready to go. It was time to open the Zeitman Clinic.

Stay cool. Tie up some loose ends.

Collect the money and the other giant debt owed her and then begin the role she was destined for...

Chapter 45

Aki and Farley were late. Drake stood in the hall just outside the main OR entrance where they'd agreed to meet. He had not let the time go to waste.

First, he'd placed a quick call to anchorwoman Tina Watt to share the warning about carfentanil and the flood of overdoses in the last hours.

A second call, also only minutes long, to Lloyd Anderson. The attorney had been in a meeting but was able to let Drake give him the bare bones of CEO Kline's proposed malpractice settlement. Drake had also shared the mortgage issue and the threat to their home purchase.

Lloyd repeated his "say nothing" caution about the malpractice case. He'd do what he could. He also volunteered to call the bank regarding the mortgage, but he'd mentioned mortgage rules were tight. Aki rounded the corner into the hall as detective Farley stepped out of the nearby elevator. They spoke for a moment and then approached.

"Sorry we're late," Aki said. "We've been stretched thin covering more OD deaths. Farley beat me here and he visited the ICU." He turned to Farley. "Anything new?"

The big, baby-faced detective in the sport coat shook his head. "The doctor is stable. The nurse told me he'll be on the ventilator for at least all of today. He's heavily sedated, so we won't be able to get anything from him any earlier than tomorrow."

"Protection in place?" Aki asked.

"A uniform is staked out at the entry, checking everyone. The nurses and physicians are aware. I don't think anyone who doesn't belong will get near him," Farley said.

"Good deal," Aki said. He turned to Drake. "Last night we cordoned off the operating room the victim had been operating in. We got warrants for his locker and the OR this morning. Our crime scene tech went through the locker, and he just started processing the OR. Lead the way, Doc, and let us know what we need to do to not mess up anything."

"We put booties over our shoes, otherwise you're fine," Drake said. "Just follow me." Drake hit the wall plate and the automatic door swung open.

He stepped into the main OR corridor and pulled blue fabric booties from a wall-mounted box and handed them to Drake and Aki. He slipped a pair over his own shoes. They walked down the main surgical corridor to the empty, taped-off scrub area outside OR six. Through the glassed portions of the door, Drake saw a gray-haired man wearing white coveralls inside.

"That's our guy," Aki said "Ted Bilger. He's the best."

Drake ducked under the tape and hit the wall plate with his elbow, opening the OR door. He and the detectives entered. The door closed behind them. The room was quiet, bright, and smelled of antiseptic.

"Ted, this is Dr. Drake Cody. He's going to give us doctor input on what we find. You went through the victim's locker already. We can put our heads together and see what we have."

The tech nodded to Drake and brought them over to a large OR table where he had a few items spread out. "I'm not familiar with the normal contents or workings of an operating room," Ted said. "I left most things in place."

Drake looked around. He spotted nothing out of the ordinary.

"I think it's highly likely," Drake said, "that Bart, er, the victim, was poisoned before he was in the room. In here, he'd have on a surgical gown, mask, and gloves."

Ted spoke up, "I have list of everything I found in his locker. If you want to take a look at that first, my tablet might be the easiest. I have notes and photos." He picked up an Apple device from the OR table, did a couple of finger swipes, and handed it to Drake.

Drake scanned through the listing: Safety razor, shaving cream, toothpaste, toothbrush, cologne, size 19 shoes— "You found a tin of Copenhagen?" Drake said.

"Yes. I was a little surprised by a doctor using chewing tobacco," Ted said. "Copenhagen sells little packets of tobacco called Bandits. It looks like he'd run out. The tin was empty."

"I never saw him spit, but as I think about it, he has stained teeth and I believe I smelled it on him before." Drake knew of a couple of the docs who were closet smokers, but chew was totally believable for Bart.

"What do you have there?" Drake asked pointing at three plastic bags sitting on the table.

"Those are from the waste receptacles. Two from in here, and one from outside the room by those sinks," Ted said.

"Have you gone through them yet?" Drake asked.

"I've gone through the two from in here but not the one from outside," Ted said. "Based on what you said, sounds like we should look."

"Surgeons scrub and get gowned and gloved out there," Drake said. "Let's see what we have."

"Absolutely," Ted said. They all moved closer as he unfurled a sheet of poly on the table, then picked up the bag. "Please let me do all the manipulating. Don't touch anything. Also, I note for the record, this is evidence-gathering pursuant to a dutifully obtained warrant and witnessed by Dr. Cody and Detectives Yamada and Farley."

He undid the loose knot at the top of the bag, then emptied the contents onto the table. The contents included a number of crumpled paper towels, the packaging from several sets of sterile gloves, and three Styrofoam coffee cups.

"It could have been put in his coffee," Drake said.

Ted set the cups aside. He gave the bag a last shake and a dark brown, bullet-shaped object slightly larger than a cigarette butt fell out.

"I think that's a Bandit," Farley said. "It matches the tin in his locker. My brother used the stuff."

They were all silent for a moment.

"It fits," Drake said. "Strychnine can be absorbed through the tissues of the mouth and gums. It also has a slightly bitter taste, so he'd be less likely to notice it in his tobacco than his coffee." The pieces fell into place with the vibe Drake felt when he made an on-target diagnosis in the ER. "If someone were to have added strychnine to one of his packets and slipped it into his locker, it would account for everything."

"The tin was empty," Farley said. "So he either used all the others before getting the poisoned one or they left only one in the tin."

"True," Drake said. "They'd have no way of knowing when he'd use it. It could have been in there a while."

"Good point," Aki said. "But if that's how he was poisoned and we can find out who put it in his locker, we have them nailed." He paused. "First step is to get that thing analyzed."

"I'll take it to the Bureau of Criminal Affairs lab straightaway," Ted said.

"Obviously tell them it's a 'right now' request and give them my number," Aki said. "We've got a lot more to do, but if that thing has strychnine on board, we're miles closer to finding who did this."

The dogged detective wore the first smile that Drake had seen on him in a while.

Chapter 46

Phoenix Halverson replayed the recorded message from the paper's local section call-in line a third time.

As an unpaid journalism intern, she'd fielded crank calls on this line before, but this was no rant. It was a clear, matter-of-fact report, much like a veteran reporter would make. There was no hint as to who had sent it, but she had no doubt it was real.

Her scalp tingled as she considered what the message could mean for her.

It was rare for any of the journalism student interns at the paper to have anything to do with a story that wasn't buried in the back pages of the metro section. If the call was as authentic as it seemed, it could be the biggest story any intern had ever broken.

Possibilities flooded her mind. The odds of getting a job as a reporter when newspapers were laying off staff daily were not good. But it could happen. And breaking a story like this would get her noticed.

Phoenix loved the Minneapolis StarTribune. Sure, some of the knuckle-dragging Neanderthals around the cities and on the radio called it the "Minneapolis Star and Sickle," and letters to the editor railed about "liberal bias," but that was just a reflection of how unenlightened they were. Writing for the StarTribune was her dream.

Every instinct told her this story was big. It could be a rocket booster to her career.

The article she was already writing in her mind fit the passions and beliefs that had driven her to pursue journalism in the first place. It had the political and social slant that the editors loved. She would craft a story with a conscience, one that challenged how people viewed healthcare and their community. The rush of excitement had her thoughts flying. Her article would shine a light on hospitals, health care, prejudice, death, and money. It would open readers' eyes to the truth.

Her schooling, particularly her college coursework, had educated her about America's rampant injustices, both historically and today. She was sickened by how few people recognized that the country was based in repression. Free enterprise was nothing more than a guise used to hide control by the rich few at the expense and abuse of the many. How it could be denied was beyond her.

And here, dropped in her lap, was a story she could use to reveal how things really were.

Patients were dying that shouldn't be dying. A number of malpractice verdicts and settlements had occurred. And a disproportionate number of the victims were people of color.

The phoned-in message outlined a story that would almost write itself.

Who had called? Why?

It didn't matter.

She started typing. This was her chance.

Her first article would make headlines.

***

What could have happened at the hospital? Rachelle paced back and forth across the kitchen.

It had to be something bad. The CEO wouldn't have called the bank to tell them Drake would be losing his job if it were a minor thing.

Why hadn't Drake let her know?

She dialed his cell phone again and it rolled to message. She'd left one earlier. She hung up the phone and walked to the window. The kids were still at play.

The rejection on the mortgage stemmed from what was going on with his job. But what? Why didn't he share more with her? Was he trying to protect her? Not knowing made it worse.

Even when he was around, he often really was not. She could see in his eyes that he was far away. Concerned about a patient, thinking about his research, or worrying about his mother—always something. She couldn't help but resent the things that kept him from her.

As she paced, she scanned the photos on the wall. His brother, Kevin—anytime Drake looked at the photo, or in those rarest of times when he mentioned him, he disappeared. He went places where she'd never been invited. There were secrets there—more things he didn't share.

At times when she was with him, they connected so intensely it was magic. She knew he felt it, too. Was it love or just desperate lonely people in a sexual blaze that masqueraded as love?

There were parts of her past she kept walled off—even from herself. He hadn't probed. She didn't know if it was them allowing each other the space they needed or two damaged people who were afraid to reveal themselves.

She had issues, but she'd grown stronger. When the children were in danger, she'd come though. She rubbed the burn scars of her wrists. She'd take that pain again and more to protect them—or Drake. She'd proved that, and it gave her strength.

But long hours on her own, and her forever enemies of anxiety and depression were smothering her once again. *Please, God.*

Losing the house was an ache at her core. She'd never wanted anything as much. When she'd called the ER, she'd said it was an emergency. Losing the house was an emergency! They said he wasn't in the ER but they'd page him and have him call. They'd been very nice and Rachelle had felt guilty.

Before Drake, anytime there'd been anyone positive in her life, she'd lost them—her mother, her brother, kindhearted Drew who she'd been the caretaker for.

Drake was so special, so loving—but other times he was someone else. She'd seen what he'd done to the woman who'd hurt her and the children. And his reaction to the neighbor who'd terrified Shane. Those times, he scared her—but in the end his violence had been all about protecting them.

After the call from the bank she'd sat on the floor, too devastated to cry. The home on the lake was a dream she'd believed had come true. Its loss ripped apart something deep inside her.

She picked up the phone, then put it down.

Whatever had happened to put his job at risk had to be painful for Drake. She should feel sympathy about what he was going through. But why hadn't he shared it with her? It was her life, too.

The wall phone rang, and she snatched it off the hook.

"Rachelle, I'm sorry. My cell went dead—they paged me. They said there's an emergency. Are you and the kids okay?"

"No. I'm not okay. We lost the house. A person from the bank called me. The mortgage application has been turned down. He told me the CEO of your hospital called and said you would be losing your job. He—" Her voice broke and she fought to avoid crying.

"Kline called the bank himself? What an incredible asshole." Drake's voice was a growl. "I'm sorry. The CEO is a serious jerk. There's been some bad things happening—"

"Why don't you share with me? Why is it that I don't hear about anything until—never mind. I don't know what to say."

"I didn't want to worry you," Drake said. "I thought I could take care of everything. There's a chance I still can, but things have gone from bad to horrible."

Horrible?

"You're really worrying me now, Drake. What's worse than losing your job and the house? My heart is breaking."

"I'm so sorry," Drake said. "I'm feeling it, too."

"Don't you trust me? You don't have to hide things from me."

"Of course. You were so happy and excited about the house. I didn't want to disappoint you, so I held back."

She took a deep breath. "Please tell me what's happening."

"Jim Torrins forced me into helping investigate a possible malpractice problem at the hospital. Patients have been dying unexpectedly. The CEO is using the malpractice issue to try to get rid of Torrins and me."

"He can't do that," Rachelle said.

"Yes, he can. Or at least he can try. But things have gotten worse. Recently I took care of a patient who was raced into the ER almost dead from a narcotic overdose and in the midst of giving birth. We were able to get her stabilized and get the baby delivered. The mother was bleeding heavily but we got it under control. She was admitted to the ICU doing better. A little later, the bleeding returned, and she died from blood loss."

"Oh my, Drake. How sad."

"Yesterday, a malpractice attorney notified the hospital, two other doctors, a nurse, and me that we're going to be sued for wrongful death."

"You?" *Malpractice and wrongful death?* A lump lodged in her throat.

"Yes. They're claiming she died due to inept and reckless care."

"That can't be true. You're the most caring and—"

"If the attorneys gain a settlement or guilty verdict, it means big money. They believe they can persuade a jury that negligence and incompetence resulted in the wrongful death of my patient. They have little to lose and could gain millions."

"Everyone knows you're a great doctor."

"I'm glad you believe in me, Rachelle, but unfortunately, that doesn't matter." The line went silent.

Her breathing came hard. Drake sounded more beaten down than she'd ever heard him. *This is a nightmare.*

"There's more," he said. "This morning, the hospital CEO told us that he intends to settle the case. He's going to admit guilt to avoid the possibility of a massive award at trial."

"That's so unfair."

"I've talked to Lloyd Anderson. We'll resist, but I'm an employee of the hospital, and the hospital pays for my malpractice. They can settle even if I disagree."

"That's not right," Rachelle said.

"It's the law." Drake sounded beaten down. "I learned long ago that the legal system doesn't necessarily mean justice."

"What happens if the hospital settles?"

"Since I'm already on probation with the state Medical Board, if I have a wrongful death settlement against me, they'll have no choice. I'll be done as a doctor."

"No!" The word jumped from her mouth.

"Even if that happens—"

"Don't say that," she said.

"Even if that happens, we'll be okay. There are jobs, good jobs that I can get. We'll be okay." He paused.

The house, his license, his career—

Her thoughts went to her medications. They were no longer in the cupboard.

"You were so happy," Drake said. "I didn't want to bring you down. I'm sorry."

"Don't give up, Drake. You're a doctor. Often, I hate it and wish you did something else, but it's a big part of who you are."

"I'm not giving up. I have a chance, but it doesn't look good. I should have told you. I was a coward."

"You're no coward, Drake." *I have to be strong.* "I apologize for whining. I was being so selfish. This has to be so hard for you."

"And so hard for you. I'm sorry. I have to get going. I have a meeting with—"

"Okay," she said. "Go and take care of whatever you need to."

"I love you," he said. "No matter what happens, we'll be okay."

He hung up before she could say anything more. His "we'll be okay" sounded like he was trying to convince himself. That worried her more than anything else—*he hadn't believed his own words.*

She needed to get out of this house and escape the screaming in her head.

Chapter 47

Drake pulled into the parking lot in front of the one-story, sandstone Hennepin County morgue building.

He'd just disconnected with Rachelle. Despite their years together and all they'd gone through, he didn't feel he could fully read her—especially over the phone. Would she be okay? One thing was sad and certain—the euphoric ride she'd been on since seeing the lake house had crashed hard.

Drake swung his car past the fluorescent orange Humvee with the "IC Dead" personalized license plate parked in the staff slot. Kip was here. There were few times he wasn't.

Drake knew no one in medicine or anywhere else who was as obsessed with their work. The study of death and its causes was his life.

Requesting the brilliant social misfit's help usually involved running a gauntlet of insult and abuse. He hoped Kip was in a decent mood today. His recent rejection for the chief medical examiner position had to have fanned his long-smoldering resentment.

Kip had more professional recognition and accolades then almost any forensic pathologist in the country, but his profanity, ego, inappropriate comments, and general "doesn't play well with others" persona had caused him to be passed over multiple times for the county's politically appointed "chief" medical examiner position.

Drake cared about the undersized, fractious eccentric and worked to be as close to a friend as the ego-stoked man was capable of having. He suspected underneath the "kiss my ass" exterior, the brilliant devotee of death might be lonely.

Drake shamelessly fed Kip's ego and didn't feel bad about it. Kip had come through big in the past, and Drake needed his brilliance more than ever before.

Drake parked in a visitor spot and tried to organize his thoughts. The Crash Room patients in the ER of his life were stacking up. He closed his eyes and leaned his head against the steering wheel. He'd told Rachelle he wasn't going to quit, but he wondered. What if he just bailed out and got a regular job? The malpractice suit and all the headaches at Memorial Hospital would be behind him. Death and opioid overdoses would be something he'd see on TV or in the newspapers. He wouldn't have to face the unrelenting pressure and responsibility of correctly diagnosing and treating each and every patient.

Beyond that, he could leave behind the doubts. Whenever a patient did poorly or died, doctors and nurses questioned whether they could have done something different to change the outcome.

Drake had lost sleep wrestling "what if" thoughts about the drug-overdosed mother. He knew he'd done nothing that rose to the level of malpractice, but could he have somehow done something different? Something that would have changed things? Might she have—

Drake slapped his hand on the dashboard. Enough! The questions were unanswerable.

Along with Kip's expertise, Drake needed the medical examiner's brutal honesty and lack of sympathy. Nothing like a dose of arrogant hardass to reality check self-pity and doubts. He opened the car door.

***

Drake's footsteps echoed down the terrazzo floor hallway. As he pushed open the reinforced door into the autopsy theater, he was met by the sickly smell of formalin and the reverberating notes of Alice Cooper's "Schools Out."

Bodies lay on all four of the stainless-steel exam tables. Three were in zippered body bags, and the wire-thin body and shock of salt-and-pepper hair of Kip was bent over the fourth. The corpse looked to be that of a young, white, adult female. Kip, in scrubs, gloves, and mask, peered through his wireless glasses into the open chest and abdomen with scalpel in hand.

The faint stink of putrefaction and death tinged the formalin fog, and the air was chilled. Dangling off the corpse's great toe hung a tag. Her personhood was gone and now she was just one of many bodies requiring markers to track inventory. Drake stopped some distance from Kip and waved his arms.

He'd approached closer or called out on other occasions, and Kip's startled reaction had started things in a bad way.

Kip sensed the motion and straightened. He flipped the scalpel onto the metal tray, the clink just audible over the music. He reached over and the music ceased with a dying echo.

"ER guy in the middle of the day?" Kip said. "I expected you much later. Your timing is bad. I'm trying to get cranking on my," he flipped the hand towards the occupied exam tables, "assembly line of overdose deaths."

"I got over here as soon as I could, Kip. I really need your help."

"Yeah, you hit me up with the 'help me or my career is over' line. Your CEO is trying for a land-speed record in settling a malpractice suit." He cackled.

"I don't see the humor in it. It's my career." Drake said. "I wanted to talk to you in person because there are a couple of other problems where you could be a big help."

"Really?" He frowned. "Are you for real? I say I'll help you with one thing, and you show up with a new job description for me? I don't need more work. I'm getting slammed here. I got bodies rolling in like UPS deliveries at Christmas time."

"I appreciate—"

"And you know what else? The 'chief' medical examiner's not around. Left on vacation right after being reappointed. How messed up is that?" Kip's face flushed, his old resentment flaring. "The opioid-death tidal wave you and your prescription-happy colleagues helped start is flooding every morgue in the country."

Kip had a point. Too many docs had written too many prescriptions for too many narcotics. Drake felt comfortable that his prescribing habits had been appropriate. The complaints that drug-seeking patients filled out on him were testimony to his care. They wanted a prescription for drugs, not a referral for addiction treatment.

"I sympathize with too much work and too little time," Drake said, "but I'm not here asking you to wash my car. What I need is your unique brain and specialized knowledge. I'm looking for the kind of help that only you are capable of providing." Shoveling praise Kip's way always helped, and Drake's words were true

"You're brighter than most, ER."

"The overdose explosion is one of the things I need to talk to you about."

"You already sent your detective bozos here. I taught them all they're capable of understanding about opioids. What else do you want? I'm already doing all the heavy lifting around here."

"You're the best," Drake said.

"So how is it that I'm not chief? I'm sick of doing the majority of the work, being the best, and being stuck as *assistant* medical examiner. It's humiliating."

Drake took a deep breath.

"Kip, I'm in the deepest trouble ever, and I don't have time to kiss your ass. Consider what I have to say if you're serious about getting the chief position." Kip shrugged. "You're a messed-up, petty grouch who treats people so bad you turn off even the few folks who can see past all your obnoxious bullshit to recognize that you're really, truly a genius."

Kip raised his eyebrows. "Jesus, ER. A hell of a run-on sentence. Take a breath once in a while when you're gutting me."

"Sorry, but I have more. When you talk to police, administrators, and the media, you're inappropriate. It's like you're a cheerleader for death. I know it's because you're passionate about the puzzles and the science, but you can't make it seem that you like death. It weirds people out. Do you understand?"

"Screw worrying about weirding people out," Kip said. "People have been trying to mess with me since I was a kid." He looked at Drake with a defiance that was as much a part of him as his bones.

Drake could only imagine how others must've picked on the scrawny, brilliant, and strange child.

"The delusion, no, the conceit," Kip said, "is that you and the others believe that everyone needs the validation of the rest of the herd. Newsflash, ER guy—total crap. I genuinely couldn't give a rat's ass what anyone thinks about me. That's their issue."

"Okay, consider this. Why is it you want to be chief? It's a political appointment. Being made chief is based, in part, on what non-medical people think about you. If you don't care what anyone thinks, then you should recognize a political appointment is not for you." Drake paused. "The police and I appreciate you. We need your knowledge, skills, and genius. No one but you cares if you're chief."

"Interesting angle, ER guy," Kip said. "But don't assume I'm all buddy-buddy with the police. I'm not for the prosecution or the defense. I'm about the truth."

"I assume nothing when it comes to you," Drake said. "I want to continue as an ER physician. I don't want to have a wrongful death settlement or malpractice conviction against me. I also need you to help me and the police put away the assholes that are getting rich selling the drugs that are killing people."

Drake indicated the corpses on the exam tables. "This is truth."

Kip looked to be listening.

"In addition, there's been a rash of mysterious deaths at Memorial Hospital that have been judged as malpractice. Millions of dollars in verdicts and settlements have been assessed. I was assigned responsibility to investigate, and something about these cases feels wrong, but I can't figure it out."

"Mysterious deaths and things you can't figure out? We've been down that road before," Kip said. "Speaking of mysterious, check this out."

He moved to one of the zippered body bags. "One of the strangest findings we see. Opioid overdose patients develop pulmonary edema. Their lungs typically weigh two or three times normal, due to the fluid that floods them. Have you heard of a *foam cone*?" He reached for the zipper. "Fluid keeps bubbling out of overdose patients' nose and mouth for as much as twenty-four hours after they die. This kid died of an OD last night, so he should have a good one." He pulled the zipper down.

Bryce's face and head came into view. The blue color and slack flesh contrasted with a glistening mound of white foam like that of a bubble bath centered over his nose and mouth. A high-pitched wail sounded inside Drake's head as small bubbles formed and burst in the high intensity beam of the autopsy table light.

"No one has come up with an explanation for the fluid," Kip said. "One of the funkiest postmortem findings ever. Seeing the new bubbles form this long after death would almost freak me out, if that was possible. It is cool. Thought you'd want to check it out."

The shrieking in Drake's head died as the grisly tableau rotated in his view. Feelings were beyond him. Somehow he nodded.

Part of his mind jammed the horrific image into a lead-lined box that was never to be opened again. He faced away.

"Kip, if you'll help me, I'll try to repay you somehow," Drake said. "Those selling drugs are killing people—just as sure as if they're pulling a trigger or exploding a bomb. We need to shut them down."

"Damn, dude. I don't need any 'save the world' sales pitch," Kip said. "You had me at mysterious deaths. I'm in."

Chapter 48

Clara swiveled her office chair to face one of her three computer displays. She accessed the most recent reports on ICU patient Dr. Bart Rainey. The image of him seizing on the floor of the ER flashed in her mind. She'd made the jerk pay.

Lab results flashed on the screen.

Two different reports identifying strychnine now appeared where there'd been nothing entered only twenty minutes ago.

The urine screen took less than a half hour, while the GC-mass spectrometer result had a turnaround time of at least two hours. The entry of both at the same time meant at least one report had been held back. For how long and why?

Why had the test results been held back?

There could only be one reason.

Strychnine had been anticipated beforehand, and they'd arranged for the report to be kept hidden if their suspicion was confirmed. Her throat tightened.

They must have known early and were lying in wait hoping to catch her. How had they reacted so quickly?

The call she'd made earlier on her untraceable burner phone showed her instincts and timing were good. She'd got the ball rolling on collecting her final payment early. The pressure was growing.

She turned to the second display screen and pulled up the security video files. She accessed the hallway leading to the male physician locker room and went back to one hour after the surgeon began seizing. Keying the digital advance, she fast-forwarded through the hours, scanning. Wait! She stopped and reversed the feed.

She checked the time: 10:30 p.m. last night. Dr. Drake Cody was leading an Asian-looking guy to the male physician's locker room. It took a second but she recalled. It was the detective who'd been in the papers when a guy had been shot by the police in front of the hospital a few months back.

How had they known to look in the locker so soon? *Not good!*

Wait. Deep breath. Think.

It would make sense to check his belongings once they knew he'd been poisoned. They must have confirmed the strychnine no later than last evening. How could it have been so quick? She swallowed hard.

Her breath came fast and she gripped the stethoscope. So close to realizing her dream and— *Stop! Calm down, Clara!*

There was no reason to lose her cool. She'd anticipated these possibilities, though she'd underestimated the speed of police involvement.

No, there was something she hadn't anticipated. Why was Drake Cody with the police? Why was he the one bringing the detective to Bart's locker last night?

Bart Rainey was no longer an ER patient. Drake Cody shouldn't have still been involved. Was he trying to play detective?

Damn him! He'd been the one to figure out the strychnine so soon. He'd have been able to have the lab result held back. No way could the police have come up with that on their own.

Drake Cody had been responsible for the death of the only man who'd ever loved her. And now he threatened her dream.

The scheme she'd put into play would make him lose what he loved the most—but it would take time. Meanwhile, he was sticking his nose where it didn't belong.

Drake Cody's reporting of Dan for domestic abuse had ended with her watching the only person who'd ever loved her die of a gunshot wound. Drake Cody's self-righteous falsehood had killed Dan as sure as if he'd pulled the trigger. He would not take anything more from her.

He needed to be stopped.

***

After receiving multiple reports of ODs on his dark web account, Q recognized they involved the distributors he and Smurf had delivered to the day before.

The rush of his all-time best money-making day crashed and burned.

He looked at his lab and its new, high-quality equipment. Had he, the self-taught superstar chemist, screwed up?

The ODs and deaths proved something must have gone wrong.

He felt like he'd been kneed in the balls. *Son of a bitch!*

He'd used the same diluted carfentanil formula and procedure several times, resulting in product that rocked but was manageable. Overdose deaths happened. If you never had any, it meant your product was lame. But the number of reports he'd received today suggested something major was going down.

What the hell had happened?

He began a step-by-step hunt for any error as he checked his measurements and procedures.

After more than thirty minutes, his brow was sweaty and he was ready to blow up. He'd checked everything. He had no explanation. *Son of a bitch!*

The weights and volumes of the raw carfentanil and fluid he worked with were minuscule. His procedure involved using a needle-thin lab spoon to transfer granules of drug powder into a beaker perched on a micro-balance. He added drug until it reached the weight his proven "recipe" called for. Next, he would add the recipe-determined amount of liquid, creating the safer and easier-to-handle diluted carfentanil solution he used to "dope" the powder and pills.

Again, he went through each step in his mind and once more felt certain he'd done nothing different. Nothing had changed— *Wait!*

He'd used a new beaker.

He'd bought the new beakers from the same manufacturer as the old one. He'd ordered the same size and model number. They looked identical.

He placed the now dry and empty older beaker on the microbalance and wrote down the precise weight. He squinted through his sweat-fogged protective glasses as he put the new beaker on the scale and checked the weight. What? *Bastards!*

The beakers were not identical. Their weight differed by just under a milligram. The amount would have been insignificant if it involved anything other than the most potent opioid drug on the planet.

This had to be it—the mistake. It was an equipment issue.

He did the calculation. To bring it up to the weight with the old beaker, he'd added almost fifty percent more carfentanil than previous runs—only a few grains different. The carfentanil solution was fifty percent more potent. Every pill and all the powder he'd made with the solution was half-again more powerful than any product he'd previously sold. And yesterday he and Smurf had delivered more product than ever before.

Heaviness draped him. Everything seemed to be crashing down. The combination of the mistake, the deaths, police attention, and the ER doctor and beautiful Tina's "the sky is falling" messages could crush his booming business.

Son of a bitch!

In a funk he got up, opened the door, stripped off and tossed his protective gear, then went down the stairs.

***

Q stared at the four fat lines of the cocaine he'd laid out on a mirror on the oak coffee table.

Usually he self-administered his drugs in measured doses, aiming for productivity and a good buzz. This blast was an attempt to chemically dynamite himself out of a soul-sucking funk. He snorted each of the lines through a rolled one-hundred-dollar bill.

The cocaine exploded in his head. He sat back with his eyes closed as the drug pulsed through him. His energy surged, but where was the head rush?

The buzzkill of failure was holding him down.

He'd worked so hard, been so smart, and things had been going so well. Now, one mistake, and his business would be set back hard. He rested his head on his hands.

He laid out two more lines of coke and snorted them. Again, he sat back with eyes closed.

His head was a hot-air balloon rising. Flashing lights appeared behind his closed lids. He opened his eyes, sniffed, and rubbed his nose.

His wasn't the first business to have something go bad. He'd read about a US chemical-manufacturing plant in India that had messed up and killed thousands. That company was still around. Hey, shit happens. Good businessmen didn't panic. He just needed to power forward and deal with the setback.

It was time to get back to work. His strength and wounded scientist pride were rebounding with the cocaine.

He went back up the stairs, unlocked the door to his laboratory, put on his protective gear, and opened his laptop.

Usually as he accessed his server, he was excited in anticipation of new orders. This time he was braced for more bad news. He connected.

What? His mouth went dry.

Dozens of messages were queued up.

It looked even worse than he'd feared.

He clicked open the first message. "Double my last buy of Oxys and packets. That which does not kill you makes you higher. Ha ha. Sales are flying."

Then the next. "Wicked stuff. Repeat my last order. Ready to take delivery right now."

And one more. "Killer stuff, dude. For real. I'll take all you can give me up to three times yesterday's delivery."

The euphoria the coke had failed to produce flooded in. He laughed.

Most of the other messages were similar.

News had spread fast in the user community. His business was not trashed. His products were what users were clamoring for. He pumped his fist. *Hell yes!*

Cocaine and his rocketing business prospects had him flying.

Chapter 49

The group text to the homicide squad read "10-79, female, drug paraphernalia, 1189 Grimley Ave N."

Farley had just pulled away from the hospital. The 10-79 "medical examiner notified" call was no more than fifteen minutes from him—another overdose death crime scene.

He texted back that he'd respond.

The number of incoming overdose deaths had tossed the normal homicide case distribution system out the window. For now, the team was going with the group-wide text notifications and allowing whoever was available to take it.

Some of the veterans were grumbling that the district attorney would be unlikely to prosecute the overdose cases they were working up. Even if a link to a particular supplier could be proved—which was rare—getting a conviction was tough. There weren't enough detectives to process every fatal OD as a prosecutable homicide. Something had to give.

This call sounded like what the homicide veterans called a grounder—as in a routine play, no big deal. The neighborhood was bad—an area where many addicts and criminals lived. Farley expected he'd be able to handle it in short order and get clear to continue investigating the kid's OD death and the poisoning of the doctor.

He turned left on Seventh Street and continued toward the Target Center. He took a right and rolled along a stretch where many of the Cities' poorest hung out. Sharing and Caring Hands and other charities for the homeless were here.

Hennepin Avenue and downtown were nearby, as was the main library, cheap liquor sales, the bus station, and the river bank, where some used the woods and bridge underpasses to drink and be left alone.

Earlier, Farley had reached out to the Minneapolis narcotics squad and the DEA. The stylized glyph on the drug packets that had killed Drake Cody's young patient was known to both teams. They called the supplier "Music Man" because the symbol marking his product looked like a musical note inside a circle. They reported the Music Man product had become widely distributed in the metro and in several outstate regions. It had been associated with previous overdose deaths but nothing like the recent numbers.

It was a good lead. All the agencies were eager to get the Music Man locked up, though they recognized that removing one source was like chopping off the head of a hydra. Others were always ready to step in and get rich selling addiction and misery. The synthetic opioids made everything even worse.

The narcotics squad and DEA suspected or knew who many of the drug suppliers were. The difficulty was doing anything meaningful about it. Nailing the street and low-level sellers did nothing—they were often back in business within a day. Convicting mid- or higher-level suppliers took a lot of time and resources and rarely happened.

Every area of law enforcement Farley had worked in had been like running on a hamster wheel. Those chasing the drug trade had it particularly hard. They saw endless ugliness, and the flow of drugs never stopped.

Farley could not work there. His memories were too raw.

He turned onto Olson Memorial Highway and passed a charter school and blocks of subsidized housing. This neighborhood was the site for the majority of police calls in the city, and its residents were disproportionately the victims of crime, drugs, and violence.

He turned right, then, half a block down, parked on the street behind a lone squad car.

The small apartment complex was run down, the pavement cracked and worn. What had been lawn was dirt and mud. There was a stripped bicycle chained to a parking rack. Farley entered the building into a dingy hallway. A uniformed officer stood beside an open apartment door.

"Farley, Homicide," he said, nodding to the officer. "What have we got?"

"It was a 911 call-in. Woman found down." He nodded toward the inside of the apartment. "I haven't touched anything. The paramedics were here but had to leave on another call. The woman is down and seriously dead. On the couch with a needle beside her. Record screen shows prostitution, drugs, and petty crimes history." He shrugged. "Looks like Darwin's theory at work. Cleaning up the gene pool."

Before Farley could think, he had the officer slammed against the wall. The uniform's face was twisted, fear flashed in his eyes.

Farley stopped himself, recognizing that he'd messed up. He shook his head, releasing the officer.

"I-I'm sorry." He attempted to straighten the officer's shirt and vest. "I lost it."

"What the hell, fat boy? No shit you lost it," the officer said puffing out his chest as if trying to erase his earlier reaction.

"I'm sorry," Farley said, though he wasn't. "I'm on a bad stretch. No sleep."

The officer shook his head. He adjusted his vest and gave Farley a hard-guy stare as if he might do something physical. "I'll let it go."

"Thanks," Farley said, letting the guy be alpha.

The job jacked almost everybody up. Everybody had to be a badass. Once more, he wondered if he really fit in homicide. Heck, if he fit in law enforcement at all.

"Did you call for a tech?" Farley asked.

"Yeah, I called for a crime scene investigator. I did my job."

Farley recognized the guy was still trying to get his pride back. Farley didn't play the tough guy game. Memories had flashed and he'd grabbed the guy before he could think.

"Maybe I need to go to decaf," Farley said.

"Yeah, right," the officer said, cutting him no slack. "Why don't you check the scene so when the tech gets here, we can wrap this up. It's not going to take Sherlock Holmes to figure out what went down. A junkie is dead. Case closed."

Farley gave up on the guy and stepped into the apartment. The body of the fortyish-looking black woman wearing sweat pants and a tank top was slumped sideways on the couch with glazed eyes open and tongue extended. Her skin looked grayish blue.

One arm hung draped to the floor, with a needle and syringe on the carpet below outstretched fingers.

He thought of Drake Cody's young patient from last evening. The bodies shared the blue-tinged, sprawled lifelessness. But this woman was gaunt and worn, and her arms showed needle tracks. The boy had been a first-time experimenter, whereas this woman looked to have long been in the grips of addiction. Had she tried to get free? How many times had she failed?

Farley knew the cost of those failed battles.

He spied something on the arm of the couch—two small empty plastic packets. He looked closer and made out the circled symbol on each of them. This woman was another victim of the Music Man, as had been the boy Drake Cody knew.

Heat flushed through Farley. Violent thoughts gripped him.

This wasn't Darwin at work—it was exploitation. Greed-stoked predators were preying on the vulnerable.

Chapter 50

Q smiled as he loaded product into tiny glyph-marked plastic bags. His Prince-like trademark glyph really meant something now. Brand recognition. Every one of his packets of powder or counterfeit Oxys would go for top dollar.

His protective glasses were fogged as they had been earlier, but now it was from working under the lights rather than from freaking out trying to find the screw-up he thought might ruin him.

The error had turned out to be good luck.

It was not what he'd expected after the ODs and deaths. He'd checked out some stuff online and found it was not a new phenomenon. In Detroit a few years earlier, a bunch of hardcore users had ODed and died. The law and TV had got the word out to warn users about where the involved drugs had been sold. Within an hour, those street corners had been swarmed with users and wannabe buyers hounding for the killer-strength smack.

Q grinned. Supply and demand. He loved the world of business. A mistake he'd feared would crush him had boosted demand so much that everything he could produce would sell at a premium. There was something about working hard that he really liked. When he was young, his momma had said that work was happiness. It hadn't made sense to him then.

It did now. When you were your own boss and you made crazy money, work kicked ass.

Once he'd figured out the mistake, it had been easy to dilute the too-potent carfentanil solution and crank out more product. Stoked on the cocaine, he'd laid out his production challenge like one of those math word problems from school.

If a businessman has ten milliliters of carfentanil solution that is fifty percent stronger than desired, how many milliliters of additional solution must be added to create a solution of the desired strength? How many milliliters of the final solution will the business have in the end?

The calculation was simple, and he ended up with enough solution for fifty percent more product, which meant sick amounts of cash just as fast as he could make delivery.

He had Prince cranking and he did a little dance move to a riff—"*This is what it sounds like when doves cry...*" Q already had prepared double the record amount of product he and Smurf had delivered the day before. And he'd negotiated higher prices.

His sales were increasing in what his online business coursework called exponential growth phase. He felt so good he thought about another line or two of cocaine, but he knew better. Too much will mess you up. He'd been blasting for over twenty-four hours.

He heard his phone and felt it vibrate. Almost no one had his cell phone number and he never got calls. Had he given it to anyone other than his lawyer?

He set down his instruments, stepped to the clean area, stripped off his gloves, and retrieved the phone. He did not recognize the number. He hit answer and held it to his ear saying nothing. There was a long pause. "H-hello? Mr. Q?"

What the hell?

"Smurf. What you doing calling me? I was just going to call your mom and see if you could help me deliver some gifts this evening."

"Momma not wake up." Her voice broke and her breath hiccupped. "I scared."

Damn. Q figured in an instant what had happened. Smurf's momma was hardcore. She always pushed it to the limit.

"She on the couch." Smurf sniffed. "She cold. Not move." She sobbed. "A needle in her arm."

"The worn-out whore had finally pushed it too far. "Where are you now, Smurf?"

"I at the Quick Treat."

"Did you tell anyone?"

"I called the 911. I run. I in trouble?"

"No, Smurf. You did good." Lucky that she'd got out of there. His thoughts were flying. "I'm going to help you. Wait for me there."

Her crying sounded over the phone. "Hurry."

Hell yes, he'd hurry. The kid didn't understand anything. Oh, man. What if—?

"Stop crying. If you cry, you'll get in trouble. Don't say anything to anyone. I'll be there soon. It will be okay."

"No." Her voice hitched. "Momma not be okay."

***

Farley examined the rest of the one-bedroom apartment and took pictures. A death investigator would come from the ME office, so he didn't need to document much. The ME and morgue had to be as swamped as his department.

The apartment's tiny kitchen was spotless, the sink scrubbed, and dish towels hung neatly. The remainder of the apartment had the same unexpected tidiness. Not the typical housework habits of an addict. Some drug users were able to function for a long while. His brother Ronnie had been like that at first, until addiction claimed more and more of who he was.

Ronnie had been nine years older. He'd been a star but never too cool to let his chubby little brother hang around. Good in school, popular, and a good enough high school linebacker that he earned a scholarship from the University of Minnesota.

A knee injury and surgery before his first season introduced him to pain pills.

From day one, whatever the narcotics gave him was something he couldn't be without. He made it through two years of college football and a second surgery with few people being aware of his addiction. Then he'd spiraled downward. It was not the rapid transition from first use to hardcore that many believed was typical. His reality was like that of so many others. His destruction had taken years.

For Farley, the family crises, progressive decline, and repeated stays in treatment centers for his brother were part of growing up.

All happiness bled out of his parents, and Farley grew up worrying every day about his brother. Addiction tormented them all.

At the age of twenty-nine, Ronnie was found cold and dead in a drug house off Lake Street. He'd been at rock bottom for some time before that.

The dead woman's apartment was too clean. Was there a roommate?

"Lord have mercy!" Farley spun to find a tiny, gray-haired, bespectacled black woman standing at the apartment's open door with her hand to her mouth.

Farley moved to put his bulk between her and the body.

"I'm sorry you saw this." Where had the uniform gone? "Are you a neighbor?"

"Are you police?" she asked.

"Yes ma'am. Detective Farley."

"I live in the next apartment. I was just going out."

The uniform must have moved to the building's front door.

"What happened?" She looked distraught.

Up close, Farley could see the woman was quite elderly. She was neatly dressed and carried a purse like his mother had owned twenty years earlier. The word that came to his mind was spry.

"Did you know her? Do you know if she had any visitors? Did you hear anything earlier today?"

The woman looked past Farley to the body.

"Poor child. She was lost. Now she's with Jesus." Her eyes were magnified by the thick lenses of her glasses as she blinked and shook her head. "So sad. I didn't know her but to say hello. She was in and out at all hours. I didn't hear anything today, but I was watching my programs."

"Do you know about friends or visitors?"

The woman raised a hand to her cheek, still staring as she answered. "She had people come but I don't know as they were friends. I think most were lost like her. The ones that shoot the junk. And there were also men visitors." She looked down. "I don't know that you'd call them friends."

She looked around the apartment as if she'd misplaced something. "Is her baby all right?"

"Baby?" *Oh, no!*

"Her child. Not a baby. Her sweet girl. Sometime here and sometimes with the child protection. I did see her the other day."

"How old is the daughter?" *Old enough to call 911?*

"Maybe sixteen or seventeen. She one of those who's always young. Her name is Tonya."

"Always young?"

"She has the Down syndrome. We need to find out where she is."

Farley pulled out his phone, ready to call it in. There could be a vulnerable, very scared girl out there somewhere. He put a hand on the shoulder of the distinguished lady and stepped with her into the hall. He closed the door.

"You last saw Tonya when?"

The woman's wrinkled face wrinkled further. "Hmm, oh my Lord, I feel foolish. It was yesterday." The old woman brightened. "And there is a friend. Or might be a relative. I saw a man drop her off."

"Can you describe him? Why do you think he was family?"

"He's nice to her. Made her laugh. She liked him. I thought he might be Child Protection at first."

"Can you describe him?"

"A tall, handsome, black man and dressed real nice." She gave a small smile.

"You don't know a name?"

"No. He drove a fancy car. That's how I know he wasn't Child Protection."

"Do you know what kind of car?"

"I'm not good with cars. One of the really big ones."

"Did he go inside?"

"Just for a minute. He wasn't like the other men who visited Tonya's momma."

"Thank you, Ma'am. I may need to talk with you later. Here's my card. If you think of anything that might help or you see Tonya, please call. Can I get your name and phone number?"

He wrote them down.

"I'm sorry you had to see this."

"It was the junk, wasn't it?" Her magnified watery eyes stared at him.

"It looks that way."

She sighed. "Lord Jesus help them." She walked out of the building.

He opened the door to the apartment and once more looked at the body. The coroner's van should be arriving soon.

This woman was another victim of the Music Man and his drugs. Minneapolis narcotics had identified him as a middle- or upper-level supplier distributor. How many had he killed so far?

Many, like the uniform cop, dehumanized addicts. They saw the ugly behavior of those addicted and it triggered anger. Because the drugs led good people to abuse and victimize others, sympathy became elusive. But Farley knew every addict was a brother, sister, daughter, or son. Opioids stole their humanity—and their lives.

Farley was going to take down the Music Man. He would see justice done.

Chapter 51

Stuart Kline admired himself in the full-length mirror as the tailor pinned the suit pants to be altered.

Dan Ogren had used this clothing store. Celebrities, professional athletes, and the very wealthiest men in the Twin Cities frequented this most exclusive of clothiers.

Stuart believed that if clothes didn't make the man, they sure as hell didn't hurt. Thinking of Dan Ogren was still like something out of a movie. Dan Ogren had been a super stud, sat on the hospital board, and was fat-cat rich. When his wife shot him and he subsequently died in Memorial Hospital's ICU, the Twin Cities had a story as wild as anything in New York, Chicago, or LA.

Stuart missed the guy, even though Dan had treated him like crap. Once in the country club locker room, Dan had tossed his underwear at Stuart and said, "Here you go, queer bait. I bet you'd like to sniff these."

Dan had been the kind of man Stuart wanted to be. Despite the abuse, Stuart had liked being around him, hoping the cool would rub off and Dan would help him get rich.

Getting big-time crazy, stupid, filthy rich had been Stuart's aim forever.

He'd come pretty close. He'd used his smarts and pharmaceutical industry contacts to try to convert Drake Cody's breakthrough drug into serious money for himself, but the ER doctor, his lawyer, and others had blocked Stuart's scheme.

The CEO position paid what most people would think was huge money. He made much more than most of the doctors, but his aim was much higher.

The pharmaceutical deal he'd tried to pull off was long gone, but now another big money opportunity had presented itself.

The money in malpractice didn't match the pharmaceutical trough, but it was significant. The big dollars and backroom possibilities of malpractice negotiations cried for the skills of a fixer and facilitator such as himself.

"How does that look to you, sir?" the gray-haired tailor said, indicating the pant-length.

"Come on, man. Are you serious? Another quarter inch lower, at least," Stuart said. "And I want this ready by Thursday. Make sure you have it done."

The tailor turned and moved to the counter.

The old man was pretty uppity for just being a damn tailor. Stuart stepped off the fitting stand. He'd bought several suits, sport coats, and other clothes here and didn't feel he was treated with the respect he deserved.

"Bill me for this and make sure it's pressed. I'll have someone come by before Thursday—"

Stuart's cell phone sounded. He reached into his suit jacket where it hung next to the mirror.

"Stuart Kline, CEO."

"This is Marcy, I have public affairs on the line. They have a reporter from the Minneapolis Star-Tribune on hold. The reporter is looking for a comment on a story they're planning to run. The public affairs person said the story focuses on malpractice. He thought you'd want to handle it. Do you want me to transfer the call to you?"

Jesus Lord. More fallout due to inept doctors and nurses. What next?

"Yes. Do it." He swallowed. Malpractice. What the hell was he going to say? What could he say? A couple of clicks sounded.

"Hello? Are we connected?"

It sounded like a young woman.

"Yes, this is Stuart Kline, Chief Executive Officer of Memorial Hospital. Who am I speaking with?"

"This is Phoenix Halvorson with the Minneapolis StarTribune. I...uh...wanted to give you the opportunity to respond to...information our research has found involving the hospital."

She sounded nervous.

"What information are you referring to? We at Memorial have a good relationship with the media and your fine paper in particular." He thought the paper was a left-wing rag with the class of the National Enquirer.

"Our source has identified that your hospital has had a rash of poor patient outcomes and deaths. Reports we received say there have been a number of malpractice verdicts and settlements, including wrongful death. Would you like to respond?"

Oh no! I knew the shit would hit the fan.

"Thank you for the call, but I'm not at liberty to discuss any specifics related to our patients. I'm sure you understand HIPPA and patient protection law. I can tell you that unfortunately, all hospitals do at times experience bad outcomes. I would note that Memorial Hospital is known for its excellence in patient care."

"Are you denying the reports?"

"I'm not addressing any specifics. I'm just sharing the truth, which is that Memorial Hospital is committed to the best care possible for all our patients."

"I see. I wanted to give you the chance to deny the reports. Your lack of denial is noted. That leads me to other specifics." Her voice had grown in confidence. "It's been reported that the bad outcomes and wrongful death cases at your hospital involve people of color at a rate much higher than the city's demographics would predict."

"Demographics? What?" *Where is this going?*

"The percentage of people of color in the Twin Cities is eighteen percent. Our source says that almost fifty percent of the patients who have had bad outcomes at your hospital are minority persons. Additionally, we've learned that there is a pending wrongful death action involving another person of color, which would make the percentage of wrongful deaths even more racially skewed. I'm seeking the facts. Why does Memorial Hospital have a program of care where minority persons are nearly three times as likely as whites to die from malpractice?"

Racially skewed? What? Oh no! This reporter was going to throw gas on a public relations fire that could burn the hospital to the ground.

" I, uh, er, certainly not. I categorically deny—"

"Several studies have identified racial disparities in national health and healthcare outcomes, Mr. Kline. Is this a reality in your hospital?"

She didn't sound at all nervous anymore.

"Phoenix...it's Phoenix, correct?"

"Yes, Phoenix Halvorson."

"Phoenix, there are no racial disparities in healthcare at Memorial Hospital. We provide the best possible care to all our patients. Our charitable care and uncollectible fees exceed forty percent. We do more than our share."

"Let me make sure I understand you." Now she sounded like a seasoned veteran. "Are you saying charitable care and uncollectible services are evidence of lack of bias? Do you have data showing that people of color are the source of your charity and uncollectible? That sounds like a bigoted assumption. Do you have any further comments on Memorial Hospital's racial disparities in outcomes and collections?"

Shit! This little wench was twisting everything he said. The more he spoke, the worse it got.

"Miss Halvorson—"

"It's *Ms.* Halvorson."

"Excuse me, Ms. Halvorson. Let me say for the record that Memorial Hospital is committed to its founding statement, which is excellence in patient care for all and contribution to the community foremost. I believe that the information you received is misguided. I recommend you discuss it with your editorial and legal staff. Is there anything else?"

His only hope was the paper's legal staff would put the brakes on her story to avoid a slander charge.

"I think you've said enough," she said. "Thank you for your time, Mr. Kline."

Damn. She was pleased with herself. Little Miss 60 Minutes had tied him in knots.

She was going to hang Memorial Hospital out to dry.

***

Jim Torrins hung up his office phone. It was the third hospital board member he been able to speak with, and each time he'd received the same troubling response.

The hospital's financial and malpractice crisis had the board members listening to Kline's outrageous recommendation. It looked as if they wouldn't stop him from immediately settling the wrongful death suit. *Craziness!*

His phone rang. Hopefully a call back from one of the board members reporting reason had returned.

"Hello, Jim Torrins, Medical Affairs."

"Torrins, this is CEO Kline. I just—"

"Stuart, I'm aware you're the CEO. When you introduce yourself as 'CEO Kline' to the people you work with, it makes you sound like a boob."

His new strategy with Kline would be bulldozer blunt.

"Whatever, Torrins. I just got off the phone with a Star Tribune reporter. They're looking to break a story tomorrow about the epidemic of malpractice at Memorial Hospital. That's your doctors and nurses, Torrins. They're also claiming racism. Are you aware that the percentage of minorities in the Twin Cities is eighteen percent, but almost half of the Memorial patients that had bad outcomes are people of color? How do you explain that?"

"Forty-eight percent of the patients who visit our emergency room are minorities," Torrins said, "which I know only because the government mandates we track it. We are the safety net caregivers for the inner city and disadvantaged. It influences our patient mix."

"Well, er, I wish I'd known that, but it doesn't matter. It sounds racist."

"I hope they're responsible enough not to print that," Jim said. "Who's the reporter?"

"It was a woman, sounded young. Name was Phoenix Halvorson."

"I know who does their health care reporting, Kline. I've never heard that name. Are you sure this call was real?"

"Yes. It came through public affairs. I think I responded pretty well, but face it, Torrins, this is all because of your inept doctors and nurses. It definitely supports settling Clete Venjer's newest claim ASAP. The reporter already knew of it. She called it 'the pending case' and it fits her narrative—another black person dead with a claim of malpractice. We need to make it disappear as fast as possible—whatever it costs."

"She knew about the case?" Torrins said. "That's surprising. Most personal injury and malpractice lawyers will try and use the media to their advantage. They can lay out their accusations and broadcast a slant without resistance. It's irresponsible reporting but the media loves it. But I can't see Clete Venjer stooping that low. He's got too much integrity for that."

"Whatever, Torrins. Somehow she knows," Kline said. "Get me those numbers on minority percentages and bad outcomes straightaway. If they turn this into a race thing on top of malpractice, it will destroy us."

"Public Affairs can give you the numbers, Kline. I'm president of medical affairs, not your errand boy. You might try to learn something about our patients and their care. You've got your head buried so deep into balance sheets and marketing schemes that you don't have any idea what this hospital is about."

"It better be about making money and stopping malpractice suits or it will be out of business," Kline said.

"Settling this case would be a grave mistake. I'll fight it all the way," Torrins said. "I'm advising the nurse and doctors involved to do the same."

Advise whatever you choose," Kline said. "The Board will support me."

Torrins hung up.

It looked like the hospital board was going to place their bet with the CEO.

Insanity.

Chapter 52

Clete Venjer spotted a loon on the lake as he walked the hiking path. Ice still covered the lakes in northern Minnesota and Canada. Loons followed the open water in their migratory return. They sometimes stayed on Lake Harriet for a week or two before heading for their northern sanctuaries.

Clete tried to get exercise every day, and walking or riding his bike around the city lakes provided physical and mental respite. Today in particular he needed it.

The earlier sunshine had disappeared, replaced by dank, gray skies. The wet earth smell of post-thaw spring hung raw and heavy. He hadn't checked a forecast, but he sensed unsettled weather moving in.

The command he'd received this morning had confirmed his fear. His uneasiness and nagging suspicions had been too little, too late. How could he have been so blind?

His cell phone rang. "Blocked" showed on caller ID. He answered.

"This is Clete Venjer."

"Clete, this is Stuart Kline, CEO of Memorial Hospital." Clete inwardly recoiled. Kline gave off a bad vibe. Of all the people involved in the deposition the other morning, it was only the CEO who had triggered Clete's distaste. "I wondered if we could discuss some business?"

"Of course, CEO Kline."

"Please call me Stuart."

"Okay, Stuart." He hoped this call was not what his instincts told him it was—what he'd known would be coming.

"Others may not recognize it, but I see us as having mutual interests," Kline said. "Our objectives are aligned."

Clete had no doubt that Kline's interests went no further than himself.

"I'm not sure I understand," Clete said. Unfortunately, he understood completely.

"You're looking out for the financial well-being of your client, who is seeking redress for a tragic loss," Kline said. "I'm looking out for the financial well-being of Memorial Hospital and its ability to continue to provide care for members of the community."

"That's very well stated, Stuart," Clete said. Well stated for noxious, self-serving fiction.

"We're dealing with issues of significant financial consequence," the CEO said. "Understandably, the loss your client experienced and the operations of the hospital both involve considerable dollars. While our goals might appear to conflict, I'd like to suggest a solution."

Clete waited. Here it comes.

"What I'm suggesting, Clete, is that you and I informally facilitate a solution. There is potential for financial advantage all around."

"I'm not sure I understand, but it sounds good." Clete understood. He fought to keep the bile from rising to his throat.

"In looking out for the hospital and its ability to best serve the community, I can help settle differences and influence the dollars that the hospital can deliver. As CEO, I'm in a unique position to recognize the value and true benefit of a quick and just arrangement."

This was bolder and more direct than Clete had anticipated. *Does Kline know what I've done? Was he a part of it?*

The demand Clete had received earlier left him helpless and sick: *"Work for a large settlement and close it quickly—or else. Do not let ethics get in the way."*

"The value of human life and your hospital's service to the community are hard things to put a price tag on. I welcome your offer to work together." Clete's stomach turned.

"Excellent." Eagerness tinged the CEO's voice. "You and I can informally work out an arrangement where your client does very well, the hospital is able to help the community, and you and I are appropriately rewarded for making things work for everyone."

Clete had stepped down by the lake's edge. The odor of rotting fish rose. Looking down, he saw the coarse scales, white underbelly, and sucker lips of a huge, dead carp lying belly-up on the shore.

"No amount of money can make up for the loss of a life." This was the first thing Clete said that was not forced. "But I can communicate your offer to my client."

"Let's approach things this way," Kline said. "I text you two numbers. The first will be the total settlement. The second number is the facilitator fee that you can subsequently provide me via an, er, uh, informal route. I'll text from this phone and you can respond whether the totals are agreeable. If you feel the need to suggest other totals, you can return text me. Does that sound like a reasonable approach?"

Reasonable for an illegal, unethical, kickback. "That's sounds good, Stuart. It could work out the best for all."

"I'll do some analysis and send you the numbers. Thank you." Excitement, no doubt stoked by greed, sounded in the CEO's voice.

Clete disconnected.

It was as if he'd been marinating in the water that lapped against the dead carp. He wanted to throw his phone in the lake and jump into a scalding hot shower.

Stuart Kline was rotten and his stink clung.

Clete had no choice but to act as if the man did not disgust him.

One mistake had cost him his integrity. He fought the urge to vomit.

Chapter 53

Drake slowed as he approached the hospital parking lot on Chicago Avenue. He turned into the lot, replaying his visit with the medical examiner.

Drake had played on the notion of helping out a friend, but in the end he believed Kip Dronen agreed to help due to his insatiable curiosity. Kip was fascinated by death—the more mysterious or unexpected the better. Regardless of Kip's motivation, having his help was like having a badass ally watching his back when he'd been targeted for a beat-down or worse behind the bars and barbed wire of the Furnace juvenile lockup.

Minutes earlier, Drake had called the mortgage banker and heard the same dismal report Rachelle had received. They were nowhere close to receiving mortgage approval. The rejection left him queasy. He couldn't imagine ever finding a more wonderful home.

He parked the car and tried to prioritize what he needed to do. He hoped to check in with Aki or Farley on the investigations into Bryce's death and Bart Rainey's attempted murder.

He needed to revisit medical records and try once more to make sense of the tragic hospital deaths, including the overdosed mother who had bled out. Was there a link he couldn't find?

It was also past time to check in with some of those close to him.

He keyed the phone in its dashboard holder.

"Call Rizz." He'd not talked to his paralyzed friend since before the malpractice deposition and other bad news.

"Michael Rizzini here. How can you help me?"

"Ha ha. I guess you have caller ID." Drake smiled. "How is therapy going?"

"I'm optimistic," Rizz said. Drake didn't know what to make of that answer. "But I want to hear what's happening with you. Last time we talked, Torrins and you had just been sentenced to duty on a malpractice crisis committee. Will my ER still have its doors open when I get back to showing you how to save lives?"

"A lot of bad stuff has happened since then."

"Tell me." His joking tone was gone.

"I can hardly keep track of it all," Drake said. "We're facing an explosion of drug overdoses and deaths. The paramedics are overwhelmed. Kip Dronen at the morgue has bodies being delivered like it's a war zone. I saw a young nephew of Patti's in the ER a few days ago. Last night he died from an overdose."

"I'd heard something about it on the radio, but it sounds even worse than that report. Brutal. Do you think synthetic opioids might be involved?"

"We proved it. Fentanyl and carfentanil are everywhere. The opioids are one issue." He paused. "I took care of Bart Rainey yesterday in the Crash Room. Someone poisoned him with strychnine. He went down while in the OR. I think he'll make it, but it's ugly. I'm trying to help the detectives with their investigation. It looks like it was probably someone in the hospital who tried to kill him."

"Unreal. Bart can be an asshole, but—"

"There's more. A complicated patient I admitted through the ER died in the ICU a couple of hours later. She'd overdosed and delivered a premature baby." Drake winced at the memory of the bloody ICU. "It was tragic. Julie Stone, Vijay Gupta, an ICU nurse, and I are being charged with causing her wrongful death."

"The malpractice courts act as if doctors are purposely trying to hurt their patients. Overdosed and a premature delivery? Anyone who knows anything would predict a bad outcome," Rizz said.

"Clete Venjer is the attorney who—"

"I know who he is. That guy is a courtroom assassin."

"Kline is looking to settle as fast as he can."

"No way! That's insane."

"He's worried about a gigantic award and the bad PR of a trial," Drake said.

"Kline would let an Aztec priest rip out his mother's heart if it put money in his pocket."

"You know the status of my license," Drake said. "A wrongful death verdict or settlement will give the state Medical Board no choice. My career will be over." He swallowed, his mouth dry. "I'd been holding out telling Rachelle as the bad news piled up. I just now let her know some of what is happening. She's devastated."

"Well no shit, of course she is." Rizz said.

Rachelle had loved Drake's wild friend even before what he'd sacrificed for them.

"There's more. We found a dream house on a lake and had an offer accepted. She was happier than I'd ever seen her. This morning the mortgage banker called her to report they'd reversed the mortgage approval. Kline had called the bank himself to inform them that my position with the hospital was not expected to be long term."

Rizz was silent, an uncommon event. He acted the tough guy, but underneath he felt other's pain.

"I'm sure you've called Lloyd. If you haven't, hang up and call now." He paused. "We have to fight this."

Rizz didn't sound confident, but his support made Drake feel better. Nothing had changed, but he felt less alone.

It reminded him that others were hurting. Jon was still seriously messed up physically and emotionally following his wife's murder. Julie Stone and ICU nurse Tracy were both reeling from the malpractice claim.

And he needed to reach out to Patti. Bryce's death had ripped Drake open—he couldn't imagine what it was like for her.

"I'm busting out of the Mayo this afternoon and headed back to my place," Rizz said.

"Don't be dumb. Continue your rehab," Drake said.

"No worries, amigo. I'm cleared for discharge and will continue as an outpatient at Kenny-Courage Rehab Center. Good timing as it's obvious you need me. Hell, I've spent most of the past four years getting your ass out of trouble."

"We've gotten through a lot of bad stuff together." Both in the emergency department and elsewhere, Rizz always came through for Drake. He never forgot for an instant that Rizz's paralysis had resulted from him taking a bullet fired at Drake and his family. "It'll be good to have you by my side, friend."

"My honor, brother."

"It's Rachelle getting knocked down again that worries me most," Drake said.

"I don't think I could have survived the stuff that has come her way. She has her demons, but that lady is about as tough as they come," Rizz said.

"You're right, Rizz," Drake said. "I just wish to God she didn't have to keep proving it."

Chapter 54

Rachelle pulled into the parking lot for the supermarket and liquor store on Central Avenue. Northeast Minneapolis was on the upswing, but pockets like this were much like the gritty, troubled areas of Cincinnati that had been too big a part of her youth. The low rent and nearness to the hospital had made it their choice.

The lake place was only miles away, but it seemed as if it was part of a different world.

As she parked the car, she noticed a thin white guy with stringy hair standing with a small basket of flowers at his feet. He was holding a bouquet and she saw him approach people as they made their way to the grocery or liquor store. She'd never seen him before, but something about him seemed familiar.

She'd called Kaye, saying they needed groceries and could she help? Kaye had driven over, picked them up and taken them to her house. She then allowed Rachelle to borrow her car. The groceries story was a lie. Rachelle just had to get out. She didn't want the kids to see her collapse, to see their mother struggling.

Now she sat in a borrowed car in a parking lot, trying not to break down.

Losing the house, followed by the rest of the bad news, had been too much.

His career was likely over. Their dream home gone. Even though it had never been theirs, in her heart she'd already moved in.

The malpractice charge against Drake made her nauseous. He pretended he could shake it off, but she knew better. Sometimes he was just so dumb. 'It'll be okay,' he'd said—as if it wasn't ripping him apart. As if it didn't mean the end of everything that he'd worked so hard for and sacrificed so much for.

No one could be more committed to taking care of the sick and injured than Drake. The ER was where he was meant to be.

Not that many hours earlier, she'd been ecstatic. Now she couldn't feel worse.

Drake had picked her up when she was down countless times. Now it was her turn to help him.

He needed her and she had to be strong but... *Oh Lord, help me!*

She wiped her eyes. So exhausted!

What she wanted was to make the fear go away—to eliminate the gnawing in her gut and silence the screams within her head. Maybe then she could do what needed to be done.

She'd flushed all of her medications.

After all the years and uncountable times she'd taken refuge with drugs, now she had none.

The opioids were the worst because they were the best. She'd stopped them long ago, even refusing them in the hospital for her burns and skin grafts.

Opioids had made her feel more "right" than at any time in her life. Shame, guilt, and remorse did not exist, and opioids took her to a place of such wondrous peace and contentment that she'd been drawn back again and again.

The job she'd got taking care of Drew and then meeting Drake had helped save her. She'd seen what the opioids did to others and recognized that she'd been falling prey as well.

She'd continued with other drugs, both illegal and prescribed, but steered clear of the opioids and their devastating appeal.

These last months she'd tested herself by keeping unopened the container of pills from the burn unit and then concluded the test with the chattering of the garbage disposal destroying them and all her other medications. No more drugs!

She would not become like her mother.

Was she strong enough, or was she still the burned, haunted little girl responsible for the death of her little brother and the mother who'd failed them? She wiped her eyes and grit her teeth. *I'll take it one moment at a time, one step at a time, one task at a time.*

She opened the car door, then stopped. Her purse sat on the seat. Inside she found the three twenty-dollar bills that she'd tucked there. She put the cash in her pocket and slipped the purse under the seat, then got out of the car.

She took a deep breath. She adjusted her collar to shield her scar and headed for the store. Even the short walk through the parking lot challenged her focus. Everything had gone so heartbreakingly bad.

"Lady, wanna buy some flowers?" The stringy-haired guy held a tattered bunch of flowers out to her. He looked gaunt, circles under his eyes, and his teeth were bad. She smelled tobacco and the sweet musk of marijuana.

"No, thank you." She knew what was coming. *Please, no!*

"Hey, I bet you like to get high. Am I right?" he said. "I got some incredible stuff. Really cheap."

He'd been easy to spot as a user. More disturbing was that somehow he'd sensed her weakness.

"What are you selling?" she said. The words had come out before she could stop them.

"Opioids. Check it out," he said. He held the tired bouquet towards her with both hands. He opened one hand, and in his palm were two white pills, each in its own packet with a symbol on it. "Oxys. Pharmaceutical stuff, totally pure, totally safe."

The screams and white noise hiss in her head shrieked like a 747 taking off.

***

Farley pulled his car into the no parking zone in front of the Hennepin County building that housed the Child Protective Services office.

He finished his second cheeseburger and rubbed his hands on the napkin. He brushed crumbs off his shirt and his pants. His belly hung, the shirt stretched like an inflated inner tube. A familiar pang of shame flashed.

He ate too much, too often, and stress made it worse. Unless he changed something, police work would make him a blimp. He'd started exercising regularly and had been surprised to find out how strong he was underneath his layer of insulation.

Inside he wasn't as strong.

The men and women on the police force seemed so sure of themselves. Doubt rode Farley like a jockey. It played out in his nothing social life and his endless second-guessing of the decisions he'd made in his short but eventful time in Homicide.

He knew things about a couple of recent cases that he hadn't even shared with Aki. He'd kept key information to himself. He'd played judge and jury in the passion of the moment and let two people avoid investigation.

Speaking out after he'd held back would ruin him, as well as those he suspected may have gotten away with murder—or, in his judgment, justifiable homicide.

If he had self-confidence, he wouldn't wrestle with the decisions he'd made. Instead doubt regularly dug in its spurs.

He opened the door and heaved himself out.

There was a young girl in trouble out there. Knowing she was alone, scared, and vulnerable pulled at his heart like a whimpering puppy.

He'd called Child Protection and learned that Tonya's caseworker was in the office, but in a meeting.

***

Farley stepped out of the elevator and opened the glass door to the Child Protection office. Three people were seated waiting, and a young black man stood behind the counter. Farley approached.

"I'm Detective Farley. Did I talk to you on the phone a couple minutes back? I'm looking for Rosie Padron."

"Yep, that was me. Rosie just finished with a family. She asked me to send you back. Through that door, turn left, she's the last office."

"Thanks much." Farley made his way to the office and knocked.

"Come on in."

Farley opened the door. A fit-looking, black-haired young woman with deep brown eyes looked up at him from her chair. Her short haircut and healthy look reminded him of an Olympic figure skater he'd had a kid-crush on many years back. A calendar on the wall behind her had a bold-faced image across the top that read "I didn't ask to be born Latina.....I just got LUCKY!" Files were stacked on her desk and one was open in her hands.

"I'm Detective Farley, Minneapolis police. I'm looking for help in finding Tonya Davis. Do you know if she's supposed to be with her mother, or has she been placed elsewhere? I understand it's been back and forth."

The woman's brow wrinkled, and she tossed the file to the side. "She's supposed to be with her mother. Why? What's happened?"

"We haven't made any notifications, so please keep this between us, but Tonya's mother died. It was a 911 call. I was just at the apartment. I learned from a neighbor that Tonya had been around as recently as yesterday. Do you have any idea where she might be?"

Rosie put her face in her hands. She remained bent for a moment. "Excuse me," she said, shaking her head. "These kids just never get a break." She took a quick breath, sat up, and met Farley's eyes. She looked as if she might cry. "I don't know where she would be. She doesn't have any relatives in the city. I can contact all the shelters and previous foster homes."

"Please do that," Farley said. "What can you tell me about her? Any idea how she might react if it was her who found her mom? The 911 caller did not identify herself. I haven't heard the recording."

"Tonya is one my favorite kids ever," she said. "I suspect you know that Tonya has Down syndrome. She has minor speech difficulties, but enough that you could tell if it was her that called. She could have. She's..." her words halted and she shook her head, wiping away a tear, "she's capable of making a 911 call. We try to teach all the kids that."

Rosie clearly cared.

She turned to the computer keyboard, and seconds later a photo appeared on the screen.

"Here's our Tonya."

The teen girl had bright almond-shaped eyes, a modest Afro hairstyle, a short neck, and a beaming smile.

"She's had a tough life, but she's a sweetheart. Her mother maybe had a tougher life. They moved here from Gary, Indiana, and her momma was trying to get straight. She wasn't very successful. They've been here for six or seven years. Lots of drug use and arrests—she'd get clean for a time and Tonya would be back with her, and then she'd fall again. She cared about Tonya, but the damn drugs..." She sighed. "Tonya was in and out of St. Joseph's, Harriet Tubman, foster homes, and other shelters. Was it an overdose?"

"It looks that way."

Sorrow showed in her face. It had to be a brutal job for someone who cared so much.

"I'm real sorry for your loss," he said.

"Thank you." A half-smile flickered. "You're a nice man."

He was sure he blushed.

This kind, caring woman triggered something in his lonely core. In his dreamer, social klutz mind, he imagined possibilities.

What would it be like to be close to a woman like this?

She leaned forward and put a hand on his. Her touch was so warm it startled him.

"Tell me what you need," she said.

"Huh?" For an instant he was lost.

"What do you need? I can email you a picture or her whole file. Most of the recent stuff is digital."

"Her, uh, yes. Do that and I'll get it out there." He refocused, still feeling the warmth of where she'd touched him. "The neighbor said a tall, good-looking, well-dressed black man in a fancy car dropped her off yesterday. She said it seemed Tonya liked him. Does that ring any bells?"

"No, but Tonya likes most everyone. She's friendly and real funny." A small smile came and went. Sadness returned. "Considering what she's faced in her life, Tonya is a miracle."

Rosie clasped her hands together and spoke as if Farley was not there. "Please God, keep her safe."

Chapter 55

Drake hit the button for the helipad in the ER's express elevator.

The doors pinged shut, and the elevator began its high-speed trip to the eighth-floor pad. Drake had called each of the accused and asked them to meet him in the ER. Dr. Julie Stone, Dr. Gupta, ICU nurse Tracy, and Drake rode in silence. The helipad was a site of guaranteed privacy.

The elevator doors opened, and they stepped onto the concrete superstructure. The copter was on a PR visit. They were alone on top of the city.

Darkening skies and skyscrapers surrounded them. Over lower buildings and between skyscrapers, the Mississippi was visible to the north, and a few of the city's chain of lakes could be seen to the south. St. Paul's modest downtown lay to the east.

"This is close enough for me." Dr. Gupta nodded toward the steel-framed landing pad, which was see-through and similar to a cyclone fence. "I don't do heights."

Looking down and through, Drake felt a hint of vertigo as downtown traffic moved far below.

The helipad was restricted to all but the ER staff and flight crew. Julie Stone was the only one who'd been up here before. He remembered with uncomfortable warmth the winter meeting they'd had here.

"We're all aware of what Kline intends to do about the pending malpractice charges," he began.

They nodded.

"I've got my own lawyer," Drake said. "He recommends that each of you get individual representation as well. Kline's interest is solely in the hospital's bottom line. He doesn't care about any of our careers or reputations. Personally, even the suggestion of being charged with malpractice makes me ill. If he settles the case as a wrongful death, I'll be out of medicine forever. And I'm sure you're aware a settlement will damage you professionally the same as a guilty verdict." He paused. "Any thoughts?"

"None of us did anything wrong," Julie Stone said. She looked pale and had shadows under her eyes. "I've gone over this case in my mind a hundred times. I don't see any error, much less anything approaching negligence or incompetence. What happened could not be predicted."

Tracy spoke next. The nurse who had taken care of his friend Jon and seen Rachelle through a life-threatening infection kept her eyes down. "I haven't been able to sleep." Her voice broke. "I can't talk to anyone about it because I'm afraid I'll start crying. I keep hoping it's just a big mistake and that the attorney will tell us he was wrong. But when he talked to me this morning, he—"

"This morning?" Drake said. Dr. Gupta made an 'ouch' expression.

Tracy looked hesitant. "Yes. The CEO called me and said that he wanted me to talk to the attorney so that they could clear something up." She bit her lip.

Drake had a sinking feeling. He'd meant to pass on Lloyd's recommendation to say nothing about the case without an attorney.

"The lawyer called me five minutes after the CEO. He was polite but—" Her eyes jumped from one physician to the other. "I'm sorry. I thought it would be okay. I was hoping I could straighten things out so the lawyer would know it was wrong to suggest malpractice."

"What did he say?" Drake asked.

"He asked me about uterine massage and controlling postpartum bleeding. He seemed very polite and I told him, much like I tell a patient or family, about the bleeding and how it was managed. I shared that I'd been doing regular massage and that the bleeding had virtually stopped." She rubbed her face, then dropped her hands and shook her head. "He asked why I hadn't done the scheduled massage just before the patient bled to death. I was confused by his question. I said I did do massage just minutes before she died. He said it wasn't documented in the medical record chart at that time. I explained that there had been a fire alarm just as I completed the massage, and when I returned to the bedside no more than three minutes later, she was bleeding more than any patient I've ever seen." She opened her mouth and then stopped and shook her head, clearly overwhelmed.

She continued, her voice small, "I said, from there on we were trying to save her. After the patient died..." She swallowed visibly. "After she died, I added a short note in the chart and identified that I had performed the massage earlier. The lawyer sounded friendly and said that it would make sense for me to chart that after what happened. I said yes, it did make sense because I was too busy with the resuscitation to document it earlier."

She hung her head but kept on speaking. "He said, 'I'm sorry, but I have to see this as it made sense for you to add the documentation after the patient died. After she died, you recognized what a big mistake you'd made by not doing the uterine massage earlier.' He talked all calm and easy as he called me a liar." Tears ran down her cheeks. "Everything I said was the truth."

Drake stepped forward and put his arms around her. Tracy laid her head on his chest, her body quaked. Julie put a hand on her shoulder.

Dr. Gupta frowned. "It was a setup. He looked at the records and found where he could trap Tracy. If she wrote she did the massage, he'd call her a liar. If she hadn't written anything, he'd say it was proof she hadn't done the massage. This is the way the game is played. Anything to win. Anything to cash in. They'll take a caring, conscientious nurse like Tracy and rip her apart to win their big-money payoff. Disgusting."

Tracy collected herself and straightened.

"It's a sick system," Drake said. "Even when they are found innocent, the medical caregivers are left emotionally, professionally, and financially traumatized. The attorneys and other accusers shrug their shoulders and walk away without even having to cover the attorney fees of those they wrongly accused."

"I've been clinically depressed since I heard the charge," Julie Stone said. She looked into Tracy's eyes, then the others. "I know in medicine, we generally tough it out alone. Despite our efforts, often our patients do poorly or die. That's reality. And we feel all alone. Tracy and any of you who want to talk can call me anytime. I'm not sure who else could possibly understand what this feels like."

Tracy wiped her eyes and nodded. She, Julie, and Vijay stood facing Drake, resolve in their eyes.

"I guess I can go out on a limb," Drake said, "and say we all agree this malpractice charge is totally bogus." He'd hoped for a smile or two but got none. "Clete Venjer has shown he's clever. He looks and acts like a choir boy, and maybe he believes in what he's doing, but his win at all costs, win regardless of the truth, means we have to be on guard. My attorney is going to do what he can to prevent a quick settlement. If we have to, I want to go to trial. Are you guys in agreement?"

They all gave tight-lipped, unhesitating nods.

"I've been in touch with a friend who's one of the county medical examiners. He was going to review the death and call me. If there's anything to be found, he's—"

Drake cell phone trilled and vibrated his pocket. He looked at the caller ID. "This may be him."

"This is Dr. Drake Cody," he answered.

"This is the forensic pathologist to the stars, Dr. Kip Dronen. I found some interesting things as I often do when you get me involved."

"About the mother's death in the ICU?" Drake asked.

"Yep, that's part of it. Not only brilliant but fast service as well. Would you like fries with your order of forensic genius?" Kip said with a high-pitched giggle.

"I'm standing here with my colleagues involved in the suit," Drake said. "I'm going to put you on speaker. Please try and behave."

"Who do you have there? I need to know how far back I need to throttle my intellect in making the presentation. With your detective friends, I needed to hit the Medical Facts for Dummies level, though the chubby cop is bright."

"I have an OB/GYN doctor, an intensive care specialist, and an ICU nurse with me. You don't have to throttle back at all." Drake said. "I was just this minute sharing that you were reviewing the autopsy findings. What did you learn?" Drake put his phone on speaker.

"Greetings, class. This is professor Kip Dronen, MD. I'm a nationally renowned forensic pathologist and medical examiner for Hennepin County. Can y'all hear me?"

"Go ahead," Drake said. Kip loved playing to a crowd. One of his trouble areas involved him and the media. Attention fanned the flames of his ego and inappropriateness.

"Okay, you who are standing in front of the firing squad," he chuckled at his tasteless quip, "I was able to perform an examination of the body in the case under question. The initial autopsy was performed by someone else, and

I won't go into the details of that, other than to say a number of significant features were not reported."

Drake sensed a collective breath-holding by those on the helipad.

"The anatomy and findings were generally consistent with the history that ER guy provided me. It has been claimed that the pathological and explosive bleeding was triggered by retained placental products. Perhaps the earlier examiner was unaware of that, but regardless, in such a clinical setting I would have documented a significant negative."

Drake cringed, fearing Kip would detour onto his familiar ego and resentment harangues.

"Kip, can you please get to what you found? We're dying here."

"Oh, all right. But you know I don't get to talk to many people in the kind of medicine I practice," Kip said.

And that is probably a blessing.

"Okay, the news flash I have for you is that I found no significant placental products within the uterus. Blood, clot, and the characteristic postpartum findings but no—as in effing zero—grossly observable placental tissue."

Drake, Julie, Vijay, and Tracy looked at one another with eyebrows raised.

"Before you get too excited," Kip said, "you need to recognize that does not rule out the possibility that trace amounts of placental material were absorbed into the circulation and triggered the generalized failure of the coagulation and clotting system. This would be exceedingly rare and something that could not be identified clinically before it happened. At a minimum, the finding argues against accepting a quick settlement. What I've shared are facts. I deal only in scientific truth."

Drake sensed that Kip's report had affected the others like it had him. Independent of the impact on the malpractice litigation, what Kip had shared lifted the burden of self-doubt. While not a guarantee of defeating the malpractice claim, it would help end any middle-of-the-night "what if" questions about their care of the unfortunate woman.

The fact that if any placenta had been retained, it was so small that none was found at autopsy meant whatever triggered the bleeding, even if it was microscopic absorption of placental material, was beyond anything that any medical provider could prevent.

The exact cause was unknown, but they were not responsible. They were not incompetent. They had not failed their patient.

"Kip, we're stunned here. You are amazing. Thank you."

"I'll need to look at that placenta," Kip said. "The pathology lab report I read does not fit with what I found. I want to examine it myself. I still have questions."

Once Kip was involved with a death, he needed all the answers.

"And ER guy, call me later. I have some information on something else we were talking about."

"Thank you, Kip," Drake said. "I'll call you. Right now, I just want to stand and smile with some people who haven't smiled in a while."

"Well dang," Kip said. "I'm the hero and I don't even get to join in the fun. There is no justice."

Chapter 56

Drake stepped off the helipad elevator with Julie, Tracy, and Vijay. No one had said much as they descended, but the elevator down had held less dread than the ride up. Kip had struck a hopeful spark.

They stood in front of the flight elevator near the back corner of the ER. Patients on gurneys were parked in the corridor and the noise level had risen.

"We don't say anything to anyone, right?" Drake said. "I'll let you know if Kip comes up with anything else."

Nods all around.

The "doctor to the radio" alarm screeched overhead.

"I'll see you later," Drake said. He moved forward while the others exited the ER.

Drake arrived at the radio room to find his partner Laura at the radio handling the call.

"...okay, 719. I understand," she said. "We're scrapping protocol. If your patient is awake and alert and has someone on hand, don't fight them to get in the ambulance. We've got too many calls out there. Warn them about the possibility of going down when the Narcan wears off. Document that they refused transport against medical advice. You copy?"

"10-4," came the static-ridden reply.

Before Drake could ask, she spoke. "It's worse, Drake. Multiple deaths and more than two dozen overdose calls just since I came on. We're dispatching ambulances and medics using a mass-casualty-disaster protocol."

"Unreal." *How many more?*

"The call I just got off was what we're seeing more of. After the medics get there, treat with Narcan, and bring them back from near-dead, they refuse transport. We can't afford to argue with them or go through the process to sign a hold and force them. In the time it takes to go through all that and transport them, others would die. Maybe you can talk to your TV people again. I don't know if it will slow things down, but it couldn't hurt."

"I'll reach out to my TV friend," Drake said.

"Thanks, partner," Laura said. "It's bad here, but the paramedics and first responders are the ones really getting pounded. They save them so by the time they get here, we just put an oximeter on them and observe. If they quit breathing, we hit them with Narcan again. Once they're clear, we offer them referrals for treatment. Most refuse and are out the door, already looking to get high again. Several have been resuscitated more than once in the same day. One paramedic said others were still shooting up while their friend was being resuscitated."

"Brutal. Hang in there and good luck," Drake said.

Narcotic addiction was diabolical. Both the addicted and those trying to help were losing the battle. He feared his city's current crisis was only a hint of what was to come. Drake looked at the clock. He was to meet Aki in ten minutes in the Security office. He also needed to stop by and pick up an order at the hospital pharmacy. As he neared the end of the corridor, he heard the "doctor to the radio" alarm once more.

How many lives would be lost?

"Hey, Bones. You need any of my clothes again?" called a scratchy baritone.

Drake turned. Stretched out on one of the carts was the Captain. He had a fresh bandage on one hand. His lifetime total of stitches had to be in the thousands.

The Captain was an alcoholic, poly-substance abusing, mentally ill street person who'd survived so many major medical and trauma emergencies that he deserved a clinical professor's degree for all the young doctors who'd learned from taking care of him.

The Captain had a very unusual psychotic condition—like everything else about him, it was unique. He believed he was an intergalactic scout from a planet in another solar system. He was scouting earth for possible colonization. The shrinks labeled it a "fixed delusional state." His belief in his mission was absolute and unwavering.

The fortyish man who appeared sixty tolerated extremes of alcohol, drugs, infection, heat, cold, disease, and trauma beyond anyone Drake had ever seen. Throughout everything, when conscious, the Captain was warm-hearted and strangely impressive. Only those who challenged the reality of the Captain's mission drew his ire. He visited the ER more than weekly, and was one of those widely identified as a "problem" patient. To Drake, he was both patient and friend.

The Captain called Drake and all other doctors "Bones." The clothes reference the Captain had made related to when Drake had borrowed the Captain's coat several months earlier under dire circumstances.

A sudden rush of concern hit Drake. "Captain, will you promise me not to take anything sold on the street? Drink what you want, but don't take any drugs. Okay?"

"Bones, as part of my mission I sample the products of earth people. Of these, alcohol is the finest I have found so far, but I do not shirk my responsibilities with other goods."

"Do you have money?" Drake dug in his pockets. "I can give you money for alcohol."

"Money?" The Captain smiled. "As a scout I investigate the commerce of the potential colony. I'll gladly accept a donation to my exploration fund. Thank you. You've always been most gracious. Do you think you could get me a sandwich?"

Drake had a ten-dollar bill and six ones. He handed them to the Captain. He put a hand on the grizzled man's shoulder and put his face close.

"I'll ask a tech to bring you a sandwich. No drugs of any kind, Captain. Please."

Maybe the Captain thought of him as nothing more than a good source of medical care and sandwiches, but Drake truly cared for the grizzled man. Several times, he'd found the Captain's comments and observations to be almost mystical. Perhaps more than anything, he admired the never-complaining, kind-hearted street-dweller.

"I have to go, Captain. No drugs, please." He turned to leave.

The weathered black man held up a hand. "Stay a moment. Someone is coming who needs you."

Drake looked around. "There's no one coming."

"They're in pain. You can help."

"I'm not working right now. Someone else can—"

"Drake," a familiar voice cried out.

He turned. Patti rushed toward him, tears streaming. She clung to him fiercely.

He hadn't seen her since Bryce... "I'm so sorry, Patti. So sorry."

She sobbed in his arms. He met the Captain's eye as he hugged his anguished friend, sharing her pain.

The "problem patient" nodded.

Chapter 57

Drake was a few minutes late as he hurried down the stairs to the basement level of the hospital to meet Detective Aki Yamada. The main security office, like the utilities, plant maintenance and other essential hospital functions, was buried in the bowels of the hospital.

Seeing Patti's grief at the loss of Bryce made the torrent of overdoses and deaths feel that much more urgent. What more could he do?

He'd completed a call to Tina Watts of WCCY. He'd shared the news about the incredible escalation of overdoses and deaths and the newer, even deadlier opioid drug, carfentanil. Tina assured she'd get a further warning on the air.

Would it help?

Unfortunately, the addicted couldn't see beyond their craving for drugs. For many, it was no longer the rush or the escape of the high, but a desperate need to have ever more drug in order to "get right." Drugs that killed were a sign of quality, a source potent enough to satisfy their limitless need.

Some users were being resuscitated from ODs multiple times in one week—or even, as Laura had shared, multiple times in the same day. The addicted were trapped on a treadmill chasing the high, and the only place it led was to misery and death.

Despite media coverage, most people had no idea how massive the problem was. Nor how it was devastating families and society. The down-and-out addicts on the street were the tip of the iceberg. Hundreds of thousands worked jobs and carried on, with no one knowing that their lives were slowly being taken over by addiction.

Drake opened the door to the security office. He faced a counter and Detective Yamada's back as he sat at a computer console with two large screens in front of him.

A closed door and glass partitioned wall were on the right. A uniformed guard with a phone to his ear was visible at a desk on the other side of the glass. Drake leaned on the counter and Aki turned to face him.

"Here's what we know, Drake," Aki said as if they'd been in the middle of a conversation. "The lab confirmed strychnine in the tobacco packet we pulled from the trash can in the OR. They also found trace components in the Copenhagen container from Dr. Rainey's locker. You nailed it." He paused. "There's no camera in the locker room, but the security guard and I have been going through video of the hallway leading to the door looking for who might have planted it in the locker." He rubbed his chin. "So far it's been a bust."

"How far back did you go?" Drake said. "It must take a lot of time to check the video."

"The software they have is incredible. We can zoom in on the section of the corridor immediately outside the locker room door and it pulls up only those times where there is motion in the view. We can see everyone who went in or came out of the locker room in no time. So far, we pulled up the five days before the surgeon went down. Security identified all the individuals entering and leaving the locker room from their ID photo log. So far everyone belongs. They're all staff surgeons. Do you think one of the other surgeons wants him dead?"

"I suppose it's possible, but hard to imagine." Drake said.

"I'm not giving up on the video, but I'm starting to think that maybe Dr. Rainey brought the tobacco into the locker room with the poison already in there. It could have been slipped in outside the hospital."

"I'd like to think it wasn't anyone from the hospital," Drake said.

"I'm pulling the other way, because if it's not somebody from the hospital my suspect list jumps from hundreds to limitless." Aki sighed. "They tell me they're going to try and wake the victim up and get that breathing tube out today. I'm hoping he'll be able to tell us something."

Drake had a thought. The emergency physicians knew all the surgeons and virtually every doctor on staff.

"Aki, my partner Rizz is going to be around soon. It might be worth having him look at the video and maybe go back a bit further."

"Dr. Rizzini? How is he?" Aki had been there when Drake almost lost his family and Rizz had taken a bullet to the spine—the day people died.

"He's working on recovering."

"Good. Let's put him to work. I'll take all the help I can get," Aki said.

"He'll be up for it. What's happening from the police angle on Bryce's death and the opioid slaughter? I thought of something."

"The overdose numbers are exploding—it's grim. We're beyond stretched." He glanced at the clock. "I'm meeting him in thirty minutes if you want to join us."

"Tell me where and I'll be there," Drake said. "I have to check something out first."

Something Rizz had said earlier caused a thought to pop into his head. His throat tightened.

He hoped he was wrong.

Chapter 58

Q squinted through the windshield in the downpour. He had the wipers maxed out, and his headlights had come on, though it was only late afternoon.

"You can chill, Smurf. Q won't let nothing happen to you."

The first thunderstorm of the year had hit fast and was mid-summer wicked. Earlier, when he'd grabbed Smurf from in front of the Quick Treat, it had been gray but with little clue of what was coming.

She'd been doing what he asked—standing by the payphone and not freaking out. If her Special Olympics-looking self had been crying, some Good Samaritan might have stuck their nose into what was happening.

The second she got into his car, she started crying, her face covered by her hands. The lot was empty, so he took the time to get her calmed down. Once she mellowed a bit, he left her in the car while he went back in the store and bought a bag load of her favorite treats.

She was torn up about her momma.

Q felt kind of bad, too, but they had work to do. He had distributors jamming for product.

He'd let Smurf know he was counting on her, and she'd come through for him. Within a couple of hours, they'd hooked up with distributors all over the metro and crushed the delivery and revenue record they'd set only a day before. His business was cranking. He smiled. His fine ride was carrying more cash than most armored trucks.

Lightning flashed and the almost immediate blast of thunder caused him to flinch. Smurf moaned and rocked back and forth.

She'd been quiet throughout the afternoon of deliveries but did her job. The kid was tough. It had probably been a good thing to keep her busy. Like usual, he'd told her they were delivering gifts and she believed him. The whack-looking kid trusted everyone. And unlike everyone else Q had ever come across, Smurf didn't lie.

She continued to rock forward and back.

"We be good, girl. My house is right up here," Q said.

The giant oaks and elms in his neighborhood were bending and twisting in the wind and the rain pounded. Q activated the garage opener on his corner lot and turned off Thirty-Second Street into his driveway and the detached garage behind the house.

He turned off the car and only then noticed that Smurf was curled up in her seat, hands over her mouth and tears running down her face.

"It's gonna be okay," he said. "Your momma is in heaven with Jesus."

"No. She on the couch." She sobbed.

Not in heaven, on the couch—such a funny kid even when she wasn't trying. He had to stuff his smile.

No doubt Q's own momma was still a member of her hellfire, come-to-Jesus congregation. Jesus was their answer to everything.

"That's the way Jesus calls people to heaven," he said.

Smurf frowned and shook her head.

"Not Jesus. A needle. Little bags like your gifts."

A trapdoor opened and Q's stomach was in freefall. *What?*

Distributors opened and checked his packages at delivery. She must have seen some product. Had she seen him give her mother the two packets of drug?

"What she had wasn't from me. You understand?"

Smurf winced as if she'd been slapped by his raised voice.

He'd scared her. She was crying harder now.

No use talking to her. Smurf couldn't say anything but truth. Trying to get her to not tell anyone about him or the packets was like asking the raindrops to rise rather than fall.

"I'm sorry I yelled at you." He liked her, and she was an incredible business asset, but—*Oh, no. Damn!*

People could have seen him at her momma's apartment.

He'd been so jacked up after the record business day with Smurf that he'd given her junkie momma two hits of product instead of one. The hardcore user had probably slammed them both. He'd been a fool.

He reached over to rub Smurf's shoulder, but she pulled away. "We'll get in the house out of the storm and have some ice cream. Everything is going to be okay." He forced a big smile.

The promise of ice cream guaranteed a smile or laugh, but she only stared, her face fallen.

"I scared," she said, her eyes wide.

His thoughts scattered, his mind looking to find a way to avoid doing what his first thought said he must.

She'd been like a wonderful pet—always excited to see him, acting like he was great. He liked her and she was useful, but the business decision seemed clear.

I don't have a choice.

Lightning struck so close, the thunder shook him.

Chapter 59

Drake entered the eight-digit medical record number for the next patient on the list of malpractice cases Jim Torrins had given him. All patient records were traceable by number only, due to privacy concerns. You never looked up a name, you looked up a number. The precaution was understandable, but the anonymity was one more thing that tended to depersonalize care

The Medical Records Office had been near empty when he'd sat in the cubby and signed in on his designated terminal. He'd viewed these same cases multiple times, but now he was searching using a lens that made everything look uglier.

When Drake had asked Kip for help with the mysterious deaths and claimed malpractice outbreak at Memorial Hospital, the wise-guy medical examiner had asked if the doctors were "intentionally trying to screw up."

When Rizz had learned Drake himself had been charged with wrongful death, he'd cursed and said, "They act as if doctors are purposely trying to harm their patients."

It had taken Aki's question this morning to finally bring into focus the vague uneasiness Kip and Rizz had triggered.

Aki had asked Drake if he thought it was possible one of the other doctors had tried to kill the surgeon, Bart Rainey.

And that ugly possibility had triggered the broader question in Drake's mind—could a doctor or nurse have intentionally harmed or killed others at Memorial Hospital?

The thought made him queasy.

There had been previous cases of such atrocities. In his native Cincinnati, a nurse who called himself the "angel of death" had murdered dozens of hospitalized patients as well as several other people. Could a similarly warped nurse or doctor be harming patients here?

Drake scanned the records, looking for physicians or nurses who'd been involved in more than one of the bad outcome cases. Instead of looking at each case thinking how one might cure or save, he'd turned his head upside down and considered how medical knowledge might have been used to harm or kill.

So far, he'd not found any nurse or doctor involved in more than one of the mysterious deaths, but he needed to look closer. He checked Torrins' list for the medical record number of the next patient who'd been hurt or died.

His cell phone pinged. A text from Aki appeared.

"Meeting Farley, new info, ambulance bay, 2 min, join if able."

***

Drake exited the hospital through the emergency department ambulance doors. The sound of rain echoed under the expansive, canopy-covered ambulance access area. The automatic lights had been triggered, though it was only late afternoon. Two ambulances were in the process of off-loading patients. The smell of rain and engine exhaust hung.

Fifty feet beyond the ambulances, he spied Aki and Farley standing next to their unmarked cruiser, in one of the four police/authorized parking spots under the canopy. Aki waved at Drake and he headed their way.

"Thanks for including me," Drake said as he joined them.

Farley nodded. "It's bad and getting worse. Twenty-one suspected overdose deaths in the past twenty-four hours and no idea when it's going to slow down." He reached in his pocket and pulled out a small package. Drake recognized it as a nasal delivery Narcan unit. "If all the police and fire/rescue weren't carrying these, who knows how many would be dead?"

"The reversal drug is a miracle," Drake said. "I just picked up a couple units myself. One of our nurses saved somebody at the gas station on her way to work. Have you learned anything about where the drug that killed Bryce came from?"

Farley pulled out a small notepad. He held it in front of Drake. "This is the symbol that was on the drug packets Bryce's friend bought. I just saw it again at another fatal overdose. It's been found at a good number of them. Our narcotic squad and the DEA folks say it's the trademark of an up-and-coming big supplier. They've labeled him 'Music Man' because the symbol looks sort of like a musical note in a circle. Other than the glyph and widespread distribution, they know nothing about him."

Drake inspected it. The stylized glyph reminded him of spray-painted graffiti on rail cars.

"So this Music Man is behind the drugs that killed Bryce?"

"Looks that way." Farley wore an expression Drake had not seen on the easy-going detective's face before. Farley had an edge.

"Can I see that symbol again?" Drake asked.

Farley ripped the sheet off the notepad and handed it to him. "Keep it. Maybe share it with your media friends. A lot of users will be attracted to it, but at least they'll be heads-up to the danger. The lab confirmed the residue from the packets that killed Bryce is carfentanil. So far, everything Music Man sells looks to be carfentanil."

"That's what was found in my pregnant patient who died," Drake said. "It's probably what's behind most of the new deaths. It's the nuclear bomb of opioids."

"Your mad professor doctor friend told us that in his 'drugs for dummies' lecture," Aki said. "Instead of running from it, the users seek it out. Insane."

"Addiction makes what seems insane routine," Drake said.

"If we can find this Music Man with drugs, we have a chance for a homicide conviction, though it's tough. If we can prove a link, we should be able to at least get him for manslaughter," Aki said.

"Fred Aplin, our hospital lab guy, talked with the Bureau of Criminal Affairs lab, and they're working together to coordinate evidence," Drake said. "Each batch of drug has a unique chemical fingerprint. If you nail a supplier with drug or residue found with a body, the link is solid," Drake said. "The only hitch is it's got to be in powder form."

"Jurors love the CSI laboratory and science stuff," Aki said. "This chemical fingerprint sounds good. We need all the help we can get. We're losing this game big time."

"It's not a game, and even if we nail them, the bastards still won't get real justice." Farley definitely had an edge. "Think how many this Music Man has already killed."

"Hey, we're with you, partner," Aki said, putting a hand on Farley's shoulder. "We're doing all we can. It's never enough, but we're fighting the good fight."

Farley was about Drake's age and baby-faced but today not so much. Whatever he was feeling added years to his appearance. The usually laid-back detective looked pissed-off and dangerous.

"People are dying, while predators are getting rich," Farley said. "And there's another sleazebag ready to take over for every drug-selling bastard we take down. If I get my hands on this Music Man—" The big detective shook his head, clenching and unclenching his fists.

A car horn blared behind them, making them jump.

Drake spun around and found the grinning maw and wild hair of Dr. Kip Dronen facing him through the windshield of his rain-soaked orange Humvee. The passenger window powered down, and the sophomoric cackle of the medical examiner sounded.

"Couldn't resist," he said. "Stay right there."

The Humvee speed-backed into the authorized vehicle spot next to Farley's unmarked car.

Kip hopped out of the car, trailing a briefcase. "ER guy and his favorite flat-foots—or is it flat-feet?"

"What are you doing here?" Drake said. Aki and Farley said nothing.

"I'm looking out for you, ER. I've got bodies flooding into the morgue, but I came to take a look at that placenta."

Aki and Farley looked lost.

"Kip is helping me figure out a mysterious death," Drake said.

"My favorite kind," Kip said. "I called and arranged to get a look at the placenta that the malpractice attorney got excited about."

"I appreciate it, Kip. Sincerely." He held a hand toward Aki and Farley. "We're trying to do what we can about this opioid slaughter. We were just talking about how the lab identification of drug can help."

"Good stuff," Kip said. "Get me on the stand with matching chemical signature evidence and I'll have jurors flipping thumbs down like they're in the Coliseum." He rubbed his chin. "Should be fun."

Drake's cell phone buzzed. "Kaye" showed on the caller ID. The retired nurse who'd been such a huge help to Rachelle and the kids never called him. "Excuse me, guys."

"Hi, Kaye. Is everything okay?"

"I'm watching the kids. They're fine." She hesitated.

"Where's Rachelle?"

"Well, uh, er, she called earlier and had me pick up her and the kids at your place. We swung back to my place and I'm watching the kids here. She borrowed my car to go grocery shopping. She called me a little bit ago and asked if I could keep the kids overnight."

Huh? "I, uh, wow. She didn't say anything to me," Drake moved further from the others and began to pace. "What did she say she was doing?" *What is going on?*

"Probably it's none of my business and maybe I'm sticking my nose in, but she sounded different. She said she felt exhausted and needed some time alone. I don't want to pry, but are you guys all right?" Kaye sounded uncomfortable.

"We've had some bad stuff come our way, but she and I are okay. At least, I thought so." They'd spoken only a few hours ago. She'd been sick about the house and all, but— Had he misread her? "Are you okay watching the kids? Can you get by without your car?"

"The kids are great and I'm not going anywhere. I just—I don't know...she just didn't sound like herself."

"Thanks, Kaye. I'll check on her. Give my best to the kids. I'll call you later."

"Drake, maybe, you know, maybe you could not let her know I talked to you. I want her to know I'm in her corner and she can confide in me. She looked exhausted, so that's probably all it is. I'm getting antsy in my old age."

"I won't mention you."

Kaye wasn't old, and Drake trusted the veteran ER nurse's impression more than almost any instrument on the planet.

A chill passed through him. *Please be okay, Rachelle.*

Chapter 60

Clara sat alone at a small table in the hospital café watching the storm and considering her next move. Timing was everything.

Her hand stopped with the coffee cup at her lips as she overheard a conversation from the next table.

"...a detective has been interviewing people from the OR, and some from the ICU," the nurse said to her companions. "The poisoning is all anybody is talking about. The cops must think it's someone who works here. How creepy is that?"

Clara set her cup down, concentrating on taking deep breaths and showing no reaction to what she'd heard. Of course they'd interview OR and hospital staff. Would they interview her? That was a test she did not want to face. She could handle it, but...

Either way, it was one more sign.

She left her nearly full cup of coffee and headed for her office. She wouldn't have the nose-in-the-air status of ivory tower staff physicians like her parents, but in the real work of medicine she'd be their equal. No one in the screwed-up, corrupt world of US medicine would ever know, but she would.

As she turned into the corridor leading to her office, the detective she'd seen with Drake Cody on the security video entered the corridor from the ER access ahead of her. Her breath caught, then eased as he headed away from her.

The Asian-American cop had been wearing a windbreaker last night when he was with Drake Cody. Today he wore a suit and was speaking on a cell phone. He turned into the hallway toward the administrative and conference room area. Probably where he was doing interviews.

She reached her office, entered and closed the door behind her. She leaned her back against the door, heart pounding.

Everything was getting tighter.

The police were moving much faster than she'd expected. Drake Cody continued to nose around. An hour earlier she'd tapped into the pathology labs order/access system and learned the Hennepin County medical examin-

er had made a request to examine the placenta. The request had been grant-
ed. She'd made a phone call and dealt with that, but it wasn't good.

She'd decided last night before sleep that the time to disappear was near.
Today, each issue was a ticking bomb threatening to blow away her future.
Now was the time to go. This was what she had prepared for. Her countdown
began now. Guatemala and her new life were waiting.

***

Clara had her two hospital system consoles and her laptop all active.

Her specially equipped laptop was linked to the hospital system as she
downloaded her hidden system administrator wormhole to the augmented
memory cache. Also on her laptop and backed up on the cloud was the evidence she held that gave her the upper hand with those in a position to potentially hurt her.

On one screen, a security camera video ran. Someone was going through
the images of the hallway outside the physician locker room. They were close,
but they wouldn't find anything. She'd covered all the bases.

On the other screen, she'd just completed reviewing Dr. Bart Rainey's
latest ICU labs and documentation. The physician notes now identified that
the patient had been poisoned with strychnine. Other entries confirmed
what she already knew. Bart Rainey had police protection and an investigation was ongoing.

She entered Drake Cody's activity code to see if he'd been on. Yes, he'd
been reviewing records again.

A faint rumble of thunder reached her ears. She smiled. Neither rain, nor
sleet, nor snow would stop her plans for Drake Cody. The scheme she'd put
in motion wouldn't kill him but it would slow him down. That was best, because her payback plan needed him alive to suffer most.

He would pay for what he'd done—forever.

Her skin tingled and her senses were wired. The whirring of the computer fans sounded clearly, the differing pitch of her laptop versus the network
processors. The tiny hairs on the back of her fingers glistened in the light and
shimmied in the faint air movement of the ventilation system. Even the faint
scent of the cookies in her bottom drawer registered clearly.

She should be scared, or at least anxious, but that wasn't what she felt. They would not catch her. She'd outsmarted them all. Was it excitement she felt? Confidence?

She smiled. It was more.

It was triumph.

*　*　*

Drake drove out of the parking lot, his wipers beating back the driving rain as he turned north on Chicago Avenue toward the river. Car headlights and streetlights were on in the darkness of the storm.

He'd called Rachelle three times with no answer. He'd been concerned after their earlier talk, and that combined with Kaye's concern had him near the edge. Working with Kaye in the ER, he'd learned that if a patient or situation troubled her, he'd damn well better check it out.

And it wasn't just Kaye. Hell—it was everything. What hadn't gone wrong—the house, his job, their future?

He should have called Rachelle immediately with the glimmer of hope that Kip's report on the young mother's autopsy provided. It was the first positive news in a while, and she needed it as much as he did.

He stopped at the light at Tenth Street, and standing in the steady rain was the Captain. His height and standard uniform of two hats and two overcoats drew looks from the small group of downtown business people. They stood clear of him under their umbrellas. Drake rolled down the passenger window.

"Captain, you're getting soaked," he said.

The Captain bent and peered into the car.

"Bones?"

Drake put the car in park and leaned over to open the passenger door. "Hop in. I'll give you a ride."

The Captain shrugged and climbed in. The scent of wet wool, body odor, alcohol, and a tinge of mint filled the car.

"Where are we going?" the Captain asked. His just-repaired hand was in a bandage, though Drake could see it was already wet. The Captain flipped the car's visor down and looked behind it, turned and scanned the back seat, then turned and opened the glove box. Sitting on top of the car's registration and insurance info were Drake's emergency medications—an epinepherine auto-injector and two Narcan nasal injectors.

"Curious, Captain?" Drake asked.

"It is my job to investigate my surroundings. That is what a scout does. Why the medical things?" he said.

"The epinepherine is for me or anyone else I may come across having an allergic reaction. It can save a life. The nasal injectors are for narcotic over-doses. They can keep people from dying from the drugs I warned you about."

"I've seen the medicine in the nose used before," the Captain said.

"Was it people you were with who needed it?" Drake asked.

"Yes, a couple of times."

"Were you taking drugs, too?"

"Yes. It is my job to experience your culture and practices. The drugs did not harm me."

The Captain had used up more than nine lives, and his constitution and tolerance for alcohol and all things intoxicating was legendary. Some paramedics and ER staff at Memorial called him the man who couldn't die. Drake imagined what incredible health the Captain would have if he was not plagued by his substance abuse and its consequences.

Drake's cell phone rang. "Kaye" appeared on the caller ID.

"Hi, Kaye. Everything okay?"

"Probably, but I can't shake my bad feeling," she said. "I tried to call Rachelle and no answer. She told me she was going to take a nap, so I don't know why I'm on edge, but I... If you're not free, I can take a cab and head over there with the kids to check on her—"

"I'm worried, too. I'm in the car and should be at the townhouse in less than ten minutes. We're probably both overreacting, but—" Drake took a left turn in front of a guy in a business suit with an umbrella. "I'll call you when I get there." He started weaving his way through the Seventh Street traffic like a jockey on a muddy track.

"You're afraid," the Captain said.

"It's my wife. I need to check on her right now. I'll have to drop you off later. Okay?" He swung a right and accelerated north on Hennepin Avenue.

"Do not worry about me. Someone you care about is in danger. Drive fast."

Drake's heart was in his throat and his jaw ached. First Kaye and now the Captain—two people whose intuition had proven on target in the past. He raced over the Hennepin Avenue Bridge through the driving rain, with the dark water of the Mississippi roiling below.

Please God, no.

Chapter 61

Drake raced down the flooded street, the tires blasting water against the undercarriage so forcefully the car shook. His hands clutched the wheel and he grit his teeth as he accelerated. The wipers provided only watery glimpses through the slashing rain.

He approached the railroad crossing near the entrance to the townhouse complex.

The Captain braced his arms on the dash just as the old Dodge hit the tracks and bucked so hard their belt restraints grabbed. The most violent of early-season storms raged.

Drake prayed his mounting fear was overblown. Rachelle was likely just taking a nap, but his heart pounded and his breath came fast.

Lightning flashed and thunder shook the car.

"The atmosphere is unsettled," the Captain said.

Drake entered the parking lot as fast as he dared in the blinding rain. As they advanced, the air in the car came alive. His scalp tingled and the hair on his arms rose. He slid to a stop in front of the townhouse just as the Captain hunched his shoulders and covered his head. "Here it com—"

Lighting and thunder exploded on top of them. Spots floated in front of Drake's eyes. Steam rose from the asphalt.

Ears ringing, he gathered himself and threw open the door.

"Stay in the car, Captain," Drake yelled over the howl of the storm.

The downpour drenched him in an instant. The burnt copper stink of ozone hung as he unlocked the deadbolts and opened the door. Before he could close it behind him, he spotted the slim arm and burn-scarred wrist and hand of Rachelle draped motionless from the couch to the floor. *No!*

"Rachelle!" he screamed. He raced to her, the door forgotten. Her olive skin was now deathly blue, her eyes closed. An open envelope and creased papers lay on her couch-sprawled body. There was no movement—she was not breathing. He ripped the envelope and papers off her and threw them aside. A cloud of white powder filled the air as if someone had clapped chalk-laden blackboard erasers. His eyes stung and a bitter taste registered on his tongue.

"Rachelle!" His anguished scream a plea.

Nothing. No reaction. He felt for a pulse, her skin cold to the touch. He raised an eyelid—her pupil pinpoint and unmoving.

The powder, no breathing, her cold and blue body... *Rachelle, what have you done? Please, no!*

He bent and gave her a rescue breath, her mouth and jaw stiff and rubbery, her body lifeless. No reaction.

His vision blurred, he struggled to stay upright. He shook his head as strength drained from him like water from a wrung sponge. He had to breathe life back into her! He tried to deliver another breath, but his body was not his own. Drugged!

Nightmare weak and helpless. Dread beyond imagination. *Rachelle!*

God, please. Have to—

He collapsed sideways to the floor.

Floating—his thoughts a fog. Agony, yet blunted. As if on fire, yet unfeeling. His body lay pressed to the floor as if gravity had multiplied. Time had disconnected. His thoughts fading—nothing mattered. An open door. Shadows. Curtains moving in the wind. An unrelenting screech. The smell of rain and an acrid tinge in the air. No pain.

A final certainty—*dying.*

The world faded to black.

Chapter 62

Drake floated in darkness. Silence.

Shadowed memory and thoughts as fleeting as smoke—everything more right than ever before.

In a place unlike he'd ever been and one he did not ever want to leave. Peace.

Small nudges, like ripples on the bow of a drifting boat, prodded him.

Hands on his face. A kiss? Smells known but now nameless. Movement around him, sensed but not seen. A strange taste.

Consciousness like a bubble in water rising. Comfort fading, ripples were now cresting waves, each one bringing him back. A continuous screech penetrated the silence. Eyes opening—fuzzed images becoming sharper like a camera lens twisting into focus.

A face. Water dripping, a white scar on a grizzled cheek. A sluggish meshing and recognition formed—the Captain?

Wait! He struggled. *Rachelle!* He must— A hand held him down.

"Breathe, Bones, breathe," the face says.

Curtains moving, an open door and the roar of a storm. A warbling shriek joined the unrelenting screech. The Captain moving above him. Memory returning.

Rachelle—had it been a dream? Pain too profound to be anything but real lanced his heart.

He'd been too late. She was gone. Rachelle!

He plunged into a chasm—endless and forever but it could not contain his anguish.

***

The bulletin on Tonya appeared on the terminal on Farley's desk. His filing of her as a "high risk missing person" assured that the Sheriff's office, Highway Patrol, and all other law enforcement agencies would receive be-on-the-lookout bulletins for the vulnerable, newly orphaned girl.

He'd listened to the recording of the earlier 911 call. The halting, child-like message left no doubt that it was Tonya who had found her mother dead. What must that have been like?

He couldn't stop thinking of the child. Where was she?

Dang it—toughen up. *I should be working in a daycare, not chasing killers.*

Her mental challenge and history put her at an especially high risk emotionally. Farley pictured the raven-haired case worker Rosie and her edge-tinged comment. "She's not a syndrome, she's a person." And now she was a person scared, vulnerable, and likely all alone.

Alone? Another worry arose. Maybe it would be best if she were alone? Who was the big guy with the fancy car that the neighbor had seen? Might she be in danger?

He looked at the bulletin's photo. Why would anyone hurt the harmless girl with the winning smile? His worry did not disappear.

His cell buzzed. "Dispatch" showed on the display.

"Detective Farley here."

"We have a request for you and Detective Yamada from an overdose crime scene. A man and a woman found down. Can you proceed?"

Overdose, crime scene, a couple—boyfriend-girlfriend overdose fatalities were becoming routine. *Very sad, but why Aki and me?*

"Dispatch, I'm working on multiple active cases. Detective Yamada is as well. Can someone else pick this up?"

"This is a request from the officer on the scene. Individuals reported as known to you and involved in one of your cases."

What? Known to him? He could think of no one, and certainly no couple he suspected would be at risk.

"What's the location?" Farley said.

"Northeast, a townhouse, 2121 Sumpter. Can you respond?"

The address was familiar. It clicked. He'd been there before, on his first case. Drake Cody's address!

"I'm on the way." He grabbed his sport coat and ran.

Drake Cody? There was no combination of events he could put together that made sense.

He chugged down the stairs, his belly pulling his shirt tail free. His un-marked car was parked right out front, in the pouring rain.

He'd sensed Drake's wife had a troubled past. He'd seen her when she'd suffered the terrible burns to her hands and wrists. Likely she'd been given painkillers. Had she become addicted?

But Drake and drugs? He thought of his brother. He imagined the stresses in Drake's life—in everyone's life. Who didn't want to escape sometimes? He burst through the door into the storm.

He was rain-soaked as he ripped open the car door and threw himself behind the wheel. The townhouse wasn't far. He started the car, turned on the wipers, and ripped into gear lurching away from the curb. Tires skidded and a horn blared. He'd pulled out in front of a pickup truck.

In the jangled nerves of the near-collision, a sober thought struck. Overdoses aren't declared crime scenes unless they involve a fatality. His throat clenched.

No matter how fast he got there, it was already too late...

Chapter 63

Rizz scanned the passing Minnesota countryside from the back of the van an hour south of Minneapolis. His phone sounded and he pulled it out of the pouch on the arm of his wheelchair. The phone showed "Lloyd–attorney."

"Hey, Lloyd, thanks for getting back to me," Rizz said.

"How is it going, and what can I do for you?" the attorney asked.

"I'm doing better," Rizz said. "I'm on my way back from Mayo. I called about Drake. Things are looking like ugly for him."

"Agreed," Lloyd said. "He believes if he gets burned on this malpractice settlement, it will cost him his career. I think he's right. Also we were working on a home purchase. It was a done deal, but with his situation at the hospital, the bank withdrew his financing. That's what I know. Is there something else?"

How much should he share with Lloyd? "Before I say more, I need to know what I can tell you."

"What do you mean?" Lloyd said.

"Attorney-client privilege. I want to discuss something that involves me, Drake, and our partner, Jon Malar."

"I'm representing all three of you on the drug research matters, and the language of my contract covers any other legal needs. Dr. Malar is the only client I've ever had who paid the bill for himself and his partners and never spoke to me in person. Are you in touch with him?"

"Not much," Rizz said. *You see, Lloyd, I can hardly talk to him because I helped wreck his life by secretly screwing his wife, letting her almost steal the research breakthrough, and being a selfish, cowardly ass.* "He's recovered better from the gunshots than from his wife's betrayal." Imagine if he learned what Rizz had done. "Her death left him rich, but he's hurting. If he can get back to work in the ER, it'll help."

"I hope he does well," Lloyd said. "We're okay on confidentiality, unless you tell me you're planning a major crime."

And what if we've already committed a crime but it hasn't been discovered?

"What I want to talk to you about involves Drake, Jon, D-44, and money," Rizz said. Now wasn't the time to reveal more.

"I'm listening."

"Drake often doesn't think to ask for help. Too much pride. Some of us know that money and power can make all sorts of things happen. Drake isn't as cynical, and in some ways he's naive. He'll take all sorts of abuse personally, but if somebody messes with his family, friends, or anybody who's vulnerable, there's another Drake. I pulled him off a jerk who hit a nurse in the ER. I believe he would have killed the guy if I hadn't stopped him."

"I'm not sure why you're telling me this," Lloyd said.

Rizz's concern for Drake had him babbling. Lloyd's main role was lawyer, not friend. He didn't need to understand Drake. Best to just get down to business.

"I have a plan to help Drake," Rizz said. "Can I run it by you?"

Chapter 64

The Captain flinched as the drumming of rain on the car's roof became a violent hammering. Marble-sized hail bounced off the windshield and the hood of Bones' car. The glistening ice-balls collected on the sidewalks, grass, and asphalt.

If not for the troubling aura surrounding Bones, the car ride and the eruption of earth's atmosphere would have been most enjoyable. The Captain's scalp tingled and his ears rang. It was as if he and Bones had been inside the lightning strike.

It had been nice of Bones to invite him into his car. The Captain could not remember when he had last been in any vehicle other than a police car, ambulance, or the van that ferried him and others from the drunk tank to the homeless shelters.

Bones was the Captain's favorite of all the healers. Most of the nurses, doctors, and medics had caring energy, though for many the strength of their batteries had worn down. Bones always cared, and he respected the Captain's scouting mission. And he provided sandwiches.

Bones had achieved a higher plane than other earth citizens—though there was also a capacity for destruction. Earth people had the potential for good and bad. The worst of them had no feelings for others—they were dangerous. The Captain avoided them.

He could not remember when he'd last been to a person's home. A faint memory pulled at him. A flickering glimpse of a woman and a small child, then shadows of pain and loss, but none of it in focus—always the confusion.

He pulled the pint bottle of peppermint schnapps from his coat pocket and took a swallow, then replaced it.

The hail stopped and the drumming of rain returned.

He looked toward the building. Huh? The door was open. That could not be right. Bones would not want his house to be wet.

The Captain opened the car door and stepped into the storm. Rain pelted him and hail crunched under his feet. As he neared the door, the continuous squeal of an alarm shrilled from inside the structure. What?

He reached the doorstep and as he stretched inside for the handle to the door—

The healer was on the floor and not moving.

"Bones!" the Captain yelled. He hurried to the doctor's side. A beautiful young lady lay sprawled on the couch, her color not right. White powder covered her shirt. Bones put his rain-soaked finger on the powder and touched it to his tongue. The bitterness. He knew what this was.

He looked around for help. There was no one else.

He felt the powder's buzz immediately—very strong. A ringing sounded through the electronic squeal—a phone. He looked at the woman, then at Bones, and then towards the ringing of the phone.

As a scout he was not supposed to get involved. That's why he lived as he did. Should he try? Was it his place to do so?

The power of the drug washed over him. It was quality earth product, and as with alcohol and all the earth products he craved, he felt less confused, less on edge. Things became clearer.

He knew what his mission was.

Chapter 65

Rachelle floated in a place without light.

Inky black but she was not afraid. There was no worry. There was nothing.

She was safe.

Now came the faintest intrusion. Someone touching her? Did she hear her brother? Again she felt movement—someone pushing on her. Something covering her mouth. A familiar but strange taste. Something in her nose?

It didn't matter. Everything was good. Again movement. Unsure if it was up or down but it didn't matter. The blackness shifted to gray. She'd been to this place before. It was where the drugs took her—the place in her mind where everything was perfect. She was at peace.

Her memory stuttered. The man with the stringy hair had been in the parking lot selling opioids. And she'd felt the desperate pull. And now she was in the drug's grip.

In her weakness she must have betrayed those she loved. The ones who counted on her. How could she have? Just like her mother. *Lord, no!*

The gray lightened. Movement—someone bending over her. Words sounded but she could not understand. She was rising but still deep.

The man in the parking lot. He'd held the drugs out to her. A packet of white powder with a symbol on it. She'd wanted the drugs, needed them—a part of her had screamed for them.

She'd thought of her mother—thought of her brother. The smell of dried urine, his skinny body trembling, the cast on his arm. What she'd done. The drugs calling to her.

No!

Relief flooded her consciousness.

She hadn't failed her children. She'd screamed at the man. Struck him. He'd run away.

It had been hard to resist, but she had.

"Breathe, pretty lady," a husky voice said. "There you go." The grizzled face of an older black man smiled above her. *Who?* His lids were half-mast and he looked ready to nod off.

She remembered getting home. Kaye would watch the kids so she could rest. She'd been so tired.

There had been letters on the floor beneath the mail slot. The packet addressed to Mrs. Drake Cody with "Thank you" handwritten on the back.

When she'd opened it, a "pop" sounded and white powder filled the air. She'd plunged into fog and then blackness.

The shrill wail of the security alarm sounded in the background. Her senses sharpened. The man wore a large, wet coat and he was on his knees bent over something on the floor. The sound of a storm and an approaching siren reached her. The last of the fog cleared.

She turned on her side. The grizzled man shifted and someone got to their knees from the floor alongside the couch where she lay. Drake!

He saw her. His mouth gaped and his eyes went wide.

Looking into his clear blue eyes, all questions about what he felt were answered. Only as a child in the time before drugs had destroyed her mother's soul had Rachelle seen such love.

Drake's mouth opened, but no words came out. Tears ran down his cheeks, and the depth of what she saw in the windows to his soul made her heart swell. To be so loved and to love so totally was a gift she would not give up. Never would Drake or her children lose that most special part of her.

She would not let drugs or anything else steal the miracle of loving and being loved.

***

The Captain moved to the side. Drake's awareness fully returned, and with it came recognition. He moaned as pain like a shard of glass sliced through his heart. He'd been too late.

Disoriented, he got to his knees. Dread-filled, he turned to look at the body of the woman he'd loved.

His heart skipped. *Oh God!*

Rachelle awake, breathing, and looking into his eyes...

Joy and disbelief burst within him like fireworks. He could not speak. *How?*

He reached for her. They hugged desperately, her tears and breath warm on his neck. She was alive!

His senses filled with the wonder of her.

Chapter 66

The storm had moved on, and Farley was surprised to see shafts of low-angled sun penetrate from the west. Puddles and scattered debris littered the parking lot.

"Please make sure everyone uses precautions, Farley," Drake said from where he sat in the back of the ambulance, his arm around his wife. "And whatever he wants, please make it happen and I'll cover it."

Farley nodded.

From the time Farley had arrived, Drake hadn't let go of his wife for an instant—as if he was afraid she would disappear. From the reports, she nearly had.

Drake had almost died as well. Incredible.

"Take care of yourselves," Farley said, "and don't forget what I asked."

Farley had requested that they have drug testing done to help in any subsequent criminal proceedings. It was not likely Drake would forget.

Someone had tried to kill his wife.

"Drake, please, I'm fine now," his wife said. "I don't want to go to the hospital."

She looked tired and shaken but overall well. The Narcan opioid-reversal drug was miraculous.

"It will be quick. We won't have to stay." Drake took her hand. "They'll watch us in the ER for a bit, do a couple of tests, and we'll be on our way. Besides, if we refuse to get checked out, the medics will worry, plus have to complete a boatload of paperwork."

"You got that right, Doc." The paramedic smiled as she climbed in the back and sat facing them. She pulled the door shut, and the ambulance moved away from Farley without lights or siren.

It was a miracle that Drake and his wife were being transported by ambulance rather than a coroner's vehicle. If not for the mentally ill street person, they'd be dead. According to the paramedics, the old man was an ER regular and he had single-handedly saved them.

Farley looked toward the tall, graying black man in the oversized coats sitting in the front seat of the unmarked cruiser. When Farley had spoken

274

with him, the man's eyes had been half-closed and his speech slow. The narcotics that had nearly killed Drake and his wife had only made the Captain high. The soft-spoken, strangely dressed man smelled of mint and alcohol.

He was the most unlikely of heroes.

The paramedics said the Captain was a known medical marvel. He'd been shot, stabbed, run over, and frozen, and had survived infections, major surgeries, and uncountable misadventures with alcohol and drugs. They said he was not in danger, and Farley had been around his addicted brother enough to know dangerously drugged from high but safe.

The responding officer and paramedics related that the Captain said he'd gone to the door and seen Drake and his wife collapsed and unresponsive. He saw the powder and recognized what had happened. The security system alarm had triggered a police alert.

The Captain had done mouth-to-mouth on Drake's wife, then ran to retrieve the Narcan he'd seen in the car's glove box. He'd brushed clear the remaining powder and administered the Narcan first to Drake's wife and then Drake, while giving intermittent mouth-to-mouth to both.

When they started to breathe on their own, he had answered the home security service's call and reported the overdoses.

When the uniformed officer arrived, the Captain had called out for him to stop at the door.

"It was clear the old dude was high, but he warned me about the powder. The guy did everything right. The doctor and his wife were groggy but hugging each other. The doctor said he'd thought his wife had died. It was intense." The officer shook his head. "Right then, the rain stopped and the medics arrived. I protected the scene, but it was the Captain who saved them."

Drake had reported that he'd found his wife unresponsive and not breathing. As he tried to resuscitate her, he'd been overcome by contact with the same powder that had almost killed her. He'd asked the officer to contact Aki and Farley.

The Captain hadn't needed Narcan. The medics said that it was his famed tolerance and indestructibility that had allowed him to withstand the drug and save lives.

The Captain now sat in the front seat of Farley's car. His eyes were still drooping, though he seemed brighter as the minutes went by. Farley would get a full statement from him.

Now the critical question was "who?" Who had tried to kill Drake's wife. And why?

The "how" greatly narrowed the field of suspects.

Farley examined the crime scene while wearing a mask and gloves. There was lots of powder—the attempted murderer had access to plenty of drug.

Farley collected a sample from the postmarked envelope addressed to "Mrs. Drake Cody." The raw drug was essential as evidence because testing of Drake or Rachelle would only tell what drugs they were exposed to. The powder would yield the all-important chemical fingerprint, which could potentially be matched to a specific supplier.

The envelope was not distinctive, the handwriting easily disguised. The spring-loaded drug launch was clever but seemed unlikely to be traceable. Farley did not expect stupid mistakes from whoever had attempted to kill in such a diabolical fashion.

Who? Why?

Did Rachelle Cody have secrets that led someone to want her dead? Was this a way to get at Drake? The use and quantity of opioids suggested a distributor and a possible response to Drake's strong antidrug efforts. Did someone try to kill his wife as a way to hurt him?

Seeing Drake and his wife together had revealed the intensity of their feelings for each other.

What must it be like to have someone like that?

God, how he'd like to know.

The crime-scene techs were working solo now. The demands of the city-wide multiple overdose deaths had stretched all the resources to the limit. The tech was finishing up, having found nothing more than Farley's initial results. The powder-flinging booby trap was simple and made with commonly available items. In short, other than the powder, they had no useful evidence.

Farley's phone sounded and "Aki" showed on the screen.

"Hi, Aki. What have you heard?"

"Enough to freak me out. I'm still at the hospital and I got word that Drake Cody and his wife are being brought in as overdoses. What the hell?"

"Attempted murder. Clearly premeditated. Somebody sent a packet full of opioid drug addressed to Drake's wife through the mail. She opened the packet and the drugs put her down. Drake showed up a minute or two later. She was out and not breathing. While trying to revive her, he went down. I'm here with an old guy who's a patient and kind of a friend of Drake's. He's a mentally ill street person. The guy saved their lives. I haven't got a full statement from him yet. He's still a little zoned from his contact with the drug. If he'd have gone down they all would've died."

Silence hung.

"This is all just too much," Aki said. "How does all this tie together?"

"The scene is clean. Not much to work with here. We did get a raw drug sample, so if we can find a suspect with opioids, we can check for a chemical fingerprint match."

"Good."

"I'm wondering if it's a supplier trying to get at Drake for his antidrug efforts. That seems a stretch, but it's someone with access to a good amount of drug—of course that could be dang near anyone these days. Could his wife have enemies? She seems like such a nice person," Farley said.

"Nice people, and especially nice women, are assholes' favorite victims," Aki said. "Speaking of victims, the reason I didn't get out there with you is that I got called to the ICU. The big surgeon woke up. They pulled his breathing tube. I just finished interviewing him."

"Does he know who did it?" Farley said.

"No, but he did volunteer that he thinks plenty of people working at the hospital are cretins. He's a rather heavy-handed individual, to put it mildly. Summary—he didn't know anything useful, and talking with him I can see why the suspect list around the hospital is long."

"Nothing is coming easy. After all these years, aren't you burnt out?"

"I bitch and moan," Aki said, "but when it gets right down to it, I can't see doing anything else. Taking the bastards out of the game lights my fire. What we do matters."

Farley thought about his brother, the dead teenage boy, the scared and vulnerable Tonya, her dead mother, and the unknown Music Man. "I'm with you there, partner."

"Roger that. Do you need me there?"

"We've gotten all we're going to get here. I'm going to formally interview the Captain, now that his buzz is clearing. After that I'll drop him somewhere. Drake asked that I treat him right. The guy is a hero."

"It was the Captain? I know who he is." Aki chuckled. "He'd rather have booze, but buy him a meal on me. Call me later."

They disconnected.

Farley heard his car door open and turned to see the Captain climbing out.

"What can I do for you, Captain?" Farley asked.

The Captain looked brighter.

"Thank you for asking. I'm just going to Bones' car to retrieve my hats."

"Let me help you."

They walked to the old Dodge. "Let me check things out first," Farley said.

He opened the car's passenger-side door. The glove box was open and there was an epinephrine injector and papers in it. A baseball cap and a Fedora lay on the car seat beside a square of notepad paper. Farley saw no other abnormalities or suspicious objects in the vehicle. He grabbed the hats and paper.

Farley gave the Captain his head gear, then turned over the paper. It was the Music Man symbol that he'd drawn for Drake earlier in the day.

"Thank you," the Captain said. "What do you have there?"

"This is a symbol that's on the most dangerous of the drugs on the street," Farley said, holding out the drawing.

The Captain leaned forward, squinting. "It looks sort of like the letter q with a circle drawn around it. What does that mean?"

Farley shook his head. "It's not a q. It's a musical note—" Wait a minute. Hey, maybe it was a small q? It was stylized and could be something else as well.

"q"—a link jumped to Farley's mind. Drugs, drug sales, and someone who hates Drake. "Q" Robinson. The assault case in the ER. The case where Farley had first met Drake. The big drug-seeking, ex-con who'd laid hands on a nurse, causing Drake to take him down. "q" or "Q"—it would be one heck of a coincidence.

Was Q the Music Man?

Chapter 67

The Captain's grizzled, life-worn face broke into a Christmas morning smile as the waitress set the rush order stack of pancakes in front of him.

"With an offer of any place in the city, you chose IHOP. You must love pancakes," Farley said with a laugh.

"Yes. I also have sausages and hash browns coming. Thank you." He leaned over the plate, closed his eyes and sniffed deeply.

"Drake requested we get you a meal befitting a hero."

"You succeeded and thank you but I am just an ordinary citizen of the universe. I did what I thought was right and look what karma has brought." He held a hand towards the pancakes, his ragged features beaming.

"Go ahead and dig in. I only have a couple of minutes to get you set up before I head to the station."

The Captain picked up the syrup dispenser and poured on as much as the cakes and plate would hold, then attacked the stack with knife and fork.

"Everyone is grateful for what you did." Farley stood and tucked a twenty-dollar bill under an unused cup.

"The experience was most rewarding," the Captain said after swallowing. "It has been my privilege to mingle with those whose souls have evolved more than most on this planet." The Captain's focus on the pancakes made it clear he needed no further distraction.

Farley hustled out of the restaurant, trying to recall if anyone had ever commented on his soul before.

Despite more than sixteen hours of effort so far today and little sleep last night, he was not tired. He was hunting an earth inhabitant whose karma in no way resembled the Captain's.

He had no time to waste.

***

The lights were on in the homicide squad room, and as Farley approached he smelled coffee and burnt microwave popcorn. He recognized he hadn't stopped at any of his usual fast food fueling sites on the way back to the station. More unusual was that he wasn't hungry. His thoughts were on the missing Tonya, the near-death of Drake and his wife, and the likelihood that Quentin Robinson was the Music Man.

Only one of the several Homicide desks was occupied. Aki looked up as Farley approached.

"How you doing, partner?" Aki looked wrung out. "Drake's wife is another high-profile attempted murder, and we've got so many overdose deaths that the Chief said we can use judgment on which ones we process. Should save time. If there is no raw drug on the scene, the odds of linking to any particular supplier are weak. The DA is advising full workups only on cases where we can get a chemical fingerprint of the drug."

"Anything on the surgeon's poisoning?" Farley wanted to get Aki's update before he broke his news.

"Nothing. I'm starting to get a bad vibe." Aki sighed and ran his hands over his scalp. "It's nice questioning people who are actually trying to help, but all I've learned is that plenty of people don't like the guy, but no one has any idea who might want him dead."

"The security video didn't help?"

"So far, it's a bust. Drake screened it this morning and didn't see anyone who stood out. His buddy Dr. Rizzini is going to go over it tomorrow morning, but I'm not optimistic. As far as a suspect, I got everyone and I got no one. All these nurses and doctors are smart enough to have pulled this off. I'm not giving up, but my gut is telling me that unless something breaks big and soon, we may never find who did this." He shook his head and gave a big sigh. "Enough on that. Catch me up on Drake and his wife. What have you got?"

"I think we've caught a break. It could be about Drake and his wife, but possibly much more."

Aki sat forward. "A break?"

"There was a lot of powder in that envelope, which suggests someone with access to a significant amount of drug. I mentioned a supplier as a suspect in retaliation for Drake's anti-drug effort. It seemed a bit of a stretch, but maybe not. You know the symbol on the killer drugs from the unknown supplier the DEA and narcotics teams are calling the Music Man?"

"Yeah, it's on the stuff that killed the kid that was Drake's patient, the high school kids by the lake, and a lot of other overdoses."

Farley leaned over Aki's desk and sketched out the symbol on the notepad. "This is it."

"Yep, I've seen it," Aki said. "They think it's a music note in a circle."

"Take another look," Farley said. "Could you see that as a small q in a circle?"

Aki shrugged. "It looks like graffiti art. Okay, so maybe it's a small q. What difference does it make? So maybe we shouldn't call him Music Man. Instead, he's—" He cocked his head towards Farley, his eyes widening.

"It fits," Farley said. "Quentin Robinson—"Q"—an asshole, a drug supplier, and a guy who hates Drake because he punched him out."

"If I remember right, he threatened Drake back then. This is huge." Aki stood up and began pacing. "Have you talked to the DEA or Narcotics to see if they or their snitches know where Q's at?"

"Made those calls on the way over. Nothing offhand, but they said they'll shake the trees."

"You need to be on this full time." Aki picked up the phone. "I'll get the Lieutenant to cut you loose. I've got nothing breaking on the hospital case, so no need to drag you down with that. You have a lead on the biggest killer on the streets and possibly the person responsible for the attempted murder of Drake and his wife. It ties a bunch of our headaches together. Would be great to nail this bastard." He punched in numbers on the phone.

Before his last few months of homicide experience, Farley would have been thrilled just to be contributing. He was beyond that now—it was personal.

His cell phone sounded.

"Detective Farley here."

"Detective Farley, this is Rosie, Tonya's child protection caseworker. I—"

"Have you found Tonya?" He moved away from Aki.

"No. None of her old contacts know anything. I'm very worried. It isn't like her to disappear."

"I have notices out all over the system." His worry about Tonya had grown continuously, with thoughts of Rosie as well. "There's been no word. I won't let up until we find her."

"Not just find her, Detective. We have to find her safe. Nothing can happen to her." Rosie's voice broke. "Damn it, if anyone hurts her..."

"Rosie, I'll do everything I can. We'll keep her safe."

"You're sweet, but," she sniffed, "you're talking crap. We can't keep these kids safe. I spend every day doing all I can, but ignorant, weak, messed-up, addicted, criminal, and sick people hurt these kids every day." Her voice went to just above a whisper and he sensed she wasn't talking to him. "Just please not Tonya. Not this time."

Farley wished there was some great sacrifice he could make to help her.

"All we can do is care and try our best," he said. "I promise you I'm doing both."

"God, I-I'm sorry. I'm a wreck. I hardly know you. Tonya is so... You must think I'm—"

"I think you're a very special person." He couldn't believe he'd said it. "I'm going to call you the minute I know anything. Will you do the same?"

"Yes, of course," she said. "And if I can help in any way, call me."

"We will." Geez, he'd finally said something personal then followed it up with an officious bureaucratic "we."

"And Farley, thank you. I'm coming to think you're special, too."

They disconnected.

"Who was that?" Aki asked. "Geez, partner, are you blushing?"

"Just talking with a contact." He turned as if to look at the clock. It was getting late, but no way would he rest.

"What are you doing?" Aki asked as Farley sat at his computer and his fingers flew.

"I'm hunting Quentin Robinson."

Chapter 68

"Drake, please let's just stay out here for a moment. I'm not ready," Rachelle said.

Her grip on his hand had tightened as they approached the door to the townhouse.

The observation and testing at the hospital had not taken long, and one of the North security people had just dropped them off. It was dark now, and the storm had left warm temperatures behind it. The parking lot light showed most of the pavement had dried, but leaves, branches, and puddles remained.

Farley had let Drake and Rachelle know the crime scene techs were done with the townhouse and assured them that all traces of drug had been removed.

Rachelle's hatred of the place could not be as readily washed away.

He wrapped his arms around her and held her against his chest.

"Why do seriously shitty things keep happening to us?" she said.

"Just lucky, I guess," Drake said.

She nudged him with her head. "Not funny."

They stood holding each other in front of the place where they'd almost died. Who had tried to kill Rachelle?

He'd called Kaye from the ER and asked if she would keep the kids overnight. He'd then given her a brief accounting of what had happened.

Kaye had been silent for a moment and Drake hoped she was not too upset. "Oh, is that all?" she said. "When I didn't hear from you, I started to think it might be something serious."

Drake had laughed and it had felt good. Most who worked in the ER used humor like Kevlar vests. It helped keep tragedy and pain from taking them down. At that moment, he'd appreciated Kaye beyond words.

It had been a long, brutal day.

It seemed impossible that it had only been about fourteen hours since Kline hit them with his intention to settle the malpractice case as a wrongful death. The CEO's focus was solely on the hospital's balance sheet. The truth didn't seem to matter.

Someone had poisoned Bart Rainey, leaving him on a ventilator.

And now someone had tried to kill Rachelle. The woman he loved and the mother of his children had been cold, blue, and lifeless.

"Drake, is there a tornado tearing through your mind, too?"

"More like a hurricane," he said.

Her smile warmed his soul. They held each other tighter.

In those first desperate moments, he'd believed she'd intentionally taken the drugs that led to her overdose. He'd assumed that she'd weakened and given in to the old urge. He was glad she was unaware of how unfairly he had judged her.

"It makes no sense, but I feel less worried now than I did before," she said.

"When I thought I'd lost you, I..." He stared into her eyes. He did not have the words to describe what was in his heart. He prayed she understood.

She stepped back, taking his hands. "I love you, Drake Cody."

"I'll bet you say that to all the guys you almost die with."

"Okay, funny guy. Have I mentioned how much I hate this crummy townhouse?"

"I've picked up on a couple of hints." His chest tightened as if in a vise. She was so incredibly beautiful.

"Let's go inside this dive of a house," she said. "We can put my tornado and your hurricane together and see what happens."

Her loveliness had him ready to burst. He unlocked the door, then she entered and led the way. He closed the door and turned to secure the two locks.

"Let's keep the lights off," she said from behind him as he attempted to enter the security code in the near-darkness. He messed up on the first try, then succeeded.

He turned and his breath caught. Rachelle stood in the soft light, naked, lovely, and flawless as a Greek goddess. Shadows flickered across her breasts as they rose and fell with each breath.

"You may have just broken the world speed record at undressing," he joked, his voice husky. She held one hand draped over the scar of her neck.

"I hate this place, but if we have to stay here, I won't let that stop us from living."

She took his hand and pulled him to her. He kissed the back of her hand where it was scarred from the sacrifice she'd made protecting the children.

His eyes absorbed her every curve. "You're more beautiful than anything I could ever imagine."

She unbuttoned his shirt slowly, her eyes locked on his. He slipped off the rest of his clothes and stood facing her. His heart throbbed throughout every part of him, his senses so tuned he could feel the air move.

She moved close but not yet touching. His body was steel drawn as if by a magnet toward her. He held his breath, vibrating in anticipation.

She pressed against him, her heat startling.

Oh, God!

The couch and floor where they'd almost died became the site where their love proved itself to be spectacularly alive.

Chapter 69

Clara looked out over Lake Calhoun from the window of her sixth-floor condo. ABBA's "Dancing Queen" played over the speakers. The lake's far southern margin was traced by the headlights of the scant traffic traveling its bordering boulevard. The still water's surface looked like polished onyx, blacker than the moonless sky.

This would be the last night Clara ever spent in the city of lakes.

She felt uncomfortable, though the sensation wasn't physical. For the first time in more than a decade, she was not connected to the electronic grid that had been both foundation and tool for her work and plans.

She'd severed all electronic links. Her dark web account, the wormhole links within the hospital system, and all evidence of her manipulations had been erased. She'd even shut down her phone account and was now using burners. She'd wiped her electronic fingerprints from the hospital network, and for the first time in more than fifteen years was not plugged into the hospital or what was happening there.

She'd been like a spider at the nexus of a huge electronic web—aware of everything going on anywhere in the system. But her escape required her to sever all ties. She'd jumped out of the plane and was hurtling towards her new life ready to pull the ripcord that would allow her to land free and safe.

After her meeting in the morning, she would disappear, her escape route foolproof. Extradition would be an impossibility. Regardless of what anyone might subsequently suspect, she'd made certain there was no proof. Her escape was as good as done.

She looked about her condo, revisiting torrid memories and missing Dan and what they'd had. But it was time to look forward. Her new life lay ahead.

She'd had no drive to binge or purge for almost two days. She was already changing.

Being off the grid left her unable to check if her plan for Drake Cody had worked. She hoped he would suffer a living hell and the endless agony of loss—that would be justice.

She picked up her stethoscope and placed it in her travel bag. All her computer equipment, electronic data storage components, and software tools had been shipped hours ago. They were on the way to the clinic—her new home. She was traveling light.

Her life as Dr. Clara Zeitman would begin when she stepped off flight 642. She smiled and lost herself in the music.

Nothing could stop her.

***

Q looked at the one remaining photograph he had of his mother. He was in fourth grade and she stood behind him smiling. He was beaming, and the junior chemistry set sat in front of them.

He'd completed one of the kit's experiments and she'd been proud.

She should be proud of him now—but she wasn't. He hadn't heard anything from her in more than a year and that was best. He thought what her response would be if his business was to be uncovered. If he appeared in the newspapers or on television, she'd see it as another black man bringing shame to black people everywhere. That was the bigoted way she thought.

His prison counselor Dr. Shabazz had helped Q to see that he could be whatever he wanted. He didn't need to fit others' idea of what a man should be—not his mother's, nor any of the people on the street or in prison.

He'd evolved.

Business was the way of the world. Free enterprise was the gateway that allowed a man to be what he wanted to be.

But it was not easy. And what business demanded he now do had his gut in a knot.

He would get it over with fast. He would make it painless. He would do what he could to make sure she was not afraid.

Smurf—no, he thought of her as Tonya now—was sleeping.

He'd tried to make her evening a special one. He'd ordered one of her favorite movies on cable, made her popcorn, and let her have ice cream. After she went to bed, he'd watched her door until he figured she was asleep and then he'd locked it.

He'd snorted three lines of cocaine and it helped. He had to prepare more product, and night was as good as day for working. He didn't think he would've been able to sleep anyway.

He wouldn't be able to sleep until he did what needed to be done. Business demanded hard decisions.

Tomorrow would be the day.

Chapter 70

Five a.m. and Stuart Kline clicked the refresh on the Minneapolis Star Tribune's eEdition site for the fifth time in the last two minutes. If the pain-in-the-ass reporter's article made it into the paper, it would be the worst kind of PR for Memorial Hospital.

The new day's front page appeared on the display. "Wave of Killer ODs Hits Region! More Than 25 Dead in Past Day." Son of a bitch. The druggies were going over the cliff like lemmings. Stuart skimmed to see if Memorial Hospital was mentioned. The morgue, police, and emergency medical services were noted to be overrun, but Memorial Hospital was not mentioned. Thank God, Drake Cody or one of the other doctors wasn't quoted encouraging addicts to come to Memorial for help.

It looked to Stuart like the druggies were taking care of themselves—natural selection at work. Memorial Hospital damn sure didn't need any more of their high-cost and low-compensation problems. Very few of them paid anything.

The rest of the front page focused on the monster storm. A second wave of thunder and rain was forecast.

He advanced to page two. All clear there. He clicked to page three—shit!

Midway down, the headline "Memorial Hospital in Midst of Malpractice Crisis" jumped at him. He began to read.

"...reports of millions in paid and anticipated malpractice settlements and awards... Special hospital committee created to deal with crisis... CEO Stuart Kline citing legal concerns declined the opportunity to deny malpractice, wrongful deaths, or a markedly disproportionate percentage of people of color among the mistreated... The troubling racial disparities raise serious questions... A recent case involving the death of a young mother of color and left her premature baby struggling for life has increased focus on the hospital and its care."

Damn it! The article was a hatchet job. It was only four columns wide and about six inches deep, but it was a marketing disaster.

The annoying Phoenix Halverson had just made settlement on the Clete Venjer suit beyond question and erased untold dollars in marketing. He pictured the political correctness warrior eating her gluten-free granola and getting her self-righteous rocks off seeing her name as the byline.

The young mother's death had not been judged malpractice yet, so mention of her or her infant was totally inappropriate. The article had tried and convicted the hospital.

As CEO, he had to minimize the damage. The amount the mother's wrongful death settlement would cost had just gone up dramatically. The hospital would have to pay whatever it took to make the case go away. His ability as fixer and facilitator would be critical.

The settlement numbers offer that Stuart had in his head to text to Clete Venjer this morning had just doubled.

The fat-cat attorney would counter with who knew how high a figure?

Regardless of the price tag, Stuart planned to have the settlement signed, sealed, and delivered before the day was over.

Memorial paid his big-time salary. The hospital was sinking, and he needed to keep it afloat.

His ability to keep focused on the bottom line was key to the hospital's future—it was only right that he be compensated accordingly.

He couldn't help but smile.

***

Rizz had been in the hospital for more than an hour.

He sat in front of the security office display screen viewing the video record showing traffic into and out of the locker room. After last evening's van ride from Mayo back to his apartment, he'd slept a couple of hours then woke up fully charged. He'd never needed much sleep. Historically, he'd had handled the extreme hours of the ER, partied whenever he could, and indulged in as much high-intensity physical activity as possible—preferably the co-ed naked type.

Since the bullet, his activity was so reduced he found it hard to sleep at all.

Before he'd left Mayo Rehab, Detective Yamada and Drake had set it up for Rizz to review the security video this morning. Drake had "volunteered" Rizz, and he'd been right on. Rizz was looking for ways to be useful.

But the security video of the locker room access had yielded nothing. The system had allowed him to screen an additional week prior to Bart Rainey's poisoning, and Rizz was viewing the motion-triggered traffic one last time.

All the people entering or leaving the locker room were surgeons. They all belonged.

He'd have to tell Aki that no one looked out of place—perhaps he could help out in some other way. Wait! What?

He reversed the video. Dr. Alan Steele, one of the trauma surgeons, entered the field of view. He wore scrubs and surgical booties and was pulling off his surgical cap as he entered the locker room—clearly he'd just got out of the OR. Alan was a friend of Rizz's. He double-checked the date and time indicator at the lower left corner of the image. It showed eleven-thirty the morning of the day before Bart Rainey was poisoned. Holy shit!

Rizz picked up his cell phone and entered Aki Yamada's number. This would blow the detective's mind.

***

"Please let me know if there's anything I can do to help you, Dr. Dronen," the medical student said. "I'm hoping to make forensic pathology my specialty. I've read many of your articles. If I can assist you, it would be my honor." The baby-faced young man in the short white coat practically bowed.

This medical student had the right attitude—Kip was a rock star in his field, and he didn't often receive the recognition he deserved.

Kip slid open the specimen tray from the refrigerated tissue repository. Security and privacy were paramount in the handling of specimens.

He understood the patient privacy mandate, yet yesterday afternoon's last-minute block to his examination of the placenta had been maddening. Only after he'd arrived and gloved in preparation had one of the hospital's legal staff entered and informed him he could not proceed. She said an objection had been raised by the attorney who represented the survivors. Memorial Hospital's head of medical records had agreed with the attorney's claim. A court order would be needed. He'd had to leave.

It had taken several phone calls, but finally last night Kip had been cleared to do the exam.

The placenta was an unusual structure. After delivery, it was no longer part of the mother and if portions of it were retained, it could trigger deadly bleeding based on its foreignness.

He opened the shallow, one-foot-square tray. The odor of iron and the chemical tinge of preservative rose. The placenta was oval and about eight inches in diameter and only a half inch thick. Its margins were irregular. Unlike most organs, placentas varied widely in shape and form—no two looked alike.

As with all human tissue, Kip appreciated the exquisite combination of structure and function. Everything a growing baby needed was provided by the umbilical cord that linked the fetus to the placenta. More than half a liter of blood flowed through it each minute, delivering oxygen and nutrients while simultaneously removing all toxins and waste products from the fetus.

While Kip's passion was death, the uniqueness of this special structure fascinated him.

The margins of all placentas were irregular, but in this specimen there was a gap, suggesting missing tissue. *Looks like trouble, ER guy.*

Proving that the missing placental tissue had caused this mother's bleeding and death would be medically impossible, but Kip had seen Clete Venjer in a court room. He could persuade a jury that the sun rose in the west.

Kip looked again, turning the placenta and examining the defect from the other side. *Huh?*

He turned, looking for a tissue microscope. The medical student was standing silent on the other side of the instrument bench with a scope in front of him.

Kip carried the tray over and placed it on the support. He positioned the scope over the tissue. He peered through the binocular eyepieces and shifted the tray while adjusting the focus. "Son of a bitch."

"What is it?" the medical student said eagerly. "May I see?"

"Look," Kip said. "But remember that being a forensic pathologist is not just looking at tissue or ordering tests, you must always be thinking. This case involves a report of missing placental tissue, and the claim that the tissue remained in the mother's body and triggered fatal bleeding—as can happen. But there is a significant finding here."

The student bent over the scope. He repositioned, then repositioned again. He straightened and his disappointment showed.

"I see placental tissue and an area of tissue loss, Dr. Dronen. I recognize no other significant finding. I must be missing something."

"Don't feel bad. A pathologist reviewed this tissue and reported nothing else of significance. Please get me your camera-mount for this scope. Let's capture some images and I'll point out the finding. I'll let you know what it tells a ninja-level forensic pathologist."

The medical student was looking at him as if he were godlike. It was almost embarrassing. Almost.

Chapter 71

Drake drove past the front of the hospital and turned right on Chicago Avenue at the parking lot. The streets were empty in the predawn grayness before rush hour and shift change.

He'd awoken very early gripped by unease. He had to act.

The magic of his and Rachelle's night together left him both appreciative and on edge. Thoughts of her made his chest tighten. Someone had tried to kill her—to take her from him. He clenched the steering wheel so hard it flexed in his hands.

He'd brought Rachelle to Kaye's house before dawn. Farley had recommended that she and the kids avoid the townhouse. Drake had no trouble convincing Rachelle to do that. They were keeping the kids out of school. As usual, Kaye accommodated as if they were family.

"Ha ha, yes, that's me. Part AARP fairy godmother and part pit bull," she'd said in response to Drake's heartfelt thanks. The sturdy nurse was one of the special people for whom taking care of others was part of their DNA.

Drake had looked in on Shane and Kristin. His sleeping children looked so innocent and beautiful, he ached. He was gripped by both his love for them and the instinct to destroy any who might threaten them or their mother.

He believed he'd been able to keep the dark side of what was going on inside him from Rachelle. Holding her in his arms and the goodbye kiss they'd shared had made his heart swell.

Seconds later as he drove toward the hospital, his thoughts were as black, rage-filled, and cold-blooded as any he'd experienced years earlier in the brutal world behind bars and barbed wire. He done ugly things there, and recently had once again taken someone's life. He'd had no choice.

Then, as now, those who harmed or threatened others loosed a part of himself he struggled to keep shackled. When he'd had to kill, it had been like nothing else. It had felt fundamentally right and good.

Drake pulled his car into the parking spot. Who had gone after Rachelle? If he found them, they would be a threat no longer. He accessed his phone.

"Call Detective Farley."

***

Farley pulled to the curb alongside the North Minneapolis apartment building. Things didn't look any better in the damp, predawn gloom.

Other than forty-five minutes on a homicide waiting room couch too small for his body, he'd worked the phones and computer all night. He'd contacted DEA and narcotics personnel and made multiple calls to their contacts and those who police records showed had been associated with Quentin Robinson in the past. Most hung up on him, but he'd heard the same thing from those who did respond. Q had gone straight. He was in real estate. He was no longer on the street. No one knew where he was living.

Farley had gone to the online license data system and found that Q had purchased a new, Lexus SUV two months before. The residence he listed on his registration was the same north Minneapolis address he'd given when arrested at the hospital several months before. He hadn't lived there for some time. Farley left messages for the landlord/owner to see if there'd been a forwarding address. He'd had no response on that.

He'd chased city records, utility user listings, water customers, and other database sites without being able to find Q's current residence.

Though it was still very early, he'd decided to visit the apartment building where Tonya's mother had overdosed and died.

He entered the same poorly lit, unkempt hallway as yesterday. It smelled of damp and mold. He walked past Tonya's mother's apartment and knocked on the neighbor's door. It opened almost immediately. The bespectacled, elderly woman was up and dressed. The apartment behind her looked spotless and smelled of cinnamon and toast.

"Remember me? I'm Detective Farley. I'm glad I didn't wake you."

"Of course, I remember. I just met you yesterday," she said. "And today is my Farmer's Market morning. If you'd got here much later you would've missed me. Have you found Tonya?" She held her hands prayer-like.

"No. Not yet."

"Lord have mercy." She shook her head.

"I have a picture to show you." He pulled it from his pocket. "Is this the man you saw with Tonya the other day? The man with the fancy car?"

She took the picture. Her eyes magnified through the thick lenses of her glasses. The picture she looked at was from Q's hospital arrest.

"Hmmm. I'm not sure." Her brow furrowed. "It could be, but this looks like a thug. Tonya was with a sharp-dressed man."

"Please take a look at this," Farley said. He took out his phone and pulled up the video of Q in the ER before the confrontation with the nurse and Drake. He hit play and held it in front of her.

"I'd bet that's him." She nodded. "He's a big man, but he's lost some weight now. But that's the way he moved. I couldn't send him to jail on it, but I believe that's him."

He pulled up another image on his phone. He showed her the image of the same model and color of Lexus SUV that Q had purchased.

"Yes. That's his car. Or at least that's the same kind of car he had."

Farley's hands became fists. His last doubts were gone.

Quentin Robinson, Q, Music Man—it doesn't matter what you're called, you're a son of a bitch, and I'm going to take you out.

"You've been a big help. Thank you very much," Farley said.

"Is he a bad man?" She directed her magnified gaze at Farley. "Would he hurt Tonya?"

Who knew what this guy might do? Hell, he'd hit a nurse. How messed up did you have to be to do that?

"We have everyone looking for Tonya."

He desperately wanted to learn that the scared, nothing-but-bad-luck kid was okay. The "she's safe" call to Rosie would be one he'd give anything to make.

His phone sounded. He nodded a thank-you to the woman.

"Detective Farley here," he answered as he walked through the rundown hallway.

"Drake Cody calling. We need to meet."

Chapter 72

Three pounds four ounces—that's what the little man Drake had delivered in the ER weighed this morning. The NICU nurse had shared with Drake that the premature drug-sickened baby was a fighter. He'd required opiates since birth to combat the jitteriness and problems of drug withdrawal, but they'd been able to taper them. He was doing well—better than expected.

The broken collar bone would heal and the nurse said he didn't seem uncomfortable.

Drake watched from the other side of the glass as the nurse held the tiny infant and delivered formula. Many said that physical touch and holding were as necessary as the high-tech medical care. Drake was a believer.

Farley had been brief on the earlier phone call. They were to meet in a half an hour.

Jim Torrins had called Drake just as he'd entered the hospital and within a minute of his hanging up with Farley. The administrator had said they needed to meet. He had not sounded upbeat.

"Hey, Drake,"

Drake turned to find that Jim Torrins had entered the room and stood alongside him, his gaze on the tiny baby.

"Is he the one?" Torrins asked.

Drake nodded.

"I heard about what happened to you and your wife. Craziness. I'm sorry, but I have something else we need to talk about right now. Have you seen today's paper?" Torrins asked.

"No." *What now?*

"An article headlining the malpractice cases and ripping Memorial Hospital made page three. They even referenced the death of this little guy's mother and mentioned him."

"Not good." A heaviness settled on Drake.

"No, it's not. I've already been contacted by several board members this morning. This has pushed them over the edge. Even some of the reasonable ones are agreeing with Kline. He has the votes. Kline is going to make a settlement offer today."

Drake sighed. His life was a speeding train hurtling off the tracks.

"Have you told him about what Kip Dronen found in reviewing the postmortem?" Drake asked. "About no placental tissue found in the uterus?"

"They all know. It virtually eliminates it as the cause of death, but it's too complicated for most juries. Bottom line, with the hospital's current standing and the anticipated media coverage, they won't take the chance of a trial. The board is supporting Kline. I'm doing everything I can to delay. This is way too fast and it's not right."

"If Kline makes a settlement offer and it's accepted, how much time do we have to challenge it?"

"None." Torrins paused, his eyes on the floor. "The minute it's signed and notarized, it's a done deal. There's no unringing the bell, regardless of what might be proved later."

The neonate wriggled and stretched in the nurse's arms, crying loudly enough to be heard through the glass. It wasn't the shrill, jittery shriek he'd made in the Crash Room but the vigorous complaint of one growing stronger.

Such a tough little guy. Drake had helped this little person. One of thousands of patients he'd taken care of. His work in the ER was the most rewarding thing he'd ever been part of. What they did there was noble. It mattered.

"I'm sorry, Drake," Torrins said. "Kline has no idea what taking care of patients or this hospital is about. It looks like he's going to get his way."

The wrongful death settlement—a bell that could not be unrung.

"Stop him, Jim," Drake said. "There's something strange going on with these patients. We need answers. You have to buy us some time."

"I'll give it my all," the graying physician-administrator said.

He did not look confident.

***

Drake stood in the ER corridor near the flight elevator. Rizz and Aki would show any minute. Rizz had said they had news related to Bart.

The big surgeon had been poisoned. Though with a different substance, that's what had happened to Rachelle. Who could be targeting Rachelle?

It had to be about me.

Did he and Bart have a common enemy? It was hard to imagine.

Rizz wheeled around the corner and Aki followed. His friend looked good.

Drake slid his keycard through the slot, and the flight elevator doors opened. He stepped in and Rizz and Aki followed. The doors pinged shut and the elevator began to rise.

"Hey, brother. You're looking great." Drake extended a hand toward his friend.

Rizz grasped Drake's hand in an iron grip and pumped it. "Missed you, amigo. You look like you just spent five minutes in the worry-microwave with the setting on high. No fear, the Rizz man is here. Who's better at getting you out of trouble than me?" The confident smile was back.

"I need help, that's for sure." After Torrins' report, confidence was hard to come by.

"Farley told me all about what happened with your wife and you," Aki said. "Glad you're okay. We're gonna find who did it."

"Who did what?' Rizz asked.

"We're okay," Drake said. "I'll fill you in later."

The elevator stopped and the doors opened. Rizz rolled out first and they moved to the edge of the concrete where the steel mesh platform began.

The helicopter sat perched and ready. Drake took in the downtown office buildings, the river, and the view of the metro area. The big storm had left warm weather, and though the clock said sunrise had occurred, the sky was dark. The air hung heavy and static-charged.

"Tell Drake what you found, Rizz," Aki said.

"Reviewing the video, I saw Alan Steele entering the locker room at 11:30 a.m. the day before Bart went down."

"Alan?" Drake said. The trauma surgeon was one of the classiest people on staff. Alan and Bart Rainey both covered trauma, but they were night-and-day personalities. "No way. Alan would never—"

Rizz held up a hand. "Agreed. Alan is a friend of mine, which is why I called Aki straight away."

Huh? "We agree Alan would never have anything to do with this, so what the—"

"Haiti," Rizz said.

"What?" Drake said.

"He's in Haiti. Alan left on his annual medical care trip the day before the date of the video. The security video has been screwed with. Someone patched in a different stretch of video and somehow edited the time imprint. It's bogus."

Drake looked to Aki.

"We are having the tech nerds figure out which sections have been changed," Aki said. "It would have been great to see a clear suspect entering the locker room, but the fact that it has been messed with tells us a lot."

"It's somebody very medically sophisticated," Rizz said. "And it's somebody who works here or can otherwise access the hospital and locker room. And now we know it's somebody who also has the knowledge and ability to mess with the hospital's high-tech video system."

Drake's thoughts were spinning. Who could it be?

His phone sounded. He answered. "Drake Cody here."

"Hey ER, where the hell are you?" sounded the squeaky voice of Kip Dronen. "I make a Medical Examiner house call to the hospital to help you out, and now I'm in your nuthouse of an ER and you're not here. I've got something you need to hear, and I don't want to share it over the phone."

"We're eight floors straight above you on the helicopter flight deck. Detective Yamada and Rizz are with me. Ask one of the docs to access the elevator for you and come up."

"That won't be happening," Kip said. "I don't do heights. If you want to hear what I found, and you sure as hell do, you come to me. I'm a forensic pathologist, not a pizza delivery guy."

Brilliant but always with attitude—did Kip have good news or bad?

"We're on the way."

Chapter 73

Clara checked her watch— three hours before her flight. The tickets were listed under her alias, and she had excellent forged identification and a simple but effective disguise. She could not be stopped. First a jump to Atlanta, and from there the flight to Guatemala City. In twenty-four hours, she'd be in her new villa. There would be no tracks.

She adjusted her black wig and clear-lens glasses in the mirror of the bathroom of the Whole Foods grocery store. The phone message she'd left at the lab identified she was home ill. She'd walked away from the condo for the last time, leaving everything as if she'd just stepped out for a moment. Her car sat in its assigned parking stall. It could be days before anyone discovered she was gone for good. She looked at her watch once more. Her cab would be out front in minutes.

Now that she'd started the countdown, her escape and the start of her new life couldn't come fast enough.

She hungered for the intellectual challenge of being fully tested and the satisfaction of triumphing. She longed to demonstrate her brilliance and reap the rewards and recognition for what she accomplished.

Back when she'd endured the medical school application process, she hadn't acted like all the other applicants and their phony I care-so-deeply-about-everyone posturing.

Fake sentiment aside, it would genuinely matter to her how her patients did. That was how physicians were judged. It was the ultimate test.

She would be on the frontline, proving that she was more than good enough. She was counting the minutes.

One meeting to collect a final massive payment and she'd be on her way.

She would have the life she'd been born to lead—the life of her dreams. Her life as Doctor Clara Zeitman.

***

Q had decided.

Business meant hard decisions. Putting things off was bad business. He'd give her a good morning, then...

He'd thought it through. The storm made it highly unlikely anyone had seen him bring her into the house. And if they had, no way in that rain anyone could have seen well enough to provide a clear identification. Nothing they could swear to on a witness stand.

He'd stick close to her—not let her near a phone and not let her outside. He'd pulled the drapes and locked the door and, as always, the alarm was on. The door to her room was locked, but at this hour he was sure she was still sleeping. He would go unlock it so when she woke she didn't freak. If she sensed something was up, it could get ugly.

If he kept things mellow it would go easier. Despite a lying junkie of a mother and some shitty foster care, Tonya had faith in people. She'd been upset yesterday but she still trusted him. How had the girl remained so sweet and innocent?

This is gonna be ugly.

More cocaine would help.

He laid out two big lines on the living room coffee table and snorted them. He leaned his head back and the chemical accelerator revved his mind and gave him strength.

He could do this.

She would disappear. It sucked, but business was not just about doing what was fun.

If it were easy, everyone would be rich.

Chapter 74

The elevator doors slid open.

Drake could judge the department's activity level by the sound. Currently, he'd estimate the place was not overrun. He turned to Rizz and Aki. "Let's find Kip and see if we can use the Crash Room. It's private there."

Drake led the way down the corridor. He spied the skinny, wild-haired Kip leaning on the counter at the unit coordinator's desk. The Crash Room across the hall stood empty.

"Let's go guys," Kip's said. "It's not like I don't have anything else to do. Corpses are showing up at the morgue like on an assembly line."

Kip's impatience stoked Drake's apprehension. *What did Kip find?*

"Let's talk in the Crash Room." Drake said as he led the way. Kip, Rizz, and Aki followed.

Drake slid the glass partition closed behind them and they positioned themselves around the bed in Bay three.

"What kind of hospital are you running here?" Kip said. "Between the zoo of an ER, the reported malpractice, the poisoning of the surgeon, and toss in what I found in the pathology lab, this place is out of control."

"Please tell me what you found that you said I 'sure as hell' need to know," Drake said. "I'm dying here. My life and dreams are on the line."

"Life and dreams?" Kip scratched his head. "Oh, yeah. I forgot about that. If you get tagged for a wrongful death you're pretty much toast."

"Please. What did you find?"

"Okay. Geez, lighten up, ER," Kip said. "I just finished examining the placenta."

"Yes, and?"

"There is missing tissue." He pulled folded papers from his pocket and unfolded them. On top was a picture of the placenta with a ruler in the frame.

"That fits the malpractice attorney's claim. It sounds bad," Rizz said.

"It looks bad, too. Particularly if you don't look close," Kip said.

"What are you saying?" Drake said.

"See these margins?" He pointed to the boundary where the tissue had been lost. "This is the area where the missing tissue separated from the rest of the placenta."

Kip shuffled the top paper, revealing a second image underneath. "This is the microscopic view of those margins. As you see here," he indicated on the image, "the margins are sharp and linear." He set the paper on the bed and shrugged. "Done deal."

"Done deal what?" Aki said, looking lost.

"Well, Officer Flatfoot," Kip said. "When tissue is torn or separated in illness or injury the margins are never sharp and linear. Never. These margins resulted from being cut with a blade or other edged tool. I would testify with absolute certainty that the missing tissue was cut free with an instrument. And, not to put too fine an edge on it," he chuckled, "I'd bet it was a surgical scissors. It had to have happened outside of the body." He smiled as if he'd just completed a magic trick. "Bottom line, ER guy. I think I saved your ass again."

"You're saying that someone cut the tissue away after the placenta came out of the mother's body?" Aki said.

"That's exactly what I'm saying. Zero doubt about it."

"Bingo," Rizz said. "That blows their malpractice claim right out of the water." He looked at Drake. "Are you reading that, amigo? They've got nothing. It was fiction in the first place, and now it's been confirmed."

Drake said nothing. Relief, appreciation, and anger all bounced around in his head. They had to get this information to Kline before he signed the settlement for wrongful death. Drake's career hung in the balance.

What had happened to the placenta was not an accident—it was another mysterious, destructive event in Memorial Hospital. Who was doing these things? Why?

"I'm just a grind-it-out, flatfoot detective like Einstein here says," Aki nodded toward Kip. "But I'm trying to put it all together. This placenta stuff is one more piece of a puzzle, but a bigger question is, how many puzzles are we dealing with? Is this hospital teeming with diabolical lunatics, or does this stuff all fit together somehow?"

"Sound thinking, Aki," Rizz said. "From Bart's poisoning, we know it's someone who got into the hospital and locker room and is medically knowledgeable. The fact that they messed with the security video means they have access to the hospital computer system at a high level and have significant expertise." He backed his wheelchair up a bit. "And what does their being able to mess with the placenta tell us? The person has to be medically aware and cunning and somehow have gotten access to the privacy-protected pathology specimen. The best fit is if we find one person who fits the bill for everything."

"Since the placenta scheme involved a wrongful death case, we should look at the others," Kip said.

"Torrins put you on that committee, Drake," Rizz said. "You've looked at those cases. Have you found anything weird?"

"Something has seemed off, but I have no answers. The last time I screened the cases, I specifically tried to figure how a medically knowledgeable person might have intentionally caused the harm or death. I—"

"Stop right there," Kip said. "You said death. No offense, but when we're talking about keeping people alive, you ain't half bad. When we're talking cause of death, I'm the ninja-master. I should look at all those cases."

"Absolutely, Kip." Drake said.

"Give me the medical record numbers and get me access on the hospital system, and I'll start now," Kip said, clearly eager. "I can let the chief medical examiner and other second-stringers handle the overdose parade. This challenge is worthy of me."

Drake reached into his pocket and pulled out the slip with the list of eight-digit medical records numbers of the bad outcome and malpractice cases. Torrins had given him the list days ago, and Drake had reviewed them multiple times. "I have these copied on my phone, so you can keep it." As he handed the list to Kip, recognition streaked across his mind like a shooting star.

He leaned back against the instrument console next to the bed and raised a hand to his head. Pieces fell into place.

Son of a—?

"Are you okay?" Rizz asked.

"Wow." Drake paused and looked each of them in the eye. "I got it. I know who poisoned Bart." He sighed. "And probably are responsible for a lot more. Several times when I looked at the records, I felt like I was missing something—" It had been a nudge, something that he couldn't nail down—like a name or fact that he knew but couldn't quite grasp. Now it had come together with slam-dunk certainty.

He had no clue as to why, but he knew who.

Chapter 75

Running water sounded from the bathroom. Q looked in the room Smurf had slept in. She'd already made the bed. Such a good kid—it made what he had to do even harder.

She came out of the bathroom. Something about her looked off. It took a second, but he figured it out—no smile.

"I've got Fruit Loops, toaster waffles, and chocolate milk—your favorites," Q said. "How does that sound?" He smiled.

"I not hungry." Not a hint of a smile and her posture like a partially deflated balloon.

"You love Fruit Loops."

"I want to see Momma."

Wow, how to handle this? This wasn't his Smurf, this was a seriously upset kid.

"You want to watch some cartoons? I can get anything you want on cable."

She looked at him, her eyes pinched. "You said Jesus took Momma. She in heaven. I don't want her there. I want her back."

Aw, damn. Talking death with a kid who still thinks Santa Claus and the Easter Bunny are real was not something he knew how to handle. *Sorry, kid, your momma was a junkie and she messed up* would not cut it.

"It doesn't work that way, Smurf. We can talk about it later. Let's go downstairs."

"No call me Smurf. My name Tonya. You yell at me. You mean. You not my friend no more." She looked ready to cry.

"That's cold," he said. *This is not good.* "I'm your friend. And you're my friend, my best friend. Let's go eat some breakfast and we'll both feel better." The hell of it was she was as close to a friend as he had. *Please, girl, don't make this harder.*

"I want to talk Rosie." She did not make eye contact.

"Rosie? Who's Rosie?"

"She my friend. She nice."

307

"After breakfast, things will look better. I'm going to take care of every-thing." He put a hand on her shoulder and her body stiffened as if she'd been shocked.

She'd never been like this before. What could he say? He wanted her to have a good morning. Before he...

She'd soon be with her momma. Damn.

***

"I have no idea why, but I know who," Drake said.

Aki, Rizz, and Kip looked at him open-mouthed. The buzz of the ER outside the Crash Room doors seemed to pause. The pieces fell into place, and his gut overrode any doubt.

"Clara Zeitman poisoned Bart, messed with the placenta, and may be in-volved with some of the other stuff that's happened in the hospital."

"Who?" Aki said.

"The head of the lab and information management? The control freak?" Rizz said.

Kip frowned.

"It's Clara," Drake said. "Everything fits. Look at what she does running the laboratory. She's brilliant and knowledgeable. Beyond that, she oversees Memorial's information technology operations and is mega-skilled. She could access the security video and alter it. She has access to the entire system and she could get in anywhere. She's definitely sharp enough to poison Bart's tobacco."

"What about the placenta?" Kip asked.

"That's another link. She was in the Crash Room the day the patient who bled out came in and delivered her baby. I can't recall for sure, but she may have been the person who took the placenta to pathology. Even if she wasn't, I'm sure she could get access." Drake paused, his belief gelling more firmly as he spoke.

"I have no idea why she'd try to kill Bart or why she'd mess with the pla-centa, but it's her. And she may have done more. I was worried about an in-sane nurse or doctor being involved with the mysterious deaths and bad out-comes in the hospital. She may be the one."

"You said something had been nagging at you. What was it that just hit you?" Rizz said.

Drake held up the list of multiple eight-digit medical record numbers.

"There are thirteen eight-digit numbers here," he said. "Jim Torrins gave them to me when he put me on the malpractice crisis committee. I went to Clara in her capacity as Chief of Health Information Services and asked for the best way for me to access the medical records."

"That's standard," Kip said." I've contacted her on medical examiner cases."

"When I showed her the list, she almost took my head off," Drake said. "She threatened to report me to the state Medical Board. She said that since I hadn't been involved in the care of any of those patients, my reviewing them would be a patient privacy violation. Her reaction shocked me."

"Did she know why you wanted to review the cases?" Rizz asked.

"No. I had only identified that I wanted to check the records and asked what she recommended. She looked at the list and flipped out immediately. It's suggestive in retrospect, but what only occurred to me a minute ago is that she could not have possibly known what linked those cases or that I had not been involved in any of them."

"I don't know if I understand what that means," Aki said.

"What it said is that without referring to anything, she was familiar enough with those cases to recognize their medical record numbers. Further, she knew enough detail to know that I had not been involved in any of them. Add that to the way all the other pieces of the puzzle fit together, and she has to be the one."

"I'm with you," Rizz said. "I've always known she was bizarre, but she may be totally nuts."

"Is she in the hospital now?" Aki said. "We have enough to pick her up. I want to arrest her now."

"She should be here," Rizz said. "She's got a reputation for pretty much living here."

"Let me call Jim Torrins," Drake said to Aki. "He should be able to help."

"Yes, I want to coordinate with him and security," Aki said. "Arrests can go bad in a hurry, especially if the suspect is unbalanced. We don't want anybody getting hurt."

"Rizz, I would really like your help and Torrins' as well," Drake said. "With what Kip found, we have to stop Kline from signing the settlement. Clete Venjer's claim is now proven groundless, but if Kline signs that settlement, it'll be too late for me. If you can call Lloyd and get him up to speed, that would help as well. I need to—"

Drake's phone sounded. "I have to take this." He turned from the group. "Drake Cody here."

"Drake, it's Detective Farley. Where are you at?"

"I'm in the ER. I was just about to tell Aki and Rizz that I was going to meet with you. Aki is preparing to make an arrest on the poisoning of Bart Rainey."

"Good. I'm eager to hear more, but everything's happening at once. I'll call Aki in a minute, but I have a question for you. When was the last time you saw or heard anything of Q, the guy who got arrested in your ER?"

"The last time I saw him was when he was getting arrested."

"It looks like he's the Music Man. He's the number one suspect for the drugs that killed your young patient, and I don't have proof of this yet, but he may be the one who sent the stuff to your wife. I just traced him to a cable TV account for a house in Uptown. It looks like he's there. I'm waiting on a warrant and scrambling a Critical Response team to hit the residence. If you're critical-incident certified, I could use a backup medical guy and somebody to ID him. I'm just pulling up to the hospital. If you're available, I can swing through the ambulance bay and grab you. Things are going to go down fast."

Drake's hand tightened on the phone and black thoughts surged. Q was the big druggie who'd hit Patti in the ER. He 'may be the one' who'd sent the drugs that had almost killed Rachelle. Drake had lost it months back when he'd taken the big man down, and now once again a pounding began in his head, and tightness gripped his neck and shoulders.

"All of us who flew medical rescue have had critical incident training," Drake said. "I'll be there in ninety seconds." He disconnected. Early in his training it had been a surprise to learn that ambulances were positioned nearby for all major law enforcement actions. Medics or emergency doctors were often part of the incursion team. Drake and his partners had been certified in case they were called on.

"Aki, that was Farley. He's got a lead on the Music Man. He thinks it's Q, the guy who got arrested here a few months back. He's got an address. He's working on getting a warrant and is putting together a CRU team to hit the house. He said he'd call you in a minute."

"I knew he was hunting Q." Aki looked torn. "Let's hope we can get this Clara into custody quick. I want to be in on it when that warrant comes through."

Drake turned to Rizz and Kip. "I'm going to meet Farley. I need you two guys to come through for me like never before. Kline has to be stopped before he signs that settlement. Torrins and Lloyd might be able to help. Can you do it?"

"I'll give it everything I've got, brother," Rizz said.

"I can convince anyone who's not a total moron that the retained placenta claim is false," Kip said.

"Thank you."

Drake left unsaid that Q looked to be responsible for the death of Bryce and the attempted murder of Rachelle. Or that he was going to grab a medical bag and provide medical support for the tactical team takedown.

Drake had been out of control when they'd pulled him off Q in the ER that day, but his instincts had been righteous.

He should have killed the bastard.

Chapter 76

Stuart Kline strode through the carpeted, walnut-appointed administrative wing holding the cup of coffee he'd just poured. Typically, he'd have his secretary perform the task, but sometimes he liked to walk through the executive office area in his hand-tailored, expensive clothes just to be seen.

Appearances and titles mattered. Stuart used his title, position, and power to acquire what he valued most—money.

The settlement offer he'd sent to Clete Venjer thirty minutes earlier had been seven figures. Stuart's coffee walkabout was in part triggered by restlessness as he awaited a response.

"CEO Kline, sir." His secretary held the phone up as he approached her desk. "Attorney Clete Venjer is on line one."

Stuart liked being called CEO. He also liked being called sir. Most of all, he liked what this phone call meant—*it's going to happen.*

"Put him through." He entered his office and picked up the buzzing phone.

"CEO Stuart Kline here." Anticipation kept him from sitting down.

"Good morning. This is Clete Venjer. I reviewed the settlement numbers you texted me."

As they'd discussed, Stuart had sent off both a total settlement figure and the amount that would come back to him under the table in recognition of his facilitator role.

"The offer represents the hospital's good-faith effort to make things right," Kline said. Venjer's counteroffer would be a bigger number. *How much will my cut be?*

"If you check your text messages now," Clete said, "you'll see my counteroffer. The patient's brother is sick with grief, and the orphan infant may have a lifetime of medical difficulties. I'm glad to hear the hospital acknowledges their responsibility, but the offer minimizes the enormity of the tragedy. Recent media coverage has highlighted just how horrific the untimely loss was."

Man, oh man, Venjer was smooth. Mentioning the media and the "orphan infant" reinforced the reality that Stuart understood all too well. This case was radioactive and needed to disappear.

Stuart pulled out his cell phone. The first number was Venjer's counteroffer total. The second was the amount that Stuart most wanted to see—his cut.

The attorney's counteroffer was more than twice the hospital's initial offer. Despite that, Stuart smiled and his heart raced. In addition to jacking up the settlement figure, Venjer had made Stuart's kickback an even greater percentage—a huge payday.

Yesterday Stuart had discussed with the Board and the insurance carrier how damaging a trial would be. They'd agreed on an upper limit for a payout. Somehow the attorney had come up with an offer that was within five percent of that.

"The hospital wants to do the responsible thing." Stuart found it hard to spit out the obligatory sober response—inside he was doing cartwheels. He'd taken a crisis and turned it into an opportunity. "The hospital agrees to your terms, Clete."

The hospital would stay afloat and keep paying his salary, and he'd reap a gigantic, off-the-books reward. *Jackpot!*

"I'm authorized to sign immediately, and the hospital would appreciate your help in maintaining appropriate privacy for both the family and the hospital. Publicity for such sensitive matters is unseemly, and the hospital requires all the standard no-discussion clauses for all parties."

"My client is ready to have this painful process behind him," the attorney said. "I have the appropriate documents, witnesses, and notary available at my office. Can you meet me there in an hour?"

Stuart felt flushed. His scalp tingled. One hour to closing the biggest deal of his life!

"Great! Er, yes, that works. Please extend the sympathy of Memorial Hospital to your client. I'm glad we have been able to put our professional abilities together to help everyone get through this challenging situation."

The attorney disconnected.

Stuart stopped in front of the full-length mirror that hung near the walk-in closet in his office. He admired himself—he had the look of a man who was one hour from becoming much richer.

He loved the look.

***

Clete hung up the phone in the study of his Lake Harriet mansion. "CEO" Stuart Kline sickened him. He'd said he was "glad we put our professional abilities together to help everyone." How the sleazy weasel could spout such garbage without choking was a mystery. Clete felt like swabbing his ear with disinfectant just from having listened to him.

Clete had been ordered to play along on the rapid settlement or he'd lose everything. He looked out over at an iron gray sky and the still surface of Lake Harriet.

All his years in the malpractice world, he'd remained clean. Malpractice was a world of money grabbers, phonies, corrupt medical "experts," and plenty of unethical behavior. A world that was driven by money.

And he'd tried to stay above that. No corruption, no kickbacks, no under-the-table payoffs, no lying—he'd held as true to his aim as possible. The settlements and verdicts he'd won had totaled many millions, but that was his tool, not his objective. His commitment was "no more Anjanees." No more mothers lost and broken. No more fathers hollowed out by guilt, regret, loss, and pain. He'd used the testimony of experts he knew were unprincipled, he'd destroyed caring doctors and pursued cases where laying blame was not fair, but he'd told himself he'd done it because it was necessary for the greater good.

Hospitals and medical people needed to constantly fear the damage they could do. Clete's work kept them vigilant. But had something he'd never intended happened?

Regret now soured his righteousness.

He'd made a bad decision. He'd compromised himself. One misjudgment, one misread, and his integrity had been lost. He hadn't slept for days.

The collusion with Kline tainted his life's work. Would other demands be made? For Anjanee's memory and his soul, he prayed not.

Chapter 77

Aki, the security supervisor, and the bespectacled lab guy stood near a complex-looking device at the back of the Memorial Hospital laboratory. They'd quietly asked the lab staff to slip out the front entrance, and the large room was empty except for the tables of glassware and high-end equipment.

"Dr. Zeitman left a phone message that she wouldn't be in today, and she's not answering her office phone," the lab technologist said.

"Is that the master key?" Aki asked indicating an orange keycard the security supervisor held.

"Yes," the security supervisor said. "If administration will give an okay, I can open her office for you."

"This is a police case involving attempted murder, and others may be at risk," Aki said. "It doesn't look like she's in there, but I need to check it out. Dr. Rizzini is talking with the president of medical affairs right now, but time matters. Give me the card and stay back." He held out his hand.

The supervisor thought for a moment, then handed over the card.

Aki walked across the main lab to the door that opened into Clara Zeitman's office. He pulled his weapon, slid the card through the reader, and the lock clicked. He crouched low and burst through the door.

The sterile, white office and desk were unoccupied.

Aki checked the lab counter and the desktop, and all looked as he would expect at the end of a workday. He hadn't liked the idea of making an arrest in the hospital, but the prospect of an arrest at her residence presented other problems.

The best case would be they found her sick in bed. *Crap!* He'd need a warrant.

Meanwhile, Farley was getting ready to hit a house in Uptown that was definitely high risk. It didn't look like he'd be able to be there for his partner.

Neither this Clara-freak nor Q were known to have weapons, but hard experience had taught him that arrests could go sideways when least expected.

He had a real bad feeling.

***

Rizz slapped the wall plate and wheeled through the door into the administrative office wing. He wheeled up to the secretary's desk outside of Medical Affairs president Jim Torrins' office.

"Hi, Doctor Rizzini," she said.

"I need to see him right away," Rizz said.

"He's on the phone, but I'll let him know you're here."

"No worries," Rizz said and wheeled up to the partially open door. "He needs to hear this right now." He pushed the door open and wheeled in.

Jim Torrins was hanging up the phone as Rizz wheeled in. "What's up, Rizz?"

"The police are going to arrest Clara Zeitman. She poisoned Bart Rainey."

"No! Clara Zeitman?"

"Yes. And the medical examiner has proved that the malpractice settlement case is a set-up. Kline needs to be stopped before he signs Drake's future away," Rizz said.

"He threatened he was going to sign as soon as he could," Torrins said. "I've been trying to slow things down, but the Board is behind him. I saw him leave his office about fifteen minutes ago. We may be too late ..."

Chapter 78

Farley pulled into the parking lot alongside a dark SUV with police plates. In the short drive from the hospital to this Uptown neighborhood park, Drake had learned about the young girl and the other circumstances surrounding Q and the evidence pointing to him as the Music Man. A narcotics officer had called Farley and reported that one of his snitches confirmed Q sold the high-grade product marked with the glyph. The contact had also said that Q used a "funny-looking girl" as a mule.

A lone man stepped from behind the open back gate of the parked SUV as Farley and Drake got out of the car.

"Hey there, Detective," the short, powerful-looking police officer said, extending a hand to Farley. "We have a skeleton crew on this one. There's a protest with people waddling onto 35W like geese, a barricaded shooter on the north side, and a couple of other raids in progress." He shrugged his shoulders, not looking the least bit concerned. "I've got my partner watching the house, and two of my tactical brothers will try to make it as soon as they get clear. If we need to move fast, it may be just us."

The black officer was pulling on a windbreaker with POLICE in large letters across the back. He wore a Kevlar vest, and his Glock was secured in a military-style holster on his right thigh. He wore combat-style boots.

He spoke into the communications mike strapped to his shoulder. "Status report."

Some static and then, "No change. Car hasn't left the garage. No visible activity." He double-clicked off.

"Nate, this is Dr. Drake Cody," Farley said. "He's a Memorial ER doc and our medical guy on the hit today. He can also identify our bad guy. He's dealt with him before."

"Nate Cray, tactical squad," the officer said, extending a meaty hand. As they shook, he eyed Drake. "Have you been critical-incident certified?"

"Nice to meet you, and yes I have," Drake said.

"Good, but as this goes down, I'm going to talk to you as if you don't know anything, so don't be offended."

"The more you tell me the better," Drake said.

"Detective Farley is calling the shots, but I'm the operations specialist," he said. "My job is to eliminate threats. I do a lot of these."

"What he means is that he's crazy," Farley said. He popped the trunk of the unmarked. He took out a Kevlar vest and handed it to Drake. He removed another and began putting it on.

"How are we going to play this one?" Nate said.

"I'm waiting on the search warrant. This guy should already be in jail for an assault in the ER a few months back, but he lawyered up, somehow got the civil liberties activists behind him, and the DA let him walk. He's been through the system and seems to be getting smarter all the time. We don't want him getting off on a technicality." Farley pulled on a windbreaker like Nate's and handed another to Drake.

"What's this about the vulnerable kid? I saw the alert and photo," Nate said.

"Her safety is our top priority," Farley said. "She was seen with Q two days ago. Yesterday, her mother died of an OD with drugs that came from him. The girl called it in but hasn't been heard from since. Her Child Protection case worker should be here any minute."

"I hope she's someplace far away and safe." Nate turned to Drake. "When we're going to do a raid we always try to scope the residence beforehand. The priority is to minimize risk to public or other innocents. A lot of the time, these assholes have kids, girlfriends, or any manner of folks around them. The observer watches for signs of anyone else in the house. I checked the garage twenty minutes ago, and his car is there. We've seen movement and shadows at windows. Best bet is he's in there, but we don't know if he's alone."

Nate checked a long weapon in the back of the vehicle, keeping it out of sight. "Anytime there are kids, we try to have Child Protection involved. In all raids, we try to have an ambulance crew standing by. This park is our staging site on this hit. Only three minutes to the house, so they're close if needed. We may not be able to have medics on hand today due to all the overdoses, but we have you. If a rig gets loose, they're going to show here."

Drake swallowed. Handling critical injuries in a fully staffed ER was very different than being alone in the middle of an active crime scene with nothing but the contents of a rescue bag.

"I'm ready to help in any way I can," Drake said.

"Roger that, Doc. To protect and serve," Nate said. "It's like city water, electricity, or gas service—the average citizen has no idea what's involved in making it happen. Actually, we're more like the sewer system." He winked. "We get rid of shitheads."

Farley's phone sounded.

"Do you have it?" he said and then frowned. "Bust into the office if you have to. We need to move." He put his phone away. "The judge is tied up on a ruling about the protesters blocking the highway. No warrant yet." He shook his head. Throughout the short car ride and the time on site, Farley had seemed less and less like the pudgy, easygoing person Drake was familiar with and more like a guy no one would want to mess with.

A red Ford Escort pulled into the lot and a dark-haired, athletic-looking, young woman jumped out and went straight to Farley.

"Is Tonya with this guy?" Her voice was strained.

"We don't know."

"Guys, this is Rosie Padron from Child Protection," Farley said. "She's the girl's case worker."

"Her name is Tonya," Rosie said. She crossed her arms as if she were hugging herself or very cold. "Seventeen years old, but think of her as an eight-year-old. Down syndrome. She's a sweetheart, but if she's in there and there's noise or yelling she's going to be out-of-her-head scared. Please, er, uh... Oh, God, just do what you can." The woman was white-faced and distraught. "Please, I just know she's in trouble." She hugged herself tighter.

"I don't like this waiting," Farley said. "Nate, are you ready to go? Drake? When we get the green light we need to fly."

"Banzai," Nate said. "And the doc is ready to go. Right?"

Drake nodded, his jaw tight. The throbbing in his temples grew. The presumption of innocence was about the courts. In the real world, people on the frontlines often knew who the guilty were—the details might be uncertain, but those who'd regularly victimized others were known.

Q had probably been who had almost killed Rachelle, and he'd killed many others with his drug business. Drake's jaw ached. Would the law and courts provide justice and stop Q for good? He took a big breath. Farley, Nate, and the rest of the team would handle Q. He needed to focus on his medical duty as a member of the team.

"Take these." Drake pulled respiratory masks and nitrile gloves out of the trauma and resuscitation bag he'd grabbed at the ER. "Before we hit that door, put them on. The drugs can take you down in seconds. If anyone has a suspected contact or any other issues, you holler out immediately—understood?"

"With you," Farley said.

"Roger that," Nate said. "But we'll have to wait for the mask part. Communication is life or death, so we can't be muffled." He didn't seem stressed.

What would they find when they went in the house—a bunch of nothing or disaster? Farley had explained how it would go down. Nate's observer partner would cover the rear door. Nate would man the ram and bust open the front door, with Farley in first, then Nate. When they called "clear," Drake would follow. He was to hang back and stay out of any action.

Rosie stood holding a fist to her mouth, her eyes closed. Farley looked hard-eyed and locked in. Nate stretched his neck and shook his arms loose.

It felt like past the time to move.

How much longer did they have to wait?

The seconds crawled.

The phone clipped to Rosie's belt sounded...

Chapter 79

Rizz finished his cell call just as Torrins hung up his office phone.

"Kline isn't answering his cell phone," Torrins said. "His secretary said he'd received a call from Clete Venjer about fifteen minutes ago and then told her he was leaving the hospital. He didn't say where he was going."

"He's probably on his way to hook up with Venjer to sign right now," Rizz said.

"He's been awfully eager to settle," Torrins said.

"He's got to be stopped," Rizz said. "If he signs, Drake is history."

They were silent for a moment.

"Have you got Venjer's number?" Rizz asked.

"Office and cell number. You have a plan?" Torrins asked.

"Plan?" Rizz shook his head. "The Life Clock is ticking and we're about out of time. My first thought was a deer rifle and parking one in Kline dead center. I figure I'd better ratchet back a bit from that."

"Maybe just a leg wound?" Torrins said, arching an eyebrow.

Ha! If things weren't so grim, Rizz would have laughed at that one. The older doc had his head on right.

Torrins was good people. Drake was the best.

We stop Kline and stop him now or I won't ever work with Drake again.

***

"What's wrong with you, Smurf? You love Fruit Loops." Q's patience had run out.

"Not call me Smurf. You not my friend!" She screamed and her words became harder to understand. She shoved the bowl. It flew off the table and shattered, with milk, cereal, and glass exploding across Q's kitchen floor.

What the hell? She'd flipped out. He'd never seen her anything like this before. Did she sense what was coming? Son of a bitch! He'd been screwing around trying to give her a good morning, like a death row prisoner's last meal. But it was only making it worse. He should have taken care of this business last night.

"If you settle down, I'll—"

"I not settle down!" She was crying and screaming at the same time. She got up, picked up her glass of chocolate milk, and threw it on the floor.

He grabbed her by the arms and shook her.

She surprised him as she put both hands on his chest and pushed hard. His feet hit the milk and shot out from under him. He slammed to his back, his head bouncing on the wood floor.

"I want my momma!" she screamed.

He jumped up, towering above her, his fist cocked. *You little bitch!*

She collapsed to the chair, cowering, face down on the table, her arms covering her head. He froze.

Her sobs were pitiful. Smurf was freaked-out, crazy afraid. No way could he hit her.

If not for the rhino dose of cocaine he'd snorted, he might not have had the strength. He had to take care of business.

Enough screwing around—no more nice-guy crap. It was bye-bye time. *Shit.*

"Smur—, er, Tonya. I'm not going to hit you." He took a dish towel and wiped milk off the back of his head and ass. He'd destroy anyone else who'd messed with him like this. There'd always been something about this kid that got to him.

She peeked out from under an arm. She looked scared sick. *Damn. She ain't no stranger to getting her ass whupped.*

This was so messed up.

"Would you like to talk to your momma?"

The crying stopped mid-sob. Tonya raised her head, looking lost. "What?"

"If you calm down and sit quiet, I'm going to see if you can talk to your momma." The stuff was upstairs. "Would you like that?"

Her mouth hung open and her brows narrowed. "Talk with Momma?" she said in a voice barely above a whisper.

"I promise. We'll go check on your momma."

She nodded her head and wiggled herself straight in the chair.

Unreal—his funky, to-the-end trusting helper still believed his shit.

He locked the kitchen door to the back steps and took the key. He stepped through the soggy cereal and mix of white and chocolate milk that looked like something that should be hosed off a slaughterhouse floor.

"If you get out of that chair, I'll know it and then you can't see your momma."

"I sit quiet." She sniffed, wiping her tear-streaked face.

"I'll be right back." He exited, locking the door to the kitchen behind himself, then moved quickly through the dining room and living room. He climbed the stairs and stopped to put on his mask and gloves. He unlocked the door to the laboratory.

It didn't matter how he wanted things to be, he had no choice. It was business.

She wouldn't feel any pain, and who the hell knew—if the Jesus stories were true—maybe she *would* see her momma.

***

Tonya heard the door lock. She looked around the kitchen.

Mr. Q had hurt her. *He bad. He a liar.*

Milk and pieces of the bowl and glass she'd broken were all over the floor. Looking at the mess, she knew she should clean up—what? Her mouth dropped open.

His phone was on the floor by the stove. She scrambled to grab it, then bit her lip as she tried hard to remember the number she'd been taught. Her hands shook as she pushed the numbers.

Ring one. *Need you.* Ring two. *Please.* Ring three. *Help me!* Ring four. *I so scared!* Click...

"Hello, this is Rosie Padron, Children's Protective Services."

"Rosie, I scared. Mr. Q hurt me."

"Oh my Lord! Tonya, honey, listen to me, baby. Where are you?"

Chapter 80

"Better if I make the call," Rizz said to Torrins. "I can lie my ass off. I'm good at it, and I can't get in trouble." *Hell, who's going to go after a poor crippled guy in a wheelchair? I'm bulletproof.*

"Use my phone," Torrins said. "Venjer should recognize the number. He's made so much money off this hospital, we're probably on his speed dial. I'll step out and use my cell to start notifying Board members. I'm sure I can get them to give stand-down orders to Kline if we can find him."

"Good luck," Rizz said. He dialed Clete Venjer's cell. They needed some luck.

"Clete Venjer, Attorney. How can I help you?"

"Mr. Venjer, this is Dr. Michael Rizzini calling."

"I expected Dr. Torrins from this number."

"We're working together. I apologize, but we've been unable to reach CEO Kline. The Board has an unresolved technical question. The settlement offer discussed with you cannot be extended at this time. The CEO's secretary believes he may be en route to a meeting with you to sign that settlement agreement. If we do not reach him before that, please ask him to call or return to the hospital to speak with Jim Torrins about the Board's decision."

"I assume you tried his cell?"

"Yes, repeatedly. No one has been able to get a response. The hospital legal staff asked me to state formally that the settlement offer you discussed with CEO Stuart Kline is not one that the hospital can agree to at this time."

"So the hospital is reneging on the agreement I reached with CEO Kline?" the attorney said. "That's unprofessional."

"Dr. Torrins, the Board, and I apologize. Given the significance of the matter and the amount of money involved, no one wants to make a mistake."

"I was just climbing into my car to meet with CEO Kline at my office," Venjer said. "Please contact me when you have settled your issue. I have a responsibility to the deceased's brother and her infant son to resolve this issue quickly and fairly. I can't assure you that our offer will remain on the table."

"Understood," Rizz said. "Thank you." He hung up and wheeled out of the office.

Torrins stood near his secretary's desk with a cell phone to his ear. He covered the phone with his hand. "I've advised one board member and he agrees on withholding the settlement. I asked him to contact others. I'm on hold waiting to speak with another. Any luck?"

"I reached Venjer on his cell phone. We were right—he was heading to his office to meet Kline and sign the settlement. I reported that the Board had rescinded that offer." He nodded towards Torrins and the phone in his hand. "Keep making those calls and make what I said true."

"Was Venjer still going to meet Kline?"

"I don't know. It seemed he accepted that the settlement was on hold, so I didn't push things."

"I don't think he'd sign after what you told him. He's a straight shooter—particularly for a guy in his business," Torrins said. "I'd still feel better if Kline answered his phone. Who knows what he might do?"

"I'm no attorney, but I'd say the notification I made to Venjer, even if it wasn't true at the time, would make a strong case for tossing the settlement, even if our weasel of a CEO did get it signed."

"You're right about one thing for sure," Torrins said.

"What's that?" Rizz said.

"You're not an attorney."

***

Farley saw Rosie go rigid upon answering her phone.

"Oh my Lord! Tonya, honey, listen to me, baby. Where are you?" Rosie's face blanched as she listened.

Farley stepped closer.

"Where is he now? Is anyone else in the house?"

"Okay, baby." She bit her lip. "Put the phone back where you found it and pretend you didn't see it. We're going to come for you. If you hear noise and yelling, just get down and cover up. Understand, sweetie? Help is coming. Hang up now and put the phone where it was. Be brave, my Tonya!" She disconnected.

Nate and Doc Cody had moved close.

"She's in there." Rosie spoke at high speed. "She said he hurt her. She's locked in the kitchen, and he doesn't know she called. She doesn't think anyone else is in the house. She's scared out of her head. Oh please!" She gripped her temples, her eyes locking on Farley's. "You've got to get her out of there."

This was it. It was all on him. Tonya said he'd hurt her. That gave a green light to go in hard—no warrant needed. Was it the way to play it?

What Farley decided—right now—might determine whether a young girl and others lived or died. Nate, Drake, and Rosie all had eyes on him. Thunder sounded from the west. A fine rain began to fall.

"Nate, radio your partner and tell him we hit in three minutes. Drake, remember what we said—when we breach the door, you stay back until we tell you to follow." He turned to Rosie, who stood with hands clasped in front of her mouth. "You stay here and update paramedics if they show. We'll call you when we have Tonya safe so you can be with her as soon as possible."

Nate was already climbing into the SUV's driver seat. Drake opened a rear door. As Farley turned, he felt a hand on his arm. Rosie turned, faced him, her hands gripping his upper arms. Tears ran from the piercing blue eyes that drilled him, her voice breaking. "Don't you let anyone hurt Tonya. You hear me? Don't let it happen."

He was no hero. What they'd find when they went through the door was uncertain. He'd come through before in a life-or-death situation, but no one knew how close to running he'd come.

This was different—no Aki. Farley was scared like before, but this time he was angry and it felt personal. A wrong decision by him would get people hurt—or killed.

Along with that, he couldn't stand to disappoint this woman who cared so much.

He'd rather die than fail.

***

Aki wore Kevlar and the black POLICE windbreaker. He had his gun drawn.

He stood with his back pressed against the wall outside Clara Zeitman's sixth-floor condo door, while the tactical officer tried the master key. The plan was to quietly unlock the door and see if it would open. If a safety chain were in place, they'd know someone was inside. One of the two uniform officers had a ram in hand. A phone call to the unit had gone unanswered.

The lock clicked softly, the tactical officer nodded, and he pushed the door far enough to see it was free. Aki pivoted and exploded through the door, crouched low with his weapon at the ready. "Police!" he yelled.

Silence.

The condo looked, felt, and smelled deserted. They'd confirm it, but he knew they'd find nothing useful. Their suspect gone and no clues or evidence—a strikeout.

Meanwhile, Farley was going to lead a high-risk raid in Uptown.

Aki was still getting to know his soft-spoken young partner. There was more to him than met the eye. He liked him more all the time. He had confidence in him, but taking down Q could put his life on the line. Aki wished he were there. *Be safe, partner.*

He and the tactical officer confirmed all was clear in leapfrog assessments of each room. The bed was made. The kitchen and other rooms were spotless.

He stood by the window overlooking the lake. Light rain had started to fall, and now angry black clouds filled the western sky.

He couldn't shake the pessimism that he'd had from the start of this investigation. They had a circumstantial case against Clara Zeitman for the poisoning, but it wasn't anywhere near enough to convict her.

She'd never called in sick before. Today she does, and now her condo looks like it's ready for *Better Homes and Gardens*. Clara Zeitman was a super-smart woman no one knew well and whose motives were a mystery. They'd always been a step behind.

He wouldn't try less hard, but everything told him they weren't going to put anyone away on this one. Clara Zeitman had thought it all through.

She was in the wind, and they were unlikely to catch her. Nothing tormented him more than someone getting away with murder. If she escaped justice, it would mean sleepless nights, sweat-soaked nightmares, and an even greater obsession with his job. When murderers walked free, the cases remained forever open in his mind. He could not quit.

Damn her to hell.

Chapter 81

Clete turned off Thirty-Sixth Street and passed between the wrought-iron gates and towering monuments that marked the entry to Lakeview Cemetery. The cemetery lay between Lakes Harriet and Calhoun and was separated from them by parkways, asphalt paths, and belts of wildlife sanctuary. The lush wooded grounds contained a small lake and was home to white-tailed deer, swans, and countless other birds. It was one of the most beautiful places Clete had ever seen.

Every time he visited, his soul bled.

He was not disappointed that his meeting with Stuart Kline had been postponed. It only delayed the inevitable—the hospital would settle soon, and his day was ugly enough without having to tolerate even a brief meeting with Kline.

The sleazy administrator reeked of things Clete hated about his job—personal greed masquerading as looking out for others, say-anything-for-money doctors who made their living testifying in malpractice cases, estranged family members feigning loss, and too many in his profession who'd do or say anything to collect a judgment.

He made the turns and drove past acres of headstones by rote. He'd traveled this route countless times. The sky had darkened, and thunder rumbled in the distance. A light mist speckled his windshield.

Malpractice law too often exposed him to people who shared Kline's obscene avarice. The system's singular focus on money fostered deceit and abuse. He believed the nature of his motivation and commitment to ethical behavior made him different. His life's work was about more than money.

But he'd made a grave error.

The CEO's clumsy kickback proposal was something Clete would have quashed with extreme prejudice if not for the threat of exposure. He pulled to the side of the narrow road.

Clete climbed out of his car. He stood among towering oaks, ignoring the mist and staring toward her gravesite.

The malpractice system was deeply flawed, but it was the only tool he had to try and protect others from suffering as he had.

His mistake and resulting compromise had tainted his efforts.

He'd believed he'd found someone who cared. A kindred spirit with access to restricted hospital records and enough knowledge to recognize when negligence may have occurred. For more than a year, the results of their collusion had furthered his crusade.

Now he knew he'd been wrong. His illicit partner did not share his commitment.

Like all the rest—it was only about the money.

They would meet within the hour, and that would be the end.

Clete looked toward the site of Anjanee's grave. Since the funeral, he'd never advanced closer. Today, especially, he could not.

***

Stuart Kline hung up with the receptionist at Clete Venjer's firm. She'd told him the attorney had advised he would not be coming in for the meeting. Kline had called after screening the multiple messages on his cell. Calls from Torrins as well as hospital board members, all with the same message. The settlement offer was a stand down. The malpractice claim appeared baseless.

Son of a bitch!

He put aside his massive disappointment and flipped into survival mode. His plan had fallen apart. He sensed instinctively that the settlement was a sinking ship. What he needed to do was cut himself free and represent himself as if he'd been on top of things. He'd do whatever was needed to assure he did not get axed. Damn! What had gone wrong? He'd been within an hour of a life-changing score.

He'd answered no calls and spoken to no one except Venjer. That was perfect. He could identify that he'd had a last-minute suspicion and had held off showing up for the meeting with the attorney.

Yes, that was it. He, Stuart Kline, had exercised keen judgment and restraint, and that had saved the hospital.

Some would scoff, but he could make it fly. Surviving was what he did best.

Chapter 82

Q worked to keep his mind in business mode as he came down the stairs. He thought about getting Smurf to one of the upstairs rooms with a bed so she'd be comfortable as she slipped away. No.

There were practical aspects to consider.

Smurf was a little kid mentally, but she weighed over one hundred pounds. That was one hundred pounds that Q would have to make disappear. Hauling that much weight down a flight of stairs was inefficient. Plus the kitchen was already a mess.

Decision made, he inserted the key into the kitchen door.

As he entered she looked up, face tear-streaked, eyes red.

"I scared," she said. "Don't hurt me."

"I won't hurt you. I promise."

He picked his way over the splashed and splattered floor and opened the refrigerator. He removed an individual serving of Jell-O butterscotch pudding, her favorite. Keeping his back to her he removed the vial from the top pocket of his lab coat. He still had his gloves on and took care as he poured a multi-lethal dose of carfentanil solution into the pudding. He took a spoon and stirred, then left the spoon in place. He turned to the girl.

"You need to eat something. I've got some butterscotch pudding here." He extended the pudding and spoon toward her.

"I no want to," she said.

"I was thinking about your momma," he said. "We'll go to her apartment. Maybe Jesus didn't take her. Maybe she woke up. Eat some pudding and we'll go check on her."

Her head shot up, her mouth open and almond eyes wide. Even now she trusted him.

A lifetime of being dumped on, lied to, and neglected—how could she still believe in people?

She reached for the pudding.

As she spooned in a mouthful, relief and regret collided in him. Tension bled away as an emptiness gripped him. She ate more.

He thought about the money. Thought about being his own man. Thought about being strong and having the balls to do what needed to be done. That's what business demanded. Life was not easy.

Long seconds passed.

Smurf's head slumped and her eyelids dropped like a falling curtain. He moved behind her and lifted her limp body, easing her to the floor on her back.

She did not move. Her chest did not rise. Her lips and the area around her mouth turned dusky and blue-tinged. The smell of the tossed milk and cereal wafted, and his stomach heaved.

He'd done what he needed to do. He couldn't look any longer.

Averting his gaze, he scanned the soiled floor and its gore-like mess. *What?*

He patted the empty pocket of his lab coat as he stepped over and picked up his cell phone. Damn.

He checked recent calls. His bowels went to ice as he found one four minutes earlier to a number he did not recognize. *No!*

He burst out of the kitchen, slipping on the floor. He regained his balance and ran to the living room. He looked out the rain-speckled front window. A bolt of lightning struck nearby, the flash and thunder startling, the hair on his arms standing on end. As he blinked, a black SUV with tinted glass lurched around the corner of Thirty-Second Street and slid to an angled halt in front of his house. *Son of a bitch!*

He sprinted up the stairs for the lab.

Chapter 83

Drake gripped the medical rescue bag in one hand and braced himself with the other as the SUV hurtled down Thirty-Second Street, the rain now a torrent. He felt afraid-to-die scared and wired. Nate had given last-minute instructions and was jaw-clenched silent now. Adrenaline surged as the engine roared.

Lightning flashed and thunder cracked right on top of them. Nate whipped a left, then locked up the brakes, and the SUV slid to a stop against the curb in front of the stately-looking corner house.

Nate and Farley threw open their car doors and sprinted through the rain towards the house as a black-jacketed officer with a weapon in hand raced across the adjoining yard toward them. Nate hand-signaled the officer toward the back of the house. He diverted without breaking stride.

Nate had the door ram in hand. Farley held his weapon in a two-fisted grip. Drake followed, clutching the medical bag, feeling as if he'd been pushed out of a plane and was hurtling earthward.

Nate paused an instant as they reached the porch. His one-second intense gaze reinforced the message he'd shared as they'd raced toward the house. It's okay for bad guys to die, but citizens and good guys no way. No room is safe until it's called clear. Never stand down until the house is secure.

Nate nodded, then crashed the ram into the door, exploding it open. Drake's heart leaped to his throat.

Farley jumped into the room with gun at the ready. "Police!" he yelled. Nate went in low and sideways, weapon poised.

"Front room clear," Nate yelled.

Drake stepped to the entry. The door and frame were in splinters where the locks had been. Farley stood covering Nate as he entered the next room.

"Dining room clear!" Nate called, his voice booming in the high-ceilinged, hardwood floor rooms. Farley advanced out of Drake's sight.

Drake heard a crash as if a door had been kicked open. Then silence. Too long.

He wanted a weapon. What had happened?

"Doc! In here!" It was Farley yelling. "One down. Not breathing."

Drake burst forward through a dining room and into a kitchen. The floor was covered in a reddish sloppy mess with scattered shards of broken kitchenware. Farley knelt over a jeans-clad body, his bulk hiding the person. He turned and looked up, agony on his face.

As Farley straightened, Drake's chest heaved. Rosie's vulnerable Tonya lay lifeless, her mocha-skinned face now blue-tinged, one eye half-open and unblinking.

"Maybe a pulse. I can't tell for sure," Farley said. "Not breathing. I don't see an injury. I called for an ambulance."

Drake dropped to his knees next to her and ripped open the medical bag. It would take a rig minutes to get here, and they couldn't come in until the building was secured. It looked like it was already too late.

"Basement, clear!" Nate's voice and his boot steps pounding up the stairs sounded through the other doorway. He entered. "Your target is here, Farley. I can feel the bastard. He's gotta be upstairs." Nate spoke quick, his body vibrating—his motor racing even as he stood still.

"Take him down, guys. I've got her," Drake said.

Farley nodded. His lip twisted and his eyes narrowed like the teeth-baring snarl of a friendly dog facing a threat to its master.

"Let's go," Nate said, yanking Farley's arm. "Go! Go! Go!"

He and Nate raced out of the kitchen like a wolf pair on the hunt.

Drake had his tools in hand and was moving. No lab tests. No X-rays. No communication or history. As combat medics and Drake's EMT and paramedic colleagues knew, sometimes one glance tells the story. He must act—hesitation guaranteed death.

Drake sealed the airway mask over her nose and mouth. She had a chance if any spark of life remained—a giant *if*.

He squeezed the ventilation bag, forcing air into her lungs. Her flesh felt as stiff, cold, and lifeless as plastic. *Please, God!*

Each of two more squeezes made her chest rise with the bellows-like flow of air. He took one of multiple Narcan delivery devices from his pocket and sprayed the reversal drug into her nose.

He repositioned the mask and continued to breathe for her. Her chest rose with his each squeeze but there was no movement otherwise—zero, nothing. *Please!*

They'd taken too long. Had the drug-pushing animal killed another innocent?

He felt her neck for a pulse with his gloved fingers. He wasn't sure if there was something there. Was he sensing his own pulse as his heart hammered with desperation and rage? He sprayed another dose of Narcan into her nose and did chest compressions, willing her circulation to distribute the drug.

Bryce and so many others dead, his Rachelle almost—the bastard.

Drake halted the compressions and again breathed for her. The asshole sold carfentanil—who knew much of the elephant-stopping drug he'd given her? He sprayed another dose of Narcan into her nose.

He checked her pupils—pinpoint and unmoving. She had no blink. Nothing.

His heart chilled as the shadow of a cold reality stretched for him—he was too late.

Lord, no.

Chapter 84

"Police!" Nate yelled from off to the side at the base of the stairwell. "No one needs to die today. You hear me, Q?"

Silence.

Farley stood in covering position with his Glock at the ready. Q's drugs had killed many already, and the girl Drake was fighting to save had shown the same blue pallor as her dead mother. It seemed they'd been too late for her.

Farley's nerves crackled and his breath came hard, but he had no thought of turning back. The anger helped. Rage trumped fear. This guy deserved to go.

Nate angled his head toward the stair. Farley stepped forward. He jabbed his head to the side, snatching peeks up the stairs. It looked clear. He nodded to Nate, who leapt to the landing with pistol trained upward.

Nate advanced, his head on a swivel. Farley followed up the stairs, in lockstep behind him.

Farley's heart filled his throat. Adrenaline had every cell in his body in overdrive.

Where are you, bastard?

A closed door stood at the top of the stairs on the left. A small table with gloves and respiratory masks sat along the wall next to it. Three open doors lined the hallway. Nate slipped past the closed door and hugged the wall. Farley followed. They were in stealth mode now—no sound. If they gave their position away, they could be shot wherever they stood.

Nate pointed to his chest then toward the first open door.

Farley nodded. He covered as Nate went in low and fast with his weapon leading. Five seconds, then Nate extended a hand with the "okay" signal.

Farley repeated Nate's actions with the second open room. Each cleared room cranked the tension higher.

Nate breached the third open door. He quickly popped back out and swiped a hand in the "safe" sign.

They both looked toward the closed door of the lone remaining room. A deadbolt keyed lock was visible, just like on the house's front door. There was little doubt Q, the supplier they'd called the Music Man, lay in wait for them on the other side.

This was the worst—going in blind on a bad guy who is set up and waiting on you—a good way to get dead.

Farley pointed at the masks on the table. He picked one up and slipped it on. Both he and Nate were wearing the gloves Drake had given them. Drake had warned that the mask and gloves were like a Kevlar vest. They helped but did not guarantee protection.

Farley stood to the side of the door and listened. What was that he heard? Water, running water—the bastard was dumping his drugs. *Shit!* Farley gestured and silently mouthed "He's dumping the drugs" to Nate. Nate nodded. He stepped back, tapped a fist on his own chest, and made a punching move toward the door. He pointed at Farley and demonstrated a ready position with his weapon.

Nate backed up, took three big strides, and leaped into the air, hitting the door feet first. His combat boots hit the door like a professional wrestler's dropkick. The door exploded open and splintered wood hung from the frame. Nate ended up on the floor on his back as Farley jumped over him into the room with his pistol in a shooter's position.

Movement near one wall, a large shadowy silhouette spinning from in front of a sink. A glint showed in his hand and his arm raised.

Boom! Boom! Two deafening shots from low and to Farley's right. Their target doubled over, groaned, and dropped.

Farley and Nate launched forward.

They ended up side by side, adrenaline-stoked, with weapons on the downed man.

"Don't move," Farley yelled, his nerves sparking and his finger tight on the trigger.

"Hands where I can see them or you're dead, asshole," yelled Nate.

Farley's heart pounded, his breath tight—resisting the urge to pull the trigger was like stopping a thrown punch in mid-swing.

A broken glass beaker and fluid lay on the floor beneath and beside the man who wore a respiratory mask and gloves.

"Racist muthas." He clutched at his upper leg and groin with both hands, writhing and moaning. "You shot an unarmed black man."

"Hands out, palms up or I'll shoot you again, asshole," Nate yelled.

"I'm goddamn bleeding to death." He raised his hands, red with blood. Nate nodded to Farley to cover, then snapped a cuff on the big man's right wrist and snapped the other to the old-style radiator against the wall. He ripped the man's respiratory mask off and Quentin Robinson's pain-twisted face showed clear.

"Don't touch anything else, Nate. It's gotta be drug." Farley nodded toward the fluid on the floor.

"Maybe so, but it ain't powder and it can't be matched to anything," Q said through gritted teeth. "I think you assholes sprayed something around here after shooting an innocent unarmed black man." He looked smug, despite his obvious pain. "No drugs around here. Unless you planted some." He winced and pressed his free hand against his groin. "I'm bleeding bad. Do something."

His pants were blood-sodden near the wound, and blood had begun to pool on the floor beneath him.

"He's all yours," Nate said in a normal volume. "I'll get the place secured and see if the doc needs help." He keyed his shoulder-mount radio. "Mendoza, I'm heading to the first floor. A citizen down in the kitchen. Suspect shot and bleeding on the second floor. The house is cleared of active shooters, but it's a drug contact risk. I say again, scene is toxic drug risk. No one in."

"You need to help me," Q said, his tone not as hard-edged anymore. "I'm bleeding to death, and I came into contact with the drugs you planted." The big man had the far-away narcotic look in his eyes. "You better get Narcan ready in case. There's some in my lockup." He nodded toward a heavy black metal cabinet whose door hung open.

"You good?" Nate said to Farley.

Farley nodded, his weapon trained on Q.

"He's bleeding heavy. Might die. Too bad," Nate said. "It would mean a lot of paperwork."

"It was a clean shoot," Farley said. "The drugs are a lethal weapon. I wasn't as fast as I should have been."

"No worries. Good work. I hope the girl makes it," Nate said and strode out.

Would Tonya make it? It had looked bad. He could have initiated the raid earlier—screw the warrant. They'd taken too long. *Please, God.*

"You have to save me," Q said. "It's your job. Protect and serve." It was a taunt. "You shot an unarmed black man. Hell to pay if I die. No weapon and no drugs that match me to anything. I'm gonna walk." His eyes were drooping and he no longer held his hand compressing his groin wound. The advancing drug effect showed. The puddle of blood grew.

Could this killer really avoid justice in court? Might he walk or be convicted of only a fraction of what he'd done?

The image of Tonya's body, her mother's, and the young kid whose death had torn Drake up so badly flashed in his mind. If Tonya didn't make it, Rosie would collapse.

This criminal and his drugs created suffering and misery for profit.

Q's eyes were closed. From the outside he looked like a normal person, but something fundamentally human was absent. How could you hurt a kid?

Only one of Nate's two shots had hit, but the bleeding proved it had to have caught the artery there. He'd be dead before long without treatment.

He was also going down from contact with his own drug—the drug that had killed so many others. That felt so cosmically just that it seemed wrong to interfere. Maybe it was best to let nature take its course.

The risk to others needed to end. Would the law and courts make that happen? Could he trust the system he was a part of? If the dealer were an animal, public safety would require he be gunned down on sight.

His brother's memory and all he'd seen screamed for him to do the right thing.

Chapter 85

Aki exited the Calhoun Beach Condominium's elevator into the underground parking garage. He approached the late-model tan Toyota Camry parked in Clara Zeitman's designated spot. A uniform officer stood watch. A crime scene technician had popped the locks, opened the trunk, and searched.

Aki felt the car's hood. He knelt and looked into the wheel wells— no moisture or debris. He'd bet the car hadn't been driven since before yesterday's storm.

The tech looked at Aki, shook his head, and gave a thumbs-down signal.

Aki's bad vibe about his suspect just kept getting worse.

He pulled out his cell phone and got an answer on the second ring.

"Karen Miller, world's greatest crime analyst."

"Ha ha," Aki said. "Prove it, world's greatest. What have you got on Zeitman, my attempted murder suspect? I just hit her condo—it had that abandoned feel to it. I've got a feeling she's in the wind."

"That stinks. Let me pull up what I have."

Crime analysts with computer skills and a small army of other investigative support staff did a lot of the digging that led to criminal arrests and convictions. Karen was one of the best. He'd put her on Clara Zeitman as soon as Drake Cody had identified her as their suspect.

"Here's what I've found—more to the point, haven't found. Her cell phone hasn't had a signal for more than twenty-four hours. A techie like her wouldn't forget to charge it. No credit card use in over forty-eight hours. No airline tickets or other suspicious purchases prior to that. The credit cards gave us zip. Bank and checking accounts are dead—no activity in days. Her internet service is likewise dead. Nothing on social media — doesn't seem to be the social type. I've run everything, and what it's remarkable for is nothing."

"Nothing?" Aki said.

"Yeah. There's so little, it has to be by design."

"Damn it." His suspect had bolted. "Excuse the French."

"If that's French, I'm fluent," Karen said. "I wish I had something for you, but she's covered her tracks—could be anywhere by now. She's done everything I'd do to disappear. It doesn't look good for us. I'm sorry, Detective."

"I'm sorry, too. We need some hard evidence. If she's left our jurisdiction, we don't have enough to extradite even if we do find her. Thanks for the effort, but it looks like we're screwed." He disconnected.

Clara Zeitman had outsmarted them all.

The uniform officer's radio squelched. He hustled over to Aki.

"Did you hear that call?" he asked.

"No."

"Shots fired and a man down on a tactical ops action. Thirty-Second and Colfax."

Aki froze.

"Damn!" His curse echoed through the underground garage.

Farley was in a kill zone, and Aki was not there to watch his back.

***

Sweat ran into Drake's eyes as he fought to fan any lingering spark of life.

He'd slipped an IV into a vein on the back of Tonya's hand and delivered two additional doses of Narcan directly into her bloodstream. He continued to breathe for her.

The lessening of the blue tinge of oxygen-starved tissue was not easy to see in dark-skinned people. Despite how desperately he wanted to, he couldn't convince himself Tonya's color had improved.

She was totally unresponsive, with zero eye movement and no chest rise other than with the air delivery he accomplished. The image of Bryce's ring and his dead blue fingers flashed.

Dread clawed at Drake's guts.

Narcan was the greatest antidote in history. Tonya now had more of the reversal agent on board than anyone Drake had ever treated, but no one knew what a massive overdose with concentrated carfentanil would require. Carfentanil had no legitimate use in people, and no human testing had ever been done.

This was unknown territory.

Boom! Boom! Drake flinched. Gun shots from somewhere above him in the house.

It had sounded like the double-tap of a trained shooter. Had they got Q?

Please, not Farley or Nate. For an instant he considered giving up on his failed resuscitation of Tonya and running up to see if they needed him.

No. She still had a chance.

If Q was the one who came down the stairs, Drake would kill the bastard.

He felt Tonya's neck for a pulse. He was unsure. He ripped off his glove and rechecked. Weak and fast but now definitely present. *Yes!*

He replaced the mask over her nose and mouth and continued the bellows-like delivery of air to her lungs. Her round face and short neck and chin made bag-mask ventilation challenging, but the rise of her chest proved he was delivering air. *Breathe, Tonya. Breathe!*

He repositioned and double-checked the airway mask. At that moment, the almond-shaped eyes of the girl Rosie had said was "the sweetest kid on the planet" blinked open as if a switch had been thrown.

Hell, yes!

He moved the mask and bag out of the way. Tonya blinked rapidly, looking lost, but most importantly, her chest rose and fell. She was breathing on her own!

The hair on Drake's scalp stood as energy coursed through him. He wanted to pump his fist and shout.

Tonya and the magical antidote had overcome the elephant-stopping drug.

She wriggled and tried to sit up.

"Take it slow, Tonya." He smiled at her. "Everything is okay. I'm Drake. You're safe, and no one will hurt you." More blinking and puzzlement, but her eyes were clear. "Rosie is nearby, and she'll be with you soon. Would you like that?"

Her eyes widened, and she nodded her head.

Footsteps approached from outside the kitchen.

Drake grabbed the stainless steel thoracostomy device from the medical bag. The oversized needle-nosed-pliers-like instrument was designed to be driven into the chest to treat a collapsed lung. Drake crouched with his medical weapon in hand, muscles tense and nerves trip-wired.

Nate entered the kitchen. He did a double-take.

Drake exhaled and turned back to Tonya.

"We're good, Doc." Nate smiled at Tonya, then spoke to Drake. "Nice work on the little lady. You're needed upstairs. The house is secure, other than the drug risk. Farley's suspect is down and cuffed to a radiator. He's bleeding. A groin hit. Ambulance should be here straightaway, but they can't enter until the house is chemically clear."

Drake heard the approaching siren. Paramedics to the rescue—among his favorite people on earth.

"We can't wait." Drake paused. "Can you get Rosie on the line and get her out front?"

"Sure." Nate pulled his cell. "What are—?"

"Grab my bag and gear, Nate." Drake turned to Tonya. "Are you hurt?"

She shook her head. "I no hurt."

Drake slipped his arms under Tonya's legs and back and lifted her from the floor.

Nate led the way through the dining room and living room, then held the ram-smashed door open as Drake exited to the covered porch.

"Rosie and some other nice people will meet you here," he said to Tonya. "Nate will stay with you." He set her on the wooden deck, her back against the house. "Keep taking big breaths."

He ran back into the living room and grabbed the blanket he'd spied on the couch. He handed a nasal-delivery Narcan device to Nate, then wrapped the blanket around Tonya. She looked stable.

"If she can't stay conscious, give the Narcan, but I think she's good for a while."

Narcan had worked its magic, and the siren sounded very near. She was out of the woods.

Drake pivoted, grabbed the medical rescue bag, and raced for the stairs.

Chapter 86

Clara directed the cab into the small gravel parking lot next to the tennis courts on the Lake Harriet Parkway Road. The one-way boulevard circled the lake, with public paths on the lakeshore side and alternating parkland and magnificent homes on the other. Clete Venjer's mansion was no more than a mile down the road. Like everything else, she'd made it easy for him.

Clara climbed out of the cab and paid the fare in cash. She opened her umbrella and put the strap of her bag over her shoulder. The rain was steady and thunder rumbled, but there was no wind. The temperature was mild.

The surface of the lake was dimpled by the rain. The weather did nothing to dampen Clara's outlook.

She was going to be born again—this birth without the pain or struggle that newborns faced. She smiled. Check-in for her flight would begin in less than ninety minutes.

She hiked up the steep hill from the tennis court area to the upper park, where a large gazebo-like picnic shelter sat among oak and maple trees. The weather had left the lakeshore and park empty of people.

A lone figure in a plain brown suit stood under the shelter's canopy. Clara had not seen Clete Venjer in person for some time. Their collaboration had begun more than a year earlier when he'd come to her office to request a medical record for one of his malpractice suits. Then, as now, his presence underwhelmed. She smiled. He looked like a wimp, but he'd made her a remarkable amount of money.

More impressive was the amount she'd made him.

This was their final meeting, and from here on she would need no one. She would be in command of her new life.

"You have my payment?" she said.

"What's with the wig and glasses?"

"The bearer bonds," she said. "Do you have them?"

"This isn't how we've done things previously," the little attorney said. "It's inconvenient to pay you in advance."

"After all the money I've sent your way, you have the nerve to complain I've inconvenienced you?"

"Our agreement was that you would identify cases where you suspected medical negligence," Clete said. "And that if I retained those cases and received judgments, you would receive a portion of the proceeds. I believed that you recognized the damage that negligent medical care could cause and shared my commitment to fight that. But now I can see that everything has been about the money."

The mousy man's usually soft brown eyes showed fierce. He was pissed. Clara could not care less.

"Maybe you believe your own self-deluding fiction, but I know better," she said. "I've seen where you live. I've read the articles describing your wealth and possessions. Pretend what you want—the reality is you love the money. My medical genius has made you a great deal of it, and you should be on your knees in appreciation."

"Self-delusion?" the lawyer said. "You're an authority on that. It doesn't require a 'medical genius' to recognize when medical disasters have occurred. You're simply a hospital employee with access to patient information. I shared the money with you as an incentive to help me protect others. You're nothing special."

Really? The attorney was yet another who failed to appreciate her abilities. His insults couldn't bring her down. What others thought didn't matter anymore. She'd proved them all wrong. "'Doesn't require a genius,' you say. Really? I thought you might be bright enough to have recognized what I did."

Those brown eyes now looked puzzled. "I have no idea what you're talking about."

"In the beginning, I referred meat and potatoes junk to you. Patient falls, medication mistakes—slam-dunk awards, but no serious money. Then I stepped things up. I made you millions."

"You didn't *make* me anything. You informed me of possible medical negligence cases. I approached the families and victims. I earned their trust and the right to represent them. I won settlements or jury awards to help them with their injuries or deal with their loss." He shook his head. "You advised me of suspicious cases. Nothing more."

"I need to get going, but I'll run through this last case in an attempt to educate you. It was my favorite," she said. "A young black female drug addict presents overdosed and in pre-term labor. She delivers in the ER and is hemorrhaging. I learned of her in the lab due to her need for a blood transfusion.

"My initial analysis—critical patient, young, minority, and a mother. Everything aligned for a possible huge award in a client demographic you dominate in the Twin Cities' market."

His brows were pinched. He looked lost. Wow, so sharp in some ways—a dunce in others.

"Translation—she met my criteria," Clara said. "A huge potential wrongful death payout in a case you would likely be able to represent. My next order of analysis—she'd overdosed on narcotics while pregnant. She was on the way to killing herself anyway and clearly was not worthy of being a mother." The memory of her own mother flashed. "Her drug addiction made her as good as dead, and removing her could only help her baby. And us."

Clete Venjer's jaw gaped. He shook his head. "What do you mean? I don't—"

"She was bleeding heavily. I was there when the placenta passed, and the perfect plan came to me in an instant. I removed some of the placental tissue before delivering it to pathology. Later I paid her a visit in the ICU." She leaned forward and peered at him. "Are the pieces coming together for you yet?"

"I don't understand. Please no." He raised his hands as if trying to stop traffic.

"When I was drawing her blood, I injected her with massive doses of two of the most powerful anti-clotting drugs known to man. Drugs that break up clots in strokes and heart attacks and are absolutely contraindicated in anyone with a wound or bleeding risk. Either drug would have done it, but with both on board, water had a better chance of clotting than her blood. As I knew it would, her post-delivery uterus bled by the bucketload, and no way anyone could stop it. End result—death by blood loss, with an impossible-to-disprove claim of retained placenta as the cause. Done deal! A wrongful death case—all you had to do was go through the motions."

She knew she looked pleased with herself, but she couldn't help it. It truly had been brilliant. "And that, Mr. Unappreciative, shows how my medical knowledge allowed you to cash in for millions."

He stood bent over with his hands on his knees as if he'd been kicked in the stomach.

"Don't worry. Like the drug-mommy, I chose only patients who were worthless other than as a malpractice payout."

His voice was a whisper. "There were more?"

"Consider these facts, and you tell me." With these pieces he couldn't help but put the puzzles together. Why shouldn't she boast? No one could ever prove anything. "Breathing nitrogen gas kills without pain or struggle. Do you recall a big payday on a mystery death in December? You also collected on a fatal post-surgical bleeding case a few months back. Hmm, wonder how that could have happened? And it's so wrong that nurses are stretched so thin in the hospital that monitor and oximeter alarms are essential. Gosh, wonder if I'd be smart enough to disable them without it being evident?" She smiled. Her medical knowledge had more than proven itself. "No one had a clue. But of course, as you say, I'm nothing special."

"Please God, no!" He dropped to one knee and gripped his head in his hands. "What you did had nothing to do with me." He continued as if talking to himself, "It's the opposite of everything I stand for."

"It had everything to do with you. I have all our business transactions documented. I never would have done any of it if not for you."

He retched and then vomited onto the cement floor of the pavilion.

Chapter 87

Drake shot up the stairs two at a time, the medical rescue bag over his shoulder.

The distant siren grew louder. Paramedics and hopefully Rosie would soon be by Tonya's side.

He reached the top of the stairs. The door to the nearest room hung splintered and open. A small table with respiratory masks and gloves sat against the hallway wall. Drake quickly replaced his missing glove and put on one of the masks.

He entered an oversized room filled with a large lab table and equipment. Farley was bent over, inspecting the inside of a heavy metal cabinet next to a desk against the near wall. He looked up as Drake entered.

"Is she okay? Did she make it?" Farley spoke rapid-fire, his eyebrows pinched above the respiratory mask.

"She made it," Drake said. "She's breathing on her own. Rosie and the medics will be with her any minute."

Farley leaned his head back, his arms dropped limp to his sides, his pistol pointing toward the floor. "Thank God."

"Where's your prisoner?" Drake said. "Nate said he's hit."

A moan sounded from the floor on the other side of the lab table.

Drake stepped to the side and saw Q on his back on the floor with one arm handcuffed to the radiator. Blood pooled under him.

Drake broke towards the stricken man.

He was pulled up short. Farley gripped his arm. The detective shook his head. "He's covered with the killer drug he tried to throw at us before Nate shot him. He's high as hell and going down. Getting near him will put you at risk. The same for the paramedics."

"Jesus, Farley. He needs direct pressure on that wound, an IV, fluids, and the hospital fast. He's bleeding out."

"Yep. He's also been bragging on how he's going to walk on any charges. Says he's an innocent, unarmed, victim shot by police. He dumped his stash down the drain. Without a chemical fingerprint match, we have no way to link him to the deaths."

Drake moved to break free, but the detective tightened his grip. Farley's eyes burned like flares.

"Think about what he's done, Drake. Think about what he'll do in the future. Maybe we should let nature and his own drug make sure he never hurts or kills anyone else?"

Farley's words resonated in the darkest places in Drake's mind. They spoke to the part of him that had unleashed merciless violence in order to survive behind bars and barbed wire. And to the primal instincts that had driven him to crush the throat of the person who'd harmed Rachelle and the kids—and to exalt in having done so. He hesitated.

"Good God, Drake," Farley said, "he tried to kill Tonya—a beautiful, innocent kid. Maybe he's too sick and dangerous to trust to the law? You and I are supposed to protect the public. What's the right thing to do?"

The law had failed Drake and others many times. If Q had been prosecuted the last time he faced Drake, how many lives would have been saved? Because charges were dropped, Bryce was dead. Rachelle and Tonya had been as close as possible to dying—it was personal. Q deserved to d—

No! Drake ripped his arm free. Farley pivoted and stepped in front of him.

Their eyes met. Doubt, guilt, regret, anger, and the ghosts of a scared, mentally ill teenage boy and a lost, hopelessly addicted big brother were part of a wordless exchange. The smell of Q's pooling blood flashed Drake to the overdosed mother's ICU death.

So much misery.

"We only get one shot at this," Farley said. "Do we let nature take its course or gamble on the system getting it right?"

Drake's heart pounded and blood roared in his ears. Rage, savage instincts and his duty to protect others pulled at him with the power of a black hole. Too often the law did not deliver justice...

Chapter 88

No! No! No! The march of his unuttered words penetrated Clete's shock.

Clara's admission had struck him like a head-on collision.

He found himself almost out of the park and approaching his car on Upton Avenue. He had no recollection of his walk.

Clara's confession—her boast—turned toxic everything he'd believed about himself and his work. She'd bragged of how she'd used her medical knowledge and position to intentionally harm others—because of him.

He stopped, feeling as if he might throw up again.

No, she hadn't just harmed—she'd killed.

Because of him.

He moaned. *God, no!*

He made it to his car and leaned his arm and head on the wet roof of the vehicle.

He'd never intended anything like what Clara had done to happen. *Never!*

After what she'd told, him, he'd been paralyzed. She'd taken her payment from his briefcase and headed down the hill toward the tennis court lot and the lakeside road. He'd stood bent, sick, and helpless.

She'd used him. She'd planned it all out and gotten away with it.

He wished that she'd just disappeared—that he'd never learned of her evil. Or of his responsibility.

His work was about protecting people from medical harm. He cared. That's what he'd always told himself.

Now Clara had made him responsible for the suffering and death of innocent people in the hospital.

Should he have known? Could he have anticipated the risk?

Responsibility. In the courtroom, when arguing malpractice cases, the determination of "proximate cause" was key. Had the action or inaction of the doctor or nurse led to the injury or death? Would the injury or death have occurred without their action or inaction? Should they have anticipated the possible bad outcome?

Had Clete's payments to Clara been a proximate cause of the deaths? He climbed behind the wheel of the vehicle and started the car. Just as he'd somehow walked from the picnic shelter across Upper Lake Harriet Park to his car without conscious thought, he now drove on Upton Avenue toward the Linden Hills neighborhood.

The rain had lessened, but the afternoon remained twilight dark. The bitterness of his stomach contents soured his tongue. He cracked his window. The air smelled of the storm's runoff and sodden debris, the odor of decay and decomposition.

He braked to a halt at the four-way stop at Forty-Fourth Street. He laid his head on the steering wheel, nausea and a cold sweat breaking out.

People had been injured and killed because of him. He moaned again.

He turned right toward the lake, instinctively headed for the road to his home.

The young surgery intern had been trying to do good that day years ago. He was well-intentioned as he'd treated Anjanee. Regardless of intent, an error had occurred in the uncontrolled frenzy of the ER, and it had taken his Anjanee's life. Clete remembered the young doctor's devastation. He'd known it was genuine and would last a lifetime.

Their daughter's death had destroyed Clete's wife and taken away any chance he'd ever had of happiness. The young doctor and all the others who were part of the tragedy had to pay.

And Clete had made many more since Anjanee pay.

Now he was responsible for Clara inflicting similar heartbreak and loss on others. Was his unintended consequence any different from that of the young doctor?

An icy realization knifed through his heart. If he were to file a suit against himself, he would easily persuade twelve jurors of his guilt—regardless of whatever an opposing attorney might argue. Clara had been right. The money mattered to him.

The money and what it bought him had been his drug. It had been what allowed him to tolerate his misery.

His collusion with Clara had made him money—a great deal of money. She would disappear, but she still had the power to turn over information that would get him disbarred, end his career, and potentially put him in prison.

He turned right on the one-way lakeside boulevard, doubling back toward his home. His beautiful house, his properties, his stock holdings, his bank accounts, his cars, his collections of art—those things and the desire for more had become part of what drove him.

The motives for his work were not pure.

He drove along the narrow road, the gray lake on his left.

Clara's deceit and greed had made him part of something that sickened his soul.

The memory of his beautiful Anjanee had been forever desecrated. He pictured his morning's visit to the cemetery and his inability to approach her grave.

He knew now that he never would. How could he live with himself?

He passed one offshoot road on the boulevard and was now nearing the lower aspect of the park. As the parking lot and tennis courts came into view up ahead, he saw her.

Clara Zeitman.

She stood in front of the chain-link fence of the tennis court, umbrella up and shoulder bag at her feet. Escape assured, she looked to be waiting to be picked up.

The worst instant of his life replayed—the scene that had acid-etched itself into his consciousness. The moment when the young intern had pulled back the blue surgical towels and exposed the horror of lifelessness.

A remote part of his brain fired to life. He was a spectator as his foot slammed the gas pedal to the floor. The high-performance engine rocketed the car forward.

He'd wondered whether Anjanee had suffered. From what he'd learned, he believed not. It was a not inconsequential comfort to him.

He braced his arms against the wheel and watched, as if in slow motion, Clara turn and face him. Her eyes widened, her jaw dropped. Before she could move, the front of his car snatched her body, folding it in half over the hood. In the next millisecond, she was crushed against the unyielding fence.

The image cut off, as if a film reel had snapped. Everything went dark as the explosive punch of the airbag struck him. A neck-snapping jolt wrenched him, followed by a sense of floating.

The concrete-anchored steel supports, cables, and fencing had stopped his car as if he'd hit a collision barrier on the highway.

He smelled radiator fluid, steam, and something raw and disagreeable.

He was done with her now.

Chapter 89

Two days later

Farley sat at his desk documenting one of the more than eighty overdose deaths from the last three days. They'd taken Q off the street, but his drugs and those of too many others were still out there causing misery and death.

"Idiots!" Aki said from in front of his computer.

"What's up?" Farley asked, turning to his partner.

"My internal affairs contact just emailed me. Nate Cray's shoot is being sent to a full review. This is political bullshit."

"Sucks for Nate," Farley said. "The shooting was totally righteous. It should have been me, but I was too slow. Thank heaven he was quick, or we both could have ended up dead and blue on the floor of that lab."

"I felt guilty I wasn't there," Aki said.

"Hey, that's not what I'm saying," Farley said. "You were chasing the crazy hospital woman."

"It didn't feel right not having your back."

Farley could relate to not feeling right. He wasn't sure how much to share. If Aki knew everything that had gone down, he'd have to wonder about Farley.

Farley was doing enough wondering himself.

Did he have what it took to be a homicide detective? Should he be a cop at all?

If it hadn't been for Drake Cody, he might have let Q die. And he hadn't resisted all the temptations that he'd faced that day. Too often he found doing the right thing and following the laws he'd sworn to uphold were not the same thing.

"It was good for me to be in charge," Farley said. "I learned from it."

"You nailed him and no one died," Aki said. "Despite the bad press, the case looks good. It's hard to stomach the crap Q is spouting. The media's eagerness to broadcast it makes it worse. He's stone-cold wicked yet playing victim. No remorse."

"I won't rest easy until he's convicted," Farley said.

"If you hadn't found one of his packets for the chemical fingerprint, I'd believe he might have dodged most everything. With it, I think he's going away. I got a call from Dr. Dronen, our friendly neighborhood medical examiner, this morning. He insulted me a couple of times but shared that the drug signature links Q to over thirty-five OD deaths so far."

Farley had identified that he'd found the two "Music Man" glyph-marked packets in the recesses of the metal cabinet in Q's lab. Q claimed they were planted.

"The ME also had a surprise. It looks like Q wasn't behind the letter that ODed Drake and his wife."

"Q denied it, but he's denying everything," Farley said.

"Fentanyl. The lab proved that's what the envelope was loaded with—not carfentanil. Likely it came from someone else."

What? Farley and Drake had been certain it was Q.

If Drake hadn't saved Q, this might have given the doc some sleepless nights. It was one more reason Farley was glad Drake had worked his magic and hadn't let the dealer die.

"Have you, Karen, or anyone else in the investigation come up with anything to make sense of what Zeitman was doing?" Farley asked. "Why poison the surgeon? What about the overdosed mother who bled to death? And where was Zeitman headed when she got killed? Seems pretty clear she was on the run."

"Mystery on top of mystery," Aki said. "And Clete Venjer happens to be the motorist who loses control of his speeding car on a rain-slicked road and kills her?"

"I can't say I feel too broken up about her death, but what are the odds?" Farley said.

"Venjer is not saying much, which is no surprise," Aki said. "I'm going to keep looking, but if there is a link between them, I'd bet my pension we won't ever find it. Or be able to prove it. I felt from the start this case would leave us scratching our heads. Zeitman's motives might have been too crazy for anyone else to make sense of—that's where I'm going to park it. It's better than beating myself up and feeling she outsmarted us all."

"Everything fits with what you told me after our first case together," Farley said. "What we think we understand we probably have wrong, and the answers we can't find means we're probably asking the wrong questions."

"I said that?" Aki said. "Wow. That's pretty good. Well, maybe not good, but it's true. Neither crazy nor evil are rational. If they start making sense, you gotta start wondering about yourself."

Farley was already doing that...

***

Rachelle had resisted coming to the lakeside park. The kids had made the request for a repeat visit. Drake had persuaded her. She'd been quiet, and he knew where her head was at—the nearby lake home that they'd thought would be theirs was now as distant as the stars.

The kids were having a ball on the playground equipment with new playmates. Drake smiled at her and she smiled back. Laughing children and the beauty of the sunny, warm, Minnesota morning were magic.

"I guess the house wasn't meant to be," he said. "But the malpractice claim against me is gone, my license is safe for now, and though Kline's doing everything he can to get me fired, it may be him who gets the boot. We have a chance of affording a lake place someday—maybe even on this lake." He tried to put a positive spin on things, but inside he ached.

"I believed it would be our home, a dream come true. Now I wish I'd never seen it." A flash of sadness so deep it almost broke Drake's heart washed over her face.

"Things will work out. We might find someplace even better someday."

"Do you know what?" she said. "Sometimes your rah-rah, cheery crap is hard to take."

"I'm trying to cheer you up."

"Whenever I tell you something bugs me, you apologize or identify how everything is fine. What's with that? You keep your Mr. Rogers' blinders on and never complain when things flat-out stink. It makes me feel like there's something wrong with me because I get sad or disappointed or angry."

"We're healthy, the kids are healthy and happy, we have some good friends, and things are looking better."

"You just did it again." She sighed. "I get it that you try and look on the bright side, but my heart is full of hurt. Nasty horrible stuff happened. We lost a wonderful place to raise the kids. You and I both almost died. Once again, this job that you have—your obsession—brought death and misery into our lives. Someone tried to kill us." She bit her lower lip. "What would have happened to the kids?"

He stood silent. She was right—he did block out the negative. Maybe he feared how he'd handle it if he let his dark side loose. Mostly he was trying to keep himself together.

"I hear what you're saying," he said. The self-analysis made his head hurt, and damned if he saw any benefit.

"I'm griping about one of the things I love about you," Rachelle said. "But sometimes you should just nod and let me get it out of my system. You're totally right that the kids are healthy and we're okay, and that is huge, but I'm sick about losing the house, and I'm going to be miserable about it for a while." She looked at him, one eyebrow raised. "Since you're so good at spouting all sorts of cheery crap and persuading people, maybe you should think about a career in sales?"

He did a double-take. *Is she serious?*

A big smile appeared on her face. She'd messed with him. Drake laughed.

Her being able to joke gave him a lift like nothing else. She would not have been able to do that in years past.

He faced her, hands on her shoulders, and looked into her incredible eyes.

"I know my work has made things incredibly hard for you. It's unfair, but you've been fantastic. But despite how much I love you," he paused, "there's no way I'm going into sales."

She smiled and mock-punched him in the chest. He wrapped his arms around her.

"I love you, Rachelle."

"I love you, Drake." They kissed.

"Oh yuck," Shane yelled. "Look, Kristin, they're doing it again."

***

Rachelle was on the playground equipment chasing the kids. Their shrieks and laughter had Drake smiling.

His cell phone sounded. "Rizz" showed on the caller ID.

"Hey, Rizz. What's happening?"

"I'm on the loose. Where're you at?"

"With Rachelle and the kids at a park by Rock Island Lake. It's beautiful. The kids are having a blast. Jim Torrins said I'm not allowed to work for at least seventy-two hours."

"I don't suppose he had to twist your arm." Rizz laughed. "How long are you going to stay there? Can you meet me?"

"We need to get going pretty quick. Meet where and why?" Drake said.

"I just met with our attorney to the stars, Lloyd Anderson. He gave me something you need to sign. Something about getting your earnest money. Fact is, he gushed about the house, and I know you and Rachelle were over the moon, so I'd love to see it. Since you're in that neighborhood, want to meet me there?"

How would visiting the home affect Rachelle?

"Maybe it's not a good idea," Drake said.

"Hey, humor me," Rizz said. "I'm curious. Vang is driving me in the van and I want to see the place."

Perhaps it was self-torture, but on this beautiful day Drake also wanted to see the place. And he hadn't been lying to Rachelle. Perhaps someday they could buy a home on the very same lake.

"Okay. I can sell Rachelle on the fact we need to hurry and get the earnest money to get us a new rental place. She's way past done with the townhouse. Tell me when."

"Let's make it thirty minutes. See you then."

Chapter 90

Drake pulled into the driveway of the Rock Island Lake home.

"No vehicle here means we beat Rizz," he said.

Rachelle nodded and swallowed big, her eyes directed at her lap.

"Hey kids, you want to look around?" Drake asked. "The lake is in the back."

"Yeah, Dad!" they said in unison.

Rachelle leaned forward as if to stop them, then sat back.

Drake got out and opened the back door and the kids piled out.

"You guys don't get within five feet of the water. Understand?"

They nodded, then scampered across the front yard and disappeared around the far side of the house.

Drake went to the passenger door. The night he and Rachelle had spent on the deck was one of his best memories ever. That sunset evening, he'd walked her blindfolded from the car to the deck. Today her eyes were open but pain-filled.

"Let's go see how beautiful it is," Drake said, as he opened the door for her. "We'll have something like it someday. I promise."

"I'm holding you to that, Drake Cody."

They walked through the small gate alongside the attached garage. A pair of cardinals flitted from branch to branch on the wooded lot in front of them. Drake took Rachelle's hand as they made their way to the deck, the place they'd made love on the magical night only days earlier.

So much had happened since then.

The sun formed dancing diamonds on the wind-riffled water. The sky shone bluebird-rich, and the lush trees crowding the lakeshore and island glowed in multi-hued greens. The scent of cedar from the tree alongside the deck mixed with the clean smell of the lake. For Drake the outdoor beauty of the place was like a cathedral—more spiritual for him than any church.

The kids were on their knees in the yard, intent on a new find. Tears ran down Rachelle's cheeks. She bit a trembling lip, her arms folded tight across her chest. He wrapped an arm around her.

"It's spectacular, isn't it?

Her breath hitched, and she closed her eyes. "It really, really is," she said in a whisper.

The sound of a sliding glass door came from behind them. He and Rachelle turned. A man stood shadowed inside the doorway, the midday sun making them squint. The legs of an aluminum walker moved into the light. Next came hands, arms, and halting steps as the figure emerged.

"Hey guys, how's it hanging?" Rizz said.

Thunderbolts, tsunamis, a shifting of the earth under Drake's feet—nothing could have rocked him more.

The amazing, wonderful, son of a bitch.

Rachelle gasped. She put a hand to her mouth.

Drake stood stunned, fireworks going off in his heart.

Along with the sadness and hope for his best of all friends, Drake had felt responsible for his friend's paralysis. Rizz had taken the bullet protecting Drake and his family, and then they'd risked his life using Drake's untried drug.

Rizz's standing upright was a soul-freeing reprieve and a rocket of joy. Drake had once had a conviction overturned and escaped a living nightmare. This pardon felt no less sweet.

Drake rushed to Rizz's side. "Do you need help?"

"I'm good, amigo. I'm going to have to sit pretty quick, though."

Rizz slowly, and with great effort, moved forward. Drake took one of the deck chairs and positioned it behind him.

"Once I start to go down, the elevator drops pretty fast," Rizz said. Drake helped lower his friend to the sitting position.

"Oh, Rizz, it's so..." Rachelle couldn't finish.

"I know you guys have lots of questions, and I'm thrilled you're happy for me—almost as happy as I am. But first, we have some business to get out of the way. I mentioned the earnest money and Lloyd Anderson."

Whatever, Drake thought. The earnest money would be good, but nothing compared to Rizz walking.

"Well, the deal with the earnest money check is that I don't have it."

"That's fine," Drake said. "I'm sure we can get it ourselves or have it direct-deposited."

"Actually no," Rizz said. "It's a little more complicated."

"Complicated?" Rachelle said.

"Yeah, I've got a sheaf of papers you need to sign and a couple of things you need to know. First," he looked at Drake, "Jon Malar is coming back. He's going to finish the last couple months of his residency training and is hoping to work with us in the ER."

"That's fantastic," Drake said.

"It is great, but I have to warn you he's not the same old Jon. Everything he went through has had an impact. But one thing is the same. He's a good man. The papers you need to sign are for a promissory note. Lloyd drafted the document. It transfers a portion of your future expected revenues from D-44 to Jon."

"I don't understand," Drake said. The drug would take several years, at least, before any possible revenues. He'd get nothing until then. Rachelle and he looked at each other, brows furrowed, then back at Rizz.

"Lloyd makes it sound pretty simple. And fundamentally it is. Jon is taking your promissory note as payment in full."

"Payment in full?" Drake said. "I don't owe Jon any money."

"You do now, my friend," Rizz said. "The closing is scheduled for two days from now. Jon advanced the money to buy the house, and the promissory note makes ownership yours." Rizz smiled huge. He pulled a key out of his top pocket and held it out to Drake and Rachelle.

"Thanks for letting me be the first guest at your new home."

The End

Thank you for investing your valuable reading time with Drake and company. The hundreds of emails, 5-star reviews, and shared recommendations are greatly appreciated.

Visit the website, www.tom-combs.com, or find 'Tom Combs author' on Facebook. Feedback and exchange at tcombsauthor@gmail.com is encouraged.

Acknowledgments

I want to thank all those I worked with and learned from at three incredible institutions: Hennepin County Medical Center, the University of Cincinnati Hospital, and North Memorial Medical Center (eighteen years at this top-ranked level-one trauma and medical facility). My special gratitude to the nurses, doctors, and many others at North Memorial Medical Center who were there for me when I needed them most.

Special thanks to Jodie Renner who, once again, went beyond the call of duty in helping me get this book to press—an outstanding editor and friend.

Thanks to Michael (Sears) Stanley, author of the award-winning Detective Kubu Mystery series, for his detailed reading and on-target writing suggestions. Thank you to Laura Childs, NYT bestselling author, for generously sharing her expertise. Thank you to author Douglas Dorow for his assistance in getting the book to print. It is an honor to be a member of a profession that includes such first-class people.

Big thanks to my many longtime friends, especially Tom Holker for his input and encouragement.

I want to acknowledge those who provided technical expertise and feedback on *Wrongful Deaths*. The list is long, and I apologize for overlooking some, as I know I will. At times, I compromised medical and EMS procedure or protocol for the sake of drama and readability. Any and all errors are mine. Thanks to: Mary Martinie (MD, OB/Gyn), Tim Combs (25-year California Police Veteran), Bob Camarillo (Police Sergeant, Supervisor of Western US Multi-agency Drug Task Force), Fred Apple (PhD, Medical Director of Clinical Laboratories, and Clinical/Forensic toxicology lab HCMC), Donna Hirschman (RN, Emergency/Critical care nursing), Scott Lloyd Anderson (Attorney/CPA), Andrew M. Baker (MD, Chief Medical Examiner, Hennepin County), Leslie Wolf Dye (Emergency MD, Toxicologist, Addiction medicine), Travis Olives (Emergency MD/Toxicologist), Shannon Suchy Hendrickson (IT Educator, Health Informatics Specialist), Rob Colbert (MD, pulmonary/intensive care), Mark Contrerato (Emergency MD, Medical Director, Chief - ambulance services), Anjanee Sooknah (MD/Author, Neonatologist), Deborah Anderson (PharmD, MN Poison Control), Alan Beal (MD/Trauma Surgeon), Joseph Clinton (Emergency MD/Administrative Chief), Jayne Klukas (Laboratory Technologist), reader Ann Bremer, Leslie Nielsen and many more.

A special thanks to the people on the front lines who shared the reality of what is happening day-to-day: Justin Snow (Firefighter/Paramedic, Nevada), Ben Gilbert (Paramedic, New Jersey), Rick Bishop (Paramedic, Minneapolis), Kristi Wright (Flight paramedic, Texas), Joanna MacKenzie (Paramedic, Columbus), Michael MacNeil (Paramedic, Boston), Michael Morse (Firefighter/Paramedic/Author, Providence), and multiple others.

Thank you to my family for their support.

I must apologize to responsible healthcare administrators—theirs is not an easy job. For the sake of storytelling, I described behaviors unlike any I have witnessed.

About the Author

Twenty-five years as an emergency physician in busy, inner-city, level-one trauma center ERs provides the foundation for Tom Combs' unforgettable characters and riveting plots.

Tom lives with his artist wife near family and friends in a suburb of Minneapolis/St. Paul.

Contact at tcombsauthor@gmail.com.

Reader reviews and recommendations are much appreciated. *Nerve Damage*, *Hard to Breathe* and *Wrongful Deaths* are books one, two, and three of the Drake Cody series. Tom is currently writing book four and more are to follow.

Made in the USA
Middletown, DE
26 July 2019